Eleventh Elementum

The Primortus Chronicles
BOOK ONE

J.L. Bond
Val Richards

The Primortus Chronicles-Book 1
ISBN 978-0-9884338-1-6
ISBN 0-9884338-1-8

Copyright © 2012
Published by Get Over It Publishing
Cover by Deranged Doctor Design

Thanks to our families and friends.
To Ruth, Shelley, Carmen, Russell, and Janna for taking the
time to read our rough drafts, answer our questions, and
reread again, your advice was invaluable.
A special thanks to Rachel for all the input and technical assistance.
Lastly, a huge thank you to Phyllis for her fantastic proofing/editing skills
and for graciously enduring a manuscript with the world's tiniest print.

Follow us on Twitter at J.L. Bond @Primortus
Facebook at http://www.facebook.com/ThePrimortusChronicles
The Primortus Chronicles Website at
http://www.jlbond-valrichards.com

Printed in the United States of America

Table of Contents

Prologue 1
1. The Birth 3
2. The Daughter 7
3. The Inheritance 13
4. The Butterfly Effect 19
5. The Stepsister 29
6. The Wedding 39
7. The Reception 51
8. Trapped in a Closet 59
9. The New Sky Tower 69
10. Cook's Farm 79
11. The Plane 93
12. The Primortus 101
13. The Humusara 111
14. The Grave 127
15. The Maori Village 139
16. The Animus 149
17. The Vision Comes True 159
18. The Secret Office 169
19. The Stinking Wonderland 183
20. The Frozen Bear 193
21. The Stolen Box 201
22. The Château 213
23. The Avalanche 221
24. The Snow Leopard 233
25. The Museum 247
26. A Helpmate Resists 255
27. The Confessions 267
28. The Silver Arrow 275
29. Brinfrost 283

I had a dream, which was not all a dream.
The bright sun was extinguished, and the stars
Did wander darkling in the eternal space,
Rayless, and pathless, and the icy earth
Swung blind and blackening in the moonless air;
Morn came and went—and came, and brought no day,
And men forgot their passions in the dread
Of this their desolation; and all hearts
Were chilled into a selfish prayer for light.

"Darkness" Lord Byron 1816

PROLOGUE

Yosemite National Park

Time had run out. For years there had been books, movies and TV shows forecasting a mega disaster. The big one—but all the predictions were wrong. The Day of Disaster wasn't caused by any of the things they had imagined. It wasn't an asteroid impact, nuclear holocaust, a deadly pandemic or the long expected zombie invasion. And it wasn't an alien attack, solar flares, a rogue black hole or even global climate change. It was the beginning of an unseen battle.

Two powerful beings came into existence. The first, who would eventually be known as Brinfrost, was born of betrayal and vengeance. The second, like no other, would be feared and called an abomination of nature. Like fire and water, darkness and light, their conflict was set in motion. Some say their arrival caused something deep in the earth's crust to shift, and others believe the world stopped spinning for a moment.

It happened on a Monday, the fifth of February. The first sign of trouble began at the peak of an immense granite cliff. As the huge rock face gave way, a large crack appeared in the valley below. It grew to a monstrous rift between the snow-covered mountains. Then, like a bolt of lightning racing through the sky, it tore across the earth's surface.

Approximately two hundred miles west in San Francisco, the ground began to violently shake, signaling the horror to come. As the dark fissure ripped through the city, buildings broke apart, the streets buckled and a large portion of Fisherman's Wharf slid into the bay.

Within minutes, the crevice had traveled thousands of miles, wreaking havoc along the way. And it didn't stop. The vast break in the earth's crust continued like a living thing, cutting a path across the land and sea, in a journey around the planet. Just when it looked like The Day of Disaster would end right where it had begun at Yosemite National Park, the unfathomable crack came to a halt near Mammoth Lakes California, barely falling short of circling the globe.

It was over in nine hours, twelve minutes and fifty-one seconds, just before midnight. Over two billion people were dead. A great, dark haze covered the skies and seas. In less than one day, the planet had fallen into chaos and humankind's continued existence hung in the balance.

ONE

〜ᵴ𝆍 ⅄ₒ 𝔸𝔸 𝓉ᅙ

The Birth

Mammoth Hospital
Mammoth Lakes, California

It was cold and dark, thick dust filled the room.

"Where am I?" asked Janis, who was lying in a hospital bed. An intravenous tube dripped a clear liquid into the delicate veins of her hand. Her thick strawberry blonde hair was clumped in mud, and her arms and legs were riddled with small, bloody scratches. Excruciating pain stabbed her in the stomach as she tried to sit up.

"No," she whimpered, rubbing her hand across her deflated belly, which was covered with a thick bandage. "My baby?"

Please God I want my baby. A million thoughts raced through her mind. *Where is she?*

In a dreamlike state she looked from side to side, realizing she was completely alone. A large florescent light overhead blinked off and on. The only window in the room had been broken and a white sheet dangled over it, flapping in the breeze. Then the television, which hung on the wall at the foot of her bed, came to life.

...Beep...
This is a warning from the emergency alert system. An emergency condition exists ... Prepare to relocate... Remain calm and stand by for further instructions ...
Beep ...Beep...Beep...

She stared at it in horror. NEW YORK said the words at the bottom of the screen, but all she could see was rubble and smoke. She gasped as she recognized the Statue of Liberty broken into hundreds of pieces. Then like a slow motion nightmare, she watched as city after city was shown in ruins. London... Berlin... Cairo... Hong Kong... Tokyo... Los Angeles... on and on.

The world is ending, she thought in despair.

Suddenly the TV flickered, and then went black as the electricity went out. A small emergency spotlight in the corner came on, dimly lighting the room. As her eyes adjusted, she glimpsed the outline of a man standing in the doorway.

"Hello, who's there?" she called out.

A shudder ran through her when he didn't answer. She carefully tried to rise and get a better look. The blurred silhouette didn't move. Why was he just standing there watching her? She blinked, to clear her vision and he was gone.

Am I hallucinating? She searched her mind and tried to make sense of what was happening. Maybe she was having a nightmare. But she knew that wasn't true. It had started at Yosemite National Park. She had gone there on a family vacation. As she struggled to remember, an image of her husband and stepson flashed into her mind.

Tears streamed from her pale blue eyes. She wiped her face and leaned back into her pillow. Painful sobs racked her chest as the memory of the earthquake flooded over her. Holding her hand over her mouth, she felt as if it was happening all over again.

She closed her eyes. *I see it...the cliff breaking apart...and the boulders...racing down the mountainside. No! I see them...they're tumbling backward...disappearing...*

Crash! Suddenly the room shook, bringing her back to the present. A long piece of florescent tubing came tumbling down and shattered on the floor. She screamed and covered her eyes. Within seconds a man rushed through the door.

"Ma'am? I'm Doctor Emerson," he said as he reached her bedside. "It's all right. Just another aftershock."

She opened her hands, squinted in the dimness and looked at his white coat, which was stained with blood. A long scratch marred his forehead, and a bandage was wrapped around his hand.

"My...my baby..."

"Your little girl made it. We had to take her by cesarean, it was touch and go for a while. I'd say she's quite the fighter."

A wave of relief washed over Janis, leaving her momentarily lightheaded. She drew in a long, deep breath. *A fighter,* she thought with a sense of pride and gratitude.

"Can I see her?"

"In awhile. You've suffered some serious injuries. You need to pace yourself."

"Uh, serious?"

"Yes, you have a concussion and deep tissue contusions on your legs, but we expect you'll make a full recovery."

She let out a soft sigh. "What about my husband and stepson? Do you know anything about them? Are they—"

"I'm sorry, I don't know. What are their names?"

"Lee and Steve Porter."

"Were they with you when it happened?"

"No, they were on a hiking trail to Yosemite Falls. I saw...I was watching from the hotel lobby when it happened. They were on the cliff."

"Oh," he said with a hesitant look in his eyes. "I'll see if I can get some info on them. But things are very hectic. I'll have a nurse bring your baby in as soon as possible. Just be aware that it might take a little while. We're short of staff, and the hospital has sustained a lot of damage. Try to be patient with us, Mrs. Porter."

"Of course, but please call me Janis," she said, sitting up as perspiration beaded her brow. "Just tell me where she is and I'll..."

"Mrs. Porter, Janis," he said, placing his hand on her shoulder to restrain her. "You're in no shape to walk down there. I promise, they'll bring her to you in just a few more minutes. Now, you get some rest in the meantime."

"Okay, doctor," she said with a lump in her throat. "Ahem...wait, can you tell me what time she was born?"

"Just before midnight."

"Thanks." Her tears returned the second he left the room. *My little girl is alive, thank you Lord,* she prayed. *Please God, let Lee and Steve be all right.*

About ten minutes later, they brought a tiny bundle to her. Inside, barely visible through a small gap in the blanket, was a baby girl. She was fair skinned with pink cheeks and fine blonde hair. As Janis hugged her daughter to her breast, she felt her pain melt away.

"We survived it, little one," she whispered, and her baby daughter opened her eyes, looking at her for the first time.

"Oh," Janis breathed in awe. "They're blue...like the sky."

TWO

_st ✗◦ ⋀⋀ ⚭

The Daughter

Fourteen years later
New Washington

New Washington, formerly Washington D.C. was no longer the U.S. capital. The most powerful city in the world had been reduced to rubble on The Day of Disaster. Nearly all of its citizens had moved south, fleeing the brutally cold weather brought on by the volcanic ash known as the "Death Haze." There were only a handful of people, survivalist types, who had stayed on, living below ground in the damaged tunnels of the Metro subway system.

It had taken four years for the politicians to get their heads together and decide on a new capital in Houston, Texas. So Washington D.C. sat in ruins, like a frozen wasteland.

Around the world, every nation had endured destruction and great loss of life. Those who survived now measured their lives by before or after The Day of Disaster, now more commonly known as The Day.

Over time, ever so slowly, the skies began to clear and it grew warmer. Naturally there had been a groundswell of support to rebuild the capital on its original site. However, after months of political debating and negotiating, a different plan was set in motion.

The capital would remain in Houston, and an SGR (special governmental region) would be set up in Washington. A region devoted to the prevention of global disasters, where experts from around the globe could come together. It would be filled with scientists, engineers, civil servants and environmentalists.

When the reconstruction began, most of the buildings and monuments were found damaged beyond repair. It took three years to rebuild the White House, which was then opened to the public as a research library and museum. But the most impressive structure erected in New Washington was "The Day of Disaster Memorial."

The entire site consisted of three parts: the Global Recovery Fountain, the Survivors Memorial Park, and the Hall of Remembrance. The Hall was a gigantic crescent shaped building on the bank of the Potomac River. A plaque at the entrance read...

Of all the questions which can come before this nation, short of the actual preservation of its existence in a great war, there is none which compares in importance with the great central task of leaving this land even a better land for our descendants than it is for us."
President Theodore Roosevelt

Upon entering the building the visitors were greeted by a massive glass wall, which overlooked the Globe Fountain. A holographic photo gallery depicting the earth from space, before and after the catastrophe, lined the interior wall. The far ends of the hall contained event rooms.

Inside one of those darkened rooms lay a neatly wrapped package, waiting to unleash its contents. Securely tucked within were two gifts that were not what they seemed. Their true worth and how deeply they were tied to The Day was yet to be revealed. After years in silence their time had arrived.

* * * * * * *

"Where are we going?" said a girl with curly blonde hair, which was piled high on her head. She wasn't the least bit comfortable with her formal dress, tight fitting shoes, and fancy hairdo. *I look like a dork*, she thought, sighing miserably. *Ugh, just what I wanted...to be a bridesmaid in Mom's wedding.*

"Just come on, Sweetie-pie," Janis Porter said, clutching tightly to her daughter's hand as they made their way down a long corridor. "I have a surprise for you."

"Me? What is it?"

"You'll see, but first I need to tell you something."

Her mother, who hadn't yet dressed for the ceremony, was wearing a bright red Japanese kimono. They came to an abrupt stop at a large wooden door bearing a bronze plaque, which was engraved with the words Bridesmaids Room. Janis smoothed her hands over the embroidered dragon on the front of her robe, cleared her throat and looked nervously at her daughter.

"After your father's death I—"

"No Mom, you don't have to talk about that, not today of all days."

"But, I want to. I need to, especially today," she insisted. "You're not honestly saying that you aren't thinking about your dad today?"

"Well, I just don't—I mean it's—um—"

"You know," her mom jumped in, clearly trying to ease the tension. "I think he would be proud if he could see you today," she continued on but her voice took on the tone of a mother cooing at a tiny baby. "Ooo...look how grown up you are in your bridesmaid dress. You're not my little baby-cakes anymore." She reached out and affectionately pinched the girl's cheek.

"*Mom.*"

Janis smiled. "Okay, but seriously, I see more and more of your dad in you everyday. Not so much in the way you look but in the way you handle yourself. I guess I named you right. Remember the story...how I waited until the day you were born to choose your name?"

"Yes," the girl said nodding slowly.

"So much happened that day..." Janis paused and swallowed hard.

"It's okay, Mom, you really don't have to," she said, not wanting to think about it. How could she think of her birthday as a happy day? The fifth of February otherwise known as The Day wasn't a date to celebrate. It was the day the world almost ended and as if that wasn't enough it was the day her father died.

"Your birth was a miracle in all the chaos," her mom continued. "You know, The Day started out beautifully with a clear blue sky. It was the bluest blue I'd ever seen, until I saw your eyes. I'd already planned to name you after your dad so I just put the two together, Sky and Lee—Skylee."

Skylee plastered a big cheesy smile on her face and playfully said, "Oooh, really? So that's how you came up with it? Who knew?"

"I know, I know," her mom chuckled. "I've told you a thousand times."

"No, only a few hundred, but who's counting," she teased, slightly rolling her eyes.

"I guess you are," her mother said warmly. "But there really is a reason I brought you here, to give you a gift before the wedding."

"Me?" she said, her eyes wide. "But you're the bride, you should be the one getting presents, not me."

"Well, I'm not just the bride. I'm your mom, and I haven't forgotten about your dad. The gift's inside...and it's from him," her mother said, pointing a finger at the door.

"Dad?" she whispered, looking surprised. "But he's been de...um, *gone* for fourteen years."

Skylee was always careful not to say the "d" word to her mom whenever they talked about her father. She usually tried to tiptoe around the subject of his death. Not that her mother was exactly a delicate flower, no one who had made it through the last fourteen years could be called delicate. After all, her mom had not only survived the cold and hunger after The Day she had somehow managed to take care of a small child.

Skylee knew it had been her mother's optimistic attitude that had helped them endure those years. It was one of the things she loved most about her. Although at times her colorful personality, kooky outfits, and tendency to use baby talk was embarrassing. And her habit of seeing the silver lining in every cloud seemed illogical, considering the fact that for much of Skylee's childhood the only thing she had seen come from the lining of a cloud was ash-filled rain.

"Sweetie, trust me," her mother said in a soothing voice. "I want to—oh, how do I explain this? Well, from the moment I woke up this morning I just knew I wanted you to have—oops, I almost told you. Now where's the fun of opening a gift if you know what's inside? You see, I really wasn't supposed to give it to you until you were fifteen, but I couldn't wait."

"Fifteen? Why? No, wait a minute. The ceremony starts in an hour and a half. Don't we need to go back to the bride's room so you can get dressed?" asked Skylee, feeling an odd mixture of guilt and excitement about receiving a gift from her dad on her mom's wedding day.

"Shouldn't I be helping you get ready?"

"That's why I have a wedding planner and a maid of honor. They'll help me. You go on inside and open it. It's what your dad wanted. Just think of it as...your inheritance. We'll talk more about it later."

"Thanks mom," whispered Skylee, giving her a hug.

"Sure, and hey...you're still my munchkin," said her mother, squeezing her a little too tightly. "I'll see you in just a—"

"THERE YOU ARE!" trilled a high nasal voice.

Skylee nearly jumped out of her skin. Turning quickly, she looked down the hall and saw Chloe, the wedding planner racing toward them.

She was a plump middle-aged woman with charcoal gray hair, which was tightly knotted in a bun. Her round face seemed to be crumpled up in a wad. Apparently she thought her job was to order everyone around at the top of her voice. Skylee thought it was ironic that someone, who seemed to live, eat and breath weddings had never been married herself.

"Goodness sakes, why aren't you two in the bride's room?" asked Chloe looking like a cat ready to pounce on a mouse.

"I'm afraid it's my fault," said Janis graciously. "I dragged Skylee down here to give her something."

Chloe's eyes were as wide as saucers as she put her hands on her hips and said, "My dear! We simply cannot have the bride out wandering around in her bath robe...you should be getting ready."

"Okay, sorry," her mother said turning toward Skylee and giving her smirky grin. "I'd better go. I'll see you after you open the gift."

"And YOU—" added Chloe in a stern voice as she pointed at Skylee. "Don't be late!"

Skylee nodded and her mom gave her a quick hug. Then the wedding planner pranced over, grabbed her mom's arm, and rushed her down the hall.

As Skylee watched her mother tagging along with Chloe she thought of her father. By the end of the day she would have a stepdad. She couldn't lie to herself. She wasn't really thrilled about it. Of course, she was happy for her mom. She deserved to have a man in her life after fourteen years alone. Still it was only normal to think about how different things could have been if her dad hadn't died.

She stood there for a moment and tried to imagine what it would be like, but it was impossible. That was the thing about death it was so final, so irreversible. She knew this because she had been to more than her fair share of funerals, having grown up in the aftermath of The Day. In fact, death had changed her life more than once.

It had only been four years since her friend, Gracie Miller, died. The Miller's moved in next door when Skylee was about five years old. Gracie was a year older and very smart, she had even taught Skylee how to read. The two of them had had lots of fun acting out the stories of their favorite books. It was a bright spot in an otherwise cold and dark childhood. Most of their time had been spent scavenging for food, gathering wood and hauling in snow for drinking water. Then one day, Gracie was gone. A lump formed in Skylee's throat every time she thought about it.

Swallowing hard, she kneaded her temples with her fingertips and returned her thoughts to her mother's words. Inheritance, she had said inheritance. Skylee's idea of inheriting something was more like being told she had her mom's wavy hair or her dad's smile. This was different, an actual gift, what could it be?

She paused and let out a long sigh before opening the door. The spacious room was eerily quiet. Her eyes were drawn to a long wooden table. It stood beneath an arched window, which was slightly obscured by long velvet drapery. A narrow shaft of light peeked through the curtains and onto the waiting package.

THREE

The Inheritance

Skylee crept into the room, carefully avoiding the open suitcases, shoeboxes and clothing scattered on the floor. Dressing for the wedding had created quite a mess. She had wanted to clean it up, but her almost stepsister insisted that her father had hired people to do such things.

As she approached the package, her pulse raced. Skylee normally opened a present slowly and carefully like a doctor performing surgery, but her excitement made her eagerly tear through the wrapping.

Inside, cushioned on a bed of crumpled paper, was a brown leather book bound with four gold rings. A diamond shape was carved into the front cover. She held the book close to her heart realizing that it could be her father's journal, a look into his soul. Turning it over, she examined it more closely and tried to imagine him holding it in his hands. Despite her feeling of excitement, a deep sadness washed over her.

Skylee reached up and pushed back the heavy curtains, flooding the room with sunlight. As she opened the book, a musty odor filled the room even though the cover looked new. She thumbed through the crisp white pages to find page after page of strange hand written lettering, which appeared to be an ancient language. Skylee squinted at the lettering and tried to make out the words.

Holding the book closer to her face, she decided it was a language she had never seen before. Her heart sank in disappointment. It wasn't her father's journal. *Why...she* wondered...*why did my dad want me to have a book that I can't read?* She softly placed it on the table and sighed. Then her gaze returned to the package. Maybe there was something else...something that would explain it to her.

She ran her fingers through the crumpled paper and found a smaller box. Her eyes widened as she opened it and peered inside. The box held a beautiful necklace, which appeared to be very old. Upon closer inspection, she realized its dark gray metal shone like new, reflecting tiny flecks of blue. She had never seen a lovelier amulet. Her eyes moved back and forth from the necklace to the carving on the book. They were exactly the same size and shape.

Plucking the necklace from the box, she held it up by its long silvery chain. The medieval looking amulet swayed and sparkled in the light as if it were covered in diamonds. Inside its circular center were four distinct etchings. She brushed her fingers across the symbols wondering what they meant, and then she turned the amulet over. On the back were more etchings. One looked like an inscription and the other was an odd symbol. They appeared to be in the same language as the lettering in the book.

Skylee didn't know what to make of it, yet she had a strong urge to put on the necklace. Draping it over her head, she crossed the room and stood at the full-length mirror. Her blue eyes narrowed as she frowned at her reflection. She had tried to tame her wavy blonde hair into some kind of twist, securing it at the crown of her head in an attempt to look more mature. Now she wondered if it only accentuated her most embarrassing feature her protruding ears. She brushed an unruly curl away from her face and examined her pale complexion. Maybe the extra makeup was too much. She usually only wore a little mascara and tinted lip-gloss. She shrugged and made a face at herself in the mirror. Then her eyes settled on the sparkling necklace, which was resting on the soft green fabric of her dress.

"So, this is my inheritance," she said, holding it up.

She curiously gazed at it and, to her surprise, white crystals were forming on its surface. Suddenly a sharp pain seared her fingers and she quickly let go, leaving it dangling from the chain around her neck. The amulet was as cold as ice. Confusion overwhelmed her. Her heart pounded loudly under the freezing metal. She took a deep breath and tried to calm down. But as if being driven by some force that she could not understand, Skylee walked to the book. She removed the amulet and, with icy cold fingers, placed it into the diamond shaped carving.

A brilliant glow grew from the heart of it, intensifying in brightness until its radiance held her gaze. Then without warning a jolt of energy surged through her fingers. She shrieked and tried to pull away from the book, but her hand wouldn't budge. It was like a heavy weight was holding it there. She yanked and tugged to free herself, but it was no use.

As she stood rooted in place, the air grew colder. Tiny clouds of white fog floated before her with each quivering breath. In astonishment, she watched as the brilliant light traveled up her arm, making its way to her chest. A tingling sensation spread across her body as if something inside her was struggling to get out.

Gasping for air, she looked down to see a whirling orb of light positioned directly above her heart. Like a bolt of lightning, energy poured through her veins and flooded her entire body. Then the orb burst forth with a column of light, which returned to the necklace still in her frozen grasp atop the book.

Skylee felt as if she were spinning around very fast. It seemed to go on forever. Then, at last, she felt herself coming to a halt. There was a prickling sensation as if dozens of sharp needles were piercing her hand. She carefully released her hold on the necklace and lifted her tingling fingers away from the book. Then, like fireflies flickering in and out, the light faded away.

Unable to look away, she held her breath as she opened the book. Shimmering words appeared on the once unreadable pages as if an unseen hand was translating a secret message. Skylee blinked wildly and shook her head in disbelief as she tried to focus on the page. More words, words she could read, materialized before her eyes. In one swift motion, she gasped, slammed the book shut, and fell back against the couch.

With her eyes shut tight, she could hear her pulse pounding in her ears. Slowly she lifted her eyelids and peeked at the book. She wasn't sure how it was possible but it seemed to be breathing. Gripped by both fear and curiosity, she edged closer. But the book had changed. Only seconds before its leather had been new and its pages had looked crisp and white, now the edges were worn and the pages were yellowed with age.

"This can't be happening," she repeated till she stood in front of the book. With trembling fingers, she opened it and again the shimmering words appeared.

It has begun...he shall not wait
to bring about a lifeless fate.

She read the phrase over and over until her head was spinning. Then she cautiously backed away from the book and stood near the door.

There was a long moment of silence, which was broken by a faint high-pitched sound. Someone was whistling a familiar tune, like a child's nursery rhyme. The slow dissonant melody sent a chill down her spine.

Suddenly a dark movement caught her eye, and the whistling fell silent. A man was standing there, at the window, his eerie silhouette backlit by the bright sunlight. Skylee's pulse pounded in her throat. She huddled in the dimly lit corner, hoping she was hidden from view. Goosebumps covered her arms as a sinister creak filled the room, and the window swung open. She blinked and tried to focus her eyes.

He was tall, with black hair, and was dressed in a dark blue uniform. His face was so smooth it looked like a mask. The sunlight tinted his high cheekbones slightly yellow, but it was his black eyes that really scared her. They were like dark holes in his face.

The room was deathly quiet. Skylee stood motionless trying not to breathe, as sweat dampened her clothing. The man peered through the open window. He seemed to be scanning the area in search of something, until his eyes stopped at the open book.

"It's true...it still exists," he said as he effortlessly climbed over the windowsill.

His swift movement into the room made her let out an involuntary gasp. He froze, then spun around and peered into the corner. The moment he saw her, a low menacing snarl rose from his throat. Terror, greater than she had ever known, swept over her. She felt paralyzed as she stared into his eyes...blue into utter blackness.

"Skylee?"

Her eyes widened. She was unsure who had called her name. A sharp knock at the door caused her to jump. In an instant, the dark stranger turned and bolted through the window, which slammed shut behind him.

"Skylee, can you come and help your stepsister?" hollered Chloe from behind the door.

Exhaling in relief, Skylee staggered forward on trembling legs and collapsed onto the couch.

"Oh, yes, I...I'm coming," she called out breathlessly.

She leaned forward and covered her face with her hands to calm herself, but the memory of the man's black eyes were imprinted on her brain. With adrenaline still pumping through her veins, she struggled to regain her composure.

After several minutes her eyes returned to the window. It seemed to have opened and closed without him ever touching it. She stood, hesitated, and then walked toward it, carefully running her hands around its edges in search of wires. Nothing. As she nervously looked around, she latched the window and checked to be sure that it was locked. She drew closer to the glass and then quickly moved back in fear of his return. *Who was he? Was he going to take the book?*

"I'd better hide it," she said under her breath. "But, where?"

Skylee explored the room looking for a hiding place. Inside a supply closet, she found a set of filing cabinets. She slipped the book into a file drawer under a stack of papers, then returned to the empty box and replaced the lid. The box shifted revealing an envelope underneath addressed to Skylee, from Mom.

She snatched up the envelope and turned to leave the room, but something stopped her in her tracks. She spun around and, against her better judgment, returned to the book. She reached out for the amulet, which was still tucked in the cover.

"Ouch," she gasped, swiftly pulling back her hand and waving her fingers through the air.

It was hot. She stared intently at it. It defied all logic. She couldn't believe it had gone from freezing cold to burning hot in mere minutes. *How? And more importantly, why?*

Grabbing a pair of jeans from the floor, she used them to protect her hand as she picked up the amulet. Almost immediately she felt the metal cooling through the fabric. She paced back and forth, holding the necklace in her hand and tried to decide what to do next. As much as she wanted to pretend she wasn't afraid, she couldn't deny her true feelings. Had her father meant to give her a book and necklace that were capable of some sort of magic? Maybe it was a test. It seemed like a challenge had suddenly been thrust upon her. Carefully touching the amulet, she found it to be room temperature. She heaved a heavy sigh, put on the necklace, and left the room. After all, it was her inheritance.

FOUR

The Butterfly Effect

Skylee ran down a long curved hallway lined with pictures depicting the earth, before and after the Day of Disaster. She glanced at each holographic image as she hurried by and thought about how life must have been before The Day. A world unaware of the looming catastrophe, where city streets were packed with people and cars, all rushing about like ants on an anthill. A place where the countryside looked like a patchwork quilt of green, dotted with herds of livestock. It seemed like a simpler time, when the young rarely encountered death. That was not the world she knew.

Skylee entered the Hall of Remembrance, before her was the brightly polished dance floor. Lush greenery and glowing lanterns hung around the room. Dashing between the round tables, which were draped in white and green linens, she headed toward the grand wall of glass at the end of the hall.

She didn't notice the splendor of the room or the girl whose eyes were shooting darts at her as she rushed toward the doors. Obviously, her relationship with her stepsister was off to a rocky start. And it wasn't because Skylee meant to ignore her, but because the only thing that mattered at that moment was unraveling the mystery behind the gifts from her father. In fact, the moment she had hidden the book her mind fixed itself on one person. She had to find him.

* * * * * * *

William Butler stood on the Memorial Viewing Platform and looked down at his reflection in the water below. A wiry boy of fifteen looked back at him, his sandy hair hung in a tangle over his brow nearly covering his brown eyes. He gazed up at the massive globe, which rotated in the center of the lake, as if magically balanced upon a cascading fountain. The sky above it had never seemed clearer, without even a hint of the Death Haze. In spite of the peaceful view, there was a battle raging inside Will's mind. And the source of his conflict was Skylee Porter. He wasn't sure when his feelings for her had shifted from friendship to something more. But he did know that for the last few weeks he had found himself wondering what would happen if he told her how he truly felt. *She'd probably punch me right in the nose,* he thought to himself.

Will chuckled as he made his way to the edge of the platform. A flock of geese floated lazily on the lake. They gracefully swam over and hovered in the water below him. He leaned forward on the railing to get a closer look.

"Eh...mate? Are ya thinkin' of jumpin'?" shouted a voice in a thick Australian accent.

Will swung around just in time to see his cousin, Airon, come up from behind and give him a shove. It came as no surprise. They were more like brothers than cousins, which meant teasing and rough housing was par for the course.

"Funny!" Will said sarcastically as he shoved him back, which was not easy, since Airon was a year older and built like a kick-boxer.

"If ya ask me, what's funny is the bloody love-sick look on yer face. Guess I know who yer thinkin' about?"

"Give it a break," Will huffed. "I've already told you Sky is my best friend and it...it's well, it's nothing more."

"Oh, I see...it...it...it's nothin' more," he mocked with an amused look. "Yeah, got ya!"

Will cocked an eyebrow at him and grudgingly laughed. The cousins had just returned from a two-week visit with their grandparents in Australia, where Airon had first begun to suspect the truth about Will's feelings for Sky.

"Remind me," said Will with a scowl. "Why did I talk you into leaving Oz and coming to this shindig with me?"

"Well, for one, yer not the one that talked me in teh comin'. And two, I'm the best lookin' date ya could come up with."

"Seriously."

"Yeah and listen, I'd like nothin' more than teh be back in Ozland."

Will knew it was true. They had been having loads of fun there, surfing, going on walkabouts and horseback riding. And they still had plenty of time for school. As far as he was concerned virtual education was one of the best outcomes of The Day. While they were in Sydney, he had finished the first semester of his sophomore year and Airon was nearing graduation. They were planning an outing to the Great Barrier Reef to celebrate when he finished. Unfortunately their trip was cut short when Will's mum received the news that her closest friend, Janis was getting married. His only consolation was that he would see Sky.

"Aren't ya even gonna ask who convinced me teh tag along?"

"No, cause I already know."

"So now yer a mind reader," said Airon, squinting oddly at Will.

"What am I thinkin' now."

"Airon, shut up," he said flatly.

"Wrong. I was thinkin' that if yer mum hadn't forced me teh come I probably would've anyway. Ya know weddings are a choice place to pick up good lookin' shelias."

"Well good luck with that, Crocodile Dundee."

"No luck needed. By the way, whatdaya think of yer mum bringin' her buddy, Levi with her?"

"Why should I care," said Will with a shrug.

In actual fact, he wasn't thrilled about it. Not that he had anything against his mum's friend, but because it meant someone else would be coming to the wedding. Someone he wasn't looking forward to seeing again. Levi would no doubt bring his cocky son, Hawk.

Over the years, Levi and Hawk Hunter had popped in and out of their lives, even when Will's dad was still alive. Sometimes, Hawk, who was a year older and at least six inches taller, would stay with them while his mum and Levi left. It was supposedly for his mum's work but something always seemed off about the whole thing. And it didn't help matters that during those times Hawk would instigate some hair-brained stunt and then blame it on him, which would inevitably get Will in trouble.

"Mate," Airon yelled, smacking the side of Will's head with his palm. "What's up? Ya look like ya been suckin' on a lemon."

"I've got things on my mind," Will mumbled as he shook his head. "Or at least I did, before you knocked me senseless."

"Ah, come on, ya got teh snap out of it. Yer face is gonna get stuck like that, and then how will ya charm that certain girl. Ya know, yer best friend that yer dyin' teh see."

"Are you just wanting to take a swim, today?" Will threatened, grabbing him by the arm.

"All right, mate," said Airon as he held up his hands in surrender. "Right, have it yer way, but I'm tellin' ya someday yer gonna have teh face it. Listen, I'm starvin'. I'm gonna go inside an' find some tucker. Ya comin'?"

"No," Will casually said. "I'll catch up with you in a bit."

Will watched as Airon shook his head and then strolled up the path toward the Hall of Remembrance. Needless to say, his cousin hadn't been fooled by his denials. Turning back to the water, he faced the Clearistic display that stood at the edge of the viewing platform.

"Display," Will ordered, which triggered an interactive screen revealing a description of the memorial.

THE DAY OF DISASTER GLOBAL MEMORIAL
DEDICATED TO THE HALLOWED MEMORY OF THE MEN,
WOMEN AND CHILDREN WHO LOST THEIR LIVES
THE DAY OUR PLANET ENDURED MASSIVE DEVASTATION

Will thought back to in his history lessons about The Day. He was a year and a half old when it happened, so he didn't remember anything. But he had seen loads of pictures and videos of the devastation. They were horrendous scenes filled with terrified faces. Faces he had never been able to erase from his mind.

To tell the truth, growing up in the aftermath had been tough. There was no time for video games or toys. Even when electricity was available he had more important things to do, like staying alive for example. And finding time for school was never easy. Fortunately he was an avid reader and never stopped learning. In fact, Will had learned about plenty of things, like hunger, blackouts, looting and desperation, but more importantly he learned about survival. He was one of the lucky ones.

It felt strange to be standing there under a brilliant blue sky. The cherry blossoms were blooming, the sun was on his face and the breeze was warm. It had taken over a decade, but the world was finally in recovery. There was only one thing missing.

I need to find Sky, said a small voice in Will's head.

* * * * * * *

Skylee rushed out of the memorial hall toward the wedding arch with the card from her mother clutched tightly in her hand. A huge cluster of butterflies flew along right behind her.

"I must bloody well be seeing things," said Will, rubbing his eyes as he headed toward her.

Meanwhile Skylee's eyes were so intently focused on the envelope, that she didn't notice the colorful insects or Will. She scampered down the sidewalk toward him.

He gently reached out, clutched her arm and said, "Sky, what's wrong?"

"Oh, Will, there you are!" she said in a distressed voice.

"What's going on, eh?" he asked, staring up at the butterflies.

Skylee smiled when she heard his voice. His normally slight Australian accent was much stronger after being in Sydney. Actually, since Airon had come to live with them, Will had picked up more and more of his cousin's Aussie ways. And Skylee noticed something else was different about Will. He had returned from his trip with blonde highlights in his wavy brown hair. She wouldn't be surprised if the new surfer-boy look had turned many an Aussie girl's head.

For some reason she didn't like dwelling on that thought, so she turned her attention to giving Will a detailed answer about the stranger, the book, the necklace, and the words that had appeared and disappeared. During her little speech the butterflies, still hovering around her, continued to distract him.

"Will?"

"Uh-huh," he grunted.

"Will?" Skylee called a little louder.

"Eh?" Will replied, with his eyes still glued to the butterflies.

"What are you looking at?" Skylee questioned grabbing his jacket.

Will finally turned his attention to Skylee and motioned with his eyes toward the fluttering creatures. He gently placed his hands on her shoulders and turned her around.

"That," he said in a matter of fact tone.

Skylee cocked her head to the side in bewilderment. A mixture of shock and awe possessed her as she gazed at dozens of colorful butterflies flying above her head. She raised an eyebrow and said, "Eastern Tailed Blues, well...their real name is Cupido Comyntas—what are they doing here so early in the spring? Okay, that's a little weird."

"Cripes, Sky! It's more than a little weird, by the look of it, they're following you." Will pointed out.

"All right, it's *really* weird," said Skylee, waving her hands in the air to shoo the butterflies away.

As she watched the purplish-blue butterflies floating into the sky she wondered if her mind was scattering with them. *I must be going crazy. Why are all these bizarre things happening today?* She shook her head, trying to clear her thoughts.

"Will, did you hear what I told you?"

He nodded but continued watching the butterflies, now tiny specks, as they faded away. Then she softly tapped him on the shoulder, which caused him to jump and look over at her.

"Sorry, I'm a bit distracted," he said with a crooked grin.

She smiled forgivingly at him. Over the last few months, there had been a change in their friendship. It was subtle, but she could sense awkwardness between them. *So what...he's still your best friend,* she told herself. In fact they had been BFFs for as long as she could remember. Her mind drifted back to when she was about seven or eight. Those were the days when she spent much of her time with Will and Gracie. They had called themselves the three musketeers, one for all and all for one. That had been their motto. Those were blissful times even though the skies were gray and even after Gracie's illness prevented them from going outside to play. They still had fun building forts out of blankets and dressing up like their favorite characters out of the books Gracie read to them. Then it all changed. Skylee wished things didn't always have to change.

She swallowed hard and fought back her emotions. She composed her thoughts and recounted the details about the gifts to Will. She decided to downplay the part about the stranger and the glowing light. It was best not to tell him too much since he was so protective of her. Will crossed his arms and chewed on his bottom lip as he listened.

"Are you all right? Did the bloke hurt you?" Will interrupted as he grabbed her hand.

"Yeah, I'm fine, just a bit shook up," she said nervously tucking a long wisp of hair behind her ear.

"Well, did you call security or your mum to tell them what happened?"

"Oh, Will, I'm okay. You worry too much, I'll tell them later," Skylee lied, trying to calm his nerves. "It's what I saw in the book that really bothers me."

"I worry too much? You just told me some bloke climbed through the window and—he could've hurt you!"

"But he didn't—I'm fine. I thought he was after the book, but come to think of it he didn't really try to take it."

"And you heard him say something about it existing?" he asked as Skylee nodded in agreement. "So where is the book?"

"I hid it. Don't worry. It should be safe. Why do you think the man said 'it still exists' like he thought something had happened to it?"

"Sky, if you see him again, let me know," he said, looking serious.

"I will," she said, letting out a sigh. "Why are you so obsessed with him? Please...tell me...what about the book? What could have made those things happen?"

"All right," Will said placing his hand upon his chin in a gesture of contemplation. "Let me get this straight, you opened the book and words just appeared?"

"Yes."

"That's impossible," he whispered in disbelief.

"I know it's impossible. So there's got to be a logical explanation."

"Right, and what did it say?"

"Well," Skylee thought about whether she should tell Will the whole story. If she said the words "lifeless fate" he would probably insist that she call security.

"Well what?" he said eyeing her suspiciously.

Skylee shuffled her feet and looked down. Will could always tell when she was lying. It was something he'd been able to do as long as she could remember.

She cleared her throat, looked up at him, and said, "I can't remember exactly what it said, I was pretty shocked, you know. But the first words were, it has begun."

"And what else?" Will asked watching her closely.

"Oh something about not waiting, I think, but what I don't understand is *how* the words appeared," she said, avoiding the fact that the words seemed like a warning.

Silence fell between them. Skylee felt an uneasy flutter in her stomach as she searched Will's face and tried to read his thoughts.

"Is there anything else," he asked. "Anything you might not want me to know?"

"What I'm trying to tell you is...that those words really did appear out of nowhere. I need you to believe me," she pleaded.

"Sky, you know I'm a skeptic. I don't believe in things like vampires and werewolves *or* Big Foot," Will added the last part with a sly grin, then he looked down at the envelope in her hand. "Was that with the gift?"

"Yes," she said curtly, feeling stung by his doubt.

"Maybe there's something in there that will explain all of this."

Skylee opened the envelope and pulled the card out.

"It's from my Mom," she said, handing the envelope to Will. She silently read it.

My Precious Pumpkin Pie,

I'm bursting with pride to have you for my daughter.

Your father, bless his soul, treasured the book and necklace. (which he always wore) In his last will and testament he stipulated that these items were to be passed on to his child. (that's you)

Love, Mom (that's me)

P.S. I found the note inside your father's book.

As soon as Skylee finished reading, she quickly closed the card. She glanced nervously at Will, hoping he had not seen her mom's kooky message. Dozens of questions raced through her mind. *There was a note in the book?* She hadn't seen it. *Was it for me?* she wondered. Her father had willed them to his child, which child? After all, her father did have a son from a previous marriage.

She looked down at the card in confusion. He treasured the book and always wore the necklace. She read it again. *He knew...he must have...about their magical powers.*

"Well, what does it say?" Will asked.

Skylee felt her cheeks blush as she cleared her throat and said, "Not that much, except mom did say there was a note. But I didn't see it."

"Hey, it's here inside the envelope," said Will, holding out an old piece of parchment with meticulous handwritten script. It was thin and fragile with a torn section at the bottom.

"Oh, let me see it," Skylee said as she reached for the parchment with trembling fingers.

She unfolded it carefully. While she looked at her father's flawless lettering, she became painfully aware of all the things she had missed. She had never heard his voice or seen his smile, and she had never held the hand that inked the words she now read.

> For My Dearest Child
>
> on Your Fifteenth Birthday,
>
> You are my hope in a dark world. You
>
> will bring light to all around you. I pass
>
> to you my treasure and reverence for the
>
> earth. Keep them safe, keep them close.
>
> You may encounter great trials
>
> before you reach your de
>
> In life you may shed tears but not al
>
> sad.
>
> I have great hope in you and I will wa

There was a long pause as Skylee tried to comprehend how her father could write her a message for her next birthday, especially before she was even born.

"Some of the words are torn off. I will ...w...a...," said Skylee as she looked up at Will with a puzzled expression. "I will—what?"

Will shrugged and stared at the parchment.

"Great trials...shed tears...I don't understand what this means," Skylee's voice grew tense. "I hate this—first the book with its strange lettering, and now this."

"And the stranger, don't forget about the stranger."

Even though Skylee knew he was only trying to help, she was frustrated with Will. He didn't really believe the book and necklace had magical powers and to make matters worse, all he could focus on was the stranger.

"This doesn't answer anything," she said, choking back tears.

Then a familiar sensation caught Skylee by surprise. The necklace was growing cold again. She could no longer hold back her emotions. A single tear streamed down Skylee's face and fell on the necklace forming a frozen droplet.

Out of nowhere, a strong gust of wind blew through the trees. Skylee and Will watched in stunned silence as a huge jet of water rose from the lake and moved toward them. Then it took shape, swirling over their heads in a perfect circle.

"What's happening?" gasped Skylee, staring up at the rotating water.

"No idea!" Will shouted in astonishment as he stuffed the envelope into his pocket.

The waterspout twirled faster and faster making their hair whip against their startled faces. Skylee had the odd sensation of being pulled upward. It was as if a giant invisible vacuum cleaner was going to suck her into the vortex. She heard Will yell out her name as her feet lifted off the ground.

FIVE

The Stepsister

Will caught Skylee by the hand, tugging her firmly down to earth. She latched on to him for dear life, as the card and note went airborne. The tunnel of water swirled lower, swooping over their heads until it seemed they could reach out and touch it.

"STAND BACK!" Will shouted as he pushed them backward. "It's coming for us!"

"Let's get outta here!" cried Skylee, trying to speak over the growing roar of the wind.

"RUN!" he yelled, taking her hand and pulling her along.

"Go right!" she called out. "No, No, to the left!"

The spiraling circle chased them wherever they went. As the water gained momentum the whirling sound grew deafening. Skylee covered her ears and stooped down. They both crouched low and Will tried to cover her with his body.

"STOP!" she screamed, looking up at the spinning twister

In that instant a ghostly stillness descended. And the great circle of water rained down around them in a torrential downpour. Skylee closed her eyes and let out a high-pitched scream, followed by silence.

"Is it over?" she whispered, opening her eyes.

"Yeah, I can't believe it."

Skylee and Will stood up and stared at the watery ring on the concrete surrounding them.

"Whoa, that was insane!" exclaimed Skylee.

"Blimey," Will croaked. "I thought you were gonna get sucked into that thing.

"Me too," she said, feeling as if her legs were made of jello.

"Wait a minute," he said, looking at her intently. "Look at your necklace!"

"My neck...lace?" she asked, picking it up and examining it.

Her frozen teardrop still clung to the amulet's cold surface. She placed her finger on the icy droplet and it melted away. Somehow she knew there had to be a connection between her necklace and the waterspout.

Out of nowhere, her card and note gracefully floated to the ground, landing at Skylee's feet. She gazed at Will, who briefly stared at them in disbelief, before scooping up the sopping wet notes and giving them to her.

Needless to say, there were several groups of tourists scattered around the park and many had seen the freakish, funnel-shaped spout. A few of them rushed up to ask Skylee and Will if they were all right. Within minutes, two security guards came and inspected the area. They asked loads of questions and finally decided the waterspout was a natural phenomenon. As Skylee watched the crowd disperse, the gravity of the situation began to soak in.

"I need to sit down," she said to Will.

"Me too," he replied. "Come on."

They walked in silence along a cobblestone path. When they reached a bench, which was nestled beneath a grove of cherry trees, they sat down.

Will gazed up at the pink blossoms, exhaled loudly and said, "Sky, I'm beginning to think there might be a Big Foot."

"Will, stop it," she said slapping him lightly on the arm. "This is serious. I think my necklace caused that water thing!"

"Okay, okay, I'm still trying to make sense out of all of this," he said. "What about the note? Did it explain anything?"

"No…it certainly didn't say anything to explain that," said Skylee, pointing down the path at the wet ring on the ground. "I don't understand any of this, but I intend to find out what it means."

"Okay, Sherlock," he said, nudging her with his elbow. "Exactly how are you going to do that?"

"It's elementary, my dear Watson," she said in a rather poor British accent as she held out the soggy notes. "First you're going to take these and dry them out."

"And how am I suppose to do that?"

"Really, must I think of everything?"

"Humph," grunted Will as he pulled the envelope out of his pocket. "Hey, there's something else in here."

It was an old photo of her mom and dad with her half brother. She took it from him, flipped it over and found the words *The Porter's San Francisco, California* written on the back.

"I haven't seen this one before," she said.

Skylee and Will studied the photo for a long while. She brushed her finger across her father's image. Lee Porter was a handsome outdoorsman with chestnut brown hair and an easy smile. Skylee squinted and held the photo closer. Her half brother looked like he was around fifteen or sixteen years old and was a younger version of their father. Standing between them was her mom with her arms draped over their shoulders.

"You know, maybe that note was for my brother Steve, not me," she said, thinking out loud. "I mean I'm not even in this picture."

"You're in the picture," Will said with a smile.

"No, I'm not!"

"Right there, your mum's pregnant with you," he said, pointing at her mother's stomach. "If your dad and brother hadn't died...if he'd lived to see you born I reckon there would've been two notes."

"You don't know that," Skylee said, looking sadly at Will. She carefully placed the damp notes and photo back inside the envelope and slipped it into the pocket of her dress. "But thanks for trying to make me feel better."

They looked at each other for a long moment. Then he gave her a lopsided grin and put his arm around her. Almost immediately she sensed an awkwardness she had never felt before. With all the changes that were happening in her life, it was the last thing she needed. They had always been so relaxed and comfortable together. She suddenly had a strong urge to ask him if something seemed different to him too. The words formed on the tip of her tongue. *No, don't do it,* she ordered herself. *He'll think you're crazy.*

"Hey, look on the bright side," said Will, who was clearly unaware of the struggle going on inside her head. "You're gaining a brother today...and a sister."

"I know," she said, feeling grateful to go along with his small talk. "I met Michael yesterday. He seems nice enough. And he's nothing like his sister."

"What do you mean?"

"Well, he fits in better with me and Mom. He lives in Thailand and he loves talking about all the environmental work he does there. Like helping grow crops, improving water supplies and stuff like that."

"And...uh, what's her name?"

"Chrism."

"She isn't like that?"

"Oh no, she hates nature."

Skylee felt a twinge of guilt as soon as she said it, but she couldn't help herself. The truth was, she dreaded having to introduce them. After all Chrism was a year older and much prettier than her. What if Will wanted to date her? Not that she cared who he dated. *But my best friend... and my stepsister,* she thought anxiously. *That would be awkward.*

"Why would anybody hate nature?" Will asked with a frown.

"I don't know, but it's true. She's never camped out before because she's afraid of bugs. And believe it or not, she isn't a vegetarian. I mean...really, who eats animal meat? I understand why older people still crave the real meat. They were use to it and so much was available back then. But Chrism grew up during the recovery—like us—when all we had was canned foods. Just the thought of canned meat turns my stomach!"

"Yeah, good old spam...glad those days are over. I don't get it. Why would she eat an animal when we have bio-meat?"

"Oh she claims it tastes weird," said Skylee shaking her head with raised eyebrows. "I tried explaining how bio-meat is made and how it's better for the environment. And do you know what she did? She whipped out her V-phone and showed me a website. It was nothing more than propaganda, obviously created by what's left of the meat industry. The site was plastered with pictures of glamorous Hollywood stars and the slogan was...Eat the real thing...be the real thing."

"Fair dinkum?" said Will.

"Yes, it's true," she replied, grinning at his Aussie slang. "The two things Chrism really cares about is how she looks and fashion," said Skylee, candidly. "I mean you should have seen the dress she picked out for me! I wouldn't be caught dead in something that sparkly."

Will eyed her dress and said, "I like what you're wearing. I thought...well when I first saw you...I thought you looked beautiful."

"And now you don't?" teased Skylee as she stood up and fidgeted with the flowing green fabric of her dress.

"No, I didn't mean that. I-I," Will stuttered. "I just meant that—"

"I knew what you meant. You aren't use to seeing me dressed as the asparagus queen," she said with a small curtsy, which made them both laugh.

"You're right," he said, rising from the bench. "I like to think of you as a...precious pumpkin pie."

"Ah-ah," she stammered. "You saw that?"

"Yeah, it was right there in black and white."

"Will!" she bellowed, giving him a knuckle punch to his arm.

"Ow," he said laughingly.

"Don't ever call me that again," she said, fighting back an urge to laugh.

"Oh, come on you know it's funny."

Skylee smiled grudgingly. Then she peered down at Will's watch and gasped. "Is that the time? I have to go find Chrism. I was told right before I came out here that she needed my help. She'll be mad for sure now."

"Just tell her you were held up by a giant, swirling, vortex of water."

"Rrrright," said Skylee, rolling her eyes at him as she hurried back to the Remembrance Hall.

* * * * * * *

Chrism Faraway scurried around the Reception Hall mumbling under her breath about her soon to be stepsister, who had walked right past her without a word. Chrism had spent the morning styling her naturally straight, brown hair into soft curls, meticulously applying her makeup and getting a manicure. She needed Skylee's help with the wedding decorations so she wouldn't spoil her look or ruin her designer dress. At fifteen and three quarters, she had often been told she could be a model and was frequently mistaken as being seventeen or eighteen.

She looked around the large room and disappointedly sighed. Chrism had already told every friend and relative in sight that things would be more organized and elegant if the wedding hadn't been announced at the last minute. She had wanted only the very best for her dad, but her new stepmother seemed to have other plans. The weird recycled fabrics, eco-theme, and cheap looking organic foods were an embarrassment. Apparently having an environmental wacko for a stepmother wasn't going to be easy on her sophisticated lifestyle. She hoped her future stepsister wasn't going to be as hopeless.

"That little dweeb didn't even stop when I called her," she muttered. "I'll never get all this done by myself."

Chrism noticed a lantern on the floor and spoke under her breath as she picked it up.

"With all the money dad dropped for this wedding, you'd think that frumpy wedding planner would've made sure this was done," she complained, as she looked up at a hook where the lantern should have hung. "If you want something done right, you have to do it yourself, even if you're paying someone else to do it."

Grabbing a chair, she impatiently scooted it along the floor until she reached the spot under the hook. She climbed onto the chair and vicariously balanced on her stiletto heels with an outstretched arm holding the lantern. She was impressed with herself. Just as she managed to hook the paper lantern, she heard a noisy clamor as her cousins burst through the door and bounded into the room.

Isabella and Gabriela Faraway were seven-year-old identical twins, who went by their nicknames, Izzy and Gaby. The redheaded girls darted around the room, up to their usual mischievous behavior. Without warning, the game of tag went terribly awry, and the girls collided with Chrism's chair.

"WHAT THE—" she shrieked as she lost her footing and fell backward toward the floor.

Chrism braced herself and expected pain, but strong arms caught her in mid air. She looked up and stared into the most beautiful pair of steel blue eyes she had ever seen. Then she noticed the stubble on his squared off, cleft chin and his disheveled hair. He wasn't really her type, a little too rugged for her taste. Still, she couldn't help but notice he had caught her like she was a feather.

He didn't move a muscle. Chrism continued to stare and immediately sized him up. There seemed to be an unapproachable look in his eyes. She had met his type before, guys who never show vulnerability. The kind of guy a girl of her caliber should steer clear of.

"Ya know, little girls shouldn't try teh stand on chairs in their mum's shoes," Airon said with a lifted brow. "But, well done on the dismount."

His strong accent fascinated Chrism, but she didn't like his mocking tone and the mention of her mother was like a jab through her heart. It was a touchy subject, because her mom had walked away from the family when she was only three. Chrism felt her temper rise as she thought of how many times her mother had waltzed back into her life only to disappear again.

"Obviously YOUR mother never taught you any manners. Take your hands off me, you pervert!" Chrism said as her faced reddened.

"Did ya just call me a bloody perve?" asked Airon with a slight grin.

"YES! TAKE YOUR HANDS OFF ME, I SAID!" she shouted, slapping at his hands as he held her tighter.

No one was going to make fun of her, even if he was a ruggedly handsome Aussie. She wiggled and squirmed to free herself.

"An' if I don't what are ya gonna do?" Airon taunted.

"I'll call security. Put me down!" Chrism spat out.

Airon looked baffled, he softened his hold and abruptly placed her feet on the floor.

"As ya wish, yer highness," he said, his voice dripping with sarcasm.

The two of them stood there frozen in place. It was like a standoff in an old western movie, without the guns, just eyes staring each other down. Obviously neither wanted to show weakness to the other but, for a fleeting moment, each had a slight look of regret, then pride took over and both looked away.

Chrism left the room talking loudly enough for Airon and anyone around to hear.

"Well, he's got nerve! I should get the security guard..."

Everyone in the room could still hear her complaining as the hall doors closed behind her.

* * * * * * *

Ten minutes later, Skylee watched as Chrism, who was wearing an irritated look on her face, entered the reception hall. Her spiked heels clicked loudly on the marble floor and her satin dress swayed with each step. She was nervously looking over her shoulder, as if she were being followed. Wobbling slightly, she turned and plowed right into Skylee.

"Sorry," Chrism muttered still looking back.

"That's okay," said Skylee pleasantly.

Chrism whipped her head around and looked at her with an odd mixture of anger and pride. Skylee dreaded what was coming. And sure enough her stepsister pointed her perfectly manicured finger inches away from Skylee's nose.

"Where have you been? I needed help and you went flying by me like you had just seen a ghost. You didn't even answer when I called you. I shouldn't have to deal with all this stuff by myself," Chrism complained, flailing her arms and pointing around the room. "So where were you?"

"I just...I just...had to do something," Skylee stuttered, taking a step back.

"Oh, you had to do something. Like I didn't?"

Chrism gave Skylee a defiant stare and put her hands on her hips. Skylee looked down at the gleaming floor. She was thankful that looks couldn't kill, otherwise she'd be dead. An uneasy silence fell between them.

Skylee cleared her throat and tried to come up with the right words. "Well...I mean....It was..." she stammered.

"Whatever," Chrism interrupted, impatiently. "But please stay around in case I find more things that the useless wedding planner didn't do."

"What did she not do?" questioned Skylee, her pale eyes scanning the hall.

"What *did* she do, is a better question," Chrism scoffed.

"I don't see anything out of place."

"Of course you don't, now that I put my life in danger to hang all of those lanterns," Chrism whined, as she crossed her arms and stared again at Skylee.

"I'm sorry, I should have been here," Skylee replied, sympathetically. "Did anything else happen?"

"Yeah—you could say that!" Chrism said, in a halting angry voice. "It was awful."

"What was?" Skylee asked, softly placing her hand on Chrism's arm. "What happened?"

"I was accosted by the biggest brainless jerk on earth and I hope I never lay eyes on him again!" she said, in a melodramatic tone.

"You're kidding?" Skylee gasped, looking around the room and wondering if it had been the stranger. "What did you do?"

As soon as the words escaped Skylee's lips regret welled up inside her. She had only gotten to know her future stepsister in the last few weeks, but she had already discovered that Chrism had a flair for the dramatic. For the next fifteen minutes, she rambled on and on about the incident with the lantern and the guy who saved her but insulted her as well. Skylee was relieved when she described her assailant's blue eyes.

As the tirade continued, Skylee glanced over Chrism's shoulder and noticed Will and Airon entering the Reception Hall. Will had changed out of his jeans and was now wearing a retro-looking pinstriped suit. Skylee felt a swell of pride as she watched her two dearest friends coming toward her, looking tall and handsome in their wedding attire.

Airon reached them first, strolling up with his hands comfortably in his pockets. He brushed past Chrism and leaned over to hug Skylee.

"Skippy, good teh see ya, been awhile," Airon said calling her by a nickname he had given her years ago. His gaze then turned to Chrism, who had stopped her tirade mid-sentence. "Why don't ya introduce me teh yer mate, or as ya say, friend?"

"Oh, she's not my friend...uh...I mean...this is my soon to be stepsister, Chrism Faraway," said Skylee as she turned to her. "And this is Airon Butler and his cousin, Will Butler."

Airon smoothly reached out his hand and in a suave tone said, "G'day, Chrism. I believe we've met."

All the color drained from Chrism's face and her bottom jaw fell open. She seemed to be unable to speak, and the silence grew.

Airon leaned in closer as Chrism's face hardened. "I'm lookin' forward teh gettin' teh know ya better."

"In your dreams!" Chrism blurted out and flipped her hair over her shoulder pushing past his outstretched hand as she headed to the far end of the room.

Will and Skylee watched in confused silence as she walked away.

"What was that all about?" Will asked Airon.

"Eh...she seems teh be ungrateful that I saved her from busting her beaut of an—"

"So, *you're* the brainless jerk?" Skylee interrupted, glaring at him. "Great," she went on, softer, but with worry in her tone. "She's hard enough to deal with and now you've gone and made her mad."

"I made *her* mad! Skippy, I saved her!" insisted Airon.

"But you did make her mad!" she insisted in a raised voice.

"Okay, keep it down, people are staring," Will pleaded, stepping between them.

"We've got heaps bigger issues teh worry about than a few blokes starin'," Airon said through clenched teeth. "Like the fact that her new sister has an attitude."

"Like you don't?" Skylee shot back.

"Listen, ya don't know the facts," Airon said firmly.

Skylee felt her face grow hot and tears welling up in her eyes. It seemed as if the strange events of the day and the stress of the wedding had weakened her resolve.

"Sky," said Will in a calming voice. "Why don't you go ahead and see your mum before the wedding."

Airon opened his mouth to say something but stopped short when Will seized him by the shoulder. Skylee choked back her tears and managed a small smile.

"Okay, but if you see Chrism again, be nice," she said, looking harshly at Airon.

"We will, won't we, mate?" said Will as he squeezed his cousin's shoulder.

There was a strained look on Airon's face, but he nodded in agreement. As Skylee turned to leave, she heard Will ask Airon to go easy on her and then he began telling him about the weird waterspout. She glanced back at them over her shoulder and felt the necklace cooling against the fabric of her dress.

* * * * * * *

Chrism furiously stomped her way down the hall, tugging at the top of her strapless gown as she went. *That arrogant jerk,* she thought. Her heart was racing. She rubbed her hands along the shiny satin of her dress wishing she'd worn something less restricting. *Where does that toad get off, trying to act like Prince Charming?*

As she trotted onward, her exasperation was quickly being replaced with a feeling of insecurity. She wasn't sure why he had gotten to her.

Really, who does he think he is? A tiny voice deep inside her mind responded...*he's the guy who caught you when you were falling.* Chrism stopped and groaned then strutted on. She had more important things to think about, like her dad getting married for one. She rounded the corner and headed for his dressing room. She wanted to see the groom before the wedding.

The groom...even inside her head it sounded strange. After all, she had not had long to get use to the idea. It had only been a month-long engagement. And it was a very good month to tell the truth.

Thanks to her father's guilty conscious, she had been able to talk him into just about anything. It had been four glorious weeks of shopping, movies, chocolate and more shopping. And her biggest accomplishment had been convincing him to hire her favorite band, Fifth of Droid, for the reception. She giggled just thinking about it. They were only the hottest band on the planet. *It must have cost dad a fortune,* she thought as she reached the groom's dressing room. *Oh well, they're worth it.*

Chrism lifted her hand to knock, but before her knuckles made contact the door swung open, and Alex Faraway stepped out. Her dad was a tall man, six four to be exact, with fine blonde hair and deep-set blue eyes. She stared in amazement at how polished he looked in his tux. She was proud of him for taking a chance on love when her own mother had shattered his heart. "Dad, you look great. You should dress like this all the time."

He gave her a fatherly hug and said, "Thanks, sweetheart, are you really okay—um—"

"With you getting married? I've told you, I am. I like Janis," Chrism said earnestly. "The whole 'green' thing is a bit much but...I would like anyone that makes you smile like this."

She hadn't seen him this happy in a long time. Truthfully, Chrism did worry a bit about how much time he would have for her now. His job kept him on the road and at times she and Michael were left to fend for themselves. She knew he worried about them although he rarely expressed it, but sometimes she could see it in his eyes. It hadn't been easy for him to be both a father and mother to them.

"Your tie is crooked. Let me fix it, I don't want you to embarrass me in front of all those people," laughed Chrism as she tugged on his tie.

Her father chuckled. "Embarrass you? We can't have that," he paused, and then spoke seriously, "Chrism, I know I haven't—"

"Dad, stop right there. I know what you're going to say—you think you haven't been around enough, now more people are going to require your attention, blah, blah, blah. Come on, we've had this conversation before and like I said, I'm proud of what you do. I mean really, how many girls can say their dad is a secret agent?"

"Chrism," he whispered, looking around nervously.

"Okay, I know hush-hush. But seriously, you save lives. That's huge! Now, you and Janis can save lives together. Honestly, when Michael decided to go to the other side of the world to help a bunch of people he doesn't even know, I'll admit...it was lonely. Now I won't be alone anymore, remember, my new little sis will be with me," she said, trying to cover her feelings of uncertainty.

"But this is a big change for you," he said.

"For all of us," corrected Chrism.

Alex smiled, "You know I love you and I'm—"

"Here for me as I am for you. Getting married won't change that, nothing will. Now, enough of this serious stuff, you're going to make me cry and mess up my makeup. I've worked really hard to look this good," said Chrism, patting his chest. "Now, there, your tie is straight. Look at the time, I better go and find Skylee, to make sure she's ready."

Chrism turned to go then stopped, looking back over her shoulder she lightheartedly said, "You nervous?"

"A little bit, but not about marrying Janis, I'm sure about that, it's just the reception and the—"

"Dance? You'll be fine. Besides we have Fifth of Droid, everyone will be watching them. And really who cares, right? As long as you're happy." Chrism knew he was a horrible dancer. Truthfully, she wondered how it would work out.

"Well, just in case, if I do make a fool of myself will you create a distraction?" he asked, sounding half-serious.

"Like what?" said Chrism. "Yell fire?"

"Desperate times, call for desperate measures," teased her dad with a wink as he opened the door. "Ladies first."

The two them made their way down the hall, holding hands like they did when she was a little girl until he went one direction and she headed off to find Skylee. This was a good day, despite the previous encounter with the blue-eyed hunk. Wait, not a hunk, a jerk and not her type, but it didn't hurt to look.

SIX

The Wedding

Several minutes had past while Skylee stood at the door to the Bride's Room thinking of the mysterious words in the book. She replayed them in her head for the hundredth time, trying to figure them out. It has begun...*what has begun?* He shall not wait...*okay first, who is he? And second, wait for what or who?* To bring about a lifeless fate... *I don't like the sound of that. A lifeless fate... meaning death? My father's fate was death. Is it a message for him or me?*

If only her father *were* alive, she would ask him. She had always wondered what it would be like to talk to him. Her mind raced back in time to when she was a small girl, curled up in her mother's lap, listening to stories about him. Her mom's voice echoed in her head.

"Okay, Baby-cakes, one more, but then it's off to bed. Once upon a time there was a brave man, a captain named Lee, who loved fighting forest fires. He wore a shiny helmet and a suit that would never burn. One day, when the captain and his men were returning after battling a ferocious fire, he came upon a lady, called Janis of the woods. She was traveling on the treacherous trail and had fallen, twisting her ankle. The captain swooped in, picked her up, and carried her all the way back to the village..."

Skylee loved her mom's kooky stories about their courtship. But how much did she really know about her dad. Something seemed to be missing. And now she felt as if his book and necklace were drawing her into a mysterious place to look for the answers.

She stared at the door and took a deep breath. Maybe her mom knew about the magical message in the book. She lifted her necklace, gazed at its beauty, and then hid it inside the neckline of her dress, fearing it might bring painful memories to her mom on her wedding day.

She could hear soft laughter through the door. Her mom and Will's mom, Ann Butler, had been friends for Skylee's entire life, so she thought of her as a family member. In fact she called her "Auntie Ann" although lately it seemed kind of childish as a girl of almost fifteen.

Ann's story was a bit of a mystery to her. Skylee knew her aunt had first been a friend of her father, but anytime she was asked about how or when they met she would change the subject.

Skylee strained to hear their conversation behind the door, although she knew she shouldn't be eavesdropping. A small giggle escaped her mouth when she heard her mom and Ann talking about the marriage proposal. Then a familiar name rang in her ears, Lee, her heart skipped a beat. They weren't talking about Alex Faraway's proposal but the day her father proposed. Intrigued, she placed her ear to the door hoping to hear more.

"It was crazy," her mom said. "He actually blurted it out—Will you marry me?—with smoke and flames surrounding us."

"That's hot," Ann said with a laugh. "Only Lee would've thought of proposing at a time like that, although, as a firefighter, he should have known better. Come to think of it, you've had two unusual proposals. I mean, the circumstances when Alex popped the question couldn't exactly be described as boring either."

"What can I say...life threatening situations seem to end up in marriage for me," her mom said lightheartedly. "And speaking of proposals, is there anything you need to tell me?"

"Huh?" said Ann.

"I've noticed you've been spending a lot of time with your friend Levi lately. I'm glad you invited him to the wedding. Did he bring his son along? Oh, um, tell me the boy's name again."

"It's Hawk and yes, he's with his dad."

Skylee hadn't seen Levi and Hawk for almost a year. She didn't know that much about them, except that Will didn't seem to like either one of them very much.

"That's right," said her mom. "I love that...Hawk, it's such an adventurous name. Any child with a name like that should be able to take flight out into the world and become whatever they want."

Skylee shook her head and thought, *thank God she didn't name me Pigeon.*

"Janis, I hate to darken your thoughts on flights of fancy, but hawks are birds of prey and go about eating the smaller, helpless creatures of this world."

"Think positive, Ann, think positive," her mom sweetly said. "That Hawk sure is a handsome guy, just like his dad," her mom continued, in an amusing tone, which made Skylee smile. "So tell me the truth, is it getting serious?"

"Me and Levi?" scoffed Ann. "Of course not. He's just a friend. Besides we're both too hardheaded to be anything else. I mean, that man would argue with a corpse."

"Friends uh? Sometimes that's how it starts and you know, when Alex and I were sent to Brazil on assignment we argued nonstop. But when our jeep slid off the road...everything changed. If he hadn't been in so much pain I don't think he would've confessed his true feelings."

"And if you hadn't been scared to death that he was going to die on you, you wouldn't have finally realized that you were in love with him. Of course I knew it all the time," Ann laughed, and then grew serious. "Actually, I think Lee would've approved of Alex."

Skylee pressed her ear closer to the door, eager to hear more about her dad.

"I do too, he wouldn't have wanted us to be alone forever. You know, a part of Lee will always be with me...in Skylee," her mom said sounding like she had a catch in her throat. "And I thought it would be good to remind her of that today. I didn't want her to think I'd forgotten her father, so I decided to go ahead and give her the things he wanted her to have. The idea just popped into my head the second I woke up this morning. So I wrapped them up for her. His most prized possessions, you know, the ones that were mentioned in his will."

"Oh, I didn't—uh—you gave them to her?"

"Yes, Lee's favorite book and—"

"His book," Ann said in a surprised tone. "I thought you put that in storage after you couldn't find anyone to translate it."

"That's what I thought too, but a couple of days ago I found it along with some other things of Lee's just sitting out on my table."

"That's strange."

"I guess they turned up while Skylee and I were packing," said her mom. "I don't really remember where they'd been. I know that Lee's will said to give them to her on her fifteenth birthday but then I got this overwhelming feeling to give them to her today.

"Them?" asked Ann sounding slightly tense.

"Uh-huh the book, a note Lee wrote before he died and a—"

Crash

The door had been slightly ajar and Skylee leaned a little too hard. She landed in a heap flattening a box that had once held the bridal gown.

"SKYLEE! Are you all right?" cried her mom, rushing over to help her up.

"Oh my gosh," she said, looking up to see her Auntie Ann, looming over her in a dark green dress. "Did I break anything?"

"Not unless you broke a bone," Ann joked with a sparkle in her brown eyes. "Are you okay?"

"Yeah, I'm okay, but I think this may not recover," said Skylee, reaching down to pick up the crushed box.

Janis and Ann were both gazing at Skylee with wide eyes. She bashfully clutched the box to her chest. The two of them were looking at her exactly the same way they did the first time she rode her bike.

"Oh, Sky," Ann said. "You look beautiful. Your dress is perfect, I can't believe how grown up you are."

Skylee felt her face turn pink. She didn't like having attention focused on her.

"She's right, Sweetie-pie," her mom said, beaming with pride. "Kiwi green is definitely your color."

"Thanks," Skylee replied shyly. "I just wanted to come in and ask a question."

Skylee took a deep breath and gathered her courage. They would probably think she was having a mental breakdown if she told them everything that had happened. This wasn't the time for that. Besides, all she really wanted was to find out what they knew about the book and the necklace.

"Mom, have you ever noticed anything strange about Dad's book?"

Her mom seemed to be searching her memory for an answer, but Skylee was distracted as she realized that her Auntie Ann's face, which was normally tan, had turned as white as a ghost.

"Well, yes, I remember trying to figure out what the lettering said. I even took it to some experts but no one recognized the language," Janis said with a puzzled look. "Why?"

Skylee didn't answer but looked at Ann, who seemed to be standing there like a tall statue. Her face was still pale and her eyes were glassy.

"What about you, Auntie Ann? Do you know anything about the book?"

Ann looked away and busied her hands by tugging on her dress. Skylee searched her odd expression but could not read its meaning.

"Well, yes your mom and I were just talking about the book. Hmmmm, let me think—"

Before Ann finished her sentence, a sharp clicking noise interrupted her. The sound came from the hallway, growing louder by the second. It was familiar to Skylee's ears. She glanced at the open door just in time to see Chrism stride into the room in her spiky high heels.

"WHAT? YOU HAVEN'T EVEN PUT ON THE..."Chrism's loud voice trailed off as her eyes locked on the dress hanging from a hook on the wall. "Is *that* your wedding dress?"

"Yes, isn't it perfect?" her mom said, happily looking up at it. "It was made just for me by an amazing eco-designer. The fabric is hemp and the dye is all-natural. It's a one of a kind creation."

"Yeah," sneered Chrism. "I can honestly say I've never seen anything like it."

Skylee had been so fixated on finding out more about the book that she hadn't even noticed the dress. *No way,* she thought gawking up at it. *She's not seriously going to wear that.* It was the brightest, greenest, tie-dyed wedding dress she had ever seen. *Yep, it's perfect all right. That is, if you're marrying the jolly green giant.*

"OMG," shouted Chrism. "The wedding begins in fifteen minutes! The best man hasn't shown up, and you haven't put, um, *that* on yet. We should be getting to our places."

"Okay, you're right," Janis said in a calm voice. "And don't worry, Chrism. Your dad called and his best man is on the way, something about a later flight. Now, you two girls go ahead or Chloe will have a fit.

I'll be ready on time. Your Auntie Ann and I have it all under control. Don't we Ann?"

"I don't—I mean—sure it's under control," Ann responded, clearly distracted.

Chrism let out a dramatic sigh and said, "Skylee, we have to go, now!"

"Just a minute," Skylee said, crossing the room to her mother. "Don't worry about me, enjoy your wedding day, I love you, Mom."

Her mom kissed her on the cheek and gave her a hug. Then she went to Chrism and hugged and kissed her too. Skylee glanced over at Ann, the same dazed expression now seemed frozen on her face. She planned to ask her about the book again, as soon as possible.

"Oh, dear, I better pull myself together," Janis said as she released Chrism and wiped tears. "Okay, we've got to get moving if I'm going to become Mrs. Faraway today."

Skylee smiled at her mom then turned and said, "Let's go Chrism."

Chrism, who nodded with watery eyes, was silent as they made their way down the hallway.

Less than five minutes later, as the new stepsisters were hurrying their way to the wedding site, Chrism had returned to her talkative self and began giving Skylee orders about the ceremony.

"Remember, we're supposed to walk up the aisle just before Ann," she instructed condescendingly as she teetered along on her pointed heels. "When we reach the front row I stand on the groom's side and you stand on the bride's side."

"Okay," Skylee said, although she was confused. "Hmm, which is the bride's side?"

"Honestly," Chrism answered with a smirk. "The *left*, of course."

Skylee didn't say anything. She was fully aware of the sarcasm, given that her mom could best be described as a left-leaning environmentalist. Chrism's dad, on the other hand, was known by the nickname Mr. Conservative. And so their parents were a perfect example of opposites attracting. In fact, their sudden wedding announcement had shocked everyone who knew them, especially their daughters.

Her mom had first met Alex while working at GEMA, a classified agency formed after The Day. Skylee liked to say she worked at G-files, which she came up with after watching a really old television series called the X-files. Honestly she wasn't sure exactly what her mom did at work, but knowing her, it had something to do with protecting the environment.

Skylee followed Chrism as they exited The Memorial Building and stopped at the top of the stairs, which overlooked the wedding site. There were dozens of cherry trees lining the water around The Memorial Grounds. The light pink blossoms contrasted with the cobalt blue water surrounding The Globe Fountain.

"Do you know why they put the Memorial here?" Skylee asked Chrism.

"Not really," she replied in a bored tone.

"It's because of those," said Skylee, pointing toward a row of older looking trees. "Prunus Serrulata or Japanese Cherry Trees. It's a miracle they survived."

"And you're telling me this dorky trivia because…"

"Oh, I just thought it was interesting."

Chrism pointed at the wedding platform, which was made entirely of hay and said, "You want to talk about something interesting? Try explaining that."

Skylee didn't know what to say. How could she explain her mom's eco-eccentric ways?

"Well at least they have nice chairs," she told Chrism, who looked unimpressed.

Of course she was right. The only normal decorations at the wedding site were a long green aisle runner and the white chairs. And true to form, her mom had insisted on plants that would be used after the ceremony to feed free-range animals. Rows of corn lined the outer edges of the platform and vegetables of all kinds were displayed like floral arrangements.

"It's weird, isn't it?" sighed Skylee in humiliation.

"No, it's not weird, it's demented," said Chrism, rolling her eyes.

Skylee let out a soft little laugh.

"Glad you find this funny. I can't believe our parents are getting married down there," said Chrism, looking at the scene in total disgust.

Skylee's embarrassment faded as her mind fixed on the words *our parents*. Those two little words meant she was no longer an only child. She really was about to get a sister.

There was a brief silence, which was broken by the sound of a steel drum band warming up to play.

"Oh great, a Margaritaville Bridal March," said Chrism. "How classy."

Without warning, a chilling sensation began on Skylee's chest, as her necklace grew colder. *Not now.* She gently pulled the necklace out by its chain, cautious of the freezing metal.

"Wow! That's beautiful," Chrism gasped, eyeing the shining amulet. "Where'd you get it?"

"It belonged to my Dad, a family heirloom, I guess."

Chrism reached out to examine it more closely, and the moment her fingers touched the amulet Skylee felt a jolt. Chrism shuddered and tightly shut her eyes. Silvery light glimmered out of the necklace and down Skylee's arm. It quickly made its way up Chrism's arm and onto her bare shoulder stopping at a diamond shaped birthmark. The faint colored mark glowed silver for a split second then turned dark brown.

Skylee felt a surge of power flow out of her. Her knees weakened as blood rushed to her head. She suddenly felt faint. *It's happening again.* Skylee pushed Chrism's hand away causing her to let go of the necklace and open her eyes.

"You shouldn't have touched it!" she snapped sharply at her.

As she struggled to regain her strength, Skylee realized that her soon-to-be stepsister seemed completely unaware of what had just happened. Nervously glancing around, she checked to see if anyone had seen the bright light, but no one was paying any attention. However, when she returned her gaze to Chrism, she was scowling at her, and then she stared angrily at the necklace.

"Well, you don't have to be so stingy! I wasn't trying to take it."

"Oh, no," said Skylee, shaking her head, "I didn't mean it like that. I just didn't want you to get hurt."

"Hurt? Why, is it a secret weapon?" mocked Chrism, narrowing her eyes at Skylee.

"No, but it's not just a normal necklace either—It's a long story. So did you, uh, do you feel okay?"

"Of course I feel okay," she said with annoyance. "What are you up to? Stop trying to change the subject. Why are you so touchy about that necklace?"

"I'll tell you about it later. I promise, but right now, we better think about the wedding. It's going to start any minute now."

"What do you mean, not a normal necklace? Why not?" Chrism asked in a persistent tone.

Before Skylee could think up an answer she felt a light tap on her shoulder.

"Hallo," said a man with a deep voice, extending his beefy palm. "I'm Samuel Muller."

Skylee nodded at him as her hand and wrist were gobbled up in his handshake. He was an enormous man, at least six and a half feet tall, with dark brown skin. His head was completely bald and his almond shaped eyes were wrinkled in a smile. As he spoke, Skylee was mesmerized by his striking appearance and lilting accent.

She soon discovered he lived in South Africa, where he was a professor of animal science and research.

"...ya see t'was years ago, Alex and meself, we were thick as thieves in our college days, and he's been like a brother ever since. So I came all the way from Cape Town for this lovely day. And, ya be the newest in the Faraway clan, then?" he asked with a low chuckle.

"Yes, I'm Skylee, it's nice to—"

"Oh, Doc Muller, I'm so glad to see you," Chrism interrupted, throwing her arms around him as he let out a long booming laugh.

Skylee watched as they hugged. She took in his brightly colored robe and hat. His jovial round face and neatly trimmed goatee didn't reveal his age.

"Well, child, ya be growing like a weed, I barely recognized ya," he said releasing Chrism and patting her on the head. "So, how is my favorite goddaughter doing?"

"I'm fine," she said, beaming up at him.

"Good, good. Well, of course ya are. Today's the day. And if ya ask me, the two of ya are already looking like sisters," he said looking back and forth at them.

"Oh...um...thanks," said Chrism, looking uncomfortable. "So when did you get here? I was afraid you weren't going to make it in time."

"It was close, but the old lady finally let me out of me cage to catch a flight yesterday. Ya knew I wouldn't miss the chance to be yer father's best man."

"Oh, you aren't fooling me. I know you have Ms. Alice wrapped around your finger," said Chrism with a giggle. "Anyway, thank goodness you're here. It wouldn't be the same without you."

He let out another deep laugh. "I thought the day would never come when I'd see me old chum get married again. I wouldn't miss it for all the tea in China. Now, can ya point me to the groom?"

Chrism's reaction to Doc Muller was yet another side of her that Skylee had never seen before. She had taken on the appearance of a small, happy child in his presence. Not the complicated teenager Skylee was accustomed to dealing with. Of course there were numerous reasons for Chrism's difficult attitude. The fact that she had a "now you see her now you don't" mom, a brother who seemed to be a saint, and a dad with a top-secret job—just to name a few.

Skylee's thoughts turned to the necklace. She didn't understand why it kept turning hot and cold, or what caused the silver light? She suddenly realized that it could be dangerous. *It could have hurt her*. She glanced at Chrism's shoulder and the birthmark was still dark brown. This wasn't the time to tell her. Maybe she wouldn't notice it.

"SKYLEE!" Chrism called, loudly. "Did you hear me?"

Snapping back into the moment, she shrugged and said, "No, what did you say?"

"I said that creeper friend of yours is escorting my Aunt Linda to her seat. Does he always wear that stupid smirk on his face?"

"Chrism, you've got Airon all wrong."

"Oh puh-lease, it's not like I can't spot a jerk when I see one."

"I know he comes off a little pushy, but he's got some issues."

"Thanks, Captain Obvious, but we all have our issues. That's no excuse," she said, glaring at Airon. "He's probably telling my Aunt the whole humiliating story about our first meeting right now."

Skylee watched Airon as he carefully guided a tall redhead toward the first row of seating, followed by her husband and two adorable girls. Chrism explained that her uncle Ron Faraway, Alex's younger brother, was a diplomat who had met and married Linda in Brazil. Their identical twin daughters looked like little red haired cherubs but looks can be deceiving. According to Chrism, the girls were a bundle of continuous thrill seeking energy. Skylee could scarcely believe her eyes when they locked arms and head-butted Airon right in the stomach as he tried to help them to their seats.

"Couldn't have happened to a nicer guy," said Chrism with a smirk.

"Poor Airon," Skylee whispered as she watched him stiffly walk up the aisle with a pained expression on his face.

"You really do like that arrogant toad, don't you?" asked Chrism, looking amazed.

"He's not an arrogant—of course I like him, I've known him and Will my whole life. They're my closest friends," said Skylee, still watching them as they escorted guests to their seats.

"So he's a friend? Nothing more?"

"Oh, no. Airon's like a big brother to me."

"And Will, what about him?"

"Will is...he's..." Skylee stammered and her face grew hot. Her mind raced. How could she explain her feelings for Will?

For a brief second, she considered telling Chrism about the change she felt in their relationship and her fear of losing her best friend. Then another option came to Skylee's mind, why complicate things any further, she would tell her what she wished were true.

"He's my best friend, always has been, always will be."

Chrism smiled. "Didn't you introduce Will and Airon as...did I hear you right...cousins?"

"Yes, but Ann adopted Airon after his parents were killed in a plane crash. Will's father was—"

"So...you and Will are best friends?" she interrupted.

"Chrism, didn't you hear what I said?" Skylee asked feeling annoyed by her lack of compassion.

"Yeah, yeah, plane crash. What about you and Will? You're sure, you're just friends?"

Skylee sighed. "I'm sure," she said, but deep in her heart she wasn't.

Expectancy filled the air as the music stopped momentarily and all eyes turned to Skylee and Chrism.

"Let's get this freak show over," scoffed Chrism. "Follow me."

"Now?" Skylee asked looking down at the crowd, which made her feel like running the other direction.

"Yeah now, unless you have something better to do than be in you mother's wedding."

Skylee stood there for another moment, she felt like an awkward geek standing next to her pretty stepsister. *Aren't stepsisters supposed to be ugly?* she thought. *Oh yeah, I'm a stepsister too.*

"Come on," demanded Chrism as the sound of steel drums started up again.

They made their way to the end of the long green carpet, walking shoulder to shoulder down the aisle. On their way to the altar Skylee felt like time had slowed down. Her legs went wobbly as a wave of weakness washed over her. She tried to calm her nerves and focused to her left looking for a familiar face.

Will was sitting next to Airon on the bride's side. He smiled and gave her an encouraging wink. Skylee weakly smiled back and then she noticed her grandparents sitting in the front row. She knew how lucky she was to have them in her life. Not many kids her age had been as fortunate.

The hardships after The Day cost many elderly people their lives. However, Skylee's maw-maw and paw-paw seemed to be able to survive anything. Her mom's only sister, Janie was as tough as nails too. Her aunt was the most unpredictable, spur of the moment person she had ever known. Skylee wondered why she wasn't sitting up front with their small family.

"I don't see my Aunt Janie," she whispered to Chrism.

"Janie? Really...they named their daughter's Janis and Janie?" she asked without changing the perfect smile on her face.

"Yeah, I know it's strange. I wonder why she isn't here?"

"She's probably here somewhere," replied Chrism, glancing over at Skylee. "Are you okay?"

"Uh-huh," she said, but she wasn't okay and somehow her new stepsister sensed how near she was to fainting. In one swift movement, Chrism locked her arm around Skylee's elbow and smoothly swung them around into two seats on the front row.

"What are you doing? I thought we were supposed to stand on the platform," she said in a weak voice, feeling grateful to be sitting down.

"I wasn't about to let you make a fool of yourself...or me!" said Chrism. "Anyway, how many of these people do you think know the difference?"

She was talking just loud enough to be sure Airon, who was sitting right behind them with Will, would hear. That's how it was with Chrism, she could somehow manage to do the nicest thing and make the snidest comment all at the same moment.

The music shifted into yet another tune and the maid of honor began her journey to the altar. Ann's graceful gait made it appear as if she were floating down the aisle. Skylee watched as her aunt's gaze shifted downward to rest upon the amulet. A look of sheer horror raced across her face, and she suddenly faltered.

There was a muffled gasp from the congregation as Ann caught her footing just in time to keep from falling flat. All the while, her eyes never left the necklace. Skylee knew how agile and unshakable she usually was, seeing her lose her footing was strange. *Something's wrong*, she thought.

In the next few minutes, more than a stumble made Skylee aware that something was wrong indeed. When the Bridal March began, everyone stood and looked up the aisle but her mother was not there. The musicians stopped. Skylee glanced over her shoulder at Alex, who looked like he had been kicked in the stomach.

"Where is she? I'll never forgive you if she leaves my dad standing at the altar," Chrism threatened in Skylee's ear.

"She wouldn't do that. She'll be here," she whispered back.

"She'd better!" Chrism said a bit too loud.

At that moment, the wedding planner sashayed down the aisle clearly trying to look as calm as possible. She whispered something in Alex's ear and quickly took a seat near the front. Alex then leaned over and whispered to his uncle, Daniel Faraway, who was presiding over the ceremony.

"Well, Well, Well," said Daniel, in a thick Scottish brogue. "It looks like my nephew's bride has gone and got herself locked inside a room, but now that she's been set free she's on her way. Seems she's determined to lose her freedom today, one way or the other."

A ripple of laughter passed through the crowd.

"I was worried there for a minute," Alex chuckled. "I thought she might have—" he stopped in mid-sentence and his mouth fell open.

Skylee's stomach flip-flopped as she turned to see her mother standing at the top of the stairs. A wreath of white flowers encircled her strawberry blonde hair and the simple silhouette of her dress was tied at the waist with a broad white ribbon. The music began again and her mom started down the aisle. To Skylee's surprise, she looked like a woodland fairy gliding along on a sea of green.

As she neared the altar, a ray of light appeared and followed her as she walked. Then a low murmur spread across the crowd as everyone asked one another if they saw the beam of light.

"It must be a good sign," Skylee breathed in Chrism's ear, although she secretly wondered if it had anything to do with the necklace's silver light.

"A thousand welcomes to you, we are gathered here today to be celebrating the union of Alex and Janis...finally," began Daniel with a laugh.

During the ceremony an odd sensation rushed over Skylee. Her necklace had grown hotter, so hot that she could feel it through the fabric of her dress. But there was something else. She rubbed the back of her neck, feeling as if eyes were piercing her from behind. She glanced over her shoulder and saw a blonde man, dressed impeccably in black, sitting in the last row. He had the face of a fallen angel, long and lean, with high cheekbones and skin so smooth it didn't look real. Skylee's eyes locked with his. *Black and soulless,* she thought. She felt as if she was once more hiding in the corner of the dark room looking into those piercing eyes.

A cool breeze blew through Skylee's hair, catching her attention and she turned to look at the altar. The wind intensified, creating a gentle swirling tunnel of cherry blossoms, which then encircled her mom and Alex. Two swirling tunnels in one day could not be a coincidence.

After a brief silence, the crowd broke into loud applause. There was a look of pure joy on her mother's face. Skylee glanced over at Ann, who was holding her hand over her heart with tear-filled eyes.

"Aye, what a bonny sight. Ye may kiss the bride," said Daniel as he waved his hands through the petals, and then winked at his nephew.

As her mom and step-dad kissed inside the spiraling pink petals, Skylee dared to turn and look again at the stranger in the back row. He glared intensely at the bride and groom, who were now making their way up the aisle hand in hand. Then he slowly turned and exited.

She watched him walk away, and a terrible thought entered Skylee's mind. The devil had attended the ceremony.

SEVEN

The Reception

Following the wedding, the guests entered the reception hall amid lively chatter. Most of their conversations were centered on the curious events that had taken place during the ceremony. As Skylee mingled with the crowd she heard all sorts of theories being bandied about. Some people wondered if the ray of light and swirling blossoms were somehow planned.

"Maybe it's a secret government experiment," one guest had said.

Others saw the occurrences as a sign from above, a blessing on the newlyweds. There were a number of guests who believed it was nothing more than coincidence. Skylee knew better, it was simply a continuation of the strangest day of her life.

She scanned the room in a dreamlike state unable to find the devil-stranger. Her thoughts were haunted by his black eyes, the same eyes she had seen before the wedding. *But how could that be?* asked a voice in her head. *He looked different than the man I saw earlier...different hair ...different clothing.*

Cheers rang out, returning her attention to the reception. The bride and groom had made their way onto the dance floor and, to Skylee's horror, were kissing in front of everyone. Not a simple kiss like during the ceremony but a passionate one that seemed to go on forever.

"Ugh, I think I'm gonna puke," said Chrism very loudly, which caused several people to turn and look at her disapprovingly.

Skylee flashed an innocent smile their way and blurted out, "Oh—er, Luke? Why no, I haven't seen Luke in a long time."

Chrism caught on immediately. "Well of course, that's Luke, always disappearing," she said in a high-pitched voice. Then she leaned in and whispered, "thanks," in Skylee's ear.

At that moment the crowd broke into a hearty round of applause. Skylee looked up just in time to see the ending of what she was sure was the longest and sloppiest kiss in the history of mankind.

"Okay, that's way too much SDA for me," groaned Chrism.

"SDA?" asked Skylee, furrowing her brow.

"Yeah, you know *Sickening* Display of Affection."

"Ha, that about covers it," laughed Skylee.

"Well at least the worst is—oh no," said Chrism, her eyes widening, as she looked across the room. "Brace yourself, things are about to get ugly."

Skylee looked up and saw Chloe and five guys, who all looked exactly alike, making their way onto the stage.

"But I thought you loved this band."

"I do," she said staring up at them with dreamy eyes. "Just look at them. They're gorgeous."

"Uh? Didn't you just say they're ugly?"

"Not them, silly! I was talking about—"

"All right everybody!" Chloe interrupted as she shouted into the microphone. "And now for Mr. and Mrs. Faraway's first dance...please put your hands together for...FIFTH OF DROID!"

As the lights dimmed the band members picked up their instruments. Then a bright spotlight landed on the bride and groom. The crowd waited with bated breath.

"Um, this might be a good time to tell you something about my dad," said Chrism as she eyed her father sheepishly.

"Okay..." replied Skylee with great interest. "Is it a good something?"

Before Chrism could respond Fifth of Droid struck up a tune. Not a slow song as Skylee had expected, but a lively rock-n-roll number. She whipped her gaze around to her mom and stepdad.

Skylee's jaw dropped. There in the middle of the dance floor was her new stepdad, doing the craziest dance she'd seen in her life. His elbows were bent at an odd angle, he was hunched over at the waist and every muscle in his body seemed to be going in a different direction. He looked somewhat like a chicken running in circles.

"Well, there's your answer," said Chrism, scrunching up her face and shaking her head.

Skylee put her hand over her mouth and laughed. "Hey, it's not all that bad," she lied. "At least he's—wait, Chrism—where are you going?"

Her stepsister had already disappeared into the crowd. Skylee considered going after her, but she talked herself out of it, deciding it would be best to give her some space. So she watched the chicken dance for a few more moments, and then joined the others as they took to the floor. She danced, drank lots of punch and made conversation until she was exhausted.

Her missing Aunt Janie finally showed up and entertained everyone with an in depth story of why she was late. She told them her sky-taxi had broken down so she tried taking the solar tram but got on going in the wrong direction. Then, in a panic she got off in a seedy area of town, where she was mugged and lost her purse. Her aunt explained that just when she thought all hope of making it to the wedding had been lost, a police officer offered her a ride on his bullet-bike. Her story ended when she introduced him as her rescuer and date.

After listening to another twenty minutes or so of her aunt's colorful stories, Skylee wandered over to an empty table and sat down to rest her feet.

"Well, if it isn't Sky Porter," said a deep voice from behind her. "Man, I almost didn't recognize you—dressed up like a girl. You should do it more often."

"Um—thanks," she said, not sure if she had just been complimented or insulted.

Skylee twisted around in her chair and saw Hawk standing there.

"Hi," she said as her stomach, which already felt sloshy from too much punch, did a funny little somersault. Then again, it might not have been the punch at all. Maybe it was the fact that he looked, just as his name implied, hawk-like with his green eyes fixed keenly on her.

He was a very distinct looking guy of Irish-African ancestry. His white shirt contrasted sharply against his brown skin and closely cropped black hair. He had grown considerably since she had last seen him. She guessed he was at least six feet tall now. And his upper body looked so strong that it was hard to believe he was only sixteen.

"I suppose congratulations are in order," he said, sitting down next to her.

"Er—yes thank you. It was a—nice day. I mean—nice for a wedding."

Nice day? Yeah genius, she inwardly berated herself. *He's gonna think I'm on drugs.*

"It sure was," he said. "Well, how do you like the music? Are you a fan of Fifth of Droids?"

"Oh, they're not bad," said Skylee. "Kind of odd though—how they all look alike. Maybe their brothers or something."

"You don't *know*," he said, in what sounded like both a question and a statement.

Skylee shrugged.

"Fifth of *Droids,*" he said motioning toward them on stage. "They're androids, you know, they only look like humans."

"No—you mean robots," she said breathlessly. "I've never seen one in person before."

"Well you have now. Actually, five of them."

Skylee stared at the band in amazement. They all seemed perfectly human to her, with their dark spiky hair, skinny-legged outfits and black boots. Upon closer examination, she noticed they truly were impossible to tell apart, with one exception. Each of them had a number (one through five) tattooed on their wrist. She was so interested in watching them that she had almost forgotten that Hawk was still sitting beside her.

"Hmm...that's a very unusual necklace," he said, reaching out and touching the amulet. "It suits you."

"Oh," she quickly said, leaning away in fear of the silver light reappearing, but nothing happened. "Um...thanks, I just got it today. As a gift."

Hawk's eyes stayed focused on her necklace. Skylee found herself wondering why he appeared so mesmerized by it. *Geesh...I'm getting paranoid,* she thought. *He's just admiring it.* Then again, he seemed to be way too fascinated by it. And she might have imagined it, but she thought she saw a look of disappointment flicker across his face. *Yup, totally paranoid.* Finally, his intense gaze moved from her amulet to her eyes.

"A gift, huh? From your boyfriend?" he asked with a lifted brow.

"What—are you talking about—Will's not my—I mean, we're friends, very good friends. So yeah, he's a boy, who happens to be my friend, but not my boyfriend."

Hawk's lips curled into a smile. "The funny thing is, you knew exactly who I was talking about."

Skylee felt like her brain had turned to mush. She could not think of a single thing to say.

"Don't worry," he bent forward and whispered. "Your secret's safe with me."

He stood and walked away. Skylee sat there and watched him go. Then she looked around to see if anyone had overheard. Will and Airon were across the room, helping themselves to yet another serving of wedding cake. Chrism, who was excitedly waving her hands about, stood near the stage surrounded by a group of teenage guys. And everyone else was either eating or dancing. No one seemed to have heard a thing.

Skylee needed a moment of solitude so she stepped outside to get a breath of fresh air. It was a chilly night, and a sickle moon was peeking through silvery clouds. Leaning her arms on the terrace railing she looked out across New Washington. Dozens of dome shaped buildings dotted the skyline like igloos gleaming in a black sea.

She lifted her necklace, held it closer to her eyes and examined the engraving. The metal felt warm against her fingers but not unusually hot. *What secret does it hold?* She held it out a little and squinted her eyes focusing on its diamond shape.

"Oh my gosh," she breathed. "Chrism's birthmark...it's a diamond."

Airon chose that exact moment to slink up from behind and poke her in the side. Skylee nearly jumped out of her skin.

"Hey, don't sneak up on me like that," she said with a shiver as she swatted at him. "It's creepy."

"All right, take it easy. I just wanted ya teh dance with me," Airon said as he tugged a reluctant Skylee back into the reception hall.

"I'm tired," she said.

Airon raised his brow. "Come on, Skippy, seems like ya had the energy to dance with everyone else and besides I'm ya best mate."

"Fine," said Skylee, rolling her eyes. "But you know I'm a terrible dancer."

"No big deal. They don't call me twinkle toes for nothin'. All eyes will be on my smooth moves, no one will notice ya at all."

I should be so lucky, she thought as she took his hand. As soon as they stepped onto the dance floor, Chrism, who was dancing with her brother, Michael, swooped past. The two of them were gliding about so effortlessly that Skylee wondered if they had taken dance lessons. It seemed highly likely considering their father's dancing skills. She watched them swirl around the floor. Their matching brown hair and formal attire made them look like professionals. Skylee couldn't help but notice that Airon had his eyes glued on Chrism. So much so that he wasn't paying attention and stepped on her toes.

"Hey, watch it," she scolded.

"Sorry about that. Have ya noticed that yer sister has danced with that older bloke several times?"

"So?" she replied, realizing at that moment that he was actually attracted to Chrism, which offered Skylee a rare opportunity. It only seemed fair to dole out a little payback for his previous attitude about her stepsister. "He's nice looking...I don't blame her."

"Nice lookin'," mumbled Airon. "Ya really think so? Doesn't matter, he's too old for her."

"Hmmm, I don't know if that's a problem." She smiled deviously. "I know for a fact that her dad is fine with them dancing together. I would go as far as to say that Alex would let Chrism go anywhere with him."

"That's just crazy," said Airon as he twirled her around. "What's his name?"

"Why, Airon, I think you're jealous."

"Skippy, yer out of yer mind. Why would I be jealous?"

"Well, look at him, he's tall, handsome and even his muscles have muscles."

Airon stopped dancing and glared at her.

"What...don't you think they make a nice couple?" she continued on teasingly. "I wouldn't be surprised if she loved him."

"No bloody way," he said in an irritated tone. "Who is he?"

"If you really must know, his name is Michael," said Skylee with a smirk.

"Michael who?"

"Michael...Faraway, as in her brother," she said triumphantly.

Airon huffed and yanked her back into a dance. The gleam in his eyes let Skylee know that she may have won the battle but eventually he planned to win the war. Until then, she would bask in her success.

Later, during a break in the music, Skylee made her way to the refreshment table. A smile crossed her face when she spotted a dish of Luck-E-Chocs, which were four-leaf clover shaped chocolate candies with a creamy mint surprise in the middle. Her mom must have included them in the reception menu because they were her favorite. Her plan to grab a couple of Luck-E-Chocs was interrupted when Izzy and Gaby, better known as the twins of mass destruction, shoved her sideways into an elderly man, nearly knocking him off his walker. Before she could stop them, they ran straight into Doc Muller, who fell against the refreshment table. The punch bowl jerked forward then backward and started to flip over.

"NOOOO!" Skylee yelled, catching the large glass bowl. Green punch spilled over the rim then unexpectedly hovered in mid air. Within seconds, part of it flowed back into the bowl while the rest dropped to the table in a big splatter. She stared down at it and then looked around to see if anyone noticed. Will was rushing toward her.

"Did you see that?" she asked as he reached her.

"Yeah," he said in amazement. "I did. How'd you do that?"

"I don't know," said Skylee.

Setting the bowl back into place, she tried to recover without bringing attention to herself. She looked down to see a few green droplets had found their way to her dress. And then she noticed the twins were staring at her. She was trying to think of something to say when Chrism walked up and grabbed them by the back of their necks.

"*What* are you two juvenile delinquents doing?" she said in a hushed angry tone. "Look what you did to Skylee's dress. You're not going to ruin this for dad and Janis. Now stop it."

"You're not the boss of us. We can do whatever we want," Izzy said as both twins stuck out their tongues.

"Why you little brats," she said with a reddened face.

Skylee glanced across the room at Michael who was looking their way. He seemed to know his sister was about to blow her top, because he crossed the room in seconds. Skylee knew he was on a mission. He had told her in their very first meeting that ever since his mother left, he was the only one who could control Chrism's fiery temper.

"Hey sis, why don't you let me take our cousins outside for a walk?" Michael asked casually. Chrism released her hold on the squirming girls and stepped back. He gave her an understanding look and turned to the twins, "Let's go outside for a bit. There might be something of interest out there to see."

"Liar," Gaby said, cheekily. "It's just a bunch of trees and grass."

"Yeah, liar," Izzy agreed as she always seemed to do with her sister.

"What? Me? Never!" Michael said in an overly dramatic tone as he started leading the twins toward the outer doors. "I've heard that there's a ghost that walks the bridge at night."

"Really?" Izzy said merrily.

Michael motioned for them to head outside as he turned and winked at Chrism before stepping out the door.

"If there is a ghost out here, I hope it takes those two little monsters away," Chrism muttered under her breath.

Skylee smiled awkwardly, turned her eyes to the dance floor, and located her mom.

"Good, they didn't even notice the commotion," she said.

"Who?" Chrism turned to look where Skylee's eyes had stopped. "Oh, yeah, them, they act like they're the only ones here."

"I know. They look happy...don't you think?"

"Yeah, they do. But I don't know what was more embarrassing watching that kiss or thinking your mom was going to back out."

"I knew my mom wouldn't do that," Skylee leaned toward Chrism. "She loves him."

"I know. I just wonder how that door got locked."

"Me too, Mom and Auntie Ann told me it was open when they left. My mom forgot her bouquet and went back to get it. She said the door slammed and she couldn't get out."

"Well, whatever. They're married now and that's what matters," Chrism said as they smiled at each other. "Wait, did you say *Auntie Ann*? Really?"

Skylee's smile faded. *I have to stop calling her that.* Looking away in embarrassment, she noticed a tall, blonde man in a dark suit watching the newlyweds from across the room. *It's him,* she thought, *the one from the wedding.* She cautiously walked toward him as he exited through the double doors.

The second she stepped into the hallway, a wave of panic overtook her. *Where is he? I know I saw him go through these doors.* Skylee listened for movement but the hall was silent. She crept down the long corridor and stopped at the door to the bridesmaid room, which was standing slightly ajar. As she reached to push it open, she felt a hand on her shoulder.

"Ahhhhh," Skylee screamed and turned to defend herself.

As the scream escaped her mouth, it was met by Chrism's much louder scream.

"What is your problem? Wha-What is going on? Were you go-going to-to hit me?" her stepsister stuttered as she backed away, holding her shoes in her hands.

"Why does everyone keep sneaking up on me?" Skylee asked. "You scared me to death! Why aren't you wearing your shoes?"

"My feet hurt," she whined. "I saw you leaving the reception and I..."

Somewhere nearby, a door slammed making both girls jump. "Quick, get in here," Skylee said as she grabbed Chrism's arm and pulled her through the door.

"WHAT ARE YOU DOING? LET GO OF ME!" she yelled, jerking her arm out of Skylee's grip. "I just thought you might need help cleaning that mess off your dress...Skippy."

A look of dread crossed Skylee's face as she realized Chrism was planning to use her nickname as ammunition to embarrass her. She shot her a dirty look and said, "Funny, real funny."

"Where did you get a name like Skippy?" she asked teasingly.

"Airon gave it to me when I was little because, well, he said when I tried to skip I looked like a baby kangaroo jumping. Honestly, this isn't the time."

"Skippy huh? Well, I guess it could be worse. You could be called—"

"Quiet, please," Skylee said as she looked around the room. The box still set on the table where she left it. She ran into the closet and pulled open the file cabinet, breathing a sigh of relief as she saw that her book was still hidden under the papers.

"What is wrong with you?" said Chrism as she stepped into the closet. "Are you like, mentally disturbed and your mom just didn't tell us?"

"No, I—It's just, I saw someone earlier, when I was in this room."

"Saw someone? In here? Do you think they took any of my stuff?"

"Focus, Chrism, anyway, I was in this room and he-he was staring at me through the window and then he came in the room and..." she fell silent when she heard whistling coming from the hallway. "That's the same tune I heard the man whistle this morning," whispered Skylee as she pulled the closet door toward her, leaving a tiny crack so she could peer out into the room. She felt the necklace warming through the fabric of her dress.

"Sounds familiar, it's a nursery rhyme, isn't it?" asked Chrism in a hushed tone and she began to hum the melody quietly.

"Oh yeah, that's 'Twinkle Twinkle Little Star'," exclaimed Skylee softly.

"You're right," she whispered in agreement. "I always thought it was a happy tune but that's just...disturbing."

The whistling grew louder as the door to the room opened and shut. She could feel Chrism's warm breath on her neck as she leaned over her to peep out of the crack. Skylee turned and placed her finger over her lips, signaling her stepsister to be quiet.

The tall man stood in the center of the room surveying his surroundings. He continued to whistle the haunting melody. Finally, after what seemed like an eternity he stopped, went to the table, and he looked inside the box. Letting out a string of curse words, he violently hit the package, sending it across the room. Chrism gasped and dropped her shoes. *Thunk...Thunk...* The man spun around and approached the closet like a lion staking its prey.

Peeking out of the slight gap in the door, all Skylee could see was a pair of dark empty eyes moving closer and closer.

EIGHT

Trapped in a Closet

Skylee's heart gave a terrible jolt. Both she and her stepsister backed away from the door. Chrism had a viselike grip on her shoulders. They held their breath as the man stared through the narrow crack.

Her necklace felt hotter than a branding iron. Without thinking, she grabbed it by the chain and held it out. The man's black eyes widened and trailed from her face to the amulet. Skylee felt Chrism's grip tighten and her sharp nails digging into her skin.

"That is not yours," the stranger snarled. He reached for the door and shoved it open. "Hand it over before—"

Grrrrr... A low growl echoed through the stillness of the closet.

The man abruptly stopped and for a brief moment everyone froze. Then he quickly looked from Skylee to Chrism and shook his head, backing away from the door. It was as if he had seen a ghost. His hands were so tightly clenched that his knuckles were turning stark white. He pointed his long finger toward the closet and the door slammed shut.

Then they heard the shrill sound of whistling. Skylee's hair stood up on the back of her neck as she listened to the eerie melody. She and Chrism didn't move an inch. Noises came from the room: shuffling footsteps, a series of creaking sounds, the click of a closing door, and finally total quietness.

"Whew, that was too close," Skylee whispered, turning to look at Chrism, who was panting and wild eyed. "Are you okay?"

"I...I..." her voice came out in a whimper. She cleared her throat and said, "I think so."

"I'm sorry," said Skylee, feeling guilty for dragging her stepsister into the situation. "I didn't think he would come after us like that. Did you see the door? It just suddenly slammed."

"It did? I must have had my eyes closed."

"Oh, I guess so," she said, slipping her hand under the collar of her dress to rub her shoulder. She knew Chrism must have been terribly frightened because her skin still smarted where her nails had dug in deep.

"Was that him?" her stepsister said a little too loud.

Skylee cracked the door open and peeked out. "Shhhhh, listen, he might come back—oh no, I hear voices."

"Is it him? Is he coming back?" Chrism whispered as she carefully pulled the closet door shut.

Skylee heard the sound of soft laughter. She leaned in and placed her ear near the door. From the other side came the murmur of voices. Chrism stepped up and pressed her ear to the door too. Both girls sighed in relief as they realized the voices were those of their parents and someone else. Skylee was pretty sure she could hear at least two other voices, those of a man and woman.

"That's right, we'll be flying into Honolulu." Her mom seemed to be talking about the honeymoon.

Skylee and Chrism shared a look of mutual agreement. Neither girl wanted to reveal herself, knowing their parents would question why they were hiding in the closet. And if they told them it would put a damper on their wedding day. So, all they could do was listen in silence.

Skylee made out the deep voice of Director Darrell Drake. He was her mom's boss at GEMA, and he was as serious as they come. "I might as well get this over," he said in a remorseful sounding voice. "Alex, Janis...there's just no easy way to say this. I have orders to send you on special assignment to New Zealand. Now, I know you both wanted some time for a honeymoon, but I need you on this."

Chrism held out both palms and exaggeratedly mouthed the word...*what?* Skylee could only answer by shaking her head and shrugging. But she did wonder what could be so serious that Drake would interrupt her mom's honeymoon. It was one of the things about her mother's job she didn't like, emergency assignments that took her to dangerous places.

"How serious is this?" Alex questioned, sounding slightly annoyed. "Can't it wait for a week or two?"

"No, I don't believe so," Drake said in a matter-of-fact tone. "Our operative in the area reported that an uninhabited island disappeared overnight."

"What?" gasped Janis. "An entire island? Was there an earthquake?"

The words rang through Skylee's mind...*An island disappeared. That's not possible or...could it be another event like The Day?*

"Were their coordinates off, faulty equipment?" Alex questioned in a skeptical tone.

"No, we sent a task force out to investigate and the island was gone," Drake said. "The bigger problem lies in our intelligence reports indicating that New Zealand is having all sorts of problems. Things we haven't seen in a while."

"What kind of problems?" asked Janis, in such an alarmed voice that it sent goose bumps across Skylee's arms.

"Well for one, odd earth tremors, you know, quakes that seem to have no epicenter," Drake said. "And secondly, something is causing the fish to die. I could go on but suffice it to say there's a whole list of strange occurrences."

"Are you sure it's all related?" Janis asked.

Skylee heard another voice responding to her mother's question. The familiar accent was that of Carmen Desoto, Director Drake's assistant, a pretty woman of Hispanic heritage. "Drake and I have gone over every single one of those reports," she said. "One of them said that the island was there one day and gone the next. And the other incidents seem to be tightly located near the site of the missing island."

There was a slight pause, and then Skylee heard a man clear his throat. She wasn't sure if it was Drake or Alex until Drake spoke, "Listen, this is top secret," he said lowering his voice. "The same episodes that happened near the missing island are happening off the coast of New Zealand now."

Skylee jerked her head around and looked at Chrism who had a shocked expression on her face.

"It does appear suspicious," Alex said. "But, are you sure there aren't other agents that could go?"

"We need the highest level of expertise, which is you, both of you. And I wouldn't ask, Alex, if it weren't urgent," Drake replied. "This directive came from the highest level."

"Are we talking oval office?" Alex asked, causing Chrism to cover her mouth with her hand.

Wow, Skylee thought. *The President wants my mom and stepdad.* So it was serious, even more serious than she thought.

"Yes, the President," Drake responded. "She believes there may be a connection to The Day of Disaster. The two of you are our top operatives in these areas. I hate to ask but I have no choice. I want you to go to New Zealand and check it out. I understand you have some contacts there, Janis."

"Me?" said Janis, sounding surprised. "Huh? I'm still trying to comprehend that we've been given a presidential order. Well, let me think...yes I do know a very knowledgeable geological researcher that lives in New Zealand. I've known him for many years. His name is Zane Cook. I think he'd be the perfect person to help us, he's very involved in land conservation and environmental protection."

Skylee recognized the name immediately. Her mom had told her many stories about him. He was her dad's best friend.

"Cook, yes, that's who I was thinking of. Sounds like he's a good starting point. Get in contact with him," ordered Drake in a thoroughly professional tone. "And one more thing, there's a man named Mr. Mogg that has agreed to meet with you."

"PHILEAS MOGG?" cried Janis so loudly that both Skylee and Chrism jumped. "You mean THE Phileas D. Mogg of The S.E.E. Corporation?"

"Si! Yes!" Carmen answered in two languages, apparently flabbergasted by Janis's outburst. "We have contacted him and he's willing to help us out. Very passionate man, Mr. Mogg, about what might be happening. So, Janis, have you met him? He seemed to recognize your name."

Skylee knew her mom hadn't met him because she would have told her if she had. In fact, every time a commercial for the S.E.E. Corporation came on T-screen her mom would go on and on about how much Mr. Mogg's company had helped in the recovery after The Day.

"No, I've never met him. But I totally respect all he's done for the planet. His foundation raises millions for the environment and the recycling his company does is invaluable."

"Well, he'll be in New Zealand on business and agreed to meet with you two at some point. Let's see...I have the contact information, uh...somewhere...is it in here...no, now...where did I put that?" said Carmen in a befuddled tone. "Anyway, you'll have to work out the scheduling. He's a very busy man."

"Oh, I know," said Janis. "I can't believe we're actually going to meet him. Can you Alex?"

"Er—well no, I mean yes," he replied sounding a bit confused.

Inside the closet, Chrism motioned for Skylee to come closer, then she whispered in her ear, "Oooh, that Phileas Mogg is so gorgeous. Have you seen him on all those save the earth ads?"

Skylee nodded. Of course she had. Who hadn't?

Chrism began whispering something else but Skylee held up her finger and lipped the words, "Just a sec." She wanted to listen to what her mother was saying.

"So, first I guess I'll contact Zane and see what he knows, if anything," Janis said. "I haven't spoken with him in a while. And then there's another little item we need to deal with," she added with a touch of nervousness in her voice. "Under the circumstances, cancelling the trip to Hawaii and all. I'd like ours girls to come with us to New Zealand. We'll arrange for them to be supervised while we're working. I hope that's agreeable."

"Sure," said Drake. "No problem."

"All right that's settled then," said Janis. "So, who's going to break it to the girls?"

"I have an idea," Alex said right away. "Since we're married now, we should do it together."

Skylee heard her mom chuckle.

"Here! Here it is!" exclaimed Carmen, sounding pleased with herself. "I finally found that number for Phileas Mogg. Here you go, Alex."

"Thanks," Alex said simply.

"Okay, then, anymore information to give us?" Janis asked.

"It's all in the file. Carmen, you don't have that with you? Do you?" Drake asked doubtfully.

Skylee smiled as she pictured the look Director Drake probably had on his face. She glanced over at Chrism who was rolling her eyes.

"Oh, yes it...it's here somewhere," Carmen answered, and then came the sound of shuffling papers. "Oh good, I did bring them." More shuffling. "I was worried. Okay, this one is for you Alex. And here's yours, Janis."

"All right, I don't want to keep you from your wedding guests any longer," Drake said with a trace of regret in his voice.

"Well, this might be a good time for us to return to the dance floor," said Carmen. "Let's go find our dates and sneak a couple more dances in. I just love the music and wasn't the wedding cake delicious, oh, and did you know it was completely organic..."

Skylee could hear her voice fading away as she carried on talking to Drake on their way down the hall.

"Honey, I'm sorry about the honeymoon," said Alex in a voice so soft that Skylee could barely hear it.

"I'm not," her mom replied. "It doesn't matter where we are as long as we're together. I'm not sure what we'll do with the girls, I mean, when we're out investigating. Oh, of course I can talk Ann into coming and she can bring along Will and Airon so—" all of a sudden she stopped talking and there was silence.

Skylee looked over at her stepsister in puzzlement, and then she heard it.

SMACK

Their parents were kissing. And the sound triggered a different reaction from each girl. Chrism rolled her eyes and poked her finger in her mouth pretending to gag, while Skylee buried her face in her hands and blushed.

"Are you trying to distract me from getting back to the reception?" Janis finally said.

Skylee heard Alex chuckle.

"It won't work, you promised to dance every dance with me and you're not getting out of it," her mom said with a laugh. "Come on, let's get back to the party. I'm sure everyone is wondering what happened to the bride and groom."

Skylee felt relieved when she heard their footsteps head toward the door. Followed by the click of the switch as they turned off the lights and exited the room, shutting the door behind them.

"I can't believe it, New Zealand!" squealed Chrism excitedly. "And what is up with that kiss? OMG, I hope they're not gonna keep this up. That's just something I don't want to see or hear."

"I know, but they did just get married and..." Skylee paused not sure where she should go with that. She quickly changed the subject and softly spoke, "I can't help but wonder why that island disappeared."

"Who cares about the island? Don't you get it—New Zealand—where they made Lord of the Rings, the best movie of all times. Seriously, you don't get that?"

"Oh, well yeah there is that but there's more, really fascinating things, like the kiwi bird. Did you know that New Zealand is the only place in the world where it's found? Kiwi birds are flightless and they don't have tails, actually their wings are pretty much useless because—"

"Hey, Miss Discovery Channel," Chrism said with a snicker. "Thanks for the science lesson."

"Oh, sorry, I was just trying to tell you how special the kiwi is because they were protected in wildlife preserves before The Day so they survived, you know, since New Zealand didn't have as much damage as some—" Skylee stopped, someone had entered the room.

She pulled Chrism to the back of the closet and they locked arms as footsteps approached. Skylee's heart pounded so loud that she was sure whoever was outside could hear it.

The doorknob turned. *Click.* Skylee felt air flowing into the closet as the door swung open. A dark figure briefly loomed in the doorway before stepping inside. Skylee's mind raced, she couldn't believe he had returned. This time she wasn't going to let him have the upper hand. She released Chrism's arm and lunged forward hoping to knock him down.

Everything happened in a matter of seconds. Skylee hit her target shoving him into the room, which took both of them down. Chrism rushed out grabbing the first thing she could find and turned to strike the stranger.

Skylee yelled, "WHAT DO YOU WANT? WHY ARE YOU FOLLOWING ME?"

"What?" said a male voice, "Sky, is that you?"

"Will? William?" Skylee asked in utter confusion. The room light came on unexpectedly and the three of them blinked while trying to adjust their eyes to the brightness. There was Skylee on top of Will and Chrism holding a shoe in her hand.

"Well, well, well, are ya havin' a bash and forgot teh invite me?" Airon teased, standing by the door with his hand on the light switch.

"You scared the heck out of us," Chrism scolded Will.

"Sorry, that was not my intention. I was worried about Sky and came looking for her," Will said never taking his eyes off Skylee.

"Well, I'm glad it was you," Skylee said. "Although, Chrism's right—you scared me half to death. We thought you were the stranger from this morning."

"And so you thought you would ram him?" retorted Will. "And exactly what were you going to do once you knocked him down? What were you thinking?"

"I...I...I decided to be pro-active." said Skylee in an unusually high voice.

"Next time," Chrism said, "let me know what the plan is." She looked down at the shoe in her hand.

Airon chuckled under his breath, "I reckon ya were gonna beat him with that, eh?" he said pointing at it.

Skylee looked up at Chrism who had her eyes fixed on Airon in a deadly stare. His slight smile faded and was replaced with a smirk.

"Airon, please," Skylee pleaded, feeling as if she had had all the drama she could stand in one day.

After a brief pause, Airon took a deep breath, "Good on ya, Chrism, it was game of both of ya have'n a go at the bloke."

Everyone looked at Chrism to see what she would say or do.

"Aaaaaah," she groaned as she looked at Airon, slightly rolled her eyes and smiled, "I give up. Honestly, I'm not sure what you just said but I'm glad both of you are here, cause that creep had the scariest eyes I've ever seen. He reminded me of a Ringwraith from Lord of the Rings," Chrism rambled on dramatically. "You know the scene where Frodo, and the other hobbits were hiding from..."

The three of them stared at Chrism in disbelief, each for a different reason. Skylee was shocked to discover how obsessed Chrism was with Lord of the Rings. Will whispered something to himself about not possibly believing that the stranger honestly looked like a Ringwraith. And Airon seemed to be trying to recover from Chrism smiling at him.

"What?" Chrism continued. "You all know what I am talking about? Right? Lord of the Rings...it changed movie making."

"Yes, we all know," Skylee said as she tried to stand up. Airon reached over to give her a hand.

As Will got to his feet, he pulled Skylee toward him, "Hey, that bloke? You think it was the same one from this morning?"

"I think so, yes, I'm almost sure, he whistled the same eerie tune. But he looked different. He looked like the blonde guy I saw sitting in the back row at the wedding. The guy from this morning had dark hair and he had on some kind of uniform. Oh, but maybe he was wearing a disguise because they both had the same dark eyes..." Skylee shivered. "Did you notice anything, Chrism?"

"I don't remember much, besides I was too scared to look away from those eyes. They made my skin crawl. Hey, I wonder where he went? I mean there he was in the door then all of a sudden he backed away like someone pushed him," Chrism prattled on. "I heard a growl and then he got a weird look on his face, I don't know, but then he was gone. He couldn't have gone out the door. Our parents came in seconds later. They would've noticed him."

"I think he left through here," Skylee said, walking to the window. She reached up and checked the lock. "It isn't locked, and I know I locked it after this morning."

"Listen mates, for the rest of the night we should stick together," Airon said in a serious tone. "Maybe he was after somethin' in this room. Still, there's strength in numbers, so let's hang together."

"Too right," Will said, looking at Skylee. "What do you think?"

"Okay, that works for me. I am a bit shaken up—I think sticking together is a good plan," she agreed, relieved that Will was staying mum about the book and necklace.

"We should probably tell someone what has happened," Airon suggested.

"No," Skylee said. "Not today, it'll ruin my mom's wedding."

"Skippy, I don't think—" Airon said.

"Please, Airon, I'll tell them, later after we get to New Zealand."

"New Zealand?" Will and Airon said together, looking confused.

"Oh, I...well we have something to tell you two. We're not going to Hawaii like we planned, now we're headed—"

"To New Zealand!" Chrism finished Skylee's sentence.

"That's right, and believe it or not you guys might be coming with us," said Skylee excitedly.

Will and Airon glanced at each other with doubtful expressions. Then Will put his hands on his forehead and said, "I think I might have bumped my head when I was knocked down by that wild eyed she-devil, cause I thought you said me and Airon are going to New Zealand."

"Will, I'm not kidding. You really could be coming with us," said Skylee happily. "It's a long story, but my mom is probably talking your mom into it right now. You just wait and see."

"Oh, I'd like nothing better," said Will, grinning. "What do you say, Airon?"

"A trip teh middle earth, eh?" he said looking over at Chrism and winked. "I reckon I could work it in, ya know as soon as I finish up my senior exams. Yeah mate, hope it works out. And there are loads of extreme sports there."

"It's so exciting. We might get to meet Phileas Mogg and I'm going to see The Shire and tour WETA—oh and I want to stay at the same hotel Orlando Bloom stayed in," Chrism said excitedly.

"So, yer into old blokes, huh?" laughed Airon. Skylee smiled hearing Airon's laughter because it was a rare occurrence since his parents died.

"Mr. Mogg isn't that old. Actually I read online that no one knows how old he really is. And okay, Orlando may be old now, but in his day he was the prettiest man alive," Chrism said, showing her fixation on the subject of famous people. "Besides, it's not just about the actors, I've read the book dozens of times."

"Brilliant, ya can read," Airon joked, causing Chrism to throw her shoe at him.

"Whoa." Airon caught the shoe in mid-air and walked straight to her with it.

Chrism backed up a step, held out her hands to stop him and pleaded, "Look, you started this."

"That's right, little sheila, and I'm gonna end it," said Airon as he knelt in front of her. He took her foot and slipped on the shoe. "Ahh, a perfect fit."

Chrism stared at Airon in total disbelief. "Thanks?" she said in more of a question than a statement.

Airon found her other shoe, grabbed it, and repeated the same. He placed her foot back on the ground and stood up, putting their faces within inches of each other. Her brows arched in surprise as Airon stepped away, bowing lowly as he retreated.

A flustered Chrism said, "Well, I for one need a drink." The other three looked at her, in stunned silence. "A soda, gees, get a grip, I'm not old enough to drink liquor, yet."

"A soda? Don't ya mean a fizzy?" Airon said.

"I'll pass on the soda but I really feel the need for some Luck-E-Chocs," said Skylee as she searched around the room for a small bag, which she could use for her book.

"Luck-E-Chocs...eat Luck-E-Chocs..." sang Will, sounding exactly like the jingle on T-screen. "Don't be a schmuck...eat one a day...to have good luck...eat Luck-E-Chocs."

"Hey mate?" said Airon, the second he finished. "Could ya do me a favor?"

"I dunno, maybe."

"Next time yer gonna sing the Luck-E-Chocs song, warn me, cause I have a reputation."

"Yeah, I've heard about your reputation, mate," said Will with a punch to Airon's arm.

As Skylee laughed at them she noticed Chrism's mouth curled in a half grin.

"Skylee," she said with a sneaky gleam in her eye. "Do you really believe that tale about the Luck-E-Chocs bringing you luck when you eat one?"

"No, I don't," insisted Skylee.

She hoped Will and Airon wouldn't bring up how she used to swear by them when she was younger. Chrism would rib her about it till the end of days.

"Hang on," said Airon. "I could tell ya—"

"Hey," interrupted Skylee. "We need to get back to the reception."

Will chuckled under his breath and said, "Sure, Sky, whatever you want." He stepped forward and offered his arm to her.

"Wait, I need to do something first."

Skylee went into the closet and got the book. She stuffed it into her bag and hung it on her shoulder. Once it was safely tucked away, she breathed a sigh of relief. She didn't know why the dark eyed man kept showing up, but she was determined not to let him steal her book.

"Come on," Skylee said lightly, as she grabbed Will's arm with one hand and Chrism's with the other. Then she paused and looked at Airon with a raised eyebrow, daring him to take Chrism's arm.

Airon raked his hands through his hair and nodded knowingly at Skylee. He took a small step forward and looked at each of them as if he was trying to decide on his next dance partner. Finally, he raised his hand in an overly dramatic fashion, batted his eyes and to everyone's surprise locked his arm through Will's.

As they all laughed, Skylee tugged them toward the door and said, "Okay, let's go see who catches the bouquet."

"I think I'll eat a couple of Luck-E-Chocs just to make sure I don't catch it," snickered Airon under his breath.

Skylee gave him a big "shut-up" glare and they all exited the room.

NINE

⎽ᴊ𝄐 ᐟᴋ ⅄₀ ∕ⴼⴼ 𝕔̄

The New Sky Tower

Inside the elegant lobby of Auckland's finest hotel, light poured through the soaring glass walls and reflected off of the marble floors. Clusters of plush couches and chairs were scattered throughout the area. A lone figure sat at the bar with legs crossed, watching the glass doors in anticipation of the Faraway family's arrival.

Dr. Ashley Hayes raised a lazy wrist and checked the time. It was almost noon, which meant another half hour of waiting. The doctor stood and leisurely walked to an ornately framed mirror, gazing deeply into the glass. The image looking back was one of a kind.

What set Ashley apart was an illusion that took years to perfect. Brushing back a strand of synthetic black hair, the doctor admired the chin length wig, which was parted on the side and perfectly styled with spiky tips. Ashley's vacant brown eyes closely inspected the refined figure in the mirror. An appearance, which had been carefully created, too beautiful to be a man yet too sharply chiseled to be a woman, attractive in either case. But the unnatural facade had come at great cost, dozens of laser treatments, electrolysis, chemical peels, and painful surgeries.

No price was too high to achieve the goal of being untraceable and that was exactly what had been accomplished. Inside the doctor's twisted mind a scenario played out.

Police officer—Can you describe the suspect?

Eyewitness—Uh...average height and build with dark hair and light skin.

Police officer—Was it a man or a woman?

Eyewitness—I don't know.

Police officer—You don't know? Well, what about the clothing? Was the suspect wearing male or female clothing?

Eyewitness—Well, a dark leather suit and white shirt, it could've been either.

Police officer—Is that it? So, I've got an average height, average build, dark haired, light skinned male or female. That pretty much describes a quarter of the people on the planet!

A tight-lipped smile appeared on the doctor's long face. The modification process, which covered almost every trace of the real Ashley, had gone much further. There were no fingerprints to leave behind, no hairs that could be traced, and no distinguishing marks to be recognized. However, there was a small chink in Ashley's armor—DNA. It was the one thing that could not be erased.

Most of the doctor's original existence had been lost but some things still remained, including Ashley's genius IQ and a photographic memory. They were part of the doctor's past, along with the peculiar odor that was best described as a mixture of smoke and rotting compost from Ashley's two obsessions, eating vegetables and smoking.

Ashley returned to the bar and pulled a thin cigar from the pocket of an expensive leather jacket, which had been draped over the chair. Then the doctor's black-rimmed eyes turned back to the entryway. Dr. Hayes held a lighter to the tip of the cigar. It glowed red hot, which matched the shade of the lipstick on the doctor's full smooth lips. A cloud of smoke filled the air.

Nearby, a young couple with a cherub faced baby, glared disapprovingly at the doctor and moved across the lobby, away from the cigar smoke.

"Good riddance," said Ashley in a strangely neutral tone.

Several minutes later, the doctor looked through the glass entryway and beyond to the street, catching sight of the Faraway family exiting a hover-shuttle. A pretty girl with a mop of curly blonde hair stepped through the sliding glass doors. The sight of Lee Porter's daughter dredged up memories, painful recollections that had long ago been buried. Ashley's eyes burned a hole through the unsuspecting girl.

As the family checked in and arranged their luggage, Ashley overheard the dark haired girl pleading with a tall olive skinned woman to take them to the Sky Tower. The doctor moved closer to listen to their conversation.

"Please, Ann," the girl begged. "Can we go to New Sky Tower? My dad will let us go if you go with us and we can walk from here, its right around the corner."

"Are you sure we should go today?" asked the woman. "Did you ask Sky and Will if they were up to it? Maybe they're too tired from the flight."

"Of course they want to go, and it won't take us that long. Skylee and I will meet you and Will right here in an hour...okay?"

"Well, I guess so," the woman said with a sigh. "Oh, wait a minute, Chrism. It looks like they can't fit all your bags on the cart. You can just tell everyone to go ahead to their rooms. I'll stay with you until we can get another bellboy for your luggage."

"Okay and thanks for going with us to the tower," said Chrism before she raced over and began organizing her massive stack of luggage.

Dr. Hayes took a drag of the thin cigar then slowly exhaled a circle of smoke. Pulling out a V-phone, Ashley carefully disabled the holographic display. It was important to handle this part of the plan flawlessly.

"Master? They've arrived...that's right...the Sky Tower this afternoon...no sir...not the parents...some woman and two other teenagers...that's right, one of them did call her Ann...I see...when shall I meet you? No, I won't go near her...yes sir...she's all yours..."

Dr. Ashley Hayes reached up to disconnect the V-phone and smiled. It was a fiendish smile. A tingle of excitement ran across every inch of the doctor's chemically altered skin. Finally, after fourteen years of waiting for their revenge, the moment had come. It was time to set their plan in motion.

* * * * * * *

Skylee set down her suitcase, dropped her backpack onto the bed and threw herself back against the soft pillows. She was happy to finally be in New Zealand. The flight had been exhausting, not the plane-ride itself, but the seventeen-plus hours of listening to Chrism complaining, whereas Skylee only had one complaint. The fact that she had to share her Luck-E-Chocs with everyone and now she was down to two pieces. However, her stepsister had enough grievances to create a list, which included the seating, the food, the "stupid" movie choices and the poor service.

At one point during their flight, Skylee had pretended to be asleep, which only gave Chrism several hours to flirt with Will. She had read to him endlessly from her V-phone about New Zealand's Lord of the Rings and Hobbit movie locations. Will sat attentively smiling and nodding at her the whole time.

During the unfortunate episode, Skylee found herself becoming increasingly annoyed with her new stepsister. She didn't know why. It couldn't be jealousy, not over Will. What was there to be jealous about? At least that's what she told herself.

Now Skylee was alone for the first time in days, and it felt nice. Her mind immediately turned to the book, which she had carefully concealed inside her backpack. Luckily, Chrism hadn't noticed when she cut the lining to create a secret hiding place. A couple of times she had even snuck a look at the book, but she couldn't find the privacy to really examine it as she wished. She knew it was pointless to fish it out now since Chrism would arrive at any moment. Exhaling loudly she relaxed into the fluffy pillows, picking up a brochure from the bedside table. She read.

Visit Ancient Maori Village
Long ago, the land was covered by rainforests...
the calls of the laughing owl and the giant Mao filled the air...
the Maori people knew no fear   Step back in time...
You'll fall in love with New Zealand.

She studied the glossy pamphlet and three words seemed to jump out at her. Fall in love. *Surely they don't think you can fall in love with a place. Or do they?* she pondered. She wasn't sure she even believed in falling in love.

All at once, her grandpa's voice, shaky and frail, seemed to fill her head. *Listen child, you can fall out of a tree or in to a hole, but you can't fall in or out of love.*

"Good old paw-paw," Skylee whispered to herself.

Well, at least loving a place can't hurt you, she reasoned. Then her mind instantly went back to the day Gracie died. That was the first time she felt the pain of losing someone she loved with all her heart. Swallowing hard, she nuzzled her head against the soft pillow. *That's what happens when you love someone too much. You get hurt,* she reminded herself. *I'm not going to let it happen again.*

Skylee recalled the months after Gracie's death when she began to worry about her mom. She had already lost her dad. What would happen if her mom died too? But as time passed her fears slowly faded, up until a couple of years ago.

She remembered it like it was yesterday. She, Will and Airon had been watching some silly reality show on the T-screen when the terrible news arrived. Will's dad, Gab Butler, had been piloting a small jet on a trip with Airon's parents, Connor and Allison. The plane was less than ten miles from their landing sight when something went wrong. All three were killed. There were conflicting reports about what had happened. Eventually, it was ruled an accident, caused by a rare winter thunderstorm.

Skylee had felt helpless at the funeral as she watched Will grieve the loss of his father. And although Airon didn't outwardly show his anguish, she knew he was devastated.

Shaking off her gloomy thoughts, she sat up and looked around the hotel room. It was stylishly decorated and thankfully had two beds. She had never shared a bed with a sibling and she didn't want to start now.

Incidentally, she wondered what was taking Chrism so long. It probably had something to do with her mountain of luggage, or she was talking on her V-phone again. Skylee grabbed her backpack and dug out the book. She might as well take advantage of whatever time she had left to examine it.

She softly placed the book on the bed and opened it. The leather felt smooth against her fingers. Her dad's torn note and the picture of her parents and brother rested on the crisp white page. Picking up the photo, she intently searched her father's image and this time something new caught her eye. He was wearing the necklace. She could see its silver chain peeking out from beneath his collar.

Letting out a deep breath, she looked at the handwritten note still lying on the book's page. She read from the torn section. *You may encounter great trials before you reach your d...e...* Her eyes narrowed and her forehead wrinkled. She read it again.

"Oh, of course...destiny, reach your destiny," she whispered.

Skylee's deciphering was abruptly sidetracked by the sensation of her amulet cooling against her skin. For the first time since the wedding, she removed the necklace and inserted it into the cover. She wondered if the brilliant light would appear again. Her hands shook as she parted the pages that were rapidly changing from white to yellow.

A tiny speck of golden light danced on the page, growing until words formed.

To reveal the gift shall be at great cost.
Keep it hidden, or lives will be lost.

Her heart raced. Forcing herself to move, she ran her finger across the page tracing the words. Suddenly a light blinded her sight. Then, vivid images appeared in her mind. She saw black eyes, the silver blade of a knife and her necklace. The objects flashed before her eyes as a calm voice spoke inside her mind. *Protect the necklace, guard the book, keep them secret. Those who learn of your gifts will be in danger. They must remain hidden.*

Skylee's vision was broken when her stepsister burst through the door with a bellboy in tow. She quickly closed the book, removing the necklace before she slid it into the backpack. She held the cool amulet tightly in her fist.

"Oh, just put those over there by the bed, dear," Chrism said in snobbish tone with her V-phone in hand.

"Yes, Miss," replied the bellboy as he struggled with the stack of luggage then stood at the door waiting for his tip.

"I know," said her sister into her V-phone. "I know...okay...I'd better go...you hang up. No, you hang up...you hang up first... Okay, lets hang up on the count of three. One...two...three...Hey, you didn't hang up...you first. No you first...okay really this time on the count of three...one...two...three."

Skylee watched as her stepsister waited a moment and finally clicked her V-phone off. Then Chrism crossed the room viewing everything as if she were doing an inspection.

"I guess this will do," she said, opening the curtains to examine the scenery. "Look, we have a view of the newly rebuilt Sky Tower. Hurry up and get ready to go! Oh, and could you give the boy a tip for me?"

"Go where?" Skylee asked as she quickly put on her necklace, hiding it beneath her shirt. Then she placed the book inside its secret spot as she dug through her backpack for cash. Chrism, who was still looking out of the window, didn't seem to notice.

"To the Sky Tower, of course, we're meeting Will and his mom in the lobby to walk over there. We have to hurry so I can change my outfit and fix my hair and make-up. I want to look my best for Will."

Skylee bit her tongue. It seemed that she would have to remain silent about more than the book and the necklace. She thanked the bellboy as she handed him the only currency her stepdad had given her, American dollars. She was embarrassed as he frowned and withdrew his hand, which held an electronic fund scanner. Skylee couldn't believe her new stepdad refused to use the new world funding method. The bellboy, who had a disgusted look on his face, reluctantly took her cash and left the room.

"What about mom and your dad, are they coming?" Skylee asked her stepsister.

"No, they said they had some business meeting or something, but I think it's just an excuse for the *honeymooners* to be alone. Ew!" Chrism said rolling her eyes.

"Well, don't you remember? We did overhear Director Drake say they had to work on this trip," Skylee reminded her.

"Sure—whatever," she said unconcernedly as she dashed into the bathroom.

Thirty minutes later Skylee and her perfectly styled stepsister met Will and Ann in the lobby.

"I can't believe you kids talked me into taking you to the Sky Tower," Ann said, shaking her head. "I haven't even had a chance to get jetlag."

"Isn't it exciting?" said Chrism, grasping Will's hand. "I can't wait to go bungee jumping. Will, will you jump with me?"

He politely nodded and awkwardly smiled at Skylee who quickly looked away, pretending not to see Chrism holding his hand.

"You know..." Will said sounding disappointed, "...it's a shame that Airon isn't here to jump today, no one loves bungee jumping more than him."

"Where is Airon?" asked Chrism in a casual tone, clearly trying not to sound too interested.

"He decided to stop over in Sydney," Ann replied. "He planned to finish his senior exams and spend some time with his grandparents. Then he'll join us for—"

"So, let me get this right," Chrism interrupted, dropping Will's hand and turning to face him. "You and Airon are cousins because your dad and his dad were brothers?"

"Yes, Chrism, that's right," Ann interjected.

Skylee knew Ann had answered for Will because the subject of his dad was still sensitive.

"I can't believe you and Airon are even related. You're so educated and polite and he—well he's a..." Chrism paused, looked at Ann then swallowed hard and said, "He's not."

Skylee wished her stepsister knew the story behind Airon's brooding nature. The terrible plane crash had changed his life forever. Losing both parents in such a sudden way would alter anyone.

"If you knew Airon like I do you'd know he's not only smart, but very faithful to his word and his friends," Skylee said pointedly.

"Okay, okay," Chrism conceded. "We'll see how he acts when he shows up, but right now I'm ready to bungee jump. Let's go."

Skylee felt distinctly uncomfortable as they walked to the tower. She made small talk with Ann who was pointing her camera in every direction taking photos. All the while, Skylee knew there was an unspoken question between them. Ever since the wedding she had noticed nervousness in her aunt.

It was a relief when they reached the corner of Federal and Victoria streets and entered the base of the Sky Tower. Skylee was pleased to learn that her book, still secretly hidden inside the backpack, could be safely secured inside a locker while she bungee jumped.

Once Ann had bought the tickets and signed the forms, they lined up for the elevator ride to the top. As they waited, Skylee felt the necklace, which was tucked under her shirt, warming against her skin. She decided to ignore it, hoping it would return to normal.

Moments later, their tour guide arrived. He explained that he would also serve as the bungee instructor for the brave few who planned to jump. He was a tall, attractive guy, even dressed in the dorky bright orange uniform and white gloves. His dark blonde hair had that shaggy but styled thing going on, and he wore trendy sunglasses. His oration about the Sky Tower turned out to be surprisingly unrehearsed. Skylee wondered if this was perhaps his first day on the job.

"The New Sky Tower is three hundred and forty meters tall," the guide began. "Uh, making it um...one of the tallest towers in the world. I think it's...yeah, it's as tall as the New Eiffel Tower." He took a deep breath and the next part of his speech flew out at high speed. "The tower was designed to withstand winds in excess of one hundred and twenty miles per hour. It even survived a nine point three earthquake on the Day of Disaster. The New Sky Tower recently reopened to the public after years of repair."

Will leaned over and whispered in Skylee's ear, "I didn't know you were so famous. You have a tower named after you, *Sky*."

Skylee rolled her eyes at him. It was hard to decide which was worst, Airon calling her Skippy or Will's Sky joke. She placed her fingers in an L on her forehead, turned toward Will and dramatically mouthed the word *loser*. Catching a glimpse of the guide staring, she quickly dropped her hand. He smiled oddly at her and she looked away, suddenly aware that he might have thought she was making fun of him.

As Skylee stepped onto the elevator she noticed her necklace warming. The sensation made her stomach churn as the elevator took off. She tried to ignore it and listen to the guide's speech.

"There are something like...twelve hundred steps...uh wait, yes, twelve hundred and eighty-five steps from the base of Sky Tower to Sky Deck," he continued, looking down at his white glove, which was covered with writing. "On a clear day you can see approximately fifty one miles from New Sky Tower."

Skylee felt the elevator lurch to a stop and someone took her by the hand. The guide was escorting her out of the elevator. This left a rather confused looking tour group to exit on their own, including Will who looked more annoyed than confused. Chrism, on the other hand, seemed to find it amusing.

Skylee could feel the guide's eyes upon her, even though his dark glasses concealed them. Her face flushed under his gaze, and the necklace hidden underneath her shirt grew hotter by the second. She wasn't sure how much longer she could bear its heat. Anguished, she let out a small sigh.

Will's mouth fell open and he formed a fist. For a second, Skylee thought he was going to punch the guide. But instead he stood frozen in place, staring loathingly at him with both fists still tightly clinched. All along, Chrism persisted in chattering to Will about their first time to bungee jump together.

Ann, who had exited the elevator behind them, was watching closely. The anger on Will's face seemed to spur her into action.

"Pardon me?" she said stepping between Will and the guide. Where's the best place to view the bungee jumping?"

The guide snapped into a professional sounding tone, "Okay...friends and family are welcome to watch from the viewing platform."

Skylee glanced over at Will who was slowly shaking his head. Then a couple of young women, dressed in orange uniforms, began leading the spectators to the platform. Ann stood motionless and watched as they prepared for the bungee jump.

"Are you okay?" Skylee asked her. "I'm sure it's perfectly safe, after all you've bungee jumped yourself, plenty of times."

"Yeah, mum, no worries. I'll make sure it's safe," Will added, without taking his eyes off the guide.

"I'm just being a mom, you know...mom's always worry," Ann replied then she slowly turned and walked to the viewing platform.

"Those of you who will be jumping tandem please stand to the right and the solo jumpers to the left," said the guide as he motioned to each side.

Chrism and Will were among the first to be suited up for the jump. Will, who had bungee jumped dozens of times, looked as cool as a cucumber.

"Oh, Will, I'm so scared," Chrism said in a childish sounding voice.

Skylee turned her head and made a face. Just then, the guide began the countdown for their jump. Her stepsister pleaded with Will to hold her until they leapt. Will complied, but his eyes were now focused on Skylee. Even as they plunged from the platform, concern was written across his face.

One by one the jumpers dived from the Sky Tower, some with squeals of delight, some with screams of terror, until Skylee alone remained. The necklace was so hot it was nearly unbearable. She considered removing it but feared she might lose it in the jump.

A shadow fell across the Sky Deck as the sun hid behind a cloud. The air grew still. It seemed that the entire world had gone oddly silent. Skylee looked across the decking in search of Ann who raised her hand in a funny half-wave. For a moment, Skylee had a weird feeling that Ann was warning her not to jump.

"Step over here, Skylee," the guide said as his hand seized the back of her waist. "I'll help you get ready."

"Okay, thanks," she said, watching him hook the bungee cord to her harness. "Wait...how do you know my name?" In that instant she suddenly realized why he had fumbled his speech about the tower. *He's not really a tour guide*, she thought. *Who is he*?

Moving with lightning speed, he shoved her away and she stumbled backward until she was at the edge of the platform. She clung to the cord for balance. A glint of light caught her eye.

A knife. He pointed it at her and raised his other hand in a slow, deliberate motion, removing his dark glasses. *No, how can this be*? Skylee asked herself as she stared into his soulless black eyes. *It's him.* The devil from the wedding had found her. Her visions were coming to life.

He slowly edged nearer, holding the knife between them. There was nowhere for Skylee to go but down and she wasn't sure her bungee cord was completely secured.

"Please...don't...who are you?" she asked, her mind racing. "Why are you doing this?"

"Give me the necklace," he coldly demanded.

"I don't have it," she said, trying to sound convincing.

"It would be wise for you to hand it over."

Skylee felt choked by fear. "Why are you—"

"Give it to me, NOW!" he shouted.

"I can't it's—it's in my room," she lied.

"No it isn't!" he barked. "You're wearing it!"

He rushed toward her, holding the cord in one hand and the knife in the other. Her feet were barely touching the edge of the platform. She struggled to peer around him hoping Will's mom had seen she was in danger. Then a sickening realization hit her, Ann could only see him from behind. She couldn't see that he was holding a knife. Gathering all her strength, she twisted and turned trying to release his grip on her.

"Be still," he snarled through gritted teeth.

A scream rose from deep inside her, but it was quickly halted as he held the blade against her throat.

"If you don't give it...to...me...I WILL TAKE IT!" he loudly growled.

Running the knife at an angle along her collar, he reached the chain of her necklace. Skylee felt the blade's cold metal and gasped as it pricked her skin.

"Okay, okay you can have it. Just don't..." she pleaded with him, but agonizing pain halted her words.

A burning sensation tormented her as the necklace slid across her chest. It eased slightly when he suspended it over her shirt, holding it by the chain with the tip of his blade. The corners of his mouth curved into a sinister grin and his black eyes sparkled as they fixed upon the amulet.

"At last, you're mine," he said, reaching for it.

The magnitude of his words triggered an overwhelming surge of willpower within her. *You're not taking my father's necklace*, she thought. Using every ounce of strength she could muster, she pushed his arm away, throwing him off balance. She looked up and saw the necklace swinging back and forth on the blade. Then a silver flash crossed her vision as the knife came down and sliced her arm. She expected sharp pain, yet she felt nothing but cold numbness. There was only one way to escape him. Moving swiftly, she grabbed the necklace by its chain and stepped backward off the tower.

"NO!" he screamed, swinging the knife wildly.

For a brief second she felt as if she were hanging in midair. Then she watched in horror as he nicked her harness, severing partway through the fabric. His other hand was still gripping her bungee cord, which was now slipping through his fingers. It slashed a gash through his glove and deeper into his flesh, leaving a bright red streak. The last things she saw as she tumbled downward were his black eyes.

Skylee felt herself falling—falling—backward. *Everything will be fine, the harness will hold,* she told herself. When she reached the end of the cord it pulled taunt and sprung back. A feeling of relief swept over her. She had escaped the stranger and the necklace was still in her hand. Soon she would be safely on the ground. On her second trip downward she heard it.

SNAP

The sliced harness had broken free. Skylee helplessly tumbled through the air watching the tower fly by. There was nothing she could do. The ground came rushing up at her.

TEN

Cook's Farm

Skylee couldn't breathe. She tightened her hold on the necklace, as it cooled in her palm. Something warm and wet trickled down her arm. *I can't die like this,* she thought. Then out of nowhere, she was engulfed by an unexplainable calm. A blast of warm air rushed up from beneath her and instead of plummeting faster she fell slower and slower. If only there had been twenty more feet she would have landed as light as a feather, but the ground arrived a bit too soon. For a second, she thought she had managed to stay on her feet but the force of the landing threw her backward and ended with a hard thud. It was over. Skylee lay sprawled out on the ground with blood oozing from her arm.

Her entire body ached and she couldn't catch her breath. All she could hear was her heart hammering in her ears. She stared up at the sky and two faces popped into view. Will and Chrism stood open-mouthed, looking down at her. They must not have seen the attack at the top of the tower only her bizarre descent.

"SKY? What happened?" exclaimed Will, dropping to his knees beside her.

"OH MY GAWD," Chrism shrieked as she gawked at her bloody sleeve.

"I'm okay, I'm okay," Skylee said in a stunned voice.

"You're bleeding!" Will blurted out. He quickly tore his shirt and wrapped it around her arm.

"I'll be all right," she said softly as she struggled to sit up.

"Stay down, Sky, till help comes," Will insisted. He motioned to Chrism to go for help. His face was stricken with fear as he hovered over her and held pressure on her wound.

Skylee's voice trembled. "Don't worry, Will, I really am okay." She was thankful to have her best friend by her side.

Within minutes Chrism had returned with an army of people, which included Ann, a police officer, the Sky Tower manager, several security guards, and a number of curious on-lookers. They asked Skylee a thousand questions, some of which she decided not to answer. She tried to stay focused on the present moment as more and more people arrived and asked questions. Deep inside, she struggled with questions of her own.

The next few hours went by in a blur. The police showed up and found the real tour guide. The poor guy had been drugged, tied up and shoved into a locker. After Skyleigh was scanned for injuries and treated by paramedics, the police asked her to help them create a hologram of her attacker. Seeing the fake tour guide's image revolving before her eyes gave Skylee the creeps. When her mom and stepdad arrived at the scene they took charge, using their government connections, and insisted that she be taken back to the hotel to rest.

At dinner that same night, Skylee tried to act normal but every time she thought of the tower her heart raced. Nothing was normal. And to make matters worse she knew the truth had to be concealed. She pushed the food around on her plate, having lost her appetite. How could she tell them her attacker was the same man that had been at the wedding without revealing that he wanted her necklace? The warning in the book was clear, it had to remain secret or lives would be lost. Her stomach felt as though it were tied in knots.

Skylee fidgeted in her chair. She took a sip of water and tried to ignore the throbbing in her arm. The deep gash had needed stitches, eight nanosutures to be exact. Her face grew hot as she remembered the scene after her fall. The most humiliating part of the whole experience had been when the paramedics treated her like a child. One of them actually offered her a lollypop, as if candy would help the situation.

Then again, maybe if I'd eaten the last of my Luck-E-Chocs it wouldn't have happened, she thought. No, that's crazy, the luck thing isn't real, it's just candy—I'm losing it.

"Hey Sky, are you listening?" Will asked waving his hand in front of her face.

"Sorry, guess I zoned out," she answered with a weak smile. "What did you say?"

"Not me—your mum. She said we're leaving Auckland. I thought you'd be happy to hear we're going out into the bush."

Skylee's eyes widened. "We are? When?"

"Yes, well as soon as the police say we can," her mom said nodding slowly. "Probably in the morning. Alex and I are working on it, we've contacted Zane Cook and he's invited us to stay at his sheep farm."

"A farm?" asked Skylee excitedly.

"That's right, Cutie Pie," her mom said reaching across the table to pat her hand. "I think you'll love it."

CLINK! The sound of Chrism's fork dropping onto her plate interrupted the conversation. Her jaw dropped open and she rolled her eyes.

"Grrreat," she said, exhaling loudly. "Why can't we stay in Auckland? There's still so much to do here!"

When her mom and stepdad suggested the countryside would offer a much-needed safe haven Chrism's eyes bore down on them in anger. Skylee felt a twinge of guilt as she watched her argue with their parents. But in the end, her stepsister could not change their minds. So in retaliation, she refused to eat her meal and would not speak to anyone for the rest of the evening.

The next morning, Skylee, feeling as if she had just lain down to go to sleep, was awakened by her V-phone.

"Hello," she groggily said. "Huh, oh...Mom. What time is it?"

It was five o'clock in the morning. Her mother, who was speaking in a very perky voice for such an ungodly hour, was telling her to wake Chrism up so they could get an early start.

"Are you sure?" Skylee said, looking over at the lump in the next bed. "I don't think she's going to like it."

But she did, because as it turned out Chrism's attempt at emotional blackmail on the previous evening had actually worked. Their parents were going to allow a stopover on their way to the farm in a town called Matamata, otherwise known as Hobbiton or The Shire.

A few hours later Skylee, Chrism, their parents, Ann and Will filed off a long hover-shuttle and onto the set from The Lord of the Rings and The Hobbit movies. Skylee felt slightly uncomfortable wearing a fancy white blouse, which Chrism had insisted she borrow. Apparently none of her own clothes were nice enough to wear to The Shire. And unfortunately her long, curly hair had been so tangled that morning that all she could do was pull it into a messy ponytail. At least she had on her favorite, comfy jeans and best fitting tennis shoes.

In contrast, her stepsister was dressed in a flowing sapphire colored sundress with shiny silver sandals. And she didn't have a hair out of place.

"Oh my gosh! It's the party tree," squealed Chrism in delight as she pointed at a large oak, which was standing by a small lake. "I can't believe it survived The Day and look at those cute little Hobbit holes. Oh, I think that one over there is Bag End."

"Wow, it's gorgeous," said Skylee, looking across the lake at the lush green hills.

As their parents and Ann followed the tour guide down the path, Chrism grasped Will by the hand and took off toward the Hobbit holes. For a moment Skylee thought about heading in the opposite direction. But today, nothing was going to go wrong, even if she did have to watch her stepsister flirt with Will across all of Hobbiton. It was better than being knifed and falling off a tower.

Most of Skylee's time at The Shire was spent taking photos of her stepsister. Chrism peering into a Hobbit hole...Chrism peering out of a

Hobbit hole...Chrism hugging the party tree...and of course Chrism holding hands with Will beneath the "Welcome to Hobbiton" sign.

The afternoon sun was baking the top of Skylee's head by the time they walked back to their auto-glider. She was glad to get into the air-conditioned passengers compartment of their vehicle. But the journey from Hobbiton to Cook's Farm in Rotorua was anything but comfortable.

In fact, it had her remembering her studies of the Spanish Inquisition. As they glided along each relative took a turn and grilled her about what happened at the Sky Tower. She felt she could relate to those poor people who had been unmercifully questioned by the inquisitors. Will was the worst of them all, asking the same questions time and time again, mostly about the guide. When Chrism began loudly reading from her V-phone about Lord of the Rings and Hobbit filming locations their questioning stopped at long last. Skylee wasn't sure if Chrism had taken pity on her and purposely distracted them or if she was tired of Skylee getting all the attention, either way she was thankful.

It was after sundown when they approached the farm. As their vehicle soared closer to the ground Skylee sat quietly and watched the shadowy scenery pass by the window. The moon hung low in the twilight sky, casting a glittering path across the water of Rotorua Lake. A herd of sheep on the hillside seemed to glow in the darkness. Skylee stared at the lunar orb and studied the "man in the moon." The effect was reminiscent of a pair of eyes watching her.

Ever since the wedding, she had an uncontrollable urge to look over her shoulder fearful of seeing the soulless eyes that haunted her every step. She had almost convinced herself that she would never see them again until the tower, where her worst fears had come to pass. It had been just as the book predicted, and it nearly cost her her life.

"Hurry up," said Chrism, who had only managed to carry one small bag into the cottage. "Dad said we can choose our room and I want to get first pick."

"I'm coming as fast as I can," Skylee replied, tugging on the strap of her backpack and then pulling two pieces of luggage over the threshold of the door.

The cottage was larger than she had expected with four bedrooms and a big open area in the middle. It was rustically furnished in dark antiques and woven rugs, which were randomly placed on the stone floor.

"Well, it's not the Taj Mahal," said her sister wrinkling her nose. "But I guess it's better than camping."

"Are you kidding? I think it's splendid," said Will dumping a load of luggage in a heap at his feet.

"Oh, yes," Chrism immediately agreed, smiling at him. "I see what you mean it is very cozy, I suppose."

After several trips between bedrooms, where Chrism pointed out the proximity to the bathrooms, the view from the window and the size of the closets, she decided on their room. It had two twin beds, a rather large built-in wardrobe and a beautiful view of a hillside covered in lush green grass.

By the time the luggage was in the correct rooms, Skylee's mom had just about finished preparing dinner. Evidently, the kitchen had been stocked for their arrival. And it was a good thing because Skylee's appetite had returned. She stuffed herself with spaghetti and bread until her stomach was so full it hurt.

After unpacking her bag, Skylee left Chrism, who was happily color-coordinating a massive pile of clothing and hanging each outfit with its matching accessories, to sort it out on her own. She headed for the main house to join the rest of the family and wait for the arrival of Zane Cook. Her curiosity had been peaked about the man whom her mom had said was one of her dad's best friends. She had so many questions to ask him.

As she climbed up the steps, she noticed a porch swing. She walked over to it and ran her hand across its worn gray surface. *Whoa, it so old, like from before The Day*, she thought.

"Real wood!" she said as she sat down on it. It was rare to see actual wood furniture. People were desperate after The Day and used their furniture for firewood. *It's sad*, she thought, rocking gently as she brushed her fingers on the wooden armrest. The feel of real wood, smoothed down and put together in a strong and sturdy swing, was nice. It was surprising, because she honestly didn't like the idea of killing a living thing just so you could sit on it. Besides, the stuff they made furniture out of now was sturdy enough and much better for the environment, but it did lack something. *So, Mr. Cook likes authentic stuff, I think I'm gonna like him.*

Skylee swung back and forth, and tried to think peaceful thoughts, but her mind instantly shifted to the humiliation she had experienced after the attack at the tower. *Oh no...it's probably going to end up in the news.* Her insides squirmed as she thought of it. There was nothing she hated more than being the center of attention. She grabbed her V-phone, scanned the local news and to her horror found several stories about her attack, most of which included video of her fall.

"Ugh," she gasped as she watched the shaky footage, which had obliviously been taken by V-phone, of herself plunging to the ground.

Some of the headlines read: *"Girl Thinks She Can Fly"*, *"Girl Falls: Accident or on Purpose?"*, *"Love Triangle Nearly Leads to American Girl's Death"*, or the best one *"Girl Jumps Desperate for Attention from Childhood Sweetheart"*

She clicked on the link and read:

Girl Jumps from Sky Tower Desperate for Attention

Thirteen year old American girl jumps off the tower,
hoping her childhood sweetheart would notice her again.
Devastated by the loss of his attention, the teen
girl throws herself off the bungee platform before her safety
harness was securely attached by the guide. An insider
revealed that the girl had been emotional since

her mother's recent marriage and that rejection from her boyfriend caused her to snap. Bystanders heard the girl scream at the boy, saying it was his fault and for him to take his hands off her...

"What a load of rubbish!" exclaimed Skylee, resisting an urge to throw her V-phone down and stomp on it.

She felt her face flush as anger built up inside her. *Where do they come up with this stuff? I am not thirteen...I'm almost fifteen!* She quickly left that site and continued scanning. Then the New Zealand Herald headline caught her attention. It read *"American Girl Attacked at Sky Tower"*, so she began reading. She was glad to see that they at least got the part about the imposter causing her fall right, but they also speculated about a love triangle being involved.

"Sheesh," she groaned.

Yet another site proclaimed it a miracle, reporting that she should have been killed by her fall. It said that a strong wind caught her jacket just right, helping her glide to the ground. Skylee knew it was something else, a supernatural something that involved the necklace and the book. The book had tried to warn her and she had not taken it seriously, from now on she would pay more attention.

Come what may, Skylee intended to find out what was really going on. Talking to Ann seemed like a good place to start. She couldn't shake the feeling that Ann knew something. Then again, it had all started at the wedding, which made her wonder if her mom's marriage to Alex could be involved. The magnitude of the situation made Skylee wish her dad was alive. She felt that somehow the truth would lie with him.

Skylee resumed flipping through the news articles on her V-phone. Another headline caught her eye *"Phileas D. Mogg to Host Sixth Annual Green Ice Ball."* She clicked on the video clip and watched Mr. Mogg being interviewed on a talk show about the charity event.

His 3-D image glowed before her with such high definition that she could count every freckle on his face, that is, if he had any. In fact, everything about him seemed to be perfect, his high cheekbones, his well-defined jaw line and his deep blue eyes. She could understand why her mom and Chrism were in awe of him. As Skylee listened to his interview she found herself fascinated with the way he looked.

His wavy brown hair was swept back and he wore a tight navy blue turtleneck, like a second skin across his lean chest and arms. The overall effect was that of a "Hollywood heartthrob" although there was something odd about his too perfect smile. She shook her head and laughed as she thought about her Mom's obsession with Mr. Mogg and his company. Maybe it wasn't *all* about the environmental activism. Still, almost every link she clicked on about Mr. Mogg and S.E.E. Corporation credited him with spearheading the recovery after The Day. She quietly looked down at his picture and realized that she might actually see him in person when her mom and stepdad had their meeting with him.

The stillness of the evening was broken by a sudden whoosh passing overhead. She snapped her V-phone shut and sat upright in fear, but she was quickly relieved to see a large black swan gracefully gliding away. The bird landed on the lake and floated on the surface of the shimmering water. Skylee was thankful to trade the turmoil of her attack for the solitude of Cook's farm.

Why am I so jumpy? It's just a bird... She leaned back in the swing, closed her eyes and tried to relax. *After all I'm sitting in the middle of nature.* Maybe being on the farm was going to be fun. She and Will could go hiking, boating and best of all Skylee didn't think her new stepsister would want to have anything to do with being outside.

Her thoughts were interrupted by a rustling noise, but she told herself it was nothing to worry about. It was just the sounds of the great outdoors. And then, she heard the noise again so she opened her eyes. The hair on the back her neck stood on end. A pair of dark eyes loomed over her. *He's here...* She opened her mouth to scream but nothing came out.

"Who are *you*?" said a large man in a gruffly voice.

A vivid scene from a horror movie flashed through her mind, the kind that's filmed in the deep woods, with a scary ax swinging killer.

"Are ya deaf, little girl?" he barked.

"N-No, I-I" stuttered Skylee. "I'm Sky-Skylee." She sat up slowly.

"Did ya say Sky-Lee?" he huskily asked.

"Yes."

Her eyes widened as his hand reached for hers, pulling her up off the swing like she was as light as air.

"Ya don't look anything like your dad," he said with a frown. "This is my place, I'm Zane Cook."

"Mr. Cook," she said in relief.

"Stop right there," Zane ordered as he leaned in over her. "If ya want to stay on my good side, call me Zane, got that?"

"Yes sir," she said swallowing hard. "I mean, yes, Zane."

"I guess for a girl, you might have some smarts. Good to know." He turned and walked toward the front door.

Skylee took in slow breaths, trying to calm down as she watched her dad's friend disappear into his house. He must have been at least six foot four and she thought she noticed some scars on his forehead. His beard hid his face so thoroughly that she wasn't sure if he had been smiling or frowning when he spoke to her.

Okay, he's creepy, she thought. *But you can't judge a book by its cover.* She decided not to let her first impression of the man influence her. Sure, he had scared her, but as she heard her mom's laughter coming from inside the house, she thought he couldn't be all bad.

Skylee laid back down on the swing and propped herself up on one elbow, making sure not to put pressure on her recent wounds. She remembered Drake saying that Zane would be a "good contact" for her mom and Alex's investigation. It seemed ironic that her dad's old friend had come into her life at nearly the same time as the book and necklace.

She pushed her worry back and closed her eyes listening to the chirping crickets.

Within minutes her relaxed state was interrupted when an auto-glider zoomed into view, stirring up dust. It came to a stop in front of the main house. Skylee stood up in time to see a tall beautiful woman with stylish brown hair step out of the vehicle.

"Hello, you must be Skylee Porter," she said with natural ease as she gracefully walked toward the porch.

"Uh, yes," said Skylee, wondering how she knew her name.

"I'm Dr. Shelley Leonard. Zane and I work together, we mostly do environmental research for the University of Auckland. He called and said your parents needed the help of a geophysicist, so I'm here to meet with them."

"A geophysicist? You study the earth's crust."

"That's right and there's a lot more. We monitor the structure and the behavior of the earth, including oil and gas deposits, earthquakes, fault lines—"

The front door swung open and Will dashed onto the porch with Chrism tagging behind him. Skylee watched as he eyed the auto-glider with his mouth agape.

"Whoa, that is some kind of hot ve—hicle," Will fumbled his words as his gazed turned to the woman.

"Thanks, so you like the red?" she said ignoring his awkward stare. "I can change it to blue, I have the paint change option."

"No, red...is...is a good choice," stammered Will shaking his head.

Skylee couldn't help but smirk as she noticed her stepsister's face. Chrism was bitterly glaring at Dr. Leonard. Then she moved her glare to Will, who looked like a kid in a candy shop.

Dr. Leonard elegantly stepped onto the porch and looked at Will. "Could you point me to the Faraway's?"

"Er, sure," he said straightening up and eagerly holding the door with his mouth still partly open. "I'll take you to them."

It caught Skylee by surprise when Will turned his gaze toward her. He managed to shut his gaping jaw long enough to give her a quick wink before they entered the house. Skylee's face turned pink. She stifled a laugh as she watched Chrism stomp into the house behind them with her arms crossed over her chest. Skylee couldn't help but wonder if Will's reaction was due to the red auto-glider or, much more likely, because of Dr. Leonard's eye-catching dress and long legs.

About an hour later, Skylee was sitting on the steps of her cottage looking up at the stars. Chrism and Will were inside. They were glued to their V-phones, trying to find media coverage of the attack, which mortified her so much that she had come outside to escape hearing about it. Ann had excused herself to her room, saying she wanted to catch up on some reading. And her mom and Alex were still at the main house with Zane and Dr. Leonard.

"Ahh...peace and quiet," she said.

Rubbing her throbbing arm, she heard the faint sound of a kitten's meow. She stood and walked slowly toward the soft cry. It took her several minutes to find the furry little thing sitting on the porch of the main house. She reached down and picked it up. It purred and snuggled against her neck. The kitten's soft fur was marked with multiple colors, which reminded Skylee of an old flat screen movie about gremlins.

"Okay, little lady I'll get you a treat." Skylee said as she entered the house.

As she made her way down the hallway she heard her mom and some others having an intense discussion. She knew she should turn around and head back to the cottage but her curiosity kept her heading toward the kitchen, right into the middle of their conversation.

Beside I really need milk for this kitten, she told herself, kissing the ball of fur on the head.

"I think it's a good idea if we go to the site," Alex said firmly.

"What site?" Skylee asked nonchalantly.

Her mom was standing at the kitchen counter, dunking a tea bag up and down in a cup of boiling water. Her stepdad, Zane and Dr. Leonard were sitting at a small kitchen table with coffee mugs set before them.

"Oh, hi cutie-pie. We're discussing a work issue right now," her mom said, somehow managing to use her baby talk voice and sound serious at the same time.

"I know," she replied smiling in embarrassment at Dr. Leonard. "I'm sorry to interrupt your meeting. I just wondered where you were going and if I'm going with you." Skylee went to the refrigerator and pulled out the milk. *Please don't make me go with you...*

"To the Bay of Plenty, the location of the island that disappeared," Dr. Leonard said. "Please feel free to call me Shelley. And I'm fine with you going. I can make arrangements—"

"No!" her mom said, spinning around with her teacup so fast that some of it slopped out onto the floor. "That is not a place for children."

"What she means," Alex chimed in. "Is that it won't be necessary for Skylee and the others to go with us." He nodded reassuringly at Skylee. "Zane assures us that you'll be safe here at the farm. Are you all right with that?"

"Of course," she said gratefully as she looked down at her mom, who was now on her knees cleaning up the spill.

"Okay," Shelley said winking at Skylee. "Whatever you want, right now everything is set to go in the morning."

Skylee grinned as she poured milk in a bowl for her little friend and sat them both on the floor at her feet.

"Maybe I should stay here," her mom stood up and said.

"No," Skylee said a bit louder than she had intended. "You have to go. It's your job." *Please go and stop hovering...*

"But Sweetie," her mom said. "You are more important than any job. You are my sunshine, my sweet butter cup, my precious—"

"MOM!"

Everyone looked startled for a moment then Zane spoke. "Janis, the kids will be just as safe here as anywhere. Safer. My farm is far from town. And my motto is—worrying about what hasn't happened is a waste of time."

Skylee smiled at Zane's matter of fact attitude. She had never met anyone quite like him. He wasn't so scary after all. Maybe he would tell her more about her father, since she couldn't get much information from her mom or Ann.

"Honey," Alex said to her mom. "Ann will be here, too. You know she knows how to handle herself."

"Yeah right," Shelley mumbled under her breath.

Skylee looked at her thoughtfully and realized that no one else seemed to have heard what she had said.

"Okay, I'll go," her mom said. "I really do want to talk to Mr. Clark."

"Who's Mr. Clark?" Skylee asked, picking the kitty up and giving it nose kisses.

"He's one of the boat captains I use for ocean floor mapping and research," Shelley said, standing to her feet. She walked over and petted the kitten, which was now cradled in the crook of Skylee's arm. "Aw, cute. I'm not sure if Jack will be there tomorrow, I haven't been able to contact him yet. But I do think you need to talk to him. He is the one that saw someone on the island before it sank."

Her mom cleared her throat. "Sweetie, where did you get that kitten?" she asked obviously changing the subject before Skylee could ask more questions.

"I found it on the porch," she said turning to Zane. "I hope you don't mind me giving it some milk."

"Just don't make it a habit," he answered sharply. "It should grow up tough so it can defend itself outside."

He stood up and walked over to Skylee looking down at the kitten. "I think this is one of my wife's favorite strays."

So, he has a wife… thought Skylee. *I wonder where she is?* Her mom and Alex were talking but she didn't hear anything they were saying. Zane seemed to be glaring at the kitten the same way he had glared at her earlier. *What's up with him,* she thought as she protectively tucked the kitty under her chin.

"Okay," Shelley said, chuckling. "I guess I should head for home. My hubby is probably pulling what's left of his hair out. I let the nanny off tonight. I think it's good for fathers to deal with their children once in a while."

"You have a mean streak, Shelley," Zane said. "Leaving him with those rowdy twins."

"He'll survive," she replied. "After all, they're boys. Skylee, one thing you need to remember—men all stick together."

Skylee giggled. She was amazed to learn that Shelley, who looked so young and slender, had twin boys. And even more surprising, she apparently had a balding husband.

"Thanks for your help," Alex said coming over and extending his hand to Shelley.

"Yes, thanks," her mom said in agreement as she cleared off the table.

"No problem what so ever," Shelley said. "So, Zane, are you coming with us tomorrow? I can always rustle you up a diving suit."

"You're diving?" Skylee asked in surprise. *Darn, I love diving...* "Maybe I should go."

"Sweetie pie, I know you like to dive," her mom said, standing at the sink with her hands in soapy water. "But you're staying here."

"And no diving suit for me," Zane bluntly said. "I prefer solid ground. But I'll meet ya at the dock in Tauranga, if I get through with my business on time."

"All right," Shelley said.

After everyone said their goodnights, Zane walked Shelley to her auto-glider and her mom and stepdad went hand in hand to the cottage, leaving Skylee alone the kitchen.

"Well, little fur ball," she said, holding the kitten up in front of her. "Looks like tomorrow we are going to be parent free—well—except for Ann. But never fear, Will knows how to talk to his mom. And I'm sure she'll let us roam about outside."

She secured the kitten with her hurt arm, holding it close to her neck, while using the other to rinse the milk bowl. She was listening to its loud purr when she felt a coolness develop on her chest.

"My book," she said softly, holding the kitten closer. Her heart pounded as she ran out the back door.

Skylee raced around the side of the house. *Thud.* She stumbled over a big log. As she fell face first the kitten jumped out of her arms. She managed to block her face before hitting the ground. Pain shot through her injured arm as if it had been cut again. The only comfort was that she landed frontward and not on her backside which was already covered with bruises.

"Oh, oh, oh." she breathed deep and slow, hoping to quiet the pain. Stunned, she laid there for a few minutes until she heard footsteps.

"What are you doing out here—ya hurt?" a low voice asked.

Skylee looked up and saw Zane. She struggled to pull herself upright when two strong hands grabbed her shoulders and pulled her to her feet.

"I'm...fi...fine," she stuttered.

"What happened?" Zane asked impatiently as his dark eyes searched hers.

"I tripped over something." She looked around, holding her arm. "That log, I guess."

"You should've stayed on the lighted path. Use your head," he said in a cantankerous voice. "Are you in pain?"

"I'm fine. I guess I just wasn't thinking about where I was going," she said as she glanced around. "Hey, did you happen to see where the kitten went?"

"It took off, it's probably in the woods." His head made a quick jerk in the direction of the forest.

Even though her arm was throbbing, she had an urge to ask him about her dad. As she looked up at his menacingly large shape looming over her, she swallowed and decided that it wasn't the best time. The way the shadows were falling across his face was scary, which made her wish she was tucked safely inside her cottage.

She smiled shyly at him as she moved to leave. "Good night, Mr. uh...I mean Zane and thanks for helping me."

"Yeah, just watch your step," he said sternly. "I promised your mum you wouldn't get hurt."

Skylee nodded and walked away, picking up her pace as she got closer to the cottage. She looked around for the kitten but didn't see it anywhere. She hoped it was okay. Maybe her mom would let her take it back home when they left New Zealand. She gave a fleeting look behind her and noticed Zane was still standing there, watching her. Skylee climbed up the steps quickly, opened the door, stepped inside and closed it as fast as she could.

"Hey, where have you been?" Will asked, staring oddly at her.

"I went for a walk," Skylee paused for a moment, holding her arm as she decided not to say anything about falling. "Well, I'm tired. I think I'll call it a night."

"Ok, goodnight," Chrism chimed in with her face buried behind the pages of a fashion magazine.

Skylee glanced at her stepsister, secretly debating with herself on whether to stay with them or go to her room. If her necklace hadn't been so cold she would have joined them. She yawned and gave Will a smile.

"G'night, Sky. Sleep tight," he said, still gazing peculiarly at her as she turned slowly and walked down the hall to her room. "Hey, are you all right? Is your arm hurting?" he called out to her.

"I'm fine. Stop worrying so much. Good night," she said as she hurried down the hall.

Skylee shut the door and put a chair in front of it. She wanted to look at the book without her stepsister barging in on her. She grabbed her backpack from her bed and pulled the book out of its secret resting place. After carefully placing the necklace in its cover, she opened it. Words shimmered onto the page. She blinked several times, not believing what she read.

"Well, that's a bit late," she grumbled.

> *Step with great care. Take a path that is clear.*
> *Keep your eyes on the sky. Danger is near.*

She shook her head and laughed softly. "I could have used that bit of information a few minutes ago."

Skylee looked up catching her reflection in the mirror and gasped, "Oh no!" Her fingers traced the grass stains that were smeared all over the front of the white blouse, which she had borrowed from her stepsister.

"She's going to kill me. Great, this is just great, so this is what Will was staring at." She let out a long sigh, and decided to hide it until she could work on removing the stains. Too tired to do much more, she shut the book and put the necklace back around her neck. After slipping into her pajamas, she quickly scooted the chair back in place and headed to bed.

Skylee could hear Will and Chrism chatting as her head hit the pillow. In truth, it made her a little uneasy but not enough to get out of her comfy bed. The moonlight flooded through the window in a watery shadow, dancing on the wall and creating a peaceful feeling throughout her bedroom. She closed her eyes and drifted off to sleep willing the next day to be better.

ELEVEN

The Plane

"Hey, wake up. Wake up!" said Chrism, bouncing up and down on the side of Skylee's bed.

"What?" she groggily muttered, squinting up at her stepsister, who was fully dressed with her hair pulled back neatly into a ponytail.

"Get up, sleepyhead. It's ten o'clock and our parents are gone, so let's go exploring."

"*You* want to go outside and...you...want...to explore?" said Skylee with a yawn as she pulled the covers over her head.

"Of course I do. And Will said to wake you up, he wants to go, so I'm going," she declared, jerking the covers off of her face.

"Naturally," whispered Skylee but all she really wanted to do was scream.

She looked at Chrism in her extravagant hiking outfit and leather boots, which were obviously another attempt to impress Will. Skylee felt like she was nearing the end of her rope when it came to Chrism's obsession with him. And to be perfectly honest, what bugged her even more was how much Will seemed to be enjoying the attention. She pushed that thought out of her mind as she got out of bed.

Later, during breakfast, the three of them convinced Ann to let them go for a hike. Will pointed out that she would have some time to herself to take photos of the scenery. Skylee was impressed with his power of persuasion when his mom finally caved.

"Stay within sight of the cottage," Ann instructed as she left the kitchen.

"Sure thing," Will said, jumping up from the breakfast table. He went to the pantry and snatched a small camouflaged backpack. "Hey, we should take a few snacks and maybe some water." He grabbed some Banquet Bars and stuffed them in the pack.

"Ew…" Chrism made a face at him. "Why are you packing those disgusting things? And that backpack is ugly."

"I like these," Will said, holding one up and reading the label. "A whole meal in one small package."

"I don't think they're that bad," Skylee said. "I mean they saved a lot of people from starving after The Day."

"Well, it's been a long time since *The Day* and its disgusting biting into one of those. It just isn't right to have a bar taste like salad or steak." Chrism stood and went to the pantry. "Doesn't Zane have something else?"

"Come on, Chrism," encouraged Will. "Be adventurous. I like them myself. Airon and I take them on walkabouts. Lightweight, easy to carry, lots of variety."

"Yeah," added Skylee. "And they're healthy."

"Whatever," her stepsister said, stepping toward the kitchen's back door. "I think they taste like paste and they stick to your teeth, so go ahead and pack them if you want. I won't be eating any."

"More for me," Will said with a huge grin on his face.

Skylee handed him some bottled water to add to the backpack. She wanted to explain the importance of the Banquet Bars to her stepsister but decided to let it ride.

"Hey, any Luck-E-Chocs in there?" Skylee asked.

"Nah," answered Will cocking his head to look at her. "I don't see any. You're not gonna be cranky now, huh?"

"No," she said sharply, but to be honest if she had one she might be in a better mood.

After Will had the snack situation taken care of, they headed outdoors. The sun shone brightly as Skylee took in the scenery around them. The hills and valleys looked like a painting that had come to life. The trees formed a tall border along the grassy fields and gently swayed in the wind. It was serene.

Skylee heard laughter and noticed Will and Chrism had gotten a little ways ahead of her. Once again, it came as no surprise that her stepsister was brazenly flirting with him.

Will looked back and said, "Sky, you sure are dragging this morning, come on," he motioned for her to catch up, and then suddenly lowered his arm, looking past her with a confusion expression.

"What now?" Skylee huffed as she turned around. To her amazement, a line of sheep trailed behind her. Two sheep dogs were with them standing at attention like they were waiting for a command. Skylee had never seen real sheep before, except in photos. After The Day a good deal of the world's livestock were killed or died later from sickness.

"Why aren't they fenced in? Do they bite?" Chrism asked anxiously, stepping behind Will for protection. "Will?"

"No worries, they eat grass," he answered. "Zane said they have free range, I reckon that means they can go where ever. Maybe they're curious."

"I don't like it. What if they step on my new boots or rub up against me?" her stepsister complained, eyeing the sheep. "Skylee, make them go away."

"*Me*? Who am I, Dr. Doolittle?" Skylee said agitatedly, although she wondered if Chrism might be right. *They're following me just like those butterflies,* she thought. It probably had something to do with her necklace, which was quickly warming on her skin.

"Well, look at them, they seem to want to be with you. So maybe you are. You do talk about nature all the time. Maybe you should talk to them," said Chrism mockingly.

Before she could come up with a witty response, a humming noise drew her attention. A small plane came into view. They all watched as it flew by, high above the treetops. The warming sensation from her necklace gave Skylee an uneasy feeling as she watched the plane go out of sight. She sighed as an involuntary shudder moved over her body.

"Hey? What is it?" Will said in an alarmed voice. "Sky?"

"I'm fine. It's just...well, a lot has happened and," exasperated, she continued, "I don't know why these sheep are following me. It's nothing, really." She noticed Will chewing on his lip. Hoping to ease his tension, she grinned widely at him and patted one of the sheep on the head.

Chrism immediately pulled on his arm. "Come on, let's keep exploring," she said, pointing up ahead. "The lake is right over there."

Skylee motioned for them to go on. She didn't want them to notice the annoyed look that was probably plastered across her face. In the meantime, she felt a tug at her feet and looked down to see one of the sheep dogs, grabbing her by the pant leg.

"Stop that. You'll put a hole in them," she scolded as she jerked her leg forward to free it from the dog's grip. The dog whimpered, looking at her with eyes that were so earnest that she stopped and reached down to scratch it behind the ears.

"It's okay, puppy dog," she said.

For a moment it wagged its tail in gratitude and pushed a cold nose against her hand. Then it stopped and cocked its head to the side.

"Ow!" groaned Skylee. Her necklace suddenly felt like a hot iron scorching her skin. As she cautiously pulled it out from beneath her shirt, she caught a movement out of the corner of her eye. It was Will running toward her, waving his arms and shouting at the top of his voice, but he was being drowned out by an increasingly loud roar.

The small plane had returned. It skimmed over the tops of the trees and headed straight for her. With a small yelp the dog took off running, Skylee wanted to follow but her feet seemed to be glued to the ground. As the cockpit of the plane came into view, she was shocked to see that no one was inside.

She stood there, frozen in fear, as the message from her book sprang into her head. *Keep your eyes on the sky...danger is near.* Her father's book had tried to warn her.

As if everything was in slow motion, she moved her eyes from the plane to Will. He was still coming toward her, but now Chrism was clinging to his hand. Then she saw her stepsister stumble and slip from his grasp. He stopped for a split second, looked down at her and yelled something. He then took off in a run, heading her way, straight into the plane's path.

"GO BACK!" Skylee shouted at him.

But her cry was swallowed by the screeching sound of twisting metal as the plane hit the ground. It dug a trench, plowing its way toward them. The horror of its approach finally freed her from her frozen trance, and she ran in Will's direction. If something didn't stop that plane he would die with her.

"NO!" Skylee screamed, looking over her shoulder as one of the wings crumpled and tore free.

Then, out of nowhere, the same calm that she had felt at the Sky Tower came over her. And something deep inside told her to stop running and face her fear. She skidded to a halt and spun around, long strands of wavy hair flying across her face. A powerful surge of energy, stronger than anything she had ever felt before, traveled through her like an electrical current. Instinctively, she threw her hands out in front of her as if she could will the plane to stop.

From the corner of her eye, Skylee saw a massive tree at the edge of the forest swaying back and forth. Then it snapped and toppled, falling slowly, almost gracefully. But she didn't see how its impact had stopped the plane, within a few feet of them, because her attention had been on a huge branch. It had broken off, flew past her and narrowly missed Will's head.

As her eyes followed the path of the limb, she saw her stepsister's face fill with shock and fear. Chrism covered her head and crouched down as it came toward her. In that instant, black smoke from the crash engulfed them. Skylee squinted and caught a glimpse of a sheep standing where she thought Chrism had been.

With burning eyes, Skylee bent over and violently coughed, trying to catch her breath. The smoldering plane had produced so much smoke and dust, that she was a little confused as to where she was. She took a step, tumbled forward and felt herself falling. Strong yet gentle hands grabbed her arms and stopped her from doing a face plant. She looked up and saw Will's worried face.

"Sky? Thank God, I thought that plane was going to..." he paused as if waiting for a reply. "Please say something."

"Are you all right?" she whispered covering her mouth as she lightly coughed.

"I'm fine, as long as you are," he said, pulling her into a tight hug.

"Oh, Chrism! Where's Chrism? That huge branch—did you see it? It missed us but I think it hit her!" exclaimed Skylee, pulling out of his embrace and scanning the grounds, which were covered in debris. A pair of leather boots was sticking out from under the limb. She pointed at them and cried in panic, "Is that her?"

"Cripes!" Will shouted, letting go of her and running toward the boots. Skylee ran right behind him.

"Chrism?" she called as she and Will grabbed the branch and threw it aside.

Her stepsister's boots fell to the ground, empty. Skylee and Will looked franticly through the branches scattered across the field. They finally spotted Chrism about fifteen feet away. She laid face down in the underbrush.

"Oh no, she's hurt!" Skylee cried in a shrill voice as they moved toward her.

"Chrism?" said Will as he dropped to his knees and gently turned her over. He bent down, placed his ear to her mouth, and sighed in relief. "She's breathing," he said, looking up at Skylee.

She knelt beside her stepsister and whispered, "Thank goodness."

Skylee watched as Will lightly moved Chrism's hair out of the way. It had been pulled loose from her ponytail and was covering her face. Blood oozed from a gash above her ear.

"Chrism, Chrism, please, open your eyes," pleaded Will.

"Eemm," she moaned. Her eyes fluttered opened. "Oooh." She lifted her hand to her head. "Oh, it hurts."

"Okay, shh... just lie still. Do you hurt anywhere else?" he asked.

Chrism brought her hand down and saw blood. She screamed, "I'm bleeding. I'm bleeding."

"It doesn't look bad," he reassured, taking her hand and patting it.

"Really?" whispered Chrism.

Skylee heard a faint cry in the distance, followed by the sound of fast moving footsteps. She looked up to see Ann rushing toward them.

"William," she said as she reached them. "Is everyone all right? What happened?" She looked down at Chrism's pale face. "Is she okay?"

"She was out of it for a while but she's awake now." He smiled down at her stepsister and lightly squeezed her hand. "Right, Chrism? Hey, can you say something?"

"Ahhhh...my head. It really hurts," she groaned.

"Move over please and let me see," Ann ordered as she knelt down to examine her. "Oh, okay. It doesn't look bad."

"But it hurts!" shrieked Chrism.

"Calm down, let me look," Ann softy demanded. "Son, help me get her up. Let's take her in the house so I can clean the wound and get a closer look."

Will reached for Chrism and helped her up but her knees buckled. He caught her as she swayed on her feet.

Skylee watched as he draped an arm over Chrism's shoulder and steered her toward the cottage. Guilt washed over her as she thought about the bad attitude she'd had toward her stepsister for the last few days. She struggled hard to hold back the tears threatening to stream down her face.

"Sky, she'll be all right. It's just a small cut. What about the pilot?" Ann asked as she looked over at the plane.

"I don't think there was a one."

"What? Are you sure?"

"Well, I'm pretty sure the cockpit was empty."

Ann stared intently at the plane without uttering a word.

Skylee felt her emotions rushing to the surface. "I don't understand why all this is happening. Chrism...she could have been killed...and Will too...could have..."

She couldn't finish. Soft sobs came out as Ann's arms went around her in a motherly hug.

"They weren't killed, so that's what we need to focus on and anyway, I should've been with you all," Ann said regretfully. Stepping back from Skylee, she gently took her by the shoulders. "Listen your stepsister's going to be fine. Come on, let's go inside, and check on them."

As they entered the house, Skylee heard Will's voice coming from her and Chrism's room. They started down the hall when Ann stopped.

"I'm going to get the first aid kit. You go on in," Ann paused and smiled at her. "It's gonna be all right."

Skylee wiped her eyes with her sleeve and stood at the bedroom door, unable to enter the room. She listened.

"My head hurts," Chrism whimpered.

"I know, but it'll feel better soon," said Will. "My mum's good at treating wounds. I've taken plenty of spills, surfing and all."

Chrism's voice trembled as she spoke, "I saw that plane and then you and Skylee were right in its path. Then that tree fell and the huge limb flew off. I...I thought it was going to hit you but it missed and came for me..." she started sobbing.

"Its okay, you're okay."

"My feet are cold," she said as she looked down at them. "Oh, no, where are my boots? Did you take them off?"

"No, they're still outside," said Will "They were under a limb. The impact must have knocked them off. You're lucky you only have a small cut. A wallop like that should have broken something."

"Sorry to disappoint you," she said in a childlike tone.

"Disappoint me—what?" Will raised her hand in both of his and said. "The only disappointment is that you were hurt at all."

Skylee watched as Chrism and Will gazed into each other's eyes. A lump formed in her throat. She sighed and entered the room, grabbing a blanket off a chair.

"Here," she said, fanning it over her stepsister. After the blanket was straightened, Skylee sat on the edge of the bed opposite Will. "Ann is getting the first aid kit. She'll fix you up."

"My head hurts. She needs to hurry up. Oh, and Skylee, make sure you get my boots. They're brand new and I don't want..." her voice faded as her eyelids fluttered.

Skylee brushed her hand over her stepsister's head and said, "I'll get your boots. Don't worry about it, just rest." Then she noticed something white in Chrism's hair. She pulled the fluffy stuff out and examined it.

"What is that?" Will asked.

Skylee handed him a piece of it. "I don't know, it looks kinda like cotton."

"Humm," he muttered as he studied it. "Could be brain matter."

Skylee giggled. She loved the way Will could find humor in the worst of times.

"What? That's not funny. Let me see," Chrism said, grabbing it out of her hand. "Yuck, this stinks. Get it out." She reached up and wildly pulled at her hair.

"Stop that," insisted Will as he grabbed both of her hands and held them still. "You're going to hurt yourself more if you keep doing that."

"Is it on my clothes? My Jacket?"

"Hold on, I'll check," said Skylee as she lifted the blanket. She spotted a few more pieces of the white stuff on her clothes but decided it was better not to mention it. "Looks good," she said with assurance as she smoothed the blanket out and covered her stepsister back up.

"Okay, I've got everything I need," Ann said as she walked into the room. "Move over, Sky, so I can get a look at her."

"Okay," Skylee said while getting up.

"Let me see…" Ann spoke calmly as she passed a portable body scanner over Chrism.

"It's bad isn't it," whispered Chrism. Tears filled her eyes and ran down her cheeks. "It's really bad. I can see it in your face. It's going to leave a scar, isn't it?"

"Calm down. No broken bones, no internal injuries," she read from the scanner. "You're not even going to need nanosutures. And I'll use Sealacut so it won't leave a scar."

First, Ann tore open an antibacterial pack, pulling out the medicated gauze and without warning began cleaning Chrism's cut.

"Ouch, that hurts," whimpered her stepsister.

"Mum," Will said, "Come on, take it easy."

Ann let out a long breath and said, "She's tough, and she can deal with this a lot better than dealing with an infection." Ann looked directly at Chrism. "You get an infection and your chances of having a scar will increase."

"Okay," her stepsister said in a whimper.

It took several attempts to apply the medicine due to Chrism twitching and crying out. Finally, Ann brushed on a layer of Sealacut and gave her stepsister a pain patch to help her rest.

Ann stood and spoke in hushed tones, "Let's go and let her sleep."

"Wait," Chrism said woozily as the medicine began to take effect. "Don't forget…"

Skylee smiled, bent down and whispered, "I know—boots. I'll get them. Now go to sleep."

"Will, p-please d-don't leave…" slurred Chrism, as she dizzily reached out grabbing his hand.

"Go on, I'll stay with her until she falls asleep," Will said without ever taking his eyes off Chrism.

Skylee followed Ann out of the bedroom but briefly paused and looked back at them. She had a strong feeling that she should stay. *No,* she told herself, *if he wants to stay with her…let him.*

"Just go and get her stupid boots," Skylee mumbled under her breath.

Once outside she glanced up at the overcast sky. The low gray clouds seemed to mirror her mood. With a heavy sigh, she headed out in search of the boots.

Fifteen minutes later, Skylee was back inside standing at the bathroom sink. She had found the "oh so important boots" and left them sitting outside their bedroom door. She stared in the mirror for a long time. *I look like a zombie*, she thought. Her face was covered in soot and dirt. Her long hair was disheveled with leaves and twigs sticking out everywhere. It took a while, but she managed to wash her face and pick most of the debris out of her hair.

Closing her eyes, images of falling from the tower and the plane careening towards her flashed through her mind. *I could've been killed...again*. Her head hurt as she tried to comprehend it. Turning away from the mirror, she headed down the hallway toward the kitchen.

TWELVE

The Primortus

Skylee stepped inside the cozy little kitchen and looked around. Open shelves lined the walls, each stacked with brightly colored dishes and glassware. Yellow checked curtains hung above the sink. Ann was sitting at a small table in the corner with a forlorn expression on her face. Honestly, she looked like she was waiting to face a firing squad. Skylee wondered why.

"Hey, have a seat," she said, pulling out a chair.

Skylee nodded and sat down. For a moment they both stared down solemnly at the table, which was set with a steaming kettle, three mismatched cups and a plate of scones.

Ann poured a cup of tea and set it down in front of her. "Drink it."

Without hesitation, Skylee took a few sips and held the warm cup in her hands. It was comforting. She absent-mindedly studied the amber brown liquid for a while. Then she wearily set it aside and laid her head on the table, closing her eyes.

A few seconds later Will came into the kitchen and said, "Mum, look at this stuff, it was in Chrism's hair. I think it might be wool."

"Humm," Ann said, examining the white fluff. "Yeah, looks like unrefined wool."

"Strange…" Skylee said, lifting her head. "I thought I saw a sheep standing where Chrism was before the smoke—"

"Wait a minute," Will interrupted. "Wouldn't we have found it there, under the debris?"

"You would think," said Ann as she turned and stared out the window.

Will shrugged. He sat down beside Skylee as his mom handed him a steaming cup of tea.

"Thanks mum."

Ann nodded, took a deep breath and spoke seriously, "I need to tell you both something. I've put this off too long."

"Put what off?" Will asked.

Ann said nothing. She seemed to stare right through him.

"What's wrong, Mum?"

"Just give me a minute to think," snapped Ann.

Skylee sat straight up. *What's going on?* she wondered.

She watched as Ann stood slowly, taking the teapot to the sink. As she rinsed it out, Skylee and Will exchanged a puzzled look.

"All right, you want to know what's wrong?" Ann asked, setting the teapot in the dish drainer. "I screwed up." She turned to face them. "But I'm going to fix it, right now. There's no easy way to tell you so, I'm just going to show you. Both of you come outside with me." She turned and walked out of the door.

"Cripes," Will said as he stood up. "This can't be good." He stared blankly at the door for a moment then followed her.

"Will?" Skylee said.

He turned and looked at her briefly before stepping out the door. "Mum…"

Skylee watched the screen door close as Will disappeared from her view. She stood up, suddenly remembering Ann's reaction when she had first seen her wearing the necklace. *She knows something,* she thought, nodding her head slowly. *Maybe I'm finally going to find out what's going on.* Skylee smiled as a mixture of excitement and hope flooded her senses.

She dashed out the door feeling oddly energized. But as she rounded the corner of the house her euphoria faded. She had landed right in the middle of an argument between Will and his mom. Ann was standing in the middle of a flowerbed, hands on her hips. Will's hands were clinched tight at his side with his head cocked slightly to the right. *What could Ann have said to make him this mad?* Skylee wondered.

"I'm not going to tell you again," Ann chastised. "Do not speak to me in that tone."

"Is everything alright?" asked Skylee.

"No," Will grumbled.

"Sky," Ann said as she waved her closer. "I've told Will the truth…about what we are and he's not happy about it."

"Blimey, Mum, how can I be?"

"What? So, what are you?" Skylee asked hesitantly.

Ann smiled sympathetically at her and said, "Not just us, we are all three the same. I think you already know that something has changed, ever since you received the gifts from your dad. Am I right?"

Skylee nodded unable to speak her thoughts aloud. *She does know.*

"I thought so," Ann said. "We're a group of beings created to help protect the earth. We're called Primortus."

"Pri-Primortus?" she whispered.

"Sky, when I saw your necklace at the wedding, I realized that your powers had been unlocked. And I nearly fell on my face," she said with a slight chuckle.

"I knew it, I knew something was wrong," Skylee said. "Why didn't you say something?"

"Now, there's a good question," Will huffed.

"Ignore him," his mom said. "He's just like his dad, can't stand too much change." Ann turned to Will and frowned. "You know what I say to that don't you? Huh?"

Skylee glanced at Will hoping he would say something, but there was nothing but silence.

"I say, he's gonna have to deal with it. So, in answer to your question..." Ann reached down and grabbed a handful of flower petals, tossing them into the air. All at once, a breeze whipped up and as Skylee's eyes widened in wonder, the petals swirled around Ann.

Will stepped up beside her and muttered, "How's she doing that?"

"I don't know," she said in awe. "Ann?"

"Listen, I didn't tell you because this life is hard and dangerous," she said. "I wanted to keep it from you and Will as long as possible but I see now that I made a mistake."

Skylee was so mesmerized by the floating petals that Ann's remark didn't faze her. "The wedding!" she said as if a light bulb had gone off over her head. "You caused those flowers to swirl around my mom. I thought it was me...but it was you."

"That's true, it *was* me. I let my emotions take control of me for a bit."

Emotions, thought Skylee, *controlling Ann?* In all the time she had spent with Will and his family, the only time she had seen her out of control was at Will's dad's funeral.

"Sky?" Ann said stepping out of the flowerbed as the petals slowly floated to the ground. "Are you all right? I know this is a lot to take in."

"Of course, she's not all right," Will interjected. "*I'm* not all right. You knew about this at the wedding and then after Sky fell from the tower you still remained silent. There's nothing all right about any of this."

"No, you're wrong," Skylee said. "This Primortus stuff, it explains a lot. Remember, the water thing at the wedding?"

"Yeah, yeah," he answered slowly.

"I caused that, I know I did," she said excitedly.

"Well, I'm not sure about the water thing," Ann said. "But the light that followed your mom as she walked down the aisle—that was you."

"Really?"

"Like I said, Sky. Our emotions, if not kept in check, can create all kinds of problems for us."

"How can a beam of light hurt anyone?" Will asked in a sarcastic tone.

"It can't," his mom replied curtly. "But if we aren't very careful, we can cause major problems. You need to realize that our power is connected to the earth. We can control the elements."

"Wow, we're like the X-men," Skylee said gleefully.

Ann laughed and said, "Well, not exactly but we are unique in our abilities. Our mission is to protect the earth from manmade disasters. Of course we can't stop all of them but we do our best."

"What do you mean? How do we stop it?" asked Skylee.

"Basically, we draw on the earth's energy through our Elementum."

Skylee looked confused. "Elementum?"

"Your amulet," said Ann.

"Dad's necklace...so, does that mean, my dad was one?"

"Yes, he was and he passed his power down to you by giving you his Elementum and book."

Will huffed loudly. "Was dad one too?"

"No, of course not but when he died I..." Ann's voice wavered and she swallowed hard. "You're father and I argued about telling you. I didn't want to, he did. We parted mad at each other that day. His plane went down...and I wasn't..."

"Mum?" Will said worriedly.

"Well, that's for another day," she said, quickly recovering. "He was right. I should have told you. And Sky, I should have told you too. I realized that when I saw you wearing the Elementum. I always thought your dad had it with him when he died, but again, I was wrong."

Skylee held the necklace tightly in her hand. "Why would you think he had it?" she questioned.

"Primortus are to wear their Elementum at all times, to protect it."

"He couldn't have, because I have it now," said Skylee as she looked down at her necklace.

"Well...maybe..." mumbled Ann, looking away.

"Seriously," Will abruptly said. "We could've died today."

"I know and I've been beating myself up for that," Ann said. "But Sky stopped that plane without my help."

Skylee looked from Ann to Will. Their expressions were complete opposites. Ann looked as if she would burst with pride, but Will was staring at her like she was an alien.

"She caused the tree to fall?" he asked his mom.

"She did. I think she called on the earth and it sacrificed a part of itself to save you," said Ann. "The power that a Primortus—that we possess can control all of the elements—any part of nature. Air, water, fire, earth, which includes every living thing, all of it is available for us to call on to protect life. But it's a very serious calling and should never be used foolishly."

"Wait a minute," exclaimed Skylee. "How did stopping that plane, save the earth?"

"Because it saved you," Ann replied. "And Will. You were saved because your destinies are to protect the earth."

"Hmph, that's ridiculous," protested Will. "People die everyday, disasters happen everyday. If the Primortus are supposed to save the earth and protect life, then I'd say they're not doing a very good job."

"Will," whispered Skylee in disappointment.

Ann sighed sadly, "You're not the first Primortus to question those things. I'll tell you what I was told. The Primortus can interfere with any disaster that is caused by man."

"That's everything," said Skylee.

"No, that's where you're wrong," corrected Ann. "The earth is a living being and it has a life cycle just like any of us. Some disasters are earth's way of moving from one stage in life to another. Those we shouldn't try to stop. If we do, it can make things a lot worse. However, on the upside, during those times we can use our power to try and save lives."

"Oh," said Skylee in amazement. She looked down at her Elementum and her thoughts suddenly raced to the book. "THE BOOK!" she bellowed energetically, causing Ann and Will to jump. "Okay, sorry, just a little excited—my book, do I have to carry it with me all the time like the necklace? It's pretty heavy."

"No, just keep it close," said Ann.

"You know, I think it might have warned me about the plane crash," said Skylee looking toward the wreckage. "I thought it was a late warning when I tripped last night but it said to keep my eyes on the sky, danger is near."

"It *was* warning you," Ann said. "Next time—"

"Next time?" said Will in a distressed tone. "There bloody won't be a next time. How do we stop this?"

Skylee glared his way, wanting to lash out at him. She was finally getting answers, learning the truth and he wanted to stop it.

"It can't be stopped by us," Ann said. "She's been activated and from what I can tell, she has chosen her path." She gazed intently at Skylee. "Am I right?"

"Yeah, I choose this path," she said happily.

"No," Will said, looking disbelievingly at her. "You can't be serious?"

"Why not? This is who I am, what my father was. I'm so in."

Ann smiled and said, "This isn't a game Sky, remember that."

"You said it was dangerous," Will blurted out.

"Right," his mom replied. "It is...but we're not alone. There are others like us and..." Ann took a deep breath and nervously cleared her throat. "The others are helpmates—actually three different types."

"Helpmates," whispered Skylee, taking it all in. "So, are their lots of them?"

"More than you would think," she paused as if trying to decide how much more to say. "A Primortus can activate one of each."

"What do they do?" Skylee inquired eagerly. "What are they called?"

"One of them is called Corporus, they're basically a shape—" Ann stopped suddenly. "Sorry, I see headlights coming. It's probably your parents and Zane. We'll have to discuss this later."

"No, you can't leave us hanging," Skylee said.

"Hanging? Hah, I feel like I'm dangling over a pit of crocs by one finger...and it's broken," smirked Will.

"William! You're gonna have to deal with this. You're one of us, and that can't be changed," his mom sternly said. "But right now we need to get ready to deal with Janis. She's going to freak out."

Skylee nodded in agreement. "Yep, you're right about that. But once we tell her it has to do with the Primortus, she'll understand, right?"

"Sky, your mom doesn't remember anything about the Primortus," said Ann as she anxiously watched the approaching vehicles. "Listen, I need to warn you that you can't tell anyone about this, not now. Just trust me on this. You must promise not to say anything, understand? Not to anyone."

"Why?" asked Skylee, feeling confused.

"It's very important, that you understand this has to be kept secret. There are certain rules and that's one of them. If this information leaked out, who knows what would happen," Ann proclaimed as she furrowed her brows.

"We won't tell anyone," Will assured her. "Besides who would believe us?"

"I guess for now I won't," said Skylee reluctantly.

Before the auto-glider came to a complete stop and settled on the ground her mom flew out of the door. Alex and Zane came right after her.

"What happened, Pumpkin?" she yelled as she grabbed Skylee. "We saw smoke—is that a plane?"

"Where's Chrism?" Alex asked, looking alarmed.

Ann raised her hands and calmly said, "She's okay. She's inside resting. A small plane crashed and a branch knocked her down. She got a cut on the side of her head but I scanned her body and she has no serious injuries. Everyone's just a little shook up."

"It was scary, Mom, but we're all fine," Skylee reassured her mother.

"Thank goodness you're okay," said her mom, hugging her tightly. "Are you sure Chrism's all right?"

"Why don't we go check on her while Zane and Will check the wreckage," said Alex as he gently patted her mom's hand.

"What about the pilot?" Zane asked.

"We...we...didn't see anyone in the plane," said Skylee hesitantly.

Her stepdad looked back at the plane and shook his head. "Maybe he bailed before the plane crashed," he suggested.

"Could be, but I don't think we'll know for sure until daybreak. It's too dark out here to see much," said Zane.

"I think it might be best to call in GEMA on this one," said Alex in a serious tone. "It's probably nothing, but there could be a connection to our investigation. I'd like to try and keep the local authorities outside the loop at this point."

Her mom and Alex rushed inside to check on her stepsister. Zane and Will inspected the wreckage for any evidence of life and made sure the fire had died down, while Skylee and Ann watched from a distance.

Later while Chrism slept, everyone else met in the living room to discuss the day's events. As the minutes clicked by Skylee grew weary of the conversation and finally excused herself, heading to her room. She opened the bedroom door slowly and peeked in first. Chrism was not just sleeping she was snoring like an old lady. Skylee was sure her stepsister would recover and eat up the attention in the morning.

"Sky?"

She turned to see Will smiling at her. Her heart skipped a beat. Even with rumpled hair, torn clothes and black smudges on his face he managed to look—her brain stopped and searched for the right word. *Good? No, fine? Oh, come on who am I kidding? He looks gorgeous.*

"It's been a long day," she whispered, feeling her cheeks go pink. "I'm gonna try to get some sleep. You should too."

"About what my mum told us tonight?"

Skylee gently pulled the door shut behind her. "Not here, too many ears to hear, let's discuss it tomorrow. I still have so many questions to ask your mom," she said with a smile.

"I don't believe it, you're actually happy about this?" he said with an appalled look on his face.

"Yeah, I am. It's good to know I'm not losing my mind. You'll feel better about it in the morning. Just think—you and me, Primortus."

"I don't even know what that means and I'm not sure I want to," he said, gazing blankly at her as he chewed on his bottom lip.

"You worry too much. Just give it some time. You'll probably be just as excited as I am once you get use to the idea," she assured him. "I really want to know more about the other beings too. There is just so much to learn."

Will shook his head. "Sky, don't do anything rash, like running out to save the earth, not till we know more. Promise me."

Skylee sensed that he needed her word. "I promise not to do anything without knowing more. Okay, happy?"

"I'm happy to see you're happy, as far as the rest, jury's still out. You have some leaves in your hair," he said, laughing as he plucked a few out and showed her.

"I really need a shower," she said, frowning down at her dirty clothes.

"I'll leave you to it," said Will quietly. "I'm glad you weren't hurt, bloody glad for that."

"I'm glad you weren't hurt too," stammered Skylee. "I don't know what I would do if I lost you."

"Lose me? I'd just like to see you try," he laughed. "Now, get some sleep."

"You too," she giggled. She waited until he left the hallway before entering her room.

Later that night, Skylee lay awake in bed. She had tried to ask her book who was behind the plane crash but it only repeated the words she'd seen before. After several attempts to learn more she gave up.

She propped herself up on the pillows and turned the necklace over with her fingers. Her stepsister moaned, flopped over in bed, and started snoring again. *Note to self,* thought Skylee, *get some earplugs.* She threw back the covers and got out of bed, drawn to the window by the bright moonlight. She could barely see the plane from this viewpoint, only a thin puff of smoke rising from the wreckage in the black sky.

Primortus...Helpmates...powers, she pondered. *What else will Ann tell us?* Exhaustion suddenly washed over her. With a huge yawn, she crawled back into her bed and pulled the covers up to her chin. *I'll check the book tomorrow,* she told herself. *Maybe it will have more answers.* She shut her eyes and finally fell asleep unaware of the danger that lurked outside.

* * * * * * *

Not far away, two heavily cloaked figures emerged from the darkness and crept along the edge of the forest. One, tall and lean, who treaded silently and gracefully, while the shorter more muscular man, straggled closely on his heels. As they moved along, they both stared in the distance at the crumpled plane, lit by the pale moonlight.

Then the taller man abruptly halted, spun around, and glared in disgust at his companion. Swearing under his breath, he held up his bandaged hand and motioned for the shorter man to head toward the plane wreckage. The short man nodded, his carrot red hair, large and bushy, bobbed up and down. With a final nod, which was more like a bow, he took off.

"Idiot," the tall man spat out as he watched him scurry across the field. A cool evening breeze wafted through the air and blew back the corners of his long black cloak revealing its scarlet lining. His pale skin and smooth features were barely visible beneath the deep shadow of his hood.

From the darkness to his left he heard a rustling sound in the underbrush. He whipped his head to the side. A tiny kitten scurried out of the forest toward him. When it reached his feet, it hissed loudly and hunched its back. His black eyes flashed with madness as he recognized the kitten's calico fur. It was the same cat he'd seen *her* holding.

Scowling down at the small creature, he swung his boot with all his might. The crushing blow broke its neck and sent the lifeless ball of fur tumbling into the woods. A low growl escaped his mouth as he viciously punched his fist in the air.

Then he turned his dark eyes to the cottage in a menacing stare as if he was contemplating some evil deed. Eventually his gaze returned to the plane. He suddenly sped toward it, like an arrow aimed at a target. His breath came hard and fast when he reached it. There was a long pause as he stared down at the twisted metal.

"Tremendous," he said nastily, his black eyes filled with rage. "Pleased with yourself?"

"Yes—yes—or well sir, n-no," the short man nervously fumbled his words.

"Blaze," he sneered, grasping the shorter man by his burly neck. "You brainless imbecile! This...is not acceptable. Is it?"

"N-no, no M-master," stuttered Blaze.

"What we have here is a failure. I don't tolerate failures," he said shoving his servant to the ground then walking around the large tree that had thwarted his scheme.

Blaze slowly got to his feet and followed him. "Yes, I-I understand."

The Master looked at him and with no warning whatsoever, raised his hand and slapped his face. Blaze flinched but made no sound as a large red welt formed. Although the servant was shorter his muscular body was much stronger than that of his slender boss, but fighting back was not an option.

"I ordered a fast plane. Does this look fast to you?"

"S-sorry sir. I...I thought..." Blaze stammered fearfully.

"You thought," his Master cut him off. "That's the problem—when did I tell you to think? You muscle bound fool. My plan would've worked if she hadn't had all that time...and if the plane HAD... BEEN...FASTER!"

"But w-we almost k-killed her, it almost w-worked."

"We?"

"Y-you Master."

"That's right *I*," said the Master in a spine-chilling voice. "But I wasn't trying to kill her. If *I* had wanted to kill her *I* would have."

"Y-yes s-sir."

"She must be alive to give me her Elementum. How many times do I have to tell you? I can only fulfill the true prophecy when she makes the right choice."

"Of c-course."

"So why aren't I holding the Elementum in my hand now?" he questioned, staring vacantly.

"S-sir, I...I..." stuttered Blaze in utter terror.

"Yes, *you* are the reason my plan failed. That plane should have taken out those two distractions. Without the boy and girl she's more vulnerable. We've seen it before, she'll be weakened if we take them from her...like she was when we took the other girl."

"G-Gracie," whispered Blaze.

"They aren't important. The Second Born will turn to me when she has nowhere else to turn. Soon enough...but you, if you fail again it will be the last thing *you* do."

There was silence as the Master locked his gaze on the wreckage, and Blaze stared down at the ground. The only sounds were the chirping of crickets and the occasional croak of a frog.

The Master's teeth were tightly clenched and thick purple veins bulged at his temples. He stood motionless, as a cloud drifted across the moon shrouding the field in darkness. He exhaled deeply and a look of superiority slowly spread over his face.

"So, she used the power of the Elementum...if she wants a fight...I'll give it to her," he spat out, then he pushed Blaze toward the plane and said, "Torch it and make sure you get it right! Not a hint of evidence left behind."

Blaze lurched forward, quickly regained his footing, and nodded humbly at his master. He backed away from the plane until he was at a safe distance. Then he lifted his hands and streams of raging fire shot out of his palms straight into the cockpit.

As the flames consumed the plane, the master stood and watched. His low sinister laugh echoed in the night. Within minutes, the fire burned red-hot. Even as the plane smoldered, the master turned and walked slowly across the field, his black eyes fixed on the cottage.

Blaze watched the tall dark silhouette moving away. He rubbed the welt on his face, reached inside the pocket of his overcoat and pulled out a fountain pen. He cast a sneaky look over his shoulder as he quickly threw the pen, aiming for the edge of the smoldering wreckage.

"W-we'll see how the g-great Brinfrost likes it w-when The Second Born finds out w-who he is."

A few seconds later, he turned and followed his master's path but unlike before, there was lightness in his step.

Meanwhile when Brinfrost reached the forest, he paused for a brief moment and glared at the dead kitten. The corners of his mouth rose in a wicked grin before he pursed his lips and began to whistle. An eerie tune filled the night air as he moved on like a ghost, fading into the forest shadows.

THIRTEEN

The Humusara

Skylee had fallen into a restless slumber. In her dream, she was back at the Sky Tower standing at the edge of the platform with no bungee cord. Her long nightgown fluttered in the breeze. She gazed out at the thick, gray clouds hanging over the city. Then large black eyes slowly came into view, moving inch by inch toward her, the dark circles blended together and formed a knife. It held up her Elementum, dangling it over the tower's edge. As the hand released the silver chain she dove after it, plummeting toward the earth. A split second before she hit the ground the dream shifted...

She was in the cockpit of a small plane, in the pilot's chair, peering out through the windshield. She spotted Will and Chrism directly in her path. She desperately pulled up on the controls, but the plane remained on course, soaring toward them...

Then the dream changed again and she was in a snow-covered forest. The air was frigid, tiny snowflakes drifted by, coating the trees and ground white. Hundreds of black eyes peered out from behind every tree trunk. Her feet suddenly took off down the forest path as if they had a will of their own.

"*Someone's after her! She can't stay here!*" A voice shouted as Skylee ran through the frozen woodland. "*No, it isn't safe here! He might FIND HER!*" the voice grew louder.

Skylee raced through the cold dense forest, dodging between the trees and bushes.

"*WHO IS HE?*" bellowed the voice. Her legs ached but she had to keep running. The path before her looked like a dark tunnel closing in around her.

"*HE'S GOING TO KILL HER!*" the voice screamed. As she ran, the tunnel seemed to lengthen ahead of her. Her breathing grew heavier and her head throbbed. She felt an icy hand grasp her shoulder.

"Let go...no...let go of me!" cried Skylee in terror, slapping the hand away.

"Ouch, hey, stop it. What are you doing?" Chrism said, sounding far away. "Careful! You almost tore my silk pajamas."

"What...Oh...Where am I? What happened?" Skylee said sitting up in bed. She looked around in a dreamlike state. Loud voices were coming from the living room.

"I don't know how you could sleep with that big fight going on," said Chrism.

"Fight?"

"Yeah, our parents—it's like Alien versus Predator out there—they woke me up thirty minutes ago. Your mom is going berserk about the plane crash. She keeps saying over and over that someone tried to kill you and she doesn't think you should stay here. She wants to take us back to the states, both of us. They told her that they think we're safer here."

"Who? Who else is in there?"

"My dad, Ann and Zane—they haven't been able to convince her that we should stay."

"Where's Will?"

"I don't know, but I bet he isn't sleeping. By the way, why were you hitting me?"

"I'm sorry...bad dreams," said Skylee, still somewhat dazed from the horrible nightmare. "Is your head okay?"

"It still kinda hurts," Chrism said placing a hand on her head. "What was the dream about?"

"Oh, you know how it is...they never make any sense," she said, pushing her curly hair out of her eyes. "It was probably brought on by all the crazy things going on.

At that moment, Skylee realized her mother's voice had made its way into her dream and had combined with her deepest fears.

Chrism rubbed her head. "I just can't believe that stupid tree almost killed me."

Skylee wanted to remind her that the so-called stupid tree had saved her and Will's lives, but she doubted her stepsister wanted to hear it. So instead, she patted her on the shoulder and said, "Thank goodness, you're okay."

"Yeah, I guess so. But didn't you hear what I said about your mom? What are we going to do? I don't want to go home right now. Will and I were just starting to have fun. Do you think—" *TAP* "we could—" *TAP* "Do you think—" *TAP-TAP* "What is that noise?" Chrism asked, looking over at the window, as the tapping grew louder.

"It's Will," said Skylee, jumping out of bed. While she struggled to lift the heavy window, Chrism dashed to the mirror, fluffed her hair, and pinched color into her cheeks.

"Well, G'day," he said climbing through the windowsill into the room. "Evidently it's a great day for a brawl."

Will stood there, shaking his head for a moment. He was dressed in faded black jeans, his favorite army jacket and a vintage t-shirt, with the words "dark knight rises" across his chest. Skylee had always admired his taste in, what he called, clothes with a story of their own.

"Sky, I've never seen your mum so bloody worked up," he said. "My mum and Alex have been trying to calm her down for over an hour. She really got miffed when Alex said GEMA wanted us to stay here and not call the New Zealand authorities."

"Well, you know she's always been a bit overprotective. But I think it would be best if we stayed here after what your mom told—" Skylee stopped short, popping her hand over her mouth.

"What...what did Ann tell you?" Chrism demanded.

"Um...she just said...that we, uh...we're lucky that no one was seriously hurt, you know," lied Skylee.

"Sure," said Chrism in an unbelieving tone as she placed her hands on her hips.

"I heard Alex say that he thought the plane was empty," said Will, who was clearly trying to change the subject. "So you were right, Sky. There was no pilot inside. And when Alex and Zane went back out at sunrise to search more thoroughly, the plane had completely burned. They were stumped as to why it caught fire again. Especially since they had made sure it was out. But Alex did find something in the ashes. It was—"

"Hey," Chrism broke in, looking determined. "So, what did you mean, we should stay after what Ann told you? What did she tell you?"

"Hold on. What did they find in the ashes?" Skylee asked Will, hoping her stepsister would give up.

"A writing pen—it was badly burned—with some sort of symbol on it. Zane told Alex he didn't recognize it. Alex said he was going to send if off to the GEMA lab."

"That's interesting. Did you hear anything else?" asked Skylee.

"Yeah, Alex said he called their boss...er...what's his name, Drake and told him about our close call with the plane. And GEMA wants Zane to help them cover up the crash because more publicity would hamper their investigation. Apparently, Drake himself is coming to New Zealand and it sounded like he's bringing loads of backup with him. When your mum heard that, it started another loud argument about our safety," said Will, glancing at the door. "Oh, and one more thing, it turns out the island they were investigating really did disappear. Your mum said it was like the whole thing just melted into the ocean."

"Enough!" shouted Chrism, stomping her foot insistently. "For the last time, what did Ann tell you?"

Skylee and Will spun around and looked at her. It was obvious. She was not going to stop until one of them told her. *She's getting on my one last nerve,* thought Skylee. *I have to tell her something but what?* Then a brilliant idea popped into her mind.

"Okay, if you must know," she said in a high-pitched whisper. "Ann told us—"

"Stop, wait a minute. I don't think you should," Will blurted out.

"Shhhh, I think I'd better let her know," said Skylee in a hushed tone. "Ann told us…um, she got a call…just before the crash, a call warning her…right…Will?"

"Right," he said with an oddly twisted smile.

Chrism furrowed her brows and skeptically said, "So, I don't understand. Why would that make you think we should stay?"

Skylee and Will exchanged nervous looks.

"Because," said Skylee very slowly, trying to come up with a good reason. "That means someone out there is trying to help us. So how much danger could we really be in? The thing is, I wish we could get our hands on Ann's V-phone to look through the images and see if we might recognize the caller."

"That wouldn't be hard. We could just sneak into her room and steal…uh…borrow it." Chrism suggested self-assuredly.

"But wouldn't they see us, if we all go?" Skylee asked, looking at Will for support.

"Right," he said, looking blankly at the ceiling.

"Yeah, that's true," said Chrism. "But I bet I could get past them, get it and be back in no time."

"If you're really sure," said Skylee as she watched her stepsister nod with confidence. "Okay, we'll wait right here for you. Won't we Will?"

"Right," he said, back to the same odd smile.

Chrism slowly opened the door and doing her best secret agent impersonation, she slithered around the doorframe into the hallway.

As soon as she was out of hearing range Will said, "Cripes! I thought you were going to tell her."

"You should've known I wouldn't put her in danger. Oh—and thanks for all the backup. How did it go? Right, Right, Right!"

"What can I say? I reckon I'm not so good at lying, maybe it's an Aussie thing, and when did you get to be such a good liar?"

"I guess, since I learned I had so many secrets to keep," she said candidly. "Listen, we should have a little time. I know your mom always keeps her V-phone in her pocket so maybe Chrism will spend a while looking for it."

"Tricky."

"Well, I do have a reason for sending her off on a fake mission. Hurry, put that chair in front of the door while I get my book."

"No, I don't think that's a good idea, Sky."

"Of course it is. Every time I've opened my book, it's tried to help me. Last night, it kept reminding me to keep the secret hidden—a warning not to reveal the gift. That's where I got the idea for the little story I told Chrism. See, I only told her a half lie."

"What if the book doesn't work with me here?" asked Will.

"Why wouldn't it? You're a Primortus too."

"Don't remind me," he said flatly.

"Just get the chair."

Skylee took the book from her backpack, placed it on the foot of the bed and they both knelt in front of it. She quickly removed her necklace and placed it in the book's cover. Will's mouth dropped open as it began to transform.

"What's bloody happening?"

"It's aging, see, here's the strange lettering," she said touching the page. "But watch—wait—there—do you see it?

"No...eh...I don't see anything, just unreadable script."

"But you have to see it, look, don't you see it?" Skylee took Will's hand and placed it on the page.

They both gasped as a brilliant light appeared. It looked exactly like the light she'd seen the first time she placed the Elementum inside the cover. There was no time for Skylee to explain. Will's body jerked, and his hand appeared to be stuck to the book. Just as before, a blaze of silvery white light erupted and formed a dazzling column of brightness that illuminated the room.

"Don't be afraid," whispered Skylee, seeing his eyes widen with astonishment.

Skylee shivered as the room grew colder and colder. She watched with tears in her eyes as Will gasped for air while the light moved up his arm to his chest. The same orb of twinkling light she'd seen days ago on her chest was now on his heart shining through the fabric of his shirt. Within seconds, the third column of light formed and returned to the book.

As the room warmed, Will stared down at the book. His hand softly rested on the page as he watched the flickering light fade. He didn't speak, didn't move. Words were appearing, shimmering across the page in front of him.

Will, I am the Humusara I am one of twelve—
The connection between the Primortus and earth.
Hear my words:

Thy Primortus awakening—the elder doth delay.
Yet the age of Heritus hath not passed away.

My words shall open the portal to thee.
My words shall reveal for thine eyes to see.
My words shall forewarn what is yet to be.

To find the way you must follow your heart—
Any other path shall tear us apart.

Skylee watched as the blood drained from Will's face. She fought back tears and cleared her throat. "Do you see it?" she softly asked.

"Yes, but I can hardly believe it—I don't..." his voice quivered. "What does it mean?"

"I'm not sure. It's never revealed this much to me. It gave you its name, the Humusara. I wonder why?" She placed her hand on his shoulder and he raised his hand to cover hers.

The words disappeared, instantly.

"That's it. You have to touch the page for it to work," said Skylee, picking up the book and laying her hand on the page.

A blinding light obscured her sight followed by clear images of her family in a vehicle. Happy voices and laughter echoed in her ears. Without warning, the vision changed to black smoke and screams of terror.

"Stop...help!" screamed a high-pitched voice.

"SHUT UP!" shrieked another voice that Skylee wasn't sure was male or female.

Skylee's heart jumped as she saw her mother being dragged by her hair through a thick forest. The vicious attacker was surprisingly average in size considering how effortlessly her mom was being pulled along. No matter how much her mom fought and thrashed about she couldn't escape the assailant's grip. Terror filled Skylee's heart as she heard her mom scream in pain. The smoke returned and gradually turned to flames blocking out the horrifying image. But her mother's scream went on and on, causing Skylee to drop the Humusara and collapse on the floor.

She couldn't see, couldn't speak, her heart was racing. Her blurred sight slowly returned as she focused on Will's face. He kneeled over her, his eyes full of distress. He carefully cradled her head in his hands and said, "Sky, Sky...What happened?"

"I saw my mom," she said with tears trickling down her face. "It was horrible, she was being taken...kidnapped."

"You mean you actually saw that?"

"Yes, my mom," she sobbed. "Wh-what if—"

"Have you ever seen anything like that from the book before?"

"Yes, just before we went to the Sky Tower. But it was different, only flashes."

"What do you mean?" he asked with a puzzled look.

"You know, like pictures quickly flashing in front of your eyes. I saw my necklace, the stranger's black eyes, and the knife. But this...this was not like that, this was much clearer. It was almost like I was there," explained Skylee as she tried to stand up on shaky legs.

Will gently took her arm and helped her sit on the foot of the bed. Then he began pacing back and forth in front of the door.

"Sky, what are you saying?" he tensely asked. "The stranger—that bloke at the tower, you're saying he was the same one at the wedding?"

"Yes, I think it is. I'm sorry, I wanted to tell you but the book—" she stopped and looked at the Humusara. "It warned me...said to keep it secret. I couldn't risk putting you in danger."

"Me? What about you? Listen, I think we better tell my mum about the stranger and about what you just saw."

"You're right, I'm gonna need her help. She has to teach me how to control my powers, so I can protect my mom," she said filled with worry.

"Skylee! Are you crazy? That's too dangerous," he said. "Let my mum protect her. You've already been hurt."

"Okay, Okay," she conceded. Will only used her whole name when he was upset. She thought it best not to argue with him, but she knew she could never stand idly by while her mom was in danger.

"I mean it, Sky. It's bloody dangerous and not after what you've just seen," he said in a stern tone. "You said so yourself that bloke's not only after you, but your mum too!"

"No, no that person—the one taking my mom. It wasn't the same guy. I'm not even sure it was a man."

"What? I thought you said you saw it clearly?"

"I did," she said. "It was so terrible. There was this...person, dressed in a fancy leather suit and boots, really weird. He, or maybe it was a she, had on lots of make-up, you know, dark eyeliner, mascara, and red lipstick. And he...uh I mean...the person wasn't all that big, but somehow my mom was being dragged by her hair."

"You're sure it isn't the same bloke that was at the wedding and the Sky Tower?" Will asked, looking worried.

"How could it be? That guy was tall, thin and definitely a man. No it couldn't be him," she insisted. Then Skylee reached over, clutched his hand, and said, "Are we going to talk about what just happened to you?"

"I don't know how to talk about something that I don't understand."

"I've seen it before," she said in a hushed tone. "I saw the same light, when I first put the Elementum in the book's cover."

"What do you think it is?" asked Will slightly squeezing her hand.

"I'm not sure, but I think it's because we're both Primortus. I wonder if the light is—" she suddenly stopped and cocked her head to the side.

A strange scraping noise came from the door. Skylee snatched her necklace from the Humusara's cover and put it on. She motioned for Will to move the chair out of the way. He spun it back into place, then quickly turned and sat on the foot of the bed. She stood beside him, facing the door as she fumbled with the Humusara. Just as Chrism dashed into the room, Skylee dropped the book on the bed behind Will's back.

"Was the door locked or something? I couldn't get in," Chrism suspiciously said, panting heavily and holding her hand on her chest.

"Well, yeah, cause we were afraid if anyone came in and asked where you were...we wouldn't know what to tell them." Skylee said in the most innocent tone she could muster.

"Nice try, but I know your hiding something. You two look like you're posing for a mug shot!" Chrism declared, pointing at them.

Skylee cleared her throat. "You were gone so long. We started to get nervous, and we—"

"Hey, have you been crying?" Chrism suddenly blurted out at her.

"Ah, yes," Skylee admitted, her mind racing to come up with a reason for it. "Because, I thought that—I'd gotten you in trouble—maybe Ann caught you snooping through her room or something."

"Fine," she snapped. "Of course, I didn't get caught. I couldn't find Ann's V-phone even after searching everywhere in her room, but I did find—hidden between the mattresses a weird bo—"

Chrism stopped talking and looked at Will who was groping with the book behind his back. Before either he or Skylee could stop her, she pounced at him and grabbed it from his hands. The Humusara was back to looking like a new leather bound journal. Chrism opened it and stared at the indecipherable lettering.

"How did you get your mom's book?" she asked, darting her eyes back and forth between him and the Humusara.

"Er...well yeah, the book...uh..." he stammered.

Chrism's eyes narrowed and she turned to Skylee. "How on earth did you two get this book? I tried taking it from Ann's room, but I...well it was weird. I dropped it on the floor, not just once but three times! Finally, I decided to come back and see if you or Will knew anything about it. But here it is."

"It's not the same book," Skylee calmly said. "It couldn't be. I was just showing my book to Will. Remember I told you that my dad left me some family heirlooms? The necklace and that—the book you're holding."

"What? Why would your dad and Ann have the same weird book?" she asked, looking confused. Then her face returned to the same suspicious expression she'd had when she first entered the room. "Okay, what's going on?"

"I wish I knew," Skylee said, telling her mostly the truth.

"Me too," said Will with a sincere smile.

"You really don't know," she said. It was half question, half statement.

"Listen Chrism," Will almost whispered. "I can honestly tell you that I don't understand the mystery behind my mum's or Skylee's book."

Something about the tone in his voice must have caused Chrism to stop questioning them. She held out the Humusara and inspected it closely, turning it over in her hands. A looked of curiosity covered her face but after a few tense seconds she shrugged and tossed it onto the bed.

Skylee sighed in relief and motioned toward the door. "Well, it sounds like the shouting match is over," she said, turning to Chrism. "So, while you were out there did you hear if Mom's going to let us stay here?"

"OMG no," said Chrism dramatically. "She's still insisting that she and Ann should take us back home. Even with all the arguing, it wasn't easy getting past them into the hallway. They're sitting around the table looking at a bunch of maps and papers. Dad said GEMA has discovered more evidence of...of...I think he said environmental irregularities, and then he said we should stay together in case of another worldwide event."

There was a long pause, Skylee was at a complete loss of words, and her apprehension seemed to be mirrored in Will and Chrism's faces. *Could it be possible? What if there was another Day of Disaster? The world might not survive it.*

The silence was broken by a soft knock on the door and her mother's voice called, "Munchkin! Are you and Chrism awake?"

Skylee rushed to the door, narrowly cracked it open and said, "Yeah, we're up. We'll be right out."

"Are you okay? Did you sleep well?" her mom asked, in a high soft tone.

"Yes," Skylee said, looking into her mother's aqua blue eyes. As the terrible vision of her mom swept over her, she struggled to maintain her composure. "I'm fine, just give me a few minutes to get dressed. Okay?"

"Sure sweetie, but hurry up. Zane's invited us to brunch at the main house."

"Oh okay, thanks Mom," she said, closing the door and turning to Will and Chrism. "Brunch...huh. Sounds like we're heading for a family meeting. Probably to tell us we have to go home." She grabbed Will's arm and led him over to the window. "We'll meet you outside as soon as we get ready, oh and be thinking of reasons we need to stay here."

"No worries," he said. "Airon and I always keep a few excuses ready, in case we need to get out of something."

"Oh, this ought to be good," said Skylee, eyeing him skeptically. "Let's hear 'em."

"All right then," he excitedly said. "How about...Sorry, I can't go until I check with my Jedi-master."

Skylee put her hands on her hips and stared straight-faced at him as Chrism giggled.

"Or, you could try...I think I'm coming down with a case of the black plague," he said, grinning broadly. "And then there's my personal favorite...I'm too busy de-linting my navel."

Skylee lifted her brow and looked at Chrism, who broke into another giggling fit.

"Like I said, think of some *reasons*," said Skylee, giving him a poke in the arm.

"Man, what do you want from me?" he said, swinging his legs over the windowsill and dropping to the ground below. His head immediately popped back up. "Hey, I've got it. We can't leave, cause the sheep ate our plane tickets."

"Yeah, bye," said Skylee as she put her hand on his forehead, pushed him back and closed the window. She smiled playfully at him through the glass, waving goodbye as she let down the blind. Then she turned her attention back to her stepsister, who had instantly stopped giggling and was now rolling her eyes. Skylee groaned and said, "You really shouldn't encourage him."

Chrism smiled deviously at her. "Take it from me little sis, if you want a guy to like you, you have to laugh at his dumb jokes."

"If you say so," she muttered with a shrug. "Well, we better get dressed. Why don't you shower first? That way you can spend some time with Will before I get out there."

Skylee had her reasons for getting her stepsister out of the room as quickly as possible. Of course, Chrism took her up on the offer faster than the speed of light. But it seemed like forever before she finally emerged from the bathroom, looking like she'd just stepped off the cover of a fashion magazine. Her thick brown hair had been flat-ironed straight and her make-up looked flawless. She had on a light blue cashmere sweater and designer jeans.

As soon as she was gone, Skylee blocked the door again and snatched up the Humusara. Placing her Elementum in the cover, she opened it and held her hand on the page.

"Tell me how can I protect my mom?" she pleaded.

To her great relief, words shimmered into view. Except the message was not at all what she had expected. She softly read aloud.

A helpmate will find you and she shall assist.
Another now hidden is found in your midst.
The others are waiting though one shall resist.

Skylee stared at the words in confusion. A helpmate, she remembered Ann saying something about other beings, she'd called them helpmates. Skylee blinked and looked down at the page to see more words appearing.

The time is at hand and you shall see—
Three powers unlocked for you are the key.

Skylee ran her finger along the text as she read. She lightly touched a blank spot below the words, setting lines and shapes into motion. She stared at the page, blinking as she slowly accepted what she saw. It was as if an invisible artist was skillfully drawing a sketch right before her eyes. The outline of a human gradually emerged with its arms and legs quickly taking shape and underneath a single word appeared.

Corporus

Spellbound, she watched as the little man sprang to life and walked across the page. After a couple of trips from side to side he stopped, momentarily looking distorted and twisted like something a child would scribble with a crayon. And then, to her surprise, the drawing transformed into a wild cat. It was a tiger with dark stripes across its elongated body.

Skylee remained stock-still, afraid that the image might somehow jump from the page. But, just as quickly as the tiger had appeared, the process reversed and the human shape returned. She peered at it in wonder. Then her eyes focused on the neatly written word below it. Corporus. What did it mean?

Taking in a deep breath Skylee realized there was an obvious explanation. *This is what Ann was talking about,* she thought, slightly nodding her head. The Humusara was telling her that a Corporus was a Shape-shifter.

* * * * * * *

Skylee joined up with Will and Chrism a few minutes later dressed in faded blue jeans and a soft green shirt. Her long wavy hair was pulled back in a ponytail.

"Hi," she quickly said. "Listen, I have an idea of how to talk mom into letting us stay. Remind her that we're a family now and families shouldn't split up when times get tough."

"Ahh, yeah right!" scoffed Chrism. "Is that the best you can come up with?"

"But it's very important to my mom, so if I—"

"Look," interrupted Chrism. "Just follow my lead. We need to use her weakness for nature, you know, tell her she can't leave when New Zealand is in danger. She'll fall for it. You just wait and see."

"No," Skylee calmly said. "I don't—"

"Come on," Chrism smugly broke in, ignoring her objection. "Let's go. I'm getting hungry."

Skylee shrugged and exchanged a droll look with Will before they tagged along after her stepsister.

The main house looked much neater than Skylee had remembered. Shelley buzzed around the living room lighting candles, fluffing pillows and tidying stacks of books. There was a roaring fire in the fireplace and a delicious smell coming from the kitchen.

"Nice," said Will, breathing in the aroma."

"Humph," groaned Chrism plunking herself down on the sofa. "What a show off."

"Shhh, she'll hear you," whispered Skylee carefully sitting down on the edge of the sofa, so she wouldn't disturb the freshly plumped pillows.

"Oh, there you are," Shelley said brightly.

"What's that awesome smell?" asked Skylee.

"I made some favorite New Zealand foods for our brunch."

"You really shouldn't have gone to so much trouble," Chrism said pretentiously, flashing a sickeningly sweet smile.

"No trouble at all," said Shelley, sounding sincere. "It seemed the perfect occasion. Oh, and there's a surprise waiting for you in the dining room. Go ahead and look."

As they entered, Skylee eyed the table, which was brimming with food. Cobalt blue plates and crystal goblets gleamed in the sunlight filtering in through the shutters. In the center of the table was a large shepherd's pie. And there were scrambled eggs, fresh fruits, stacks of pancakes, potato hash and an overflowing basket of homemade breads. It was the grandest feast Skylee had ever seen.

"It looks amazing," said Will licking his lips.

Chrism looked absolutely disgusted, no doubt because once again Shelley had stolen Will's attention from her. A deceitful smile revealed her true feelings as she slowly walked around the table and said, "Oh, what a surprise, *food* for brunch."

A voice came from behind the kitchen door. "Ya might want teh look around a bit, that's not the surprise."

"Airon!" cried Skylee and Will together.

The door flung open and there he was. He looked taller than she remembered standing there with his thick brown hair tousled to the side. He wore dark blue jeans, a plaid shirt, and cowboy boots. Skylee noticed that his eyes immediately focused on Chrism.

"G'day mates, did ya miss me?"

"Of course we did!" Skylee exclaimed.

She raced to him, nearly knocking him off his feet as she threw her arms around him.

"Whoa," he chuckled. "Hey Skippy, give me some air."

"Aw—no mate I can do better than that," said Will coming over and wrapping both of them in a bear hug that lifted Skylee off her feet. Then the three of them turned and looked at Chrism.

"Nice teh see ya again. Do ya need a hug too?" said Airon stretching his arms out to her. "Ya know that sweater brings out the turquoise in yer eyes."

Total silence filled the room. Skylee watched, as Chrism seemed to struggle to remain in control. Her mouth was clamped shut, her eyes bulged, and her face was bright pink. For a second, she thought her stepsister's head might pop off.

"So—Airon, did you finish your exams?" she said trying to distract him.

"Yeah, yeah," he answered.

"Brilliant," Will said.

"No big deal," Airon said pulling candy out of his pocket. "But this, this is a big deal, eh, Skippy?"

"Luck-E-Chocs!" squealed Skylee.

"Sure is." He tossed the bag to her.

She caught it, ripped it open and stuffed a candy into her mouth in a matter of seconds. It was the best thing she had eaten for a long while. Skylee found a happy place and ignored the rest of the conversation.

By the time all of the brunch guests had arrived, Chrism's color was almost back to normal. Skylee, on the other hand, turned red as a beet when her mother showed up in bright green bell-bottoms and a yellow t-shirt with the words "Don't Mess With Mother Nature" plastered across the chest. In sharp contrast, Alex was dressed in neutral tones and his shirt was buttoned so tightly at the neck that Skylee wondered how he could possibly swallow. *Yeah, they're quite a pair,* she thought as she watched them coming her way.

"There's my little buttercup," her mom said, smiling dotingly at her. "How are you holding up? Is your arm okay?"

"It's just a flesh wound," teased Skylee, grinning over at Will. "You know I've always wanted to say that, and I finally got the chance."

A moment later Zane, who had actually smoothed down his unkempt hair and trimmed his beard, showed them to their seats. The entire group seemed in high spirits, except for Chrism, who sat glumly staring down at her plate.

Zane began by thanking Shelley for helping him with all the preparations. Then he welcomed Airon to the farm, asking him to tell them about his visit to Australia. Skylee noticed that Zane and Airon seemed to take an instant liking to one another. *Probably because they're both avid outdoorsman*, she thought.

As the meal progressed, Skylee became keenly aware of Ann's somber demeanor. Her usual relaxed manner had been replaced by an awkward-looking stare. It seemed like no one else had noticed, except possibly Will.

Clink-Clink-Clink. Skylee looked down to the end of the table, where her mom was tapping her spoon against her water glass. "I'd like to propose a toast," she said, now rising up the goblet. "To Shelley, for preparing this bountiful feast."

"Here-Here," they all responded clinking their glasses together.

Except for Chrism, who refused to toast with Airon. Instead, she turned her back on him and held her glass against Will's. Then Skylee spotted Airon trying to force his glass in between. She swiftly crammed her goblet into his, spilling some water and making a loud clank.

"Oops," she said, shooting Airon a disapproving look.

"What are you two up to?" her mother said lightheartedly.

"Eh, nothing. Skippy just got a bit excited about the toasting," said Airon, giving Skylee a mischievous look.

"Airon, please," Skylee whispered. "Don't embarrass me."

"Isn't this shepherd's pie delicious!" said Will loudly. He was obviously attempting to help.

"Mmm, it sure is," Alex agreed.

"Dad? I couldn't help overhearing your discussion this morning," Chrism said out of nowhere. "Are we going home?"

Skylee watched as Alex dropped his fork and looked at her mom, who seemed to be trying to swallow her food without choking.

There was a long pause. "Well, Chrism," her mom finally said. "We did have a rather spirited...um, discussion this morning. And I do think it would be best to take you and Skylee back to the states."

"But shouldn't you stay here?" asked Chrism. "Aren't you worried about New Zealand? Isn't the environment in trouble?"

"Well, of course I'm concerned," she replied patiently. "But honey, I'm also concerned about you and Skylee. You know, your safety. And I don't want Will or Airon to be in danger either."

"Danger?" Airon blurted out. "Crikey, what danger?"

"I'll tell you later, mate," said Will, raising his hand between them.

Chrism turned to face Shelley. "But Doctor Leonard," she said in a high-pitched voice. "Aren't you worried about New Zealand?"

"Yes," said Shelley, who looked a bit confused to suddenly be part of the conversation.

"Wouldn't it be best for the investigation if my stepmom stays?" insisted Chrism, beginning to sound like a lawyer questioning a defendant.

Shelley nervously cleared her throat. "Yes, but—"

"Isn't there a real danger to the environment?" Chrism pressed on.

"There seems to be but, as a mother I can understand," said Shelley, looking supportively at Janis.

"But you said the environment—the whole place is in danger. There could be damage to the eco-system, right?" persisted Chrism, her voice rising passionately.

"Well, that's possible but if your parents think—"

"Tell her!" she barked. "Tell her, we shouldn't go!"

"CHRISM!" snapped Alex. "That's enough."

Everyone at the table stopped eating. Chrism looked dumbfounded. Shelley was clearly relieved that the questioning was over. Both Zane and Ann sat extremely still neither had spoken a word. Skylee thought they were wise to stay out of it. And even her mom, who was seldom at a loss for words, gazed at Alex in silence.

Skylee glanced at Will. He looked like he was trying with all his might to blend into his chair. Airon, on the other hand, wore an amused expression. He had leaned forward on his elbow and was gazing at Chrism, apparently impressed by her spunk.

After a few moments, everyone returned to their meal. Zane tried to ease the tension by entertaining his guests with a story about the scar on his face. A tale of how he rescued a baby grizzly bear from a trap. And as a thank-you, the little bear had smacked him across the face, breaking his nose. In addition, there was lots of kidding between Zane, Will, and Airon about Aussie life versus Kiwi life.

Chrism still looked stung by her unsuccessful attempt to talk Janis into letting them stay. Skylee watched as her stepsister pushed the food around on her plate with her fork. She hadn't eaten a bite.

As Will warmly smiled at Skylee, handing her the breadbasket Chrism scowled at them. "Hey Skylee, or is it *Skippy*, would you like some butter?" she needled, holding out the butter-dish.

Skylee frowned, ignoring her, then took a big bite of the hearty meat pie and slowly chewed.

"The shepherd's pie really is fantastic, this bio-beef is so tender," her mom said, looking in approval at Shelley. "How did you cook it?"

"Oh it's not bio-beef," replied Shelley cheerfully. "It's lamb. We're very lucky in New Zealand. We have real meat. Did you know that more sheep than people survived The Day here?"

Skylee stopped mid chew. Her mind flashed immediately to the cute, wooly sheep that had followed her just before the plane crash. Her eyes began to water and she couldn't swallow. The pie seemed to be growing in her mouth.

"Are you all right?" asked Will, who had apparently noticed her appalled face.

She nodded and tried to look normal, while everyone else returned to small talk. *Lamb, I am not eating real lamb,* she thought. *But how can I get rid of it?*

Her strategy began with a light, little hacking sound while placing her napkin to her lips. Then she would fake a cough and spit out the meat. But at that precise moment, Airon sharply slapped her on the back. The partially chewed glob of lamb exploded out of her mouth so violently that it flew across the table.

PLOP. It landed in Chrism's goblet and slowly sank to the bottom. Laughter erupted. Zane guffawed so hard he almost fell out of his chair. The atmosphere around the table was uproarious. Even Chrism snickered under her breath.

When the laughter died down, and Skylee had gotten her stepsister a fresh glass of water, they had a lively debate about the pros and cons of bio-meat. Everyone agreed, with the exception of Chrism, that it was practically identical in taste to the real thing.

Later on, as they gathered in the living room, Shelley and Ann cleared the dishes. When they brought out the tea and coffee, Skylee detected tension between them. Ann had a strained expression on her face. And when Skylee studied Shelley more carefully, she could see her hand shaking as she poured the steaming liquid into the cups. No one else seemed to be aware of it.

Everyone chatted while sipping the hot drinks, and Skylee noticed her mom, who was sitting on the sofa with Alex, looking more relaxed. It finally seemed like the right time for her to bring up the subject of them staying in New Zealand.

"Mom?" she gently called, coming over and sitting by her. "I understand why you think we should go home, but what about Alex?"

The question seemed to catch her mom off guard. She fidgeted in her seat and said, "Well Sweetheart, he'll have to stay here alone for a while, but as soon as I'm sure you and Chrism are safe I'll return to New Zealand."

"But aren't we a family now?" asked Skylee sincerely. "Shouldn't we stick together?"

"Well, yes. But Alex understands, I just want what's best for you girls."

Skylee exhaled deeply and spoke from the bottom of her heart. "Mom, we want to stay here, together, as a family."

"A family," Skylee's mom said thoughtfully, her eyes suddenly brimming with tears as she looked to Alex.

"It's up to you," he said. "We're a family, what ever you decide."

"Can we stay?" Chrism chimed in.

Janis paused and took in a deep breath before saying, "Okay my little Munchkins, we'll stay...the Faraway family is sticking together."

FOURTEEN

The Grave

After brunch, Chrism insisted on going along with Will to show Airon the farm. For once Skylee was glad her stepsister was up to her usual obsession with boys, because it would give her a chance to talk to Ann alone. Although she wasn't looking forward to telling her aunt about her terrible vision or that a light had appeared when Will touched her book. Not to mention having to confess that Chrism had almost taken her Humusara. But she could no longer avoid it. She gathered up her courage and invited Ann to go for a walk with her.

It was late afternoon, and the grass was swaying gently in the breeze, by the time they strolled along the meadow trail. Ann seemed to be deep in thought.

"Auntie Ann," said Skylee, hoping that calling her auntie might soften the blow of all she was about to tell her.

"Yes," she replied suspiciously.

Skylee wasn't sure exactly where to begin so she jumped in and said, "Something happened this morning with the book...um...the Humusara. I let Will see it and—"

"What?" Ann broke in, looking shocked. "You showed him the—how did you know it's called the Humusara?"

"That's part of what I need to tell you. It gave Will its name. I just wanted to show him how it works. I know I should have waited or asked you first, but I thought it might help him to see it, to understand it. The thing is, well, it didn't work out exactly how I thought it would."

"Oh," said Ann with concern on her face. "What happened?"

"I don't know. I mean—I was shocked when the light appeared, the way it did with me...just before the wedding.

"A silver light?"

"Yes," answered Skylee as she watched Ann shut her eyes and rub her temples. "Are you okay?"

Ann nodded but didn't say a word.

"I'm sorry," said Skylee avoiding her eyes. "I don't understand—the light—it acted the same way it did with me. But the book didn't. It revealed more, the words were written to Will, directly to him. It even wrote his name."

"Was he—what did the Humusara tell him?" she asked quietly.

"We were both kind of shook up," admitted Skylee nervously. "I can't remember everything. There was something about his Primortus awakening being delayed. Oh...and the last thing it wrote was for him to follow his heart. Why would it act differently with him? Did you hear me? Are you upset?"

Ann walked forward, stepping off the trail. Skylee couldn't read her emotions as she watched her stop and lean back against a tree.

"I'm all right," she finally said. "Just a bit shocked. I know it's hard to understand but Will's power, like yours, has now been awakened."

"What? Did I—was it because of me?" Skylee asked her voice unnaturally high.

"It's okay, Sky, and besides you didn't know," she said shaking her head. "Will should've already been activated, he's fifteen—well into the year of the Heritus," she continued. "You on the other hand are ahead of the game—fourteen—you shouldn't have the Humusara or the Elementum yet."

"Why not?"

"I wish I could explain it all to you in a few words, but that's not possible. This just isn't the way it should be."

"Did I do something wrong?" Skylee asked worriedly.

"No, you didn't do anything wrong," Ann said as the corners of her mouth turned up in a small grin. "The light you saw, it appears when a Primortus gains their power. And that happens when the three are joined the first time, the Humusara, the Elementum and the Primortus."

"So Will and I both—"

"Sky," interjected Ann in a very serious tone. "Now that you've received the power of the Elementum, you can use it to connect to the Humusara. Then it will reveal what you need to know."

"I knew it!" exclaimed Skylee. "You have to be touching the Humusara to make it work, that's what I told Will—oh and the necklace turns cold whenever there's a message, right?"

"That's right, the Elementum grows cold when the Humusara wants to communicate with us."

"And why does it turn hot?"

Ann looked confused. She sighed and said, "I don't know, my Elementum has never turned hot. Are you saying yours does?"

"Yes, I wonder why?"

"I'm not sure what it means."

"Well, maybe we can test it in some way to find out," replied Skylee in an eager tone. "You know like a science experiment."

"Listen to me," said Ann, her voice very firm. "The Humusara and the Elementum are not a game or magic tricks to show off. You must respect their powers."

"I do," Skylee said at once. "I really do. But I need to learn more about it. So, all three must be touching for the words to appear?"

"Yes," Ann said as she walked back to the path. "And in some rare cases the Humusara will choose to show the Primortus more than words, in the form of a vision."

"Rare?" asked Skylee, feeling perplexed. "But that's what happened this morning and it happened before. This was the second time."

Ann abruptly stopped, and turned to her, "You've already had two visions?"

"Yes, just before the tower and today, two different visions. That's why I wanted to talk to you. The vision was clearer this morning, like I was actually there and it was terrible," said Skylee as her voice grew more and more distressed. "I saw my mom being dragged through the woods. I could hear her screaming then there were flames and smoke. Oh Ann, you have to help me protect her, PLEASE!"

"Hey, calm down," said Ann as she placed both hands on Skylee's shoulders and lightly shook her. "You know I'll try to protect her. I understand that this is upsetting, but remember you're a Primortus. You have to reach deep inside to connect to your power—it's a source of great strength."

Skylee let out a deep sigh and tried to do as Ann said. *How do I reach deep inside?* she wondered. "Auntie Ann?" pleaded Skylee in a much calmer voice. "I don't want my mom to—"

"Your vision doesn't have to come to pass," she broke in assuredly. "That's why the Primortus are allowed to see into the future. To warn us, so we can intervene and change it.

"So we *can* stop it," said Skylee hopefully. "Do you think that's why I saw it—even though I'm new at this?"

"Well, I'm not sure, probably, but there might be another reason. Visions are usually only given to powerful, experienced Primortus but you are..." she stopped as though the words wouldn't come. And then she breathed in deeply and spoke again, "You're a bit of a mystery like no other before."

"Me?" asked Skylee with a look of concern.

"You-you were your father's second child," she calmly said. "There's never been a second born before you. Since the beginning of time, the Primortus are given one child—only one to which we pass on our power. Sky, I honestly wish I could tell you more, but I can't because there are things I don't understand. None of us do."

Skylee felt numb. She gazed down at her trembling hands. Her brain knew Ann wouldn't lie to her, yet deep inside she wondered how her words could be true? She looked up as sunlight peeked out from behind a cloud and shone upon Ann, who's young-looking face seemed to age with worry. Her normally straight posture was slumped forward as if a heavy weight rested on her shoulders. Ann smiled sadly at her.

"Fourteen years ago, when your father died, I was asked to watch over you and your mother. I first received a message from my Humusara telling me to go to California. Several other Primortus were drawn to the area too, but we couldn't stop it. After the disaster a helpmate told me where to find you. Luckily I was able to get to the hospital right after you were born. Your mom was in shock—traumatized after seeing your father and his son fall into the crevice during the massive earthquake. It was hard to believe that the two of you even survived...or maybe it was meant to be? I've always wondered if Lee used his power to save your mother instead of himself."

"You mean he died because of..." Skylee's words faded.

"No," Ann cut in with a wave of her hand. "No, I don't know what happened that day but for some reason it doesn't appear that he used his power to save himself. For all these years, I believed your father's Elementum was buried deep in the earth's crust with him. So we, the eleven remaining Primortus, feared the power of the twelfth Primortus was lost forever. Our hope was renewed with your birth. My task was simple, to guard you—teach you the ways of the Primortus and once you turned fifteen—if you could be awakened—train you to wield the power of the Elementum."

"But you thought I didn't have one?"

"That's right, I planned to use my own to train you. Then right before the wedding your mom told me some of Lee's things had shown up. She seemed confused as to where they'd been. There's more to that story," said Ann as she held up her hand to forestall Skylee's questions. "I'm sorry, I should've prepared you sooner for all of this. It was my mistake. I allowed myself to get too close, and I put your happiness before my duty. As the years passed by, I watched you growing up, and I wanted you and Will to experience all the normal joys of childhood. Things like climbing trees, riding bikes and skinning your knees, if I had told you, everything would've changed. I wanted more time. So from this moment on we must be ready. I'm going to help you, okay?"

"Okay," Skylee said as she nodded and swallowed hard. "I just want to make sure nothing happens to my mom. Can we protect her?"

"We will," said Ann, taking Skylee by the arm and walking them to a sunny spot where they sat down. "You know I love your mom. I'll do everything in my power to watch over her until we know the danger has passed.

"Thanks, that makes me feel a lot better. Oh...um...Auntie Ann," said Skylee, sitting cross-legged on the ground and nervously brushing her hand across the grass. "There's something else, and you're not going to like it."

"Go ahead," said Ann, raising an eyebrow.

Skylee decided to quickly spit the words out and get it over. She inhaled deeply and said, "Chrism found your Humusara—it was all my fault—she tried to take it—but it's fine, nothing happened to it. She didn't get it."

Skylee was quite surprised by Ann's reaction. She chuckled to herself and said, "Of course she didn't get it."

"What-what do you mean?"

"The Humusara is an ageless vessel of the Creator. Do you really think it would let her steal it?"

"No," said Skylee, mulling things over in her head. "I guess not but how did it stop her?"

"What did Chrism say?"

"Only that she was nervous and dropped the book. Oh yeah! She said she dropped the Humusara like three times."

"That's right, it wouldn't go with her," said Ann. "The Humusara is alive and protects itself. It can't be stolen. If the pages are torn or damaged, it will mend. If it's burned, it will heal itself. It's imperishable."

"Nothing can destroy it?" Skylee asked in astonishment.

"That's right, nothing," she responded in a reverent tone. "Both the Humusara and the Elementum are everlasting. But remember you must guard your Elementum at any cost, because it can be taken. And without it you can't use your power or communicate with the Humusara."

"Somehow, I already knew," said Skylee, reaching for her Elementum and holding it in her palm. "Maybe that's why I protected it from the man at the tower."

"Are you kidding me?" Ann snapped. "He wanted the Elementum. Why didn't you tell me?"

"I was afraid. My book, my Humusara, kept warning me. It said to keep the gifts secret or lives would be lost. How could I risk telling anyone?"

"I see," said Ann sounding more sympathetic. "But now that you know we're both Primortus you must tell me if he comes back."

"Oh, I will, it's such a relief to finally be able to talk about it," said Skylee. "Before I got the warning, I did tell Will a few things and he saw my power although neither of us knew what was going on. And speaking of my power how exactly does it work?"

"Your power is tied to your emotions. Therefore you have to practice controlling them and that takes time. There's so much to learn and we've only begun," said Ann, pointing her finger at a patch of tiny mushrooms, which sprung forth from the ground growing to five times their size. "With your power you will do great things."

Skylee felt a rush of excitement. She thought of her father, her Primortus father, for the first time in her life she felt close to him. But several questions nagged at the back of her mind. *If I'm really the second born, I wonder what that mean? And how did I end up with my dad's Elementum? Do the missing words on his note reveal the answers?* Skylee wanted to ask Ann if she knew the answers. Then she looked over at her worried expression and the words wouldn't come out.

At that moment, Ann stood up, stretched her legs, and said, "Come on, let's get back to the cottage. We'll talk more about this later. I want to get to my Humusara and keep a close eye on your mom."

Skylee scrambled to her feet and trotted after her. "Guess what, I think I know what a Corporus is."

"You do?" asked Ann, smiling curiously at her.

"Shape-shifters, right?"

"Yes, but how'd you figure that out?"

"My Humusara showed me," she said as she and Ann continued down the pathway. "And it told me there's a helper in my midst. Do you know who it is?"

"I'm not sure, but I wonder if—" Ann's words were suddenly halted as Skylee let out a loud screech.

"OH NO!" Skylee stood looking down at a mangled clump of calico fur. The kitten's eyes were frozen open and its neck was at a strange angle. She turned away with her hand held over her mouth as Ann leaned down and closely inspected the kitten.

"I'm sorry, Sky. It's dead."

"No! Can't you do something? Can't we use our power?" Tears streamed down her cheeks. "Please...do something."

"I'm sorry," repeated Ann softly. "I wish I could but even the Primortus don't have power over death." She pointed at the ground, which slowly opened up and then formed a small mound over the kitten. Skylee looked over her shoulder to watch as Ann waved her hand and a carpet of tiny purple flowers covered the grave.

Skylee was shaking all over. A feeling of grief possessed her and dredged up a dark memory. A ghost from the past. She thought of her childhood home, of the bright yellow swing-set in her backyard, where she loved to play with her best friend. Skylee remembered the day Gracie was taken to the hospital. *Why can't she play with me?* Everyday she would ask her mom about her friend before going out to swing—alone.

A deep ache filled her heart as she recalled one especially cold and dreary day. The day Gracie died. Her mom explained it to her over and over, how she had an illness, a breathing problem that was brought on by the ash-filled air. Skylee didn't believe it. Not as a child of ten and not at that moment, as she stood there with her tear-streaked face.

"It seems like when I love something too much...it dies," she said in a hollow voice.

Ann didn't say a word; she simply wrapped her arms around her. After a long while, she took Skylee's hand and said, "Don't worry, I'm going to help watch over your mom. We'll keep her safe."

"Ann?" said Skylee looking down at the purple flowers. "What you did for the kitten...thanks."

* * * * * * *

A few mornings later, as the sun rose over Rotorua Lake, Chrism stood at her bedroom window and gazed out at the farmland. She rested her forehead against the cool glass and sighed. Pale yellow light softy glowed on her face.

Across the room, Skylee was fast asleep. Chrism listened to her soft steady breathing. *Must be nice,* she thought with a yawn.

She raised her droopy eyelids and focused on a line of sheep, which were trotting across the hillside toward the barn. Ever since the plane crash, she found herself inexplicably drawn to them. It didn't make any sense. She had always hated filthy farm animals.

Chrism watched as the sheep, one by one, entered the barn door. A lone sheep dog was herding them along. She assumed they were going inside to be sheared. No doubt Airon was helping Zane with the dirty creatures. She closed her tired eyes and frowned. *Why should I care what he's doing?*

As much as she hated to admit it, Airon's arrival at Cook's farm had caught her off guard. Her eyes involuntarily fixed on the barn as she recalled their first meeting. The mental image of Airon catching her in his arms made her blush. She shook her head, trying to remove him from her thoughts. No matter how attractive he was, he was not cultured enough for her.

I would never date a farmhand...but who would know...it might be a lot of fun... then again there is Will...but Airon's older and well, he is ripped...maybe I could get him to dress better...

Chrism gazed at the tranquil countryside. She had been surprised by how much she enjoyed the farm. It was more beautiful than she'd expected. Zane Cook however was exactly what she expected of a sheep farmer, with his scruffy beard, grungy hat, and awful plaid shirts. Chrism wondered how his wife could put up with such an unfashionable husband. Still, he had been very considerate and invited them to stay a few days longer, which was a much-needed breather after that stupid tree limb had hurt her.

Another yawn escaped Chrism's mouth. She normally liked to sleep late, but she had gotten out of bed after spending the wee hours of the morning tossing and turning. Her sleepless night was the result of overhearing her dad and step-mom in another big yelling match over the danger surrounding their assignment. Their fight had stirred up one of Chrism's greatest fears, seeing her dad hurt again. She couldn't bear to see another women break his heart the way her mother had.

The damp morning air sent a chill over her. She shivered and looked down at her thin silk pajamas. Crossing the room for her robe, she heard muffled footsteps coming down the hall. Then the front door to the cottage softly opened and shut. Chrism returned to the window to see who was going outside at such an early hour.

It was her stepmom. Janis was standing at the top of the porch steps looking out over the farm. Suddenly Chrism heard more footsteps coming from the hallway, this time she recognized them. Her father softly passed by her door on his way outside. *Oh great,* she thought, *exactly how I wanted to start the day...listening to the battle of the newlyweds.*

Chrism stood next to the window with her back to the wall, carefully staying out of view. She couldn't help herself. Their arguments reminded her of a new reality show called War of the Roses, which pitted divorced couples against each other in a competition to win the grand prize, a million dollars. She hated it, yet somehow couldn't stop watching. She pressed her ear to the window frame and listened.

"Hey, I heard the door, is everything okay?" asked her dad in a sleepy voice. "What are you doing up so early?"

"Oh, I just wanted to commune with nature, it helps to clear my head. I was thinking about the case, something's nagging me," her stepmother replied. "The island, the way it collapsed into the ocean. I've never seen anything like that before. You know, those underwater formations, can't be natural."

"Agreed."

Although her father only spoke one word, Chrism could hear anxiety in his voice. He had always been a man of few words.

"Has GEMA reported back about the data we sent?" her stepmom asked.

"Yes, the analyses points to a man-made incident," said her dad in a serious sounding voice. "So, not to bring up a sore subject, but that's why we shouldn't put off the meeting with Jack Clark. Now that Drake and his team have arrived we'll have plenty of back-up."

"I know," she said. "But, like I said last night, I'm convinced those attacks on Skylee and Chrism are somehow related to our case."

Chrism's eyes widened. Why was her stepmom so sure someone was after her and Skylee? The thought sent a chill down her spine.

Her dad spoke in a low voice. "I understand, and about last night..."

"Don't," said Janis in a hushed tone. "You've already apologized and we both said things we shouldn't have."

Yeah that's for sure, Chrism thought rolling her eyes.

"So, does that mean we're going back to our investigation?" asked her dad.

"Mr. Faraway?" her stepmom said brightly. "Did anyone ever tell you that you have a one tracked mind? Yes, go ahead and set up the meeting with Clark."

"Are you sure?"

"Yes, see if he can meet us at Ancient Maori Village, like we planned. Just one stipulation, from here on out we have to make sure the girls are being carefully guarded. Tell Drake we want our best security agents watching over them."

"Done," replied a relieved sounding Alex as Chrism peeked around the window frame to see her dad kissing her stepmom.

"Awk," gagged Chrism, sounding like a cat with a hairball. "And I thought the fighting was bad."

* * * * * * *

Skylee awoke shortly after nine o'clock from the first good night's sleep she'd had for days. She looked over at her stepsister's empty bed and blinked. *Wow, Chrism's up early,* she thought in surprise. *Now what is she up to?*

For a few moments, Skylee lay motionless in bed, staring at the ceiling and thinking about being a Primortus. Was there a reason she had received her power just before coming to New Zealand?

One thing was certain, when she suggested that they stick together as a family it had worked well, maybe a little too well. For the last few days, her mom had been determined that they all stay together every second of the day. Skylee hoped she would ease off soon.

There had been few chances to spend time with her Humusara except late at night, when Chrism was asleep. She had hoped to find out more about her vision or the helpmates. But most evenings the book only repeated the warning to keep the gifts secret.

The one new piece of information she had learned was about another type of helpmate called an Animus. They seemed to have the ability to read minds. Skylee almost laughed each time she thought of the old-fashioned words in her Humusara, words like Corporus, Animus, and helpmate.

Half an hour later Skylee was in the kitchen pouring herself a cup of tea. Will and his mom had finished eating breakfast and were clearing up their dishes in silence. She sat down and began munching on her cereal. Tension filled the air.

Will was extremely quiet as he took each dish from his mother, dried it and stacked it on the shelf. Skylee knew he was resentful that Ann had kept him in the dark for so long. He had made it perfectly clear that he wasn't interested in being a Primortus. In fact, for the last few days he had withdrawn and hadn't said a word about it. A wave of guilt consumed her. If only she hadn't been so impulsive, if she hadn't awakened his power maybe they all would be talking and laughing as usual.

All at once it seemed like the sugary cereal had sunk to the pit of her stomach. Dropping her spoon into the bowl, she hurried over to the sink to help with the dishes. She tried making small talk, hoping to lighten their moods. They talked about Airon, who had gotten up before sunrise to help Zane around the farm, and Chrism's whereabouts were a bit of a surprise. It turned out that she had been up for hours and was at the main house preparing lunch for everyone.

"Cooking? Chrism is cooking?" asked Skylee wide-eyed, making Will and his mother chuckle. "Well, that ought to be interesting."

At first, although shocked to hear her stepsister was preparing lunch, she was impressed by her thoughtfulness. Then she remembered her reaction to Shelley's brunch and Chrism's true motivation dawned upon Skylee. Naturally, it was an attempt to show her up and grab more of Will's attention.

Around noon they all arrived at the main house and were greeted by the smell of burnt food. A thin haze of gray smoke filled the air. Chrism sat on the sofa in tears.

"I...it wasn't my fault," she sobbed. "Th-the oven here is di-different."

They all stood still and stared at her in silence. Finally Airon stepped forward.

"Whew," he said wiping his hand across his forehead. "I was worried that we were gonna have teh eat some sort of fancy French food, like snails or mashed up liver. What a relief!"

"Huh?" said Chrism, looking up at him pitifully.

"Hey, I've got an idea. Let's have a picnic, eh?"

"That's a great suggestion," said Skylee smiling at Chrism, who was wiping her eyes with a dishtowel and looking at Airon with a strange expression on her face.

Within minutes, they were all in the kitchen cleaning up Chrism's mess and making sandwiches. Skylee noticed the smoke had miraculously cleared and she wondered if Ann had secretly used her power. By the time her mom and stepdad joined them everyone was relaxed and cheerful.

After packing the sandwiches, some fruit, and a jug of lemonade into a picnic basket, they set out for the lake. Together they walked over the hills of Cook's Farm. Skylee watched her mom and stepdad holding hands. Ann walked just behind them with her hand on Will's shoulder. Airon and Chrism were talking and walking so closely that their arms were almost touching. Skylee wished she could freeze that moment in time. But then again, as she looked around at the trees and flowers, the insects buzzing in the tall grass, and the birds soaring overhead, she realized she didn't want to stop time at all. What she really wanted was more time. Because at that very instant, it was as if she could feel the Primortus blood coursing through her veins, and her only desire was to learn to use her power.

By three-thirty that same day, Skylee was at the dining room table with her V-phone. Every afternoon she was supposed to go online and do her schoolwork. Her eyes scanned a transparent display, which surrounded her. A series of words and images floated around her head. At one touch, she could research multiple web sites on the circular readout. Almost everyone referred to the holographic display screens as halos because they resembled a glowing ring when in use.

Much of Skylee's afternoon was spent on V-web searching for clues about the Primortus. It was becoming clear to her that their world was extremely well hidden.

Ann had been taking her role as schoolteacher very seriously, making sure that she, Will, nor Chrism fell behind in their studies. Skylee envied Airon, who was having a grand time hiking and fishing with Zane, since he had plenty of time before he had to start his virtual college courses.

Skylee looked at the digital clock on her screen. It was now almost half past five and would be getting dark soon. She brushed a long wavy strand of hair behind her ear. Just a few more sections of mind-numbing math problems and she would be finished with the chapter. She stood, rubbed her eyes and stretched her arms above her head. Needing a break from staring at the halo, she grabbed her jacket and slipped out of the room.

The brisk evening air invigorated her. Jumping lightly from the front porch, she zipped her jacket and took off in a slow jog. Within minutes, she stood at the kitten's grave. A light fog hung in the air. The purple flowers were beginning to close their petals for the night. Skylee wondered what happened to the poor kitten. *What kind of animal would do this?* A mixture of sadness and anger welled up inside her. She remembered Ann's words...*the power is tied to my emotions.*

Grasping her Elementum, she focused on the grave and concentrated hard. A large, smooth rock nearby rolled slowly over the leaves and into place at the head of the grave. Skylee fixed her eyes on the stone, held out her hand, and willed the words to etch into its surface.

Rest in Peace
Little Lady
So small, so sweet, so soon

As she gazed down at the grave with glistening eyes, her lips parted in a tender smile. She had controlled her power for the first time.

FIFTEEN

~Sᵆ Ⅹ₀ 爪 ⚓

The Maori Village

The next day, Skylee joined the group as they gathered in the driveway for their departure to Ancient Maori Village. The assembly included all four Faraways, the three Butlers, Shelley, and Zane.

Skylee was surprised that her mother was allowing them to attend a Hangi meal and visit the village. More than likely the trip was yet another way for them to stick together. Whatever the reason Skylee was curious about experiencing Maori foods and customs.

It was midmorning and the sun shone brightly as they pulled away from Cook's Farm. Just to be cautious Skylee brought along her book, which was hidden inside her backpack. She knew it could protect itself but she felt more comfortable having it with her. Despite the fact that she had spent the last few days wishing that she could escape the boredom of her schoolwork, she felt extremely nervous about the outing. The horrible images of her mother being kidnapped were never far from her mind.

After a short journey into Rotorua, they ate lunch and rode on the skyline cable car. Skylee remembered her ride to the top of the Sky Tower as they glided up the side of Mount Ngongotaha. She looked over at Will, who was talking with Airon on the other side of the car. She turned and gazed down at Lake Rotorua and tried to calm her nerves. As she breathed in deeply, the pungent smell of sulfur filled her nostrils.

"Eww, it's like rotten eggs," Skylee whispered to no one in particular.

"I know, it's hard to get use to," said Shelley. "But I've lived here so long I don't even notice it anymore. What you smell is part of the geothermal activity of this region and a natural marvel of our volcanic homeland.

"Natural marvel?" scoffed Chrism. "Yeah, if you call smelly feet a marvel."

Everyone chuckled at her stepsister's blatant honesty. Minutes later as the gondola came to a stop Skylee thought for one horrifying second that the guide (who was directing them out of the doors) might grab her. Nothing happened. After the ride, they spent some time in the gift shop, which seemed to make Chrism happy. Will and Airon had no interest in shopping, so they went outside to walk around. Skylee was disappointed when she asked the salesclerk if they had any Luck-E-Chocs.

"Oh we don't carry *American* candy," she had said, as if she were uttering a curse word.

It was Skylee's first time out in public since her run in with the stranger, and she was nervous. She hated feeling so vulnerable. Fortunately, when she asked for directions to the restroom Shelley offered to go along with her.

As Skylee stood holding her hands under the auto-sterilizer, Shelley stepped up to the next station. Glancing over at her reflection, she shuddered when she saw her eyes. They were no longer brown, her pupils had totally disappeared and she seemed to be in a trancelike state. Skylee fought an urge to run away.

"*Keep them safe,*" said Shelley in a deep voice. "*Keep them close.*"

Skylee stiffened. She stared disbelievingly at her and murmured, "What did you say?"

There was no change, Shelley looked vacant as she stood facing the mirror. Then her lips moved and the weird, male-like voice returned.

"*You may encounter great trials before you reach your destiny. In life you may shed tears but not all tears are sad. I have great hope in you and I will watch over you from afar.*"

SLAM! The bathroom door swung open and Chrism walked in.

"Hi," she said as she pulled a brush from her purse and headed for a mirror. "I have to fix my hair before we leave for the village."

Skylee watched in amazement as Shelley blinked once and her eyes returned to normal. She smiled and nodded at Chrism, who hadn't seemed to notice a thing. And then as if nothing had happened Shelley turned to Skylee and said, "Okay, are you ready?"

"Uh-huh," replied Skylee still in shock. "Oh well, no you go on, I'll stay here with Chrism. We'll meet you back in the gift shop later."

"Okay," she said nonchalantly as she left.

Skylee leaned against the wall and tried to figure out what had just happened. How could Shelley know about her father's note? And why did it seem like she didn't even know what she had said? As Skylee looked over at her stepsister who was now brushing her hair, she wished she could talk to her. Then three words came to her mind, *keep them safe.*

A short time later, they boarded a brightly painted glider-bus to take them to the village. Skylee was glad to see Will's mom seated directly behind her mom and stepdad. She knew Ann was keeping her promise to watch over her mom.

As Skylee followed Chrism down the aisle to some empty seats at the back of the bus, she noticed people staring at her. She felt a growing sense of embarrassment as more and more eyes focused her way.

A rather plump lady with squinty eyes and a prominent nose whispered, "It's her," to the man sitting next to her.

"They're staring at me," Skylee nervously said to Chrism.

"What—no, don't be silly," her stepsister replied as she located a seat behind Will and Airon. "They're probably just looking at my Prada bag."

As Skylee sat down by her, she glanced across the aisle at two middle-aged women, who were excitedly whispering behind their hands. One of the women had excessively tweezed eyebrows, which caused her to appear permanently surprised and the other looked remarkably like a bulldog. The surprised one tapped a man sitting in front of her and whispered in his ear, all the while pointing at Skylee.

"Did you see that?" she asked Chrism, doubting her own eyes.

"Yes...um...they do seem to be looking at you, but why?"

Looking toward the front of the bus Skylee spotted her mom and Alex, who were several rows ahead of them. They had both turned in their seats and were giving their daughters reassuring smiles. Skylee sat up straight and returned a smile, tying to appear unfazed by the unwanted attention. A moment later, a muffled voice behind her whispered a familiar utterance, *Sky Tower*.

Just then, Skylee realized what was happening. How foolish not to think of it. Of course, she was the girl who had been attacked at the Sky Tower. Her picture had been plastered all over New Zealand, in glorious 3D. They had been reading those awful stories about her and seeing the video of her fall on their T-screens all week.

Skylee felt her face redden. She looked at her stepsister and anxiously slithered down in her seat. Chrism nudged Skylee's arm, formed a sly grin, and stood up with an air of confidence.

"Don't you know, it's impolite to stare?" she said in a sugary sweet voice to a gawking lady across the aisle, whose mouth flew open. Then Chrism sharply clapped her hands and said, "Okay people, the show's over, talk amongst yourselves."

Skylee giggled softy and grabbed her hand giving it a light squeeze. The whole bus seemed to sheepishly look away from them. *Maybe having a bossy stepsister was going to come in handy,* thought Skylee.

A large Maori man stepped onto the bus, thankfully drawing everyone's attention as he spoke through the microphone.

"Kia ora! That's Maori for hello...but many of you are from other parts of the world...so as we make our way to the village I'd like to say hello to you... Aloha...do we have any Hawaiians on board? Yes...and bonjour to our French passengers..."

The glider-bus headed for the village as he continued on, working his way through greetings from around the world. While his deep voice rang out over the speakers, Will and Airon turned and faced Skylee and her stepsister.

Will put his arm on the seat back and grinned at Skylee, and then looked at Chrism. "Well, I guess you set everyone straight."

"Of course I did," she proudly said, flipping her hair over her shoulder and glancing at Airon. "I can't have everyone gawking at my sister...can I?"

"Apparently not," said Airon, then he whispered in Skylee's direction. "Cause if they're lookin' at you, they can't be lookin' at her."

Skylee suppressed a laugh and shook her head at him, and Will pressed his lips together in a firm line.

"I *heard* that," Chrism snapped at him with a burn-him-at-the stake look in her eyes.

He raised one brow and stared back until she looked away. "So anyway, Skippy, are ya excited about eating at the Hangi? Eh, they might have your favorite...lamb."

"For your information," Chrism answered for her as she looked down at a brochure about the Maori village. "A *Hangi* is an ancient Maori method of cooking food using super-heated rocks buried in the ground in a pit oven and yes, they will have lamb and pork and chicken. Oh, and it says here they have sweet potato, they call it *kumara*, and salad and stuffing and..."

"..Hola, to our Spanish friends... and to
our guests from Japan, Konnichi wa..."

Skylee looked out of the bus window and wondered who would talk the longest, her chatty stepsister, or the long-winded tour guide. Her vote was on Chrism. She never seemed to run out of things to say.

"Eh, Chrism," said Airon. "I hate teh interrupt yer incredibly fascinatin' pamphlet readin' but I need teh ask Skippy another question."

"Sure," Chrism said in a lofty voice while holding up the brochure between them. "Why would you be interested in what this says? It's all about Maori customs and culture, keyword being culture. Something you clearly don't have!"

"Good on ya," Airon scoffed. "I reckon not all of us are royalty...Duchess."

"What?" barked Chrism. "What did you call me?"

Airon smiled devilishly at her. "You heard me, Duchess."

"If you came all the way from Thailand, I would like to say
Sa-wa-dee-krap... and if you are from India...Namaste..."

Skylee was glad the guide had broken into their conversation. She glanced at Will signaling him to stop Airon's teasing before things got out of hand.

"Hey mate," he said tapping Airon on the shoulder. "What were you going to ask Sky about?"

Airon looked suspiciously at him, plainly aware that he was trying to sidetrack him. After elbowing Will in the ribs and winking at Skylee he said, "What's this I hear about ya bungee jumpin' with half a cord?"

"Yeah, but I don't recommend it...hard landing and all."

"Bloody good thing ya weren't badly hurt. So let's see," Airon said as his brow furrowed. "Will tells me you fell because some crazed bloke was after yer dad's necklace."

"Necklace?" said Chrism taken aback. "You didn't tell me he was after that."

Skylee froze and looked wide-eyed at Will. *What did he tell Airon? Didn't he understand Ann's warning not to tell anyone who wasn't Primortus?* Her train of thought was disrupted when the voice over the speakers broke in again.

"Now that I've greeted everyone...we must choose a chief for our tribe," said the man on the microphone. "Our chief will go through the ritual of welcome when we reach the village. He must meet the chief and show that we come in peace not war. Do I have any volunteers?"

Chrism stared at Skylee while Skylee glared at Will. Airon appeared to be amused. None of them paid any attention to the man looking for a chief. There was an unspoken conversation going on between them, each trying to discern what the other was thinking. Skylee continued to look at Will with a mingled expression of hurt, anger and alarm.

"Hang on!" Will finally blurted out, raising his hand between them.

"Good...good we have a brave volunteer...
...come on up here young man."

The passengers on the bus turned to look at Will. Airon excitedly grabbed his shoulders and spun him around.

"Yer our chief, mate," he said, and then he pulled Will up and began a chant. "Hail teh the chief! Hail teh the chief!"

Skylee watched in astonishment as a confused looking Will wandered up the aisle toward the man on the microphone. Chrism was rendered speechless, at least for the moment. The entire bus continued to chant, Hail to the chief, until Will reached the front.

"Ladies and gentlemen, may I introduce you to..." he held the microphone to Will's lips.

"Ahem, Will."

"Chief Will!" the man said holding his arm above their heads. "So where are you from?"

"America, well, I'm also half Australian, but I live in the U.S."

"No worries, mate," mocked the man. "Ya know, Kiwis and Aussies like to poke fun at each other but at the end of the day, were all mates. Right, Chief Will?"

"Eh, right," he said agreeably.

"Well folks, we are about to arrive at the village. Our chief here is going to meet a warrior at the gates. Chief Will," he turned to him and said. "You will accept the warrior's offering showing that we have come in peace. If all goes well the warrior and you will share the Hongi. This is the pressing of the noses together, our Maori greeting. And it should be taken very seriously folks, no laughter or jokes."

Will nodded at the man and then smiled at Skylee. She could see the apprehension in his eyes. How could she stay mad at him in his current predicament? She would just have to wait to tell him off later.

The glider-bus hummed to a stop and they exited onto a stone paved courtyard. Large, spear shaped logs formed a fence around the village and a tall gate stood before them. Four wooden tiki statues seemed to be standing guard over the entrance.

The tour was met by a small group of Maori, dressed in traditional tribal clothing. Skylee's eyes were drawn to their necklaces, which appeared to be made of jade. Each amulet was intricately carved into a tiki figure, fishhook, or swirling pattern and reminded her of the carvings on her own necklace.

Looking over her shoulder, she saw a tall man dressed in dark khaki pants and a black shirt. He was standing at the far right side of the tour group. She scanned to the other end and saw another man who was the mirrored image of the first. Both of them had their hands in their pockets, and they appeared to be watching her. *Great, now I'm being stalked by the lookalikes?*

She questioned their identities in her mind. She thought about the stranger at the wedding and her attacker at the Sky Tower—two tall men or were they the same man. It bothered her that she now imagined every stranger as potentially dangerous.

An ear-piercing scream rang out from the forest giving Skylee a start. The loud cry was that of a Maori woman who stood on a platform above the gate. She sang out the words.

"haromai, haromai, haromai"

The guide explained that the translation of haromai was come hither, the customary Maori salutation of friendship and hospitality. The shrill sounds seemed like an odd way to welcome guests.

Skylee watched as the woman with wavy black hair sang. Her small frame was wrapped in a black and red weaved top. A skirt made of flax swayed around her hips. When her song ended, Will, in his role as newly appointed chief, followed the guide to the middle of the courtyard.

When the wooden gate opened three Maori warriors appeared. The largest man, who stood in the middle, threateningly approached Will. He was muscular with deeply bronzed skin and he wore little except facial tattoos and a short reed skirt. Skylee's pulse quickened as she watched him come within inches of Will. He stomped around wielding a spear, sticking out his tongue, and making his eyes bulge.

"Arghhhh" the warrior shouted.

Will maintained a somber expression and stood perfectly still. But the wild-eyed warrior shouted and prowled around him, thrusting the spear at him. Skylee's knees grew weak and her heart pounded as he loudly chanted and called out intimidating grunts leaning in close to Will. After a few more nerve-wracking minutes the warrior finally retreated, picked up a silver palm leaf, and returned to place it on the ground at Will's feet.

"That guy is really scary," Chrism whispered in Skylee's ear. "I can't believe how brave Will is."

"Um…yeah," she replied uncomfortably. "He makes a great chief."

"That's what I like about him. He seems much older than fifteen. Don't you think?"

"Yes, his mom says he has an old soul," said Skylee with her eyes fixed on Will.

As the crowd watched in solemn stillness, Will gazed down at the peace offering. He nodded at the warrior, who moved in and placed his tattooed face inches away from him. Then they pressed their noses together sharing the breath of life.

There was complete silence except for a tiny giggle from a small girl in pigtails. Skylee looked on with a feeling of pride as Will calmly stood nose to nose with the powerful Maori warrior. One of the things she admired most about him was his ability to remain composed in almost every situation.

His only sign of discomfort was the movement at the corner of his mouth as he slightly bit his lip. It was a nervous habit he'd had since childhood. Skylee found it endearing. As the warrior stepped back and welcomed the tour group into the village, Airon leaned in and whispered in Skylee's ear.

"What a shame, Skippy. Ya missed out, now ya can't be Will's first kiss," he said. Then he turned to Chrism and spoke softly over her shoulder. "Since ya seem so interested in learnin' the Maori customs, Duchess, maybe we should try that one out, eh?"

"Shhh," both Skylee and Chrism hissed at him.

Skylee glanced at her stepsister, who was unsuccessfully trying to look insulted. There was no doubt about it. Chrism obviously was enjoying Airon's attention. And although Skylee found it rather entertaining, her mind had gotten stuck on two of Airon's words, *first kiss*. She wasn't fooling herself. Of course Will had kissed a girl before, probably several girls for all she knew. Why did her stomach suddenly feel queasy and her mouth dry? She forced herself to smile at Airon.

Just as she had expected, the moment Will rejoined them, Airon picked on him non-stop and insisted on calling him the chief. Even Chrism joined in and poked fun at him, especially about the nose kissing as they had taken to calling it. Will took it all in stride and accused Airon of being jealous of his "chiefness."

All four were still laughing and joking as they walked along the path to the village. It was a relief to feel like a normal teenager for a while. Skylee knew it wouldn't last so she tried to relax and enjoy the moment. In the back of her mind, the impending discussion with Will about keeping the Primortus secret loomed. Not to mention that Chrism would surely begin asking questions again at some point.

When they entered the gate and made their way down the trail, Skylee was surprised by the sheer size of the place. For some reason she had expected the village to be sitting neatly on a cleared plot of land, but it stretched out across a wide expanse of forest. It was as if the Maori had created a place that perfectly blended with nature.

There were about a dozen huts, each showcasing a different theme: warrior training, weaving, wood carving, tattooing. At the end of the path they came upon a large dimly lit structure, called a whare. It had a high thatched roof with intricately carved beams and posts that were painted bright red. They met the rest of the family at the entrance for the show.

Skylee followed her parents, Ann, Zane and Shelley to the front as they all sat on a long wooden bench. Will sat beside her. Airon and Chrism were tightly squeezed onto the end of the row. Skylee scanned the area and noticed the lookalikes were standing at the back on the room. The lights dimmed, a rhythmical drumbeat began and dozens of Maori performers in traditional costume danced onto the stage.

"Sky, I've been wanting to ask you," Will spoke into Skylee's ear over the loud drums. "You did tell my mum about the vision, right?"

"Of course, and she promised to do all she could to protect my mom. Didn't you notice how she's been sticking so closely to her tonight?"

"Yeah, no worries then," said Will looking more relaxed. "She'll make sure nothing goes wrong."

"And besides, I haven't gotten any more warnings from my Humusara," said Skylee trying to convince herself that everything was fine.

"Maybe you should put that thing away, until you're a bit older."

"Older? Like you're so much older than me. When will you ever stop treating me like a kid?"

"I'm not treating you like a kid. Believe me, I don't think of you like—" Will abruptly stopped, looking nervous.

"Really? Then why are you constantly telling me what I should and shouldn't do and why did you tell Airon about the necklace?" Skylee said louder than she intended.

Chrism leaned forward and curiously looked at them. "Hey, is something wrong? You're not arguing, are you?"

"No, no the music is just loud," said Skylee, thinking fast. "Sorry, we were just talking about the...ah...dancing. You know, what it means, that's all."

"Hum, if you say so," said Chrism skeptically. "Why does it always seem like the two of you are keeping secrets?"

Skylee and Will shrugged and she shook her head. Sooner or later, Skylee knew she was going to ask them again about the book and the necklace. How were they going to explain it? It wasn't going to be easy to keep her overzealous stepsister in the dark.

During the show, Skylee noticed Chrism seemed preoccupied by Airon's interest in the beautiful Maori dancers. At one point, she even dropped her purse on the floor right at his feet, clearly trying to distract him. True to form, Airon leaned down, picked up her purse and sat it in her lap, all the while his eyes remained fixed on the dancers. Skylee and Will softly laughed as Chrism gave him a dirty look and tightly crossed her arms across her chest.

"Ladies and gentlemen," a Maori dancer said. "We hope you are enjoying yourselves in our village. Now, you are all invited to join us for the Hangi feast!"

The crowd filed out of the meetinghouse and into a large dining hall. The Faraway's and their friends were seated around a large circular table that was filled with various meats and vegetables. Skylee was careful to identify each food item before she ate it, sticking mostly to vegetables. Airon would never let her live it down if she repeated the lamb-spitting episode.

Unfortunately, she could still feel the tension between herself and Will. She didn't like being at odds with him. Settling back against her chair, she looked over at him and felt her frustration level rise. She wanted to protect their secret, to learn all she could about what they were, to know how to control their powers and *he* undoubtedly didn't.

After dinner, everyone went their separate ways. Her mom, Alex, Shelley, and Ann rushed away for a meeting with Jack Clark. Zane went with Will and Airon to explore the village sights. She and Chrism promised they would stay in the courtyard until Zane and the guys returned.

As the sun dropped behind the tall trees, a chill filled the air. The stepsisters warmed themselves by a large bonfire. Skylee's prediction had been right. The questioning had already begun. Chrism stared at her with a dogged look of determination.

"So, again. Why didn't you tell me that guy at the tower was after your necklace?

Skylee didn't reply.

"Okay then, how did you and Ann end up with the exact, same book?"

"How many times are you going to ask?" Skylee said exasperatedly.

"Well, I haven't asked you that much about the necklace because I DIDN'T KNOW! And I guess I'm gonna keep asking until you decide to tell me the truth," she shot back.

"I've told you all I can."

"Oh, I see," said Chrism with her turquoise eyes blazing. "You seem to talk to Will about everything. You just don't trust me. Do you?"

"It's not that—I wish I could tell you."

"Tell me what?"

"Ahhh, Chrism!" breathed Skylee as she placed her hand on her forehead. "All I can say is, my dad gave me the necklace and the book and, yes, Ann has the same book too. I'm still trying to make sense of it all myself, really."

"Maybe I should just ask her about it myself."

"And exactly how are you going to explain that you've seen her book?" Skylee asked matter-of-factly. "Are you going to tell her you broke into her room and tried to take it?"

"Who broke into what?" said Airon as he and Will strolled up to them.

"I...no, it wasn't me...I mean..." stammered Chrism.

"What's this I hear, eh?" he asked. "The Duchess has sticky fingers?"

"No I don't have sticky fingers!" said Chrism. "But there's a finger I'd like to show you," she added under her breath as she turned her back on him.

"Where have you two been?" asked Skylee, hoping to change the subject.

"Watching the jade carving demonstration," said Will as he held up a black jade pendant that hung from a leather cord. "This is a Koru symbol, meaning the beginning of life. The spiral is like a silver leaf fern unfurling."

"That's awesome," said Chrism, eyeing the jade amulet. "You have such great taste. What did Airon get?"

"Oh no, Duchess. I'm not a necklace kind of fella," said Airon.

"That's right," added Will. "He doesn't believe in jewelry, but ask him about his tattoo."

"Tattoo?" Skylee and Chrism said together.

"When did you get a tattoo?" asked Skylee wide-eyed.

Airon punched Will's arm and said, "Thanks a lot mate!"

"You mean you really did," said Skylee. "You have a real tattoo?"

"Listen Skippy, you and the Duchess need teh keep this under wraps, Ann wouldn't like it. I got it while I was in Oz, went into Sydney for it. Grandpa Gene went along and signed for me since I'm not eighteen yet."

"I can't believe it," said Chrism clearly appalled. "Your grandfather encouraged you to mutilate your body, it's disgusting!"

Airon ran his hand through his hair. He leaned toward Chrism with his jaw clenched and said, "Ya might want teh lower your voice, and take a bloody look around. Do ya notice anythin'? The Maori don't think tattoos are so disgustin'."

"Well, that's—it isn't the same," she said, her face turning slightly pink. "Because, you are not Maori—wait a minute—what kind of tattoo and where is it?"

"That's a bit personal Duchess, now isn't it? But if ya really want teh know we could arrange a private viewin'."

"As if..." Chrism raised her purse over her head to strike.

Airon gave her a smirky grin and said, "First, ya try teh beat Will with your fancy shoes and now you're tryin' to hit me with your glittery purse. What's next? Are ya gonna have a go at somebody with your sparkly belt?"

Skylee and Will burst into laughter. As Chrism lowered her purse and glared at him, her face went past pink and quickly approached fiery red. As a matter of fact, she didn't look quite like herself. Her usually pretty face resembled a cornered snake ready to strike. Skylee wasn't sure what she would do next.

At that very second, a petite Maori woman stepped up to them.

SIXTEEN

The Animus

Skylee recognized her right away. She was the woman who had sung out the welcome when they arrived. Her bronzed skin was aglow in the firelight and her erect posture gave her a regal appearance. An aura of energy surrounded her. Her piercing brown eyes made Skylee feel like she could see right into her soul.

"Kia ora, I'm Hera Marama," she said to all of them, and then she gazed at Chrism. "Is—is everything all right?"

"Oh yes," Chrism hastily said as her death-threatening expression melted into a sweet smile. "I was just trying to show my friend how scary those faces are, you know, that the warriors make. Wasn't I, Airon?

"Right, and I must say *my friend* has a real knack for scary faces."

Chrism stood perfectly still and continued to smile at Hera but Skylee knew her stepsister was boiling mad inside. Her true emotions were only visible in her crimson red face and a small twitch in her right eye.

"Oh I see, those scary expressions, as you put it, are all part of our ancient Maori tradition, a way to see what the intentions of a stranger entering our village might be," said Hera as she turned to face Will. "Aren't you the young chief that met our warrior at the gate?"

Will slowly nodded his head and said, "Yes, I'm Will, uh—Chief Will I guess, that's what my mates have taken to calling me."

"Well done, Chief Will. It's best to embrace life's challenges, even the one's you may not wish to," said Hera before turning to call out to another woman standing nearby. "Nika...Nika, come and meet the Chief and his friends."

A young woman wearing a long colorful dress came toward them. She had waist-length black hair with chunky blonde streaks. Silver bracelets wrapped around each of her wrists and long silver loops swung from her ears. There was an intricate Maori tattoo on her left upper arm. Skylee wondered why she wasn't wearing traditional Maori clothing like Hera.

"Hi, how's it going?" Nika asked smiling shyly at them. "I see that you've met my Mom. Has she been trying to teach you our Maori ways? It's her favorite thing to do."

"Of course I am," said Hera in a motherly tone. "I have to make sure the younger generation doesn't forget our traditions."

"As you can tell Mom takes her job very seriously," Nika said with a soft laugh. "So, what part of America are you—"

Her words were cut short when Chrism let out a loud gasp, pointed at Will and yelled, "BUG!"

Everyone froze. There, sitting on his shoulder, was the largest bug Skylee had seen in her entire life. The brown creature resembled a giant cricket with long hairy looking legs. It was so big in fact, that if Skylee could have mustered up the courage to pick it up it would have barely fit on her palm. Usually, Skylee wasn't afraid of insects but she found herself taking a small step back as chill bumps rushed over her arms.

Will slowly craned his neck around and was eye to eye with the enormous insect. He closed his eyes for a split second and when he reopened them, they were as wide as saucers. He looked straight ahead and didn't dare move an inch.

"KILL IT! KILL IT!" screeched Chrism.

"NO, don't! Don't hurt it," ordered Nika, holding her hands up.

"Maybe it will jump off," Skylee quickly said as she considered how she might use the power of the Elementum to control the huge creature.

"What should I do?" whispered Will, trying not to disturb it.

"Hold still mate," said Airon with a bewildered look on his face. "Crikey, what is the bloody thing?"

"It's a weta bug. I haven't seen one in years," said Hera in a hushed voice. "They...they almost went extinct after The Day. So, we should try not to harm it."

"Weta? Well, do they bite?" asked Airon curiously.

"I don't think so, unless they're feeling threatened," said Hera. "Stay still. Let's think, what can we do to keep from harming it?"

"WHAT IS WRONG WITH YOU PEOPLE? SOMEBODY, JUST SMACK THAT UGLY THING!" screamed Chrism frantically shaking her hands in front of her.

"Hey, I've read about these," said Skylee, leaning in for a better look. "There are lots of different species. They're flightless so, I don't think it will jump off. It must have crawled on your shoulder when we were under the trees. Oh, do you think it is a tree weta?"

"Possible, yes," answered Hera.

"They're nocturnal, normally. Will, you must have woke him up," Skylee said smiling at the bug.

"Hopefully, he's a good sport about it," he replied as he glanced at her.

"He seems calm, he hasn't raised his back legs in defense, so you should be okay."

She placed her hand over her necklace, hoping she could use her power without having to pull it out for everyone to see. She might be able to control the weta. Skylee searched her mind for the right thoughts to concentrate on.

Almost at the same time, Zane bounded up to Will. He smiled broadly and bent forward looking closely at the bug. Then to everyone's amazement, he calmly picked the gigantic insect up and looked admiringly at it.

"Well, take a gawk at that!" he exclaimed. "I thought I'd never see a weta again. Little fella, you better find somewhere else to sit. I'm afraid you're not welcome here." He walked over to a tree and carefully placed the bug on a branch.

"Little," gasped Chrism. "You call that terrible monstrosity little?"

Zane started to speak but Will reached out and placed his hand on his shoulder. "Thanks, mate. I wasn't scarred of it or anything but I just, well, I didn't…"

"Of course," he said as he patted Will on the back then turned his attention to Chrism. "Let me clue you in on a secret, little lady. What you call a terrible monstrosity is a survivor and we should all consider ourselves lucky to have seen it."

"That's right," said Hera nodding her head. "It's a sign…a cause for hope."

Chrism's eyes got big. "I don't get it! You're saying that awful looking thing is some sort of special sign?"

"Don't you see?" said Skylee. "The weta bug means the natural world is continuing to recover—the planet is healing."

Her stepsister rolled her eyes and said, "Okay, okay you don't have to go all environmentalist wacko on me. I get it, that gross, horrid bug is mankind's link to utopia, yeah, whatever."

"No, it's not like that," said Skylee, frowning. "You don't understand."

"Yeah, I do," Chrism shot back. "But what I'm trying to comprehend is why Weta Studios is named after something that hideous. Go figure."

Before Skylee could respond, Hera and Nika chimed in and tried to get through to her, explaining the significance of protecting the fragile environment. Skylee's heart sank for she could see from Chrism's bored expression that their words fell on deaf ears.

* * * * * * *

Nearby, inside a cottage at the edge of the village, Alex crossed the room with an outstretched hand. Janis, Ann and Shelley were lined up beside him.

"Hello, I'm Alex Faraway, you must be Jack Clark. Thanks for meeting with us."

"No problem."

A short silence followed as Alex carefully shook hands with the odd looking person. An odor of cigarettes and rotten vegetables hung in the air. Alex and Janis showed no emotion on their faces. They had encountered many unusual characters in their line of work, so they exhibited no surprise at the unusual appearance and smell of the person before them. Ann shot a quick look in their direction.

Shelley looked confused. She softly cleared her throat and said, "Oh, I'm sorry, Alex. This isn't Jack. I thought...I..."

"Can I help you?" said the stranger, almost in a whisper.

"Yes, we were, I mean, Mr. and Mrs. Faraway and their friend Ann are here to meet with Jack," Shelley said nervously. "Uh, do you know him, Jack Clark?"

"No, don't think so."

"There must have been a mix up," said Alex now looking suspiciously at the person before him. "May I ask your name?"

Without the slightest pause came the reply, "Ashley, Doctor Ashley Hayes."

The confused look on all of their faces gave the doctor a wicked thrill. Before anyone could say another word, Ashley hurled a gas-filled vial on the floor at Ann's feet. A blast of dark smoke rose in the air, forming a toxic cloud around her. She covered her nose and mouth with her hand then fell unconscious on the floor. Alex rushed forward as Shelley broke into violent coughing.

"Don't move," ordered Ashley, gripping Janis's hair with one hand and a second vile in the other.

* * * * * * *

Meanwhile, Will had excused himself from the group saying he needed to go to the loo. It wasn't true. He was feeling embarrassed about how he had handled the weta bug and he needed to get away. *Cripes, it had to be a bug.* His entire life he had dealt with all kinds of creatures, snakes, sharks and even crocs with no worries, but for some reason bugs made his skin crawl. *Sky probably thinks I'm a jelly-kneed sook,* he gloomily thought.

Will suddenly stopped dead in his tracks. Up ahead, crouched in the bushes he saw the shadowy outline of a man. Carefully placing his feet on a bare spot in the path, so he wouldn't step on any twigs, he held his breath and waited to see if the bloke had heard his approach. But there was no movement, so he slowly exhaled and silently crept behind a tree. Then he peered around its large trunk.

Hidden from view he watched the figure, which was facing in the opposite direction. Will's pulse quickened as he noticed the stranger was dressed in dark clothing and seemed to be talking to himself. There was something in the bloke's hand.

One or two minutes of silence passed as Will waited to see what he was going to do. When a deep voice finally broke the silence, he recognized it. It was Director Drake.

Will watched as Drake held some night-vision lenses up to his eyes looking towards a nearby cottage. *Why is the head of GEMA here?* Will thought. He jumped as Drake swore through gritted teeth and cupped his hand over his ear.

"Wombat," Drake said in a raspy tone into his handset. "This is Lone Wolf. Do you read, over?"

A crackled response came back. "Lone Wolf, this is Wombat, loud and clear, over."

Will chewed on his lip as he tried to decide what to do. He leaned around the tree for a better look at Drake, who suddenly leapt to his feet and looked at his watch. Then he held the night-vision lenses to his eyes again.

Without warning there was a blinding flash of light and the thud of an explosion. Then a plume of black smoke rose from the back of the cottage. Will caught sight of two figures exiting the door and moving through the thick underbrush. It appeared to be a man dragging a woman to safety. *Wait...that looks like...* Will felt his stomach lurch as he realized it was Sky's mother. He couldn't believe it. Sky's vision was coming to life right before his eyes.

Will flinched as a forceful voice loudly rang out.

"Commence extraction," Drake ordered as he rushed toward the cottage. "Repeat, Wombat, do you read? Commence extraction. Now!"

Will didn't stop to think. He took off chasing after Sky's mother and her abductor. He knew he had to reach them even though they had a head start on him.

"*Where's mum?*" he thought as he ran down the dirt path. *This isn't right. She should be here*. The thought of anything happening to his mother made his heart race.

Ahead of him in the thick forest, Sky's mom was screaming out in pain. It spurred Will onward and made him pick up his pace.

* * * * * * *

"What's taking Will so long?" asked Chrism as she stepped up to warm her hands by the fire.

Skylee craned her neck around to look for him. "I don't know. He should be back by now."

"You wait here, I'll go find him," her stepsister ordered as she spun around on her heels.

"Okay," Skylee called out to the back of her head. "Hey, be care..." She didn't bother to finish since Chrism had already dashed across the courtyard.

Skylee stood for quite a while watching the fire, mesmerized by the orange flames, which were dancing up the sides of the logs. As she stared into the blaze, her thoughts turned to Will. He had been gone much too long for just a bathroom break. *Maybe he wanted to get away from me*, she thought with a frown. She had noticed him keeping to himself more and more since the day she had accidentally awakened his power.

Glancing around the courtyard, she saw no sign of him or Chrism. But the two men that she had seen earlier, the ones who were dressed alike, were there. An uneasy feeling washed over her. How had she managed to end up standing there alone? She wished Zane and Airon hadn't gone back to the dining hall for more dessert.

Skylee took a calming breath and placed her hand on her chest. Her Elementum felt cool through the fabric of her shirt. She focused her pale blue eyes on the fire and remembered Ann's words. *The power is a source of great strength.*

Her tranquil thoughts were interrupted when a dark shadow swept past overhead. She spun around half expecting to see another plane heading for her, but nothing was there, only the sound of fluttering wings and frantic chirping.

"What?" she said, looking up just in time to see a little bird as it screeched and swooped at her from above.

"Hey, watch out!" she yelled as she ducked and narrowly escaped being struck in the head.

She threw her hands up and covered her face, nervously peeking through her fingers to see if anyone was watching. The lookalikes were staring at her in stunned silence. *Why are they still watching me?* Skylee nervously thought.

The persistent little bird squawked and regained her attention with another dive at her head. Then it circled around, stopping a few feet from her face where it hovered like a hummingbird in mid-air.

Skylee had never seen another quite like it. It was small, covered in silver-grey feathers and flew with incredible speed. With a final loud screech it dove toward her, stopping short just before striking her face. Then the bird darted back and forth from the fire to the forest, like a dog trying to convince her to play chase. Without thinking, Skylee took off after it leaving the lookalikes staring at one another with their mouths open.

Gazing upward as she raced toward the tree line, she tried to keep up with the soaring bird. She followed it deeper into the woods veering off the path and through a prickly patch of underbrush. Branches popped and snapped underfoot and thorny limbs snatched at her jeans.

As she ran over the treacherous ground, the Elementum turned colder beneath her shirt. There was no time to consider what it meant. Her legs seemed to move on their own. She jumped over a fallen tree and nearly fell into a gully on the other side. Barely keeping her balance, she raced on. Her breathing grew fast and shallow as she struggled to keep up with the flying target.

For a moment she lost sight of it, so she stopped and searched all around. It looked as though the chase had ended just as abruptly as it had begun. And in a way that was true, the little bird reappeared and darted through the trees circling back to her. Its silvery wings gently swooshed each time it glided by her.

"What are you do—" uttered Skylee breaking off her words as she slapped her palm against her forehead. "Great, now I'm talking to birds!"

As if the feathery creature understood her, it landed on her shoulder and began chirping a melodic tune. Skylee stood as still as possible for fear of frightening it away. When it finished singing she let out a soft giggle as it excitedly walked down her arm, tickling her skin with its tiny claws. Holding up her finger as a perch, she watched it hop on.

The bird was a magnificent silver color with the exception of a small black spot on its left wing. It fixed its shiny eyes on her for a moment, then launched itself from her finger soaring skyward above the trees and out of sight. As soon as the bird had gone there was a rustling sound in the bushes.

"Now what?" she said, spinning around to see what might be coming toward her.

The branches parted to reveal Hera's small face peering through the green foliage. She stepped forward and said, "Are you lost?"

"Oh, sort of, I guess," said Skylee. "I know this might sound crazy but I followed a bird out here and..." her voice faded off as she gazed up at the treetops, where the bird had flown.

"Doesn't sound crazy to me," Hera chuckled. "Nature has a way of drawing you in, doesn't it?"

"Sure does, especially lately."

"Can I help you find your way back?"

"Well, um, yes, thanks."

Hera grasped Skylee's hand and led her to a long, shadowy trail. A strange tingling feeling overwhelmed her as their hands touched, like tiny electrical shocks in her fingers. She tried to convince herself that it was nothing more than static in the air. Or perhaps it was because she felt awkward holding hands with someone she didn't know very well.

As they walked, hand in hand, a brilliant pink and orange sunset peeked through the tree canopy. It created a warm glow around them. The trail carried them beside a stream that was surrounded by lush green ferns. Skylee felt as if they were entering an enchanted forest like something out of a fairytale. Enveloped by nature's beauty, her worries seemed to melt away.

The woods were cool and utterly quiet except for the sound of their footsteps crunching along over the scattered leaves.

Skylee?

"Uh-huh?" she murmured giving Hera a sideways glance, thinking she had called her name. But the Maori woman seemed deep in thought as she walked along, her skirt swaying with each step.

Skylee? Once more she thought she heard her name. Yet she saw no movement on Hera's lips.

As the two of them continued, Skylee began to feel tense. She wondered if they were even going in the right direction. After all, she barely knew this woman.

Skylee? She heard it again, this time the voice seemed to be inside her mind. She jerked to a halt and spun around to face Hera.

"Did you say something?" she asked with her eyebrows arched in confusion.

"Why?" Hera gently said, letting go of her hand. "What did you hear?"

Skylee started walking again. "Nevermind."

They walked a while longer and reached a clearing near a small bonfire, which was attended by two Maori warriors. Hera motioned to the men, who nodded and then moved away.

Skylee looked around nervously. "I thought you were taking me back?"

"There's something I must tell you," said Hera with her dark brown eyes fixed on her. "I can help you understand your gift."

"Gift?" she repeated, wondering if she knew about her Elementum.

"Yes," said Hera so softly that Skylee could barely hear. "It is rare. You should treasure it for it came at great cost."

"I...I'm not sure I know what you mean?" she stammered, looking down at the ground. "You think...I have a..."

"Gift."

"Okay, well do you have one too?" Skylee felt like they were speaking in a secret code.

"We all have a gift, but you..." Hera's words faded as she looked into the fire.

Skylee didn't know what to say. Then a question came to mind. "What am I supposed to do with the gift?"

"Only you can know," she said, still staring into the flames.

"But you seem to know," Skylee said in an uncertain tone, "something."

"Yes, I know that you will have to choose. If you do not fulfill your true destiny all will be lost," Hera said as she returned her gaze to her.

There was that word again. Destiny. She swallowed hard and said, "I don't understand. What is my destiny? What am I suppose to do?"

"What does your heart tell you?" said Hera, placing a hand on her shoulder.

A tiny shock wave raced through her body. And for the first time she noticed that Hera had an arrow shaped birthmark below her right ear. Once more a voice called her name inside her head.

Skylee...I'm an Animus. You may know me as a helpmate. I can hear your thoughts, feel your emotions and see what awaits you. My daughter Nika is also a helpmate, a Corporus. Do you remember, the little bird that brought you to me?

Skylee nodded with her eyes transfixed on Hera's closed lips. It seemed incredible, but she was actually speaking without moving her mouth. Her voice echoed again, like a soft breeze through Skylee's mind.

She brought you to me so I could help you. I can see that there are things you have not been told. Things the second born must know.

A wave of panic washed over Skylee. She opened her mouth to speak but Hera's words continued on in her head.

There are two prophecies concerning the second born. I choose to believe only one of them. It tells of a second born, who will rise on the day of doom and hold the fate of the world in her hands. If she turns from the shadow of darkness the earth will not pass away.

Skylee's mouth felt dry and her lips quivered. "And the other one?" she asked in a low, anxious voice. "What does it say?"

Hera gave her shoulder a light squeeze. *I wish I could spare you from it...the other prophecy proclaims the second born as an abomination of nature. A child, that should not have been possible, even for the strongest of the Primortus. It foretells that she will bring about the end of mankind.*

Skylee gasped in surprise.

You mustn't believe it, Hera's voice quickly ordered. *Many of us consider it to be a false prophecy. But there are those who believe it, and their voices are no longer silent. You should guard against them. Most importantly you must know that there is another, a powerful oppressor that seeks to destroy you. His name is Brinfrost. He will not stop until he has taken your gift. Protect it at all costs. If you do not defeat him—our power will fall into his hands.*

"Brinfrost? I don't...how can..." Skylee's words trailed off as she heard Hera speaking again.

He is a deceiver, who yearns to rule us all. You must not fail. I know you feel alone but remember...from one choice another is made. And through you, the second born, the earth may endure.

Skylee looked away from her intense gaze. Somehow hearing the words second born deep inside her mind made it seem more real to her. But how could all be lost because of something she would or wouldn't do? Was she supposed to believe that the fate of world depended on her alone? As more and more questions came into her mind she realized that Hera could hear her thoughts.

Are you sure, it's me? I'm the one who must stop him? Shouldn't it be someone older, more powerful—more experienced?

Hera briefly closed her eyes and lowered her head. Then she looked up, gazing somberly into Skylee's eyes. *Have you ever wondered why you and your mother survived The Day even though you were right where it all began? Or why your father perished on the day of your birth? You were destined to arrive that day.*

Skylee's blinked back tears. *Am I some sort of abomination? And could I somehow be responsible for The Day...and for my father's death?* She thought of the note he had left for her and the bizarre encounter with Shelley. Maybe her dad had known all those years ago. Could he have written it, knowing he would die? And somehow, only hours ago Shelley had completed his message. How was that possible? All Skylee knew for sure was that her father's message had finally gotten through to her.

She stared intently at Hera. *Tell me how to find—this Brinfrost—and how to defeat him?*

The fire warmed the side of Skylee's face as Hera responded. *I cannot find him. I can only tell you that he has already set his plan in motion. Time is running out. You must seek him. It is within you and you alone.*

Skylee's next words came from deep within. "I feel alone."

Hera didn't say a word. She took Skylee's hand and guided her to a nearby tree. As they walked she heard Hera's voice. *Danger approaches, but do not fear. Use your gift. When the time is right, remember the forest trees and plants will help you.*

They came to a stop beside the stream. Hera pulled a withering leaf from a low hanging branch and placed it in Skylee's hand. *Tell it to live.*

"What?" she blurted out in astonishment.

Tell it.

Skylee held the leaf close to her lips and breathed, "Live." And it slowly transformed, from dull greenish-brown to vibrant green. She shivered as a cool breeze caught the leaf, carrying it above their heads and into the water where it rode along on the current. Hera watched until it was out of sight. After a long pause, she looked back at Skylee and took both of her hands.

This is your path, said Hera's voice inside her mind, *you feel alone because you alone can determine your destiny, but like the leaf you must follow the stream where it leads. Farewell my Child, Kia kaha. Be strong.*

The dreamlike moment was broken by the sound of a woman screaming in the distance. Skylee turned and saw a strange looking person dragging her mom by her hair through the forest. Her heart seemed to turn over in her chest then it throbbed wildly against her ribs. *This can't be happening!* But it was happening just as the Humusara had shown her.

SEVENTEEN

The Vision Comes True

"STOP—help!" Skylee's mom screamed as she kicked and twisted her body struggling to free herself.

"SHUT UP!" yelled Ashley, yanking harder on her hair.

Skylee shot a terrified look at Hera who cried out, "Go! Go, and use your power."

"Mom! Let go of her!" Skylee shouted running straight toward them. She felt the metal of her Elementum cooling upon her skin. A mixture of fear and anger swelled inside her as she hurtled through the thick underbrush.

She moved with lightning swiftness. Gnarly branches pulled at her hair and protruding limbs slapped against her arms and legs. But she still raced after them, stumbling along on the uneven ground. She couldn't take the time to consider any physical limitations, if she didn't stop the abductor she might never see her mother again.

Skylee watched aghast as Ashley, still moving quickly, bashed something against her mother's head. There was a flash of light. Then a plume of dirty white smoke encircled her mom's face leaving her motionless.

"No!" Skylee shrieked.

Terror rushed through her. She *had* to get to her mom. Another flash of light appeared, which quickly formed a cloud of smoke only yards ahead of her. As she rushed past the toxic haze, it felt like all the air escaped her lungs and fire burned in her chest. Lunging forward she fell, smacking her face hard on the ground. The taste of blood filled her mouth. And when she rolled over the outline of the abductor came toward her.

Skylee leapt to her feet and frantically looked for her mother. She was lying face down on the forest floor beside Ashley.

"Get away from her!" she screamed with tears steaming from her eyes.

She staggered forward. But before she could reach them, the abductor had forcefully grabbed her mother and was once again dragging her limp body away. Mustering all of her strength, Skylee sprinted after them.

As she ran the forest grew oddly silent except for the pounding of her heart and the rustling leaves under her feet. Something inside her told her she must find a way to use her power. And then Hera's words suddenly returned to her. *The forest trees and plants can help you.*

With a burst of adrenalin, she ran onward. The sound of her own rapid breathing filled her ears. The gap between her and the abductor was closing. Instinctively she raised her hands and willed the roots and branches to help her. The ground shuddered beneath her feet and a terrible creaking sound filled the air. Dozens of panicked creatures scampered out of their burrows and dens, running across the forest in fright. To her amazement the tree roots and limbs sprung to life, like huge skeletal fingers, reaching out for the abductor. They came from all directions.

Then she saw Ashley throw something at her. A shiny object flew pass her and broke open on the ground. Once again, a flash of light and rancid fumes filled her nose. She coughed and tried to hold her breath. *Keep going...just keep going,* she told herself, fighting off an intense wave of dizziness.

How she managed it she never knew, but she threw her hands out in front of her and a huge gust of wind cleared the air. At the same moment, a massive hand-shaped root burst forth from the ground. It captured and tightly gripped Ashley's arms and legs. Skylee willed the limbs to catch her mother, who fell free from her attacker's hold.

"Ow!" screamed Ashley in a loud, high voice, as a shower of leaves and twigs pelted the hostage taker.

The roots, vines, and branches clutched brutally at the menacing kidnapper. They coiled around every part of Ashley's body before slamming their tightly wound package into a large tree trunk. Skylee watched her mother's attacker land hard on the ground, knocked totally senseless. Then the trees and plants returned to their rightful places as if nothing had happened.

"Mom!" wailed Skylee as she reached her side. "Can you hear me— Mom?"

Her mother was being gently cradled in a thick canopy of soft green branches. She was bruised and battered but looked like she was in a peaceful slumber. For a second Skylee thought she might be dead.

Then she opened her eyes as if she were waking up from a nap and said, "Hey Pumpkin, what's going on?"

"Are you all right?" Skylee said, kneeling on the ground beside her.

"I think so, what happened?"

Skylee didn't answer. She heard the sound of someone running through the forest toward them.

"Shhh," she said, placing a finger to her lips.

She defensively jumped to her feet and held up her hand. Will came into view and rushed toward her. He stared down at her mom, who was staring up blankly, and then he looked over at the unconscious kidnapper.

There was a look of shock and dismay on Will's face. "Is she—?"

"She's alive."

Will looked into Skylee's eyes for a long moment. Then his piercing gaze rested on her Elementum, which had slipped out during the chase.

"You used it—your power?" he asked looking intently at the amulet.

"Yes, I wasn't sure I could do it...but..." Skylee's voice broke as she looked down at her mother.

"Are you hurt? There's—there's some blood on your lip."

Skylee touched her mouth. "I fell, but I'm all right."

"Let me see," he said gently grasping her chin. He brushed his thumb across her lip, wiping the blood. "Well done," he whispered.

Within minutes, the forest was swarming with GEMA agents. Director Drake showed up and took charge of the scene.

"What happened?" Drake asked Skylee. "How did you stop him, or her, well the kidnapper?"

"It all happened so fast," she replied. "It looks like the um, kidnapper tripped over some branches and got knocked out."

"Pretty lucky, huh?" added Will.

At that moment Ashley, who had come to and was now in handcuffs seated against a tree only a few feet away said, "Luck? This isn't over. Your luck is about to run out."

Skylee could barely breathe. Had she only been lucky? Was luck all that got her and her mom through safety? No she had used her gift, just like Hera said she would.

Drake stepped over and firmly pulled Ashley up. "You have the right to remain silent, in other words—shut up!"

Ashley Hayes was taken into custody after a long discussion, between Drake and a local police detective, over who had jurisdiction to arrest him. Drake only looked annoyed for a moment and then he cleared his throat and smoothly convinced the man to permit a few of his GEMA agents to accompany them to the jail so they could question Ashley. Skylee remembered her mother telling her that Drake had the ability to talk people into almost anything, now she had seen it firsthand.

Two paramedics dressed in white uniforms arrived, carrying a hover-gurney. They scanned her mom's vital signs and wrapped her in medic-foil. Within minutes, she was completely covered in the shiny material with only her face exposed. Skylee watched helplessly as they placed her mom on the gurney and started it up for the long trek back to the village. As the paramedics grasped the floating gurney, her mother raised her head and smiled. Then they smoothly guided her down the trail. Skylee placed her hand on her Elementum. *Thank you.*

As soon as she was out of sight, Will bent down and whispered in Skylee's ear, "I'm worried about my mum. I don't know where she is.

Why didn't she use her power to stop all this? And where's your stepdad?"

Skylee had been so focused on chasing down her mother's kidnapper she hadn't thought of Ann or Alex. A feeling of dread overtook her. Will was right, something horrible must have happened because Ann would have done anything to protect her mom.

"Come on, we better go find them," she said, taking Will's hand.

As they tramped through the underbrush toward the trail, Skylee heard muffled discussions going on all around them. There were more than a dozen people standing around, all wearing dark clothing and as far as she could tell most of them were trying to figure out how the attacker had been stopped.

The lookalikes were there too and apparently, the GEMA agents were in big trouble. Standing before them was a squatty man with his finger pointed up at their faces yelling. She only caught bits and pieces of his rant. But she heard things like, "brainless, incompetent and lost girl." The lookalikes glared over at her. She nodded guiltily at them, realizing she was the reason for their predicament.

As she moved on, she suddenly became aware that she was still holding Will's hand. The warmth of his touch seemed to be making its way up her arm to her face. She gave him a sideways glance, and his worried expression made her heart sink. He was clearly distressed over his mother's absence. She squeezed his hand tightly and pulled him along the trail a little faster.

In the distance, she heard the faint sound of a woman's voice calling out "Hello...hello?"

As the voice grew louder, Skylee whipped her head around to see Carmen De Soto entering the trail from the thick underbrush. She rushed past at full speed with her dark hair flying wildly about her shoulders. She didn't even seem to notice them as she continued on her mad dash, one hand full of paperwork and the other loaded down with various electronic communication devices. All the while she cradled her V-phone on her shoulder and talked non-stop. Skylee glanced back to see her meet up with Drake, who was now only a few yards behind them. She handed him some papers and then rushed off toward the other GEMA agents.

Drake jogged up the path and tapped Will on the shoulder, "Where are you two going?"

"We're going to find my mum and Sky's stepdad."

"I can help you with that, son. Now, I don't want you kids to get upset because everybody's all right, but there was a fire and—"

"A fire?" Skylee gasped.

Will's face turned white.

"Listen, they're okay," Drake said reassuringly. "We got them out in time, nothing more than a little smoke inhalation. Come on I'll take you to them."

Skylee and Will followed him out of the forest. A group of medics was busily moving in and around several people that were sitting on the ground. Skylee saw a woman being carried out on a gurney and realized it was Ann. Will went straight to her as Skylee headed toward Alex. Behind them were the still burning remnants of a cottage. The realization of what could have happened hit her hard and tears spilled down her cheeks. As she reached Alex, he stood up and put his arms around her in comfort. The horror of the day would stay with her but at that moment, she had a small sensation of what it felt like to have a father. It felt good.

* * * * * * *

"She sounds like a kook."

Skylee and Will were alone in the hospital waiting room. And she had just told him about her first encounter with an Animus.

"Abomination," he said flatly. "Yeah, that proves it, she's a loon."

"She is not." Skylee declared, crossing her arms over her chest. "Hera knew what she was talking about."

"Oh Hera, so the two of you are buddies now? Don't tell me you actually believe all that rot about The Second Born and the two prophecies."

"Well I do," she said as he shook his head disbelievingly at her. "What? Am I not supposed to take the word of an Animus?"

"This is insane," he said, exhaling loudly. "You just met her, she's a complete stranger."

"Yes and an Animus."

Will stood up and began to pace. "So on nothing more than what this woman said you think you're...I can't even say it."

"An abomination," said Skylee calmly.

"That's the most ridiculous thing I've ever heard."

"Listen, I didn't say *I* think I'm an abomination, but there are others who do."

Will stopped pacing and stared at her. "Others?" he asked in a worried tone. "Like who?"

"Well, I took it she meant other Primortus. I mean who else could it be?"

"Right," he said, nodding contemplatively.

"And I think you're forgetting something. Hera was the one who told me to use the forest against Ashley, which was what saved mom. Everything she said and did was to help me."

"Okay, I'll admit it's a good thing that she gave you that warning and a few pointers with your power. But cripes Sky, you can't seriously think you're supposed to go up against some bloke named Brinfrost or the world will come to an end."

Skylee stared at him for a moment before saying, "I don't know what to think. Actually I'm not sure how I feel about a lot of things."

Will seemed taken aback by her comment. "Is there something else?"

"Yes as a matter of fact there is," she said, feeling more annoyed with him by the minute. "I'd like to know how much you've told Airon."

"Not much," he said, looking away from her.

"Sure? He seems to know an awful lot. For instance, like the fact that the tour guide at the tower tried to take my necklace. What else have you told him?"

"If you're asking me whether or not Airon knows we're Primortus, then the answer is no," he said in an offended tone. "You know, I'm not stupid."

Unfortunately Chrism and Airon choose that precise moment to return from the hospital gift shop. Skylee felt ashamed of herself for accusing Will of spilling their secret. She wanted to tell him she knew he wasn't stupid but all she could do was give him an apologetic shrug.

The next two days flew by and Skylee found herself, sitting in the auto glider anxiously waiting for her stepdad to bring her mom out of the hospital. Her mom's injuries had included smoke inhalation, bruises, and cuts. Alex and Shelley had managed to come away with minor injuries from the fire. Ann was back to normal. *It's probably because she's a Primortus,* thought Skylee.

She watched as rain spattered against the window and ran down the glass in tiny streams. She jumped when her V-phone rang loudly.

"WHERE'S MY BLOUSE?" Chrism's voice blared as her face popped into view. "You know, the one you borrowed."

"Oh, oops," said Skylee, putting the phone down on the seat. "Must be a bad connection, you know the rain and all."

"Well I don't care. We're planning a homecoming party for your mom and I WANT TO WEAR THAT BLOUSE! Where is it?"

Skylee moved the V-phone back and forth across the seat and said. "Sorry you're breaking up...I...can't even see you. We'll talk when I get back."

She quickly hung up the phone and vowed to never borrow her stepsister's clothes again.

* * * * * * *

Will watched intently as the rock he had tossed skipped across the surface of the lake. The rain had stopped and patches of blue sky were visible through the low hanging clouds.

One word echoed in his mind. *Primortus.* Sky was determined to follow through with the whole thing, even though some of them were evidently against her. How could they believe someone as perfect as Sky was an abomination? It filled him with doubt. He still wasn't sure if he wanted to be a part of it but he couldn't let her face the fall out alone.

He hated to admit it, even to himself, but if he'd had an Elementum at the Maori village he could have intervened sooner and maybe her mum wouldn't have been injured. He picked up another rock and tossed it, but it sank in the water.

"I'm done for," he moaned.

"Don't get yer knickers in a twist," snickered Airon as he approached him.

"Rat bag," Will grunted under his breath.

"Hey mate, it's not astrophysics," Airon said. "Just toss it using your wrist."

"What would you know about astrophysics, huh?" he said, never taking his eyes from the lake.

"More than you know, mate," Airon continued, "I would've thought ya would be in a better mood since you and Skippy are spendin' a lot of time together. Have the two of ya talked yet?"

"Talked about what?" asked Will with a huff as he tossed another flat rock across the water's surface.

Airon twisted his lips into a smirk and said, "About how ya feel there, Chief. The stuff we discussed on our walkabout just a few weeks ago." He reached up and popped Will on the back of the head. "Ya gone brain dead, mate?"

Will swatted his cousin's hand away. He wanted to tell Airon what was really going on with him and Sky but he knew he shouldn't, not after his mum's warnings. Even though Sky had already accused him of it.

Will shook his head and said, "No, I haven't said anything to her. Every time I start to she looks at me with those blue eyes and, I don't know, too much going on right now."

Airon picked up a rock and examined it. "If ya wait for the right time, it's never gonna happen. Just man up and do it." He threw the rock with a snap of his wrist and watched it hop over the calm surface of the lake.

"Man up," Will grumbled, "You're one to talk."

Will squatted down at the water's edge and fumbled with the stones. In the last few days, it had become clear to him that Airon had his eye on Chrism.

Airon grinned knowingly and said, "My plan is workin' just fine. I can handle the Duchess."

Will decided on a rock, stood up and tossed it. It bounced once then sank. "If I push, I could mess it up. She's my best friend, I don't want to lose that."

"That's not gonna happen," Airon said as he patted Will on the back, "Mate, ya can stand around and mope about it or make a move, any move, just get things rollin'."

Will stared out over the water as he played out different ways he might approach Sky.

"So Chief, what's it gonna be? Mope around or man up?" Airon asked as he swung his leg hitting Will at the knees.

Will fell but not before he head-butted Airon taking him down with him. The two wrestled around until they both tumbled into the lake.

* * * * * * *

Later that evening at Cook's farm, everyone gathered at the cottage. Skylee was overjoyed to have her mom back with them. The conversation during her homecoming dinner was filled with random topics, like the weather in New Zealand, the state of the economy and how everyone was doing with their school studies. No one dared mention the attempted kidnapping or the arrest of Dr. Ashley Hayes.

By eight o'clock, everyone except Skylee and Will had gone to their rooms. Skylee couldn't believe Chrism had left them alone. *Maybe her obsession with him has shifted elsewhere,* she thought, grinning to herself.

After a lengthy discussion about whether they should or shouldn't spend some time with her Humusara, Skylee and Will decided to just relax and watch an old classic movie, "Lethal Weapon."

"I love flat movies," said Skylee cheerfully as she bounced down on the couch. "The 3D stuff is great but I just like being able to watch without the lenses."

"Me too, cause they mess up my hair," stated Will as he held his nose in the air and ran his fingers through his hair.

"All right, Chrism," said Skylee as she giggled.

"Good guess, must be my acting skills," he said, flashing her a fake smile. "Anyway, I think the older movies are fun to watch. I mean take this one, you got police chases, jumping off buildings, shooting bad guys *and* its funny."

"And don't forget the cars blowing up," Skylee said as she continued to giggle.

"Can't forget that," he laughed as he sat down beside her. "The movies today are too political, they preach at you and want you to think and feel."

"Hey, there's nothing wrong with feeling and thinking, but I do realize that thinking is a struggle for you," she said teasingly.

"Very funny," Will said as he squeezed her knee. "You could make a cat laugh."

Skylee started laughing and pushing at his hand. It tickled and also hurt a little as he tightened his grip. She pleaded in-between her laughter, "Please, Will-William, stop—all right—you think—you think, you're a great thinker—I give."

Will released her knee but not before giving it one more light squeeze. "And don't forget it," he said in jest.

"You know, you have a strong grip. I think I'm gonna have a bruise," said Skylee, rubbing her knee.

"Nah, I know what you're up to," he chuckled. "You're trying to make me feel guilty, but it won't work this time."

"Ha, I could start crying and then you would feel bad but I won't because it feels too good to laugh," Skylee said with a smile.

Will pulled his lips in over his teeth and spoke in a weak shaky voice like an old man, "It's like your paw-paw always says—laughter's the best medicine."

"He does say that a lot, and I think you're right because I feel better than I have in a long while."

"I'm right?" said Will, acting shocked. "How about that, I'm right."

He relaxed back into the couch and put his feet up on the coffee table. Skylee settled into the soft cushions beside him as the movie began. Within minutes, they were engrossed in a tense nail-biting scene. Skylee reached past Will for a handful of popcorn and at that exact moment...*Boom*! The loud on-screen explosion gave Skylee a start causing her to drop the popcorn all over him.

"Hey, what a waste," he said laughingly.

"Sorry," she snickered.

Will began picking up the popcorn, then suddenly stopped, looked at his handful and tossed it at Skylee. His action initiated a popcorn war, which lasted until the bowl was empty. They both laughed until tears came to their eyes. As they glanced around the room, another round of laughter broke out. It looked like a popcorn machine had exploded scattering the fluffy white kennels all over the place.

"Look at this, your mum's gonna kill us," he said with a funny grimace.

"Not if we clean it up," she said as she started picking up.

As Will joined her, she thought back to when they were kids. They used to have so much fun climbing the only tree in her backyard. At first they were happy using a cardboard box as a tree house, but Will's dad apparently saw the danger in that and built them a real one. There, she, Will, and Gracie would play for hours pretending to be musketeers.

Skylee sighed quietly as she went back to picking up popcorn. She still missed her friend, after all these years. After her death, Skylee refused to climb into the tree for a long time. She remembered that it was Airon who had finally convinced her to get back in the tree house. He insisted that Gracie was an adventurer and wouldn't want it to go to waste. Skylee knew in her heart that he was right and so she, Will, and Airon became the new three musketeers.

"What are you thinking about?" Will asked tossing popcorn into the bowl.

"Oh, you know, I was thinking about the things we use to do as kids. Stuff like this," she said with a grin.

"Making a mess?"

They both laughed. It felt like old times. And then, just as they settled back to enjoy the rest of the movie, they heard a loud shriek.

"Waaaa—OH NO!" bellowed Chrism as she stomped into the room and shook her shirt in Skylee's face. "What is this?"

EIGHTEEN

⟋ᵴ⨍ ⅄ₒ 𝔸𝔸 ⻝

The Secret Office

Skylee jumped to her feet. "I'm sorry, Chrism, she quickly said. "I've been trying to fix it—"

"Really, so I guess the question should be why does it need fixing? I let you borrow my favorite white blouse and now it has grass stains all over it," barked Chrism. She looked at the shirt and then shoved it toward Skylee. "LOOK...AT...THIS...BLOU...GRRRR..."

Skylee's breath caught in her throat and she glanced at Will, whose mouth hung open in amazement. Right before their eyes, Chrism's appearance had changed. Her teeth suddenly elongated and sharp points began to appear as her words turned into a growl. Then her eyes went from blue to rich gold and back. Skylee and Will involuntarily took a step back when she began to snarl.

Skylee instantly knew what was happening. It was true. Chrism was a Corporus, and they needed to calm her down before something terrible happened.

"Chrism," she gently said. "Please take it easy, I..." Skylee turned to Will and pleaded with her eyes for his help.

"Ahem, maybe we should sit down and talk this over," Will said, holding up his soda can to her like a peace offering. "Would you like a soda or something?"

Skylee's head snapped around to glare at him. She mouthed the word "really," and he gave her a serious nod.

"Grrr—Oh, you want to offer me something to drink? Is that supposed to somehow help?" Chrism said, sounding a little more human. Then she held up her shirt again. "What about this? She destroyed my favorite blouse."

Skylee watched as her stepsister's teeth returned to normal and her turquoise eyes re-emerged. Somehow when Will distracted her it had calmed her down enough to stop her from shape-shifting completely.

Will took a step forward and positioned himself between the two girls. "She said she was sorry."

"Yes, yes, the saint said she was sorry and so everyone should forgive her," Chrism flippantly said to him. "Well, let me tell you something, she isn't a saint!"

"I tried to wash..." Skylee stopped, unsure of what to say next.

"What? You washed it, in water?" Chrism's face turned several shades of red and then she straightened her back and put on a defiant face. "It is dry clean ONLY. I should have known better than to let you borrow anything of mine. You're just too stup—"

"Right, that's enough," Will interrupted her. "I'm sure Sky will replace it and you don't want to say something you'll regret."

Chrism stared at Will and shook her head. She gave Skylee a "this isn't over" look, then rushed down the hall and slammed her bedroom door.

Alex popped his head out of the master bedroom and said, "Everything all right?"

"Yes sir, everything is fine," Will assured him.

"Okay, well keep it down a little, Janis is trying to rest. Good night," Alex said as he shut the bedroom door.

Will put his arm around Skylee's shoulder and gently squeezed. "She'll get over this. It's just a shirt."

A warm feeling washed over her. She sighed and said, "I hope so. You did see her change, right?"

"I saw it all right. And I can't believe it—Chrism—a Corporus," Will said in a surprised tone. "I thought they were supposed to be helpmates. Looked like the only thing she wanted was to *help* take off your head."

"I know," said Skylee. "It's just—I can't imagine a shirt would upset her so much that she would shift, even though I know she treasures her clothes. I get the feeling that it's something else."

"How could she change like that and not even know it?" asked Will looking down the hall and shaking his head.

"I don't know," she replied. "But I think we're going to need your mom's help when we tell her, you know, what she is."

"We?" he questioned with raised eyebrows. "Oh no, this one—you and my mum can handle on your own."

Will put his other arm around her and drew her to him gently, which caused warning bells to ring in Skylee's head. He had hugged her many times before but this hug felt different. Her stomach did a little flip-flop.

"It's not that I don't want to help you," he said in a low, gentle voice.

"I know I can't blame you. Chrism has really been on edge, well, guess we're all on edge," she said quietly. Skylee realized that she, herself, was on the brink of falling off if she didn't step out of Will's embrace.

"Hey," Will said as he held her in place.

"I really need to..." she paused, trying to come up with something, but what she really needed was to put some space between them.

"Wait," he said, brushing his hand through her hair as she took a tiny step back from him. "I think you have a piece of popcorn—see." He pulled out a fluffy kernel and showed her. "What else have you got? Popcorn...twigs...too bad you don't have any stain remover in there."

"Funny! Glad you found that," Skylee said as she watched him toss it into the bowl. "Although, I could've saved it for later but..."

His attention was back on her. She noticed his eyes move from her eyes to her lips and back again. Her heart seemed to miss a beat. She swallowed hard, unable to move as he gazed at her. For a brief moment, she let herself wonder what it would feel like to kiss him.

She nervously licked her lips. It was an automatic move, definitely not something she had planned to do. Then she saw Will grin, and her eyes widened as she realized his lips were coming closer to hers. *He really is going to kiss me,* she thought in a sudden panic.

"What are you doing?" she blurted out. She backed away from him, placing her hand on his chest. "I...no we can't, this isn't, we just can't..."

Will shook his head and bit his bottom lip. "I don't see why we can't. Sky, this could be a good thing, you and me," he said as he reached for her again.

"No—you're my best friend and—" Skylee stopped and stared at him. Although she didn't want to admit it a big part of her wanted to say yes. But a bigger part reminded her of the risk if she did. She could lose him forever.

"No," she said in a tone that sounded much surer than she felt.

"Right," he sighed, placing both hands in his front pockets and staring down at the floor as he rocked back and forth on his heels.

Skylee had a huge lump in her throat as she saw a wounded expression cross Will's face. She hadn't seen this look since his father died. She had hurt him, the one thing she hadn't wanted to do was cause either of them any pain. She almost broke her resolve and reached out to touch his cheek. But one of them had to be strong. She wanted them to stay best friends. All of a sudden her chest felt like something was pressing against it, squeezing her lungs. She had to get out of the room before the walls came crashing in. Her eyes darted to the door, increasing her desire to run away.

"Um...sorry but I need to go and check the holo-fax projector at the main house. I'm expecting an assignment from my science teacher," Skylee quickly said. "And I want to check my Humusara cause there might be a message."

"You need to give the whole Primortus thing a rest," he said in an indifferent tone as if addressing a stranger.

Skylee had never heard Will speak to her this way. His voice was completely void of feeing. For a moment she felt unnerved, then anger welled up inside her.

"Give it a rest! Are you kidding me?" she said in an angry, hushed voice. "Have you forgotten something? It was my power—my Primortus power that saved my mom. I thought after you saw what happened—I thought you'd realize how important our power is. You do see that right? It saved my mom?"

"I didn't mean—"

"No, I know what you meant," she abruptly said. If she didn't stop him she might say something that she would regret. She was furious with him, not just for his comments about the Primortus but because he had truly tried to kiss her. Why was he trying to change their relationship when she had so much to handle already?

Will shuffled his feet and dug his hands deeper into his pockets. He seemed to be trying to think of something to say. His lips parted but nothing came out. Closing his mouth in a thin frown, he looked at her with pain in his eyes.

"Listen," she said in a quivering voice. "I need to find out more and I can see, you don't feel the same way but I have to follow this path. I'm a Primortus just like my father. It's my connection to him. It's all that I have of him. Why can't you understand that? You do things to stay connected to your father." She quickly wiped the tears that streamed down her face. She hated to cry in front of him and now that she was it just made her angrier.

"Sorry," Will said quietly. "I just think this Primortus stuff is moving too fast. And it's dangerous. I didn't mean to upset you. I guess I'm just worried about the others. In case you've forgotten not all of the Primortus are in your corner."

"I'm not worried about them, well maybe a little, but there's nothing I can do about it. And besides, it doesn't change the fact that I've accepted who I am...a Primortus. Why can't you understand? Why do you have to...to be..." Skylee's last words were impossible to hear through her soft sobs.

Quickly turning away from him, she darted across the room. He followed, right behind her. More stuttering sobs shook her body as she ran out the front door, letting it slam in his face. She understood his concern about the Primortus who were against her, but why was he acting like she was some helpless damsel in distress. Just the thought of it infuriated her. But somewhere deep inside, she knew that she was mostly angry with herself for wanting Will to be more than just her best friend.

"Sky, wait," he called out as he opened the door. "I just meant, please come back—what about the movie? Sky..."

Skylee didn't look back, but she could feel Will watching her as she ran away. She went straight in the front door of the main house stopping in the entryway to steady herself. The hallway was dark and quiet. There was a sliver of light coming from beneath one of the doors.

"Hello? Anyone home? Zane?" she called out, but no one answered. "I've come to download a holo-fax from my teacher."

Skylee made her way down the hall, stopping in front of Zane's office. She suddenly realized that she had never been inside.

"Zane? You in there? I need to get my assignment." she said, pressing her ear up against the door. She heard nothing. "Hello?" said Skylee as she opened the door and stepped inside.

The office was a mess. Papers and unopened boxes were stacked everywhere. Old hardcover books sat on almost every surface. As she scanned the room for the holo-fax projector, something caught her eye. There was a large bulletin board covered in photographs hanging on the wall. She moved toward it to get a closer look. Picture after picture of the devastation from The Day lined the board. Newspaper and magazine printouts were haphazardly tacked around its edge. *Why would Zane want to look at this everyday*? Skylee wondered. She touched one of the news reports and began reading...

A massive earthquake has occurred in Yosemite National Park.
The first eyewitness accounts state that a huge crack has appeared and traveled west. There is no Richter scale reading for the event available at this time due to damage at the monitoring stations. Reports of deaths and injuries in the thousands are unconfirmed.

Skylee knew she was reading one of the first reports about the day her father died. She tore her eyes from the board as she searched for the holo-fax projector. Nearby, there was a large glass case placed a few feet from the wall. It looked like the kind of case that would be in a jewelry store. Peering down, she was surprised by her own reflection. It was too dark for her to see inside. She reached around its edges and flicked on the light switch. The light blinked on and off a few times before revealing the content of the shiny case.

"Wow," she softly said.

Numerous knives lined the case. Some were tucked inside some sort of leather sheath while others were laid bare on the green lined shelves. She glanced back at the open door and listened for any movement. The house was still quiet.

"Creepy," she whispered to herself. Her eyes passed over the knives. Some were made of stone, but most of them seemed to be forged out of metal. There was one spot that was empty. The only evidence that a knife had been there was a darkened outline. She rubbed the scar on her arm, which was now covered in chill bumps.

Looking around the office she wondered what else she might find. She rummaged around on the desk, trying to find a secret compartment. No luck.

Then she slowly walked along the paneled walls carefully looking for any hiding places. She stopped when she felt a slight breeze cross her face, causing a long strand of hair to flutter in her eyes. She tucked it behind her ear as she looked at the wall behind the case and saw what she thought might be a hidden door.

She walked around the case to run her hand over the panel. *Wait,* she thought as she felt a groove in the paneling. *There's a door.* She knew she shouldn't open it but her curiosity took over. She placed both hands on the panel and pushed. The door creaked softly as it swung open.

Skylee wished Will had come with her, but after the scene she had just made he would probably be mad at her for a long while. She felt on the inside wall for a light switch but couldn't find one. She frowned, and then glanced down, noticing a flashlight leaning against the backside of the glass case. Without taking time to think she grabbed it, turned it on and stepped through the doorway.

Slowly, she shone the beam of light around the room until she came to a wall lined with maps. She stepped closer to get a better look. The largest one was a world atlas with black arrows placed in various locations all pointing west. She ran her fingers over the arrows as they passed through Japan, Africa, Italy, Washington D.C., up to Canada, and finally to California. She realized that it was the direction of the crack on The Day.

A second map of New Zealand hung just to the right. Several places were circled but she couldn't make sense of it. There was a large x on the South Island near Picton. Another smaller map displayed a series of small islands. Two of the islands had an x marked over them. *Could one of these be the island that disappeared?* she thought.

The eerie stillness of the room made her think of all the scary movies she had watched. *Why does Zane have all this stuff?* she wondered. She needed to quickly find out as much as she could and get out before she got caught. As she hastily turned around, she slammed her thigh into a desk.

"Ow!" she said much louder than she meant to, listening to hear if anyone was coming.

With nothing but silence radiating from the office area, she scanned the desk. Setting the flashlight down, she quickly shuffled through the cluttered paperwork. As she looked down her eyes followed the beam of light. It spotlighted the opposite wall, revealing a large board covered in papers and photos. *They look familiar.* Stepping in to get a closer look, she heard the front door open and close.

Stunned, she hurried to get the flashlight and succeeded in turning it off, but accidently dropped it on the floor. Footsteps echoed from the hallway so she ran out of the secret door, turning off the light in the glass case as she went. There was no time to pick up the flashlight, but she hoped everything else was in place as she ran toward the door, looking back. Which was why she didn't notice Zane until she slammed right into him.

"Whoa," he said as he caught Skylee before she fell back after bouncing off him. "What are you doing here?"

Skylee stammered, "I...I...the holo-fax—couldn't find it. I was looking for the projector," she scanned her brain for anything to say. "And then...I thought I saw a big spider."

Zane let out a huge laugh and let her go. As he stepped past her, his eyes passed over the room stopping on the glass case. She held her breath, hoping he didn't notice anything out of place.

"Spider, where?" he asked with furrowed brows as he slowly turned back to her.

She swallowed hard and said, "It was over there...by that glass case. I was trying to find the holo-fax and..." Everything inside her screamed, *RUN*.

"You probably scared it back into hiding. No wonder you couldn't find the projector. It's covered with these printouts," Zane said in a grumpy tone, removing the papers to reveal it. "I really miss my wife, she keeps things a bit neater than I do." He turned on the projector and a large 3D image appeared, rotating in circles. Zane touched the image and in a few seconds one of Skylee's teachers appeared. "Yours?"

Skylee looked at her science teacher and said, "Yes." She pulled her V-phone out of her pocket and placed it in the download slot. After her assignment was loaded she grabbed her V-phone and backed toward the door. Then she paused and said, "Zane?"

"Yeah," he answered without looking up at her.

"Thanks for letting me use your projector."

"Um-hum," mumbled Zane as he leaned against his desk.

"Ah, I hope you didn't mind me coming in here without permission," said Skylee, trying to calm herself down.

Zane raised his eyebrows, smiled and said, "No harm done."

"Okay, thanks again." As she turned to go, she caught his expression. His smile had been replaced by a scowl. And even worse his eyes were fixed in the direction of the secret office. Skylee stumbled against the doorjamb as she rushed out.

Walking as quickly as possible she made her way down the hallway and out the front door. Within seconds she was inside the cottage, tiptoeing towards her room. She leaned against her door for a long time, needing to clear her mind in case her stepsister was awake. But all she could think of was what she had seen in Zane's office. *What's he doing with all that stuff...and those knives? Who needs that many?* It made her skin crawl. She eased into her room and turned on the lamp by her bed. She was relieved to see Chrism was sleeping. As she sat down on her bed, she touched the bandage on her arm. *Man! He could've caught me snooping around,* she thought, letting out a long sigh.

In all the excitement, she had almost forgotten about her scene with Will. He would never have gone in there on the spur of the moment like she had. He always had to have a plan of action. She smiled and tried to convince herself that she and Will would be fine. Maybe she had misread his actions. Maybe he really wasn't trying to kiss her. *Yeah right, he was just practicing his CPR,* she thought. Of course, he had tried to kiss her. *I'll just deal with him later. Right now I need to check my Humusara.*

Skylee quietly grabbed her backpack, but she suddenly dropped it on the floor as she remembered leaving the flashlight in Zane's secret room.

"Oh crap!" she exclaimed, jumping up.

"Stop making all that noise," muttered Chrism, rolling over to face the wall.

"I'm not...you're dreaming," she whispered in a high singsong voice.

She stood perfectly still, staring down at her stepsister until she was sure she had gone back to sleep. Then she crept over to the door and gripped the doorknob. *What am I doing? I can't go back in there now,* she told herself, letting it go.

Skylee sneaked back over to her bed and sat down, resting her head in her hands. *Maybe I'll luck out and Zane won't notice the flashlight.* Sooner or later she knew she would have to go back to Zane's office and check on it.

She reached into her backpack grabbing her Humusara and her father's note fell to the floor. As she picked it up her thoughts returned to the strange encounter with Shelley. She quietly rummaged through the nightstand for a pen. Opening the note, she tried to remember all that Shelley had said so she could fill in the missing words.

She read the first line and wrote...*destiny*...that much she had figured out on her own. Moving on, she read the next line. *In life you may shed tears but not a*—her mind went blank. Shaking her head, she continued to the last line. *I have great hope in you and I will wa*—she held her pen on an empty space below the sentence willing the words to come back to her...*watch over you from a far*. She smiled briefly but then furrowed her brows as she struggled to remember the still missing words.

Frustrated that she couldn't recall them, she turned to her Humusara for answers. She laid the book open near its center and waited for it to speak to her. A light gust of wind blew through the room and the pages of the book quickly fanned, coming to rest on the first page. Skylee was surprised to see the once ancient lettering transform to readable text...

> *I. Behold, The Creator hath brought forth a separate*
> *set of beings called Primortus.*
> *II. The twelve Primortus are one and shall protect*
> *and defend the Earth.*
> *III. The Primortus world shall remain hidden*
> *from humankind.*

Ann had told her there were rules and here it was again about keeping it secret. She read on...

> *IV. Each Primortus shall bear only one child. Unto this heir the*
> *Task and Elementum is bestowed. No Primortus shall*
> *be born with a double portion of power.*
> *V. Year ten and five begins the right of passage. This shall be*
> *called the Heritus. At the beginning of the Heritus the*
> *parent shall bequeath the Elementum to the*
> *young Primortus. During the Heritus the elder Primortus*
> *shall thus begin transformation into Provectus Primortus.*
> *The young Primortus shall learn to wield the power of the*
> *Elementum under the counsel of the Elder Primortus.*
> *After one year of training The Heritus shall be fulfilled.*

Heritus, that was a word Ann had used. Skylee sighed heavily, she wasn't fifteen, and yet she had come into her power. She placed the Elementum back around her neck and smiled as she examined it. It was exquisite in design. She could barely believe it was hers. She looked down at the Humusara. It had returned to its new self and the indecipherable scribbling was back. With a soft sigh she closed the book realizing she couldn't remember all she had read. But one thing stood out in her mind. Each Primortus shall bear only one child. *Maybe that's why I'm an abomination of nature.* She was reminded of something Hera had said about a child who shouldn't have been possible.

"Ah," she softly gasped as an orb of light suddenly rose from her Elementum.

The light spun around revealing the four symbols on her necklace. All at once, it shot right into her chest causing her to fall back on the bed. The pain hit her hard but quickly eased as a cool breeze wafted over her, making the hair on her arms stand up. She managed to sit up, rubbing her arms to warm them as she looked to see if the window was opened. Then she heard water dripping as the small lamp on her side table flickered and went out. Her eyes widened as she felt the bed under her grow cold. She swallowed and placed her hands to her sides, feeling the surface of the bed cooling. Looking down, she found that she was no longer sitting on the bed but on a large stone.

A light spread out around her and revealed the once painted walls were now rock. She stood straight up and turned quickly around. Skylee was in a cave and Chrism was nowhere to be found. A fire roared from the center and thirteen figures stood around it. She watched as the one that was brighter than the others gave each of them two items, a book, and an amulet.

Skylee shook her head in disbelief but the scene did not change. *What's going on*? she asked herself, watching them in confusion. As each figure around the fire received a book and amulet they bowed and disappeared. Then the Brightest One turned to face her with an outstretched hand.

To her surprise she wasn't afraid. She reached out and he placed something heavy in her hand. She gazed down and saw that she held a miniature globe. As the earth rotated in her palm, she saw strange etchings appear, four in total. Then the symbols dissolved and a forked path appeared in their place.

"I don't understand," she said.

The Brightest smiled solemnly and when he spoke his voice was strong but gentle, "There are two paths before you, one leads to life and the other to death."

Skylee's face went pale. "How will I know which one leads to life?"

"The choice is in your hands. When the time comes you will know."

"But..." she looked up and he was gone. She was alone in the cave. All that remained was the glowing fire and the small earth still rotating in her hand.

Without warning, a sharp pain struck her as the orb flew out of her chest and back onto the Elementum. She closed her eyes, rubbing the skin beneath her necklace as she sat down. When she opened them again, she was back in her room. She looked over at Chrism, who had curled up in a ball under the bed covers and was snoring loudly. She sat motionless on her bed. Then she felt something in her hand and slowly looked to find that her Elementum rested in her palm. She held it close to her heart feeling overwhelmed. *The carvings,* she thought, holding it out to look at them. *They're just like the ones I saw.*

This vision was completely different than the others. She still felt the dampness of the cave. Her heart skipped a beat as she realized the one that spoke to her could have been the Creator. *Could it have been real?*

She suddenly found herself wishing that Will had been with her for a couple of reasons. One, it might help him understand how important their power was. And two, he could give her his opinion on what it all meant. She sent him a text, hoping he was still awake. Then she held the book close to her chest and laid back on her bed waiting for him to reply. Sometime later she drifted off to sleep.

She woke the next morning still holding the Humusara. Her first thought was that she needed to tell Ann what had happened. She got dressed and headed down the hallway. On her way to Ann's room she heard voices from the direction of the kitchen. She watched as her mom, stepdad, Drake and Carmen headed out the back door.

As soon as they left Skylee went to the dining room table, which was covered with folders, maps, and stacks of papers. *I seem to have a new hobby...snooping,* she thought as she picked up an evidence bag and examined its contents. Inside was a charred writing pen. *This must be the one they found in the wreckage,* she thought, holding it up to examine it for a moment. As she placed it back in the bag she noticed a single piece of folded paper inside. She opened and scanned it quickly.

"Unidentifiable, partial print...hmm?" she said to herself. Then she read on, barely above a whisper, "Analysis of writing pen...recovered at scene...crafted from silver and stainless steel with a brass ball-point." *So it was expensive.* "Circular carving appears to be a company logo or possibly engraved initials with one of the symbols resembling an S. Unable to determine origin due to damage sustained in fire. Huh, odd."

She folded the document, returned it to the bag, and ran her fingers over the stacks of papers as she walked around the table. She couldn't believe GEMA was still using paperwork in this day and age. It was probably a throw back to The Day, when the government lost a lot of electronic information. Then a particular file caught her eye. It was labeled Ashley Hayes. Tossing the bag aside, she looked around the room, and opened the folder. The top of the page said.

Name: Ashley Hayes
Male in mid-forties - DNA confirms
Identifying characteristics: none
Fingerprints surgically erased

So he's a man, she thought. Even after her close encounter with him, she hadn't been sure. The report also revealed that Ashley Hayes was not his real name. However, the G- file agents had not been able to find out his true identity. *No fingerprints...*Skylee wondered whose print was on the pen.

According to the report, during his questioning, Ashley had rambled on and on about destroying the earth. He also said that a man was dead. Ashley's quote was written down as, "Clark saw too much, so now Jack's ash."

Jack Clark...Oh, no that's the man that Shelley knew. Skylee closed the folder and as she laid it down on the table, she bumped the computer and it came to life, displaying a hologram of a newspaper article. She stared at it for a moment, and then read softly.

"Good Samaritan Killed. Man found dead on Hawthormden Drive. The body was burnt beyond recognition. Several witnesses reported seeing a car parked on the shoulder of the road with its hood raised. According to the eyewitnesses a motorcyclist slowed down and stopped. He dismounted his bike and headed toward the vehicle. The witnesses stated that the motorcycle driver suddenly burst into flames. Then they saw a red haired man run to the car, close the hood and drive away."

Skylee felt nauseous and her knees wobbled. She sat down with her arms crossed over her stomach. She remembered hearing that Mr. Clark had seen someone on the island before it sank. Her thoughts rushed together...the island vanishing...life being destroyed...*Is this why I'm here?* she asked herself. She quickly stood up and ran out of the room just as her mom and the others came back into the house.

Skylee rubbed her head as she headed toward her room. Her mind was jumbled with too many thoughts to talk to Ann right away. She knew deep inside her that it was all connected. Her thoughts were interrupted when she found Will and Chrism talking in the hallway.

"What are you two doing?" asked Skylee.

"Trying to decide what to do today. It seems like we've been at this farm forever," complained Chrism.

"Too long, maybe," agreed Will.

Skylee noticed he barely looked at her. She knew he was still upset with her about last night. She longed to tell him all the things she'd learned and what she had just found out. She started to say something but Chrism stopped her.

"Now, don't go all saintly on us. You've got to admit that spending all our time on a sheep farm is not what we thought this trip would be," said Chrism. "On second thought, you probably like being stuck here with a bunch of animals."

Skylee waited for Will to tell Chrism to back off but he was silent. She looked at him, and then dropped her gaze to the floor, feeling more alone than ever. For the first time she could remember Will didn't take up for her.

"G'day," said Airon as he strutted down the hall. He put his arm casually around Skylee's shoulder. "What's this face for, Skippy?"

"My name's not Skippy!" she snapped, shoving Airon's arm away as she glared at him.

"Clearly not," Airon said with raised eyebrows. "A bit touchy today?"

Skylee knew she shouldn't have taken it out on him. She really didn't mind that Airon called her Skippy. She was just confused and hurt at Will's behavior. And of course, the information she had just found out from the GEMA documents still had her thoughts racing.

"Sorry, Airon, I...shouldn't...I..." Skylee stuttered.

"No worries, we all have our moments," Airon replied kindly. "So, who's up for some boatin' today?"

"I am—wait—what kind of boating?" asked Chrism.

"Canoes," said Airon excitedly. "Zane helped me bring 'em down yesterday. C'mon...let's get goin'. It'll be an adventure."

"I'm in," Will said. "Well Chrism, you were wanting off the farm and technically, you will be—in a boat on water."

"Okay, I guess it's sorta off the farm," said her stepsister.

"Skippy?" Airon said with raised eyebrows. "Up for an adventure?"

Airon and Chrism looked at her and waited for an answer. She glanced at Will hoping he would ask her to go, but he didn't even look in her direction. She felt a knot form in her chest.

Airon's brow furrowed, he leaned in slightly and whispered, "Come on, Skippy, it won't be as much fun without ya, eh." It wasn't often that Airon showed tenderness and when he did, it was hard to resist.

"Okay," she said barely above a whisper.

"Splendid," said Airon, swatting Skylee on the arm. The tender moment turned to jesting as he whispered, "Maybe this time ya'll stay in the boat and not under it."

Skylee let out a loud sigh as she remembered the one time, well maybe two, that she fell out of the boat. Airon seemed to remember everything. She was glad no one else heard him.

As the four of them headed to the boat ramp, Skylee felt invisible. Airon and Chrism were walking up front, discussing the correct way to paddle a canoe. Will walked an arm's length away but he still hadn't said a word to her.

As soon as they reached the lake Airon jumped in a canoe with Chrism leaving Will to share with Skylee. She noticed he was hesitant at first but in the end, Will pulled the other canoe into the water and motioned for her to join him. By midday, he started talking to her again.

As Skylee paddled in sync with him, she felt happier with each stroke. She gazed across the smooth water at Chrism and Airon, who were laughing and joking with each other as they floated along. Airon even let Chrism go on and on about Lord of the Rings without ever making fun of her. At one point, Skylee thought a war might break out when Airon splashed water on Chrism but she just sneered at him and splashed him back.

Once they were back at the farm, they tied off the canoes and headed back to the cottage. Airon and Chrism chatted away as they walked ahead of Skylee and Will.

"Hey," Will said as he placed a hand on her arm. "About yesterday, I'm sorry, I know you've had a lot to deal with and I mean I still think we should talk but I don't want to push."

"It's okay, really, it took me by surprise and—" she paused wanting to tell him she felt the same way. "I just don't want anything to ruin our friendship. You're my best friend."

Will smiled and said, "So you're not mad at me, huh?"

"No, I'm not," Skylee paused as a debate went on in her head about mentioning Zane's office and the vision. "Can I tell you something without making you mad?"

"About the Primortus?" he said turning to stare out at the water.

"Yeah, I had another vision," she softly spoke as her voice cracked.

"Okay," Will said, turning to look at her. "What was it about?"

Skylee told him everything as he listened closely and never said a word.

"Well, what do you think?" she asked anxiously.

Faint lines showed up on Will's forehead. "It seems that the symbols mean something, maybe each one represents a different power. Mum did say something about the necklace connecting us to our power and the book connects us to the earth," he said. "And the paths, well, everyone has to choose a path to go down."

Skylee sighed loudly and sat down abruptly on the ground. She leaned forward and rested her head on her knees. Her stomach churned when Will's leg touched hers as he sat down. From the corner of her eye she saw him reach out to touch her. His hand paused briefly, and then dropped down to pick up a twig instead. She felt a pang of disappointment.

"Sky?" he said in a concerned voice. "You okay?"

Skylee lifted her head. With one small tear streaming down her cheek she said, "What if I choose wrong?"

NINETEEN

⌇⫤ ⅄ ⺕ ⫿

The Stinking Wonderland

The next morning Skylee woke up feeling better than she had in quite some time. Actually, she felt like a weight had been lifted off her shoulders since talking to Will. And his reaction had surprised her. Instead of arguing about her safety or telling her what to do he had simply listened.

They had spent a long time discussing a variety of topics including her mom's investigation, Chrism being a shape-shifter, and the two prophesies. She hadn't been brave enough to tell him about snooping around in Zane's secret office, but she planned to. Skylee smiled as she brushed through her tangled hair, remembering how supportive he had been. He even referred to the Primortus as "their calling."

Unfortunately, she still hadn't found the right time to talk to Ann. In truth, seeing the report of Jack Clark's death had shook her up so much she had wanted to avoid the whole thing.

After breakfast, Skylee and the entire group, with the exception of Shelley, headed toward Wai-O-Tapu, a thermal wonderland near Rotorua. In the last two days, Shelley had not been at the farm. Actually they hadn't spoken a word since she had gone all zombie on her in the bathroom. Her absence made Skylee wonder what else she was hiding.

The trip to Wai-O-Tapu was the first time they had ventured away from Cook's Farm since her mom's attack. Her parents probably believed they were no longer in danger since Ashley Hayes was in jail. Skylee wished that were true, but now she knew Brinfrost was out there and he wanted her Elementum.

Even so, she was glad Zane had suggested the excursion. She wanted to see more of New Zealand and was particularly excited to go to the nature park. Zane had told them the area was a lot like Yellowstone National Park. He explained that Wai-O-Tapu means sacred water, named for the park's colorful pools that were formed by volcanic activity. And he said it had reopened five years after The Day.

Skylee propped her elbow on the armrest of her chair and rested her chin in her hand. She gazed out of the window, watching the scenery pass by in a blur as if seeing it with a remote on fast-forward. Her thoughts drifted back to the night Will had tried to kiss her. She began arguing with herself, wrestling back and forth, whether it would change their relationship for better or for worse. *It would only complicate matters,* she told herself. *I can't risk losing my best friend. But he's more than that,* another part of her mind insisted. *He's Primortus. Maybe it's meant to be. Ugh...when did I turn into such a sap.*

Skylee felt Will scoot over in his seat, closer to her. Even though her stomach tightened, she turned and gave him a bright smile.

"Are you hearing this?" he whispered as he nodded his head in Airon and Chrism's direction.

"No," said Skylee, tucking a stray wisp of hair behind her ear. "What's up with them?"

"They're like Jekyll and Hyde, one minute they're fighting and the next they're like this," Will said shaking his head.

Skylee watched as Airon flirted with her stepsister. The look on his face reminded her of the summer when he and Will had stayed at her house while Ann was on location somewhere in Africa. Airon had all the girls in her neighborhood wrapped around his little finger. They followed him around like a bunch of lovesick puppies. Not a single girl had been able to resist his charm.

Grinning broadly, Skylee watched as he used that same smooth charm on her stepsister. Of course, Chrism had attracted more than her fair share of male admirers or at least that was what she told her. Maybe Airon had finally met his match. She couldn't help but giggle as she looked over at them. It was nice to see the two of them getting along.

Skylee slid over towards Will until their heads nearly touched. She spoke barely above a whisper, "I guess we better enjoy this while we can. Who knows when they'll start fighting again?"

"No telling," chuckled Will.

"Hey, I was able to read some more from the Humusara last night." Skylee looked around to make sure no one was listening. "I wish you had seen it."

"More visions?" he asked in an uneasy tone.

"No, but it showed me these pictures...they were like drawings of the Elementum," she continued on as he nodded slowly. "Remember the night I had that vision of the first Primortus and those symbols appeared?"

"The carvings, like on the Elementum," he said.

"Yes, well last night the Humusara explained what the symbols mean."

"All right," Will said, looking at Skylee eagerly as he waited for her to respond. "And?"

"You really want to know?"

"Believe it or not, yes," he said, sounding sincere.

"Okay," she said, glancing at Airon and Chrism, who were still deep in conversation. She then pulled out her necklace and pointed to a symbol on the right side of its face. "This means fire."

"Bloody oath, of course. It looks a bit like flames," he said softly.

"I know. And this one to the left, it's air, and here's earth, and water," she said excitedly as she pointed at each symbol.

"I see...and did you find out what the inscription on the back says?"

Skylee gave him a huge grin. Her face lit up as she said, "Yes, it says Protect Life."

"Protect life," echoed Will, looking at her Elementum. "Makes sense."

"This might sound crazy but I've always felt..." she stopped and searched around for the right word. "...a connection with the earth, always," she said feeling apprehensive about what Will would say.

He reached out and touched her Elementum. "My mum told me the same thing about herself the other night."

"So, you and your mom are talking about it?" she asked, somewhat surprised.

"We're talking. That's not to say I agree with it, but..." Will's voice faded.

"I know but it's good you're thinking about it."

The auto-glider suddenly lurched, throwing them forward in their seatbelts. Will protectively held his arm out to hold Skylee back in her seat. They paused there for a second with their faces close together.

"Here we are," Zane belted out at the top of his voice, causing Skylee to jump in surprise as Will nervously looked at him.

As they pulled into a large parking lot, Skylee quickly tucked her necklace under her shirt. She looked around at the variety of trees, which surrounded the lot and the adjacent buildings. There were a few larger ones that had obviously survived The Day while most were new growth.

"Why aren't we getting out?" Chrism asked impatiently.

Skylee's mom, who was wearing a huge green hat with silk flowers around the rim, turned around in her seat. "Your dad and I are going to get the tickets. So everyone just hang tight till we get back."

As her parents got out and started to walk away, Alex abruptly stopped and pulled her mom into a long kiss. Skylee looked away and sank down into her seat.

"That is just disgusting," Chrism said, squinching up her nose. "Do they have to do that out in public?"

"They're newlyweds," said Ann. "It's to be expected."

"Well, it's totally sick—Hey, is there a lot of walking here?" Chrism asked, rolling her eyes as she looked out of the window at her parents, who had stopped kissing and were now holding hands.

"It's a nature park...as in nature trails," replied Ann with a droll look.

Airon laughed under his breath. "Yeah, Duchess, how can ya not know that, eh? We were talkin' about it at dinner last night, how it's like a walkabout."

"I wasn't listening to that conversation," she said as she pulled a compact from her purse.

Airon shook his head as he watched her apply more lipstick. Then he glanced down at her feet and said, "Yer always wearin' the wrong shoes."

Skylee chuckled as Chrism gave him a dismissive look and continued to put on her lipstick.

"Do ya own any normal shoes?" he asked.

Chrism looked down at her boots and smiled. "You know, these are normal."

"Not for hikin', those are nice, they make yer legs look—" Airon stopped and shook his head. "Ya need real boots for an outin' like this."

"These *are* real boots," she said as she stuffed her makeup back into her purse and turned to face him. "Just because you're fashion challenged doesn't give you the right to criticize my shoes. You know, I paid a lot of money for these."

"I don't care if ya gave yer kidney, they're still not for hikin', they're just ants pants," he said dismissively.

"What on earth are ants pants?" mumbled Chrism.

"Oh, it's an Aussie term," said Will, laughing slightly. "Airon's way of saying your shoes might be the height of fashion but not practical."

Chrism groaned, made an exasperated face and turned to look out of the window.

Skylee noticed Will open his mouth, probably to make a sarcastic comment, but with a look of warning from Airon he snapped it shut.

For the next few minutes they all lapsed into thoughtful silence. Skylee found her mind wandering back to the Maori village and her talk with Hera. *Maybe she's wrong,* she wistfully thought. *Maybe I'm not the second born.* As much as she tried to convince herself she could feel the truth in her soul. And sooner or later she would have to face it. She looked over at Will who seemed to be deeply immersed in his own thoughts.

"This is gonna be fun, eh? Hey, Chief, ya listenin' teh me?" Airon asked as he waved his hand in front of Will's face.

"I am now," he replied.

"Do ya know if there are any caves that we can explore at this park? I feel the need for some adventure." Airon extended his arms, clasped his fingers together and cracked his knuckles.

"Adventure!" Chrism said loudly. "Are you crazy...wasn't the wonderful 'lets drag my stepmom off and burn up my dad' enough adventure for you?"

Airon turned slowly to her. "Duchess, I don't consider that an adventure. I'm talkin' about fun, somethin' ya could use a little of, I believe."

Chrism lifted her chin defiantly. "You wouldn't know fun if it bit you in the—"

"Hey!" interrupted Ann, snapping her head around to give her the evil eye before turning to look outside.

Skylee watched in silence as her stepsister's face turned a bright shade of pink. Then Chrism huffed loudly, looked at Airon and said, "I read the brochure on this place, and I didn't see anything about exploring caves, so you'll just have to deal with it."

"Well of course ya read the brochure," Airon said, smirking.

"Yes, unlike you, I like to be well-informed," Chrism smugly said. "So no, there isn't a cave to explore, but there are places that you'll be familiar with."

"What's that, Duchess?" he inquired with raised eyebrows.

"Oh you know, 'Devil's Home', 'Devil's Ink Pots', 'Sulfur Mounds'...oh and I guess there is a cave...'Devil's Cave'..." Chrism's voice faded as Airon moved closer and gazed into her eyes.

"What are ya trying to say, that I'm a devil?" he smoothly asked.

Chrism looked flustered. "I...well...maybe..."

Before she could finish her muttering, Skylee's mom and stepdad returned with the tickets. Everyone piled out of the vehicle and entered the park. As they started toward the walking trail, Ann insisted on stopping to take a group picture. While lining up for the photo, Skylee noticed her stepsister had chosen to stand very close to Airon.

Once on the trail, Skylee glanced around and found that Will, Airon, and Zane were in a conversation about cave exploring.

"Spelunking is the correct term," Zane insisted in his deep booming voice.

Airon punched Will's shoulder. "We're spelunkers, mate."

"No you're the spelunker. I prefer to think of myself as a cave dweller," said Will.

And on it went as usual with the two of them trying to one up each other. Skylee smiled as she continued on.

"Munchkin..." her mom called out in a sing-song voice. "We're going to stop here for a minute so Ann can take some pictures of us. Don't get too far away."

"I won't," Skylee called back as she headed down the trail, slowing slightly. She looked back and grinned when she spotted her stepdad pick her mom up for one of those classic newlywed poses.

Skylee's brief moment of happiness faded as she watched Chrism approach her with a mixed expression of fury and determination on her face. It seemed like a good idea to put some distance between them so Skylee picked up her pace. Chrism followed suit and with a great amount of effort she managed to close in on her.

"Skylee—Sky—Skippy, wait up," she flippantly said, struggling along on her spiked heels.

"Don't call me that," she demanded, still moving along, although not as quickly.

Chrism, who now was walking right beside her, laughed sarcastically, "Fine, you know I have a bone to pick with you."

"Really, what is it now? I got a speck of dirt on your purse?"

"No, I mean, what—you got dirt on my purse?" she paused briefly and examined it.

"No, geez," Skylee said, shaking her head.

Chrism hurried to catch up, waddling in her tall boots. "It's about the blouse that you ruined, you know, it's one of my favorites."

"I said I was sorry," Skylee walked faster trying to put more space between them. She suddenly realized that if her stepsister got too upset she might shift in front of everyone. "You know, it wasn't like I meant to stain it. Anyway, mom said she would buy you a new shirt."

"It's a blouse, not a shirt and she can't replace it. My mom gave it to me the last time I saw her." Chrism's voice grew louder.

Skylee stopped abruptly and her stepsister nearly collided with her. "What do you want me to do? I can't just make the stain go away. I tried everything I could think of, I'm sorry!"

"The way you're saying that makes me think you aren't really sorry."

"Maybe because I've been saying it repeatedly for days."

Skylee waited momentarily for a response, and then continued down the trail. As they walked on in silence, she breathed a sigh of relief, hoping the subject had finally been dropped.

Slowing down her pace, she glanced back at Chrism, who now looked miserable. "What's really upsetting you?" she asked with a sigh.

"You lied to me."

"What are you talking about?" asked Skylee in total confusion.

"You said that you and Will were just good friends but there's more to it than that, isn't there?"

Again Skylee glanced back as she continued to keep a few steps ahead of her. *Did she see Will try to kiss me?* She wasn't ready to discuss it with anyone, especially not her stepsister.

"Hold it," Chrism ordered, grabbing her by the arm.

"Ouch!" Skylee cried as she pulled away. Then the pain from her injured arm caused her to snap. "That hurt! Why did you do that?"

"Sorry," she whispered as sadness filled her eyes. "I didn't mean to hurt you, really I didn't...but you aren't answering any of my questions. And I just wanted to get your attention."

"Well, you have it now," she said, rubbing her scar.

Chrism shook her head. "I don't understand why you won't talk to me. We're sisters or at least I'm trying to be."

Skylee heard the sincerity in her voice and thought she might actually be able to discuss the dilemma over Will with her. After all, Chrism herself seemed to be having mixed feelings for Airon, so maybe she would understand. The thought had barely crossed her mind when all of a sudden Chrism's face scrunched up in a look of disgust.

"What is that gawd awful smell?" she complained as she cupped her hands over her mouth and nose.

"It's sulfur."

"That is disgusting. I hope it doesn't seep into my pores or anyone else's for that matter. I would hate to have to travel with a bunch of smelly people."

"Well, if we all smell the same you won't be able to tell," Skylee said as she started walking down the path again.

"Skylee!"

"What?" she barked in total frustration. "What do you want?"

"An answer! Are you and Will like 'together'?"

The two of them had turned a corner in the path and were now out of sight from everyone else.

"I can't tell you," Skylee said. "Cause I don't know for sure. Besides why do you need to know? He's younger than you and I thought you and Airon—"

"That's not really an answer and okay, Will is younger but only by a year and well Airon and me—I'm not sure about that...yet."

Man, she's got nerve, thought Skylee, trying hard not to roll her eyes at her. "Can we talk about this later?" she said, looking up the trail to see her parents and Ann, who were being closely followed by Will, Airon and Zane.

Chrism glanced over her shoulder at them and said, "Okay for now, but we're not finished with this discussion."

For the next thirty minutes they followed trail number one, which looped back to the entrance. They stopped now and then to gaze at the thermal pools and craters along the way. Skylee had never imagined such a strangely beautiful place. Once they reached the entrance again, they loaded back into the auto glider and headed for a presentation about the effects of The Day on the park's thermal activity.

It was mid-morning by the time they gathered on a large wooden platform. It overlooked a small formation that reminded Skylee of a miniature volcano. Several tourists stood around talking. A few of them stared at her and exchanged hushed whispers. Deciding to ignore their "Sky Tower Girl" comments, she stepped up to the railing. A three dimensional sign displayed...

**Lady Knox Geyser
once active
lies dormant
in the wake of
The Day.**

"Okay, we walked all the way over here to see a hole in the ground," said Chrism as she walked to the other side of Skylee. "Is it going to do anything?"

"No, didn't you read about this in your brochure?"

"I might have," she said with an unconcerned shrug.

"Look, the sign says the geyser has been dormant since The Day. I would've loved to see it erupt. When I was studying for one of my science projects, I read that the park attendants used to put soap in it to make it erupt," Skylee said in excitement as she thought about her project.

"So, are they going to do that now? If not, it seems like a long way to walk to just stand here and stare at a hole," said Chrism in an irritated tone as she shuffled her feet, and then took turns standing on one high heeled boot at a time.

"I don't think the soap works anymore, thus the word *dormant*," Skylee said, holding up her fingers to form quotation marks with her last word.

Her stepsister looked away. "This is boring," she huffed, checking her V-phone.

"So what do you want? Do you think that I can just say ERUPT and it'll happen?" As soon as Skylee said the words, the ground began to rumble.

"What is that?" Chrism tightened her grip on the railing and looked down at her feet.

"I don't know," Skylee said quietly.

All of a sudden, Lady Knox spewed forth a huge geyser, spurting high into the air. Skylee's eyes widened as she took a step back. The other tourists in the area ran to the viewing platform and watched in amazement.

"Wow," Skylee said as she looked up at the geyser that was now gushing more rapidly.

"I thought you said it was dormant," Chrism said in disbelief.

"It has been," said Skylee as she focused on the geyser. Then it hit her. Maybe she had caused it. She had called for an eruption and that's exactly what happened. A heartfelt smile crossed her face.

"Okay, enough of this," said Chrism as she grasped Skylee's hand and pulled her away from the crowd, which was quickly gathering around the geyser.

Skylee looked at Will and the rest of their group, who were all gazing up at it. "Wait," she insisted. "I want to watch—Chrism—What are you doing? This is historic. Stop!" She felt Chrism's grip tighten on her hand as she pulled her away from the crowd, to a clearing in the forest.

The second they stopped Chrism started in on her. "Level with me about you and Will," she demanded. "I know something is going on, with all the sneaking off to talk in dark corners."

"Chrism, I'm missing it! What is so important about Will and me? Besides it looks like you're interested in Airon."

Her stepsister frowned and placed her hands on her hips. She rocked back and forth on her spiked heels, and then said, "That's not the point."

"Really, so you want both of them?"

"Yes...well...no...I like Airon. I mean Will, darn it! I meant to say Will," stuttered Chrism, suddenly looking flustered.

Skylee felt like laughing. "Well, who is it, Will or Airon?" she asked impatiently.

Chrism glared at her and blurted out, "Fine, all right, I do like Airon. But if you tell him that I swear..."

"You'll what, talk me to death. I can't believe you dragged me over here for that."

"Actually, I just want to know what's going on. I mean, really, Will isn't my type. You know, he chews on his lip and I can't kiss a guy that chews his lips. He's too polite and the only time he talks is when he's speaking up for you. He doesn't really dress for my taste either. And he should do something with his hair—"

"Will's nice looking," Skylee interrupted defensively.

"Look at the way he dresses, vintage shirts! That is so not in right now. Oh and his nose, has he broken that before?" Chrism continued, "I think he may be a little slow, I mean, has he even kissed you yet?"

"That is none of your business," said Skylee through gritted teeth.

"Of course he hasn't, because he is either too slow or he doesn't think of you that way. I mean you are younger than him. He might really just see you as a child, a little sister—like Airon does."

"Do me a favor and shut up," demanded Skylee feeling her face grow hot.

"I'm just being honest," she continued with her list of things about Will that didn't interest her anymore.

Skylee had never resorted to violence before but Chrism was making her consider it. The past week had worn her down, and she wanted to blurt out that Will had tried to kiss her. That would shut her up or maybe it would just make her go on and on some more.

"Give it a rest," said Skylee angrily. "I don't...I don't want to talk about Will with you or anyone. I can't believe you dragged me away from the geyser to badger me about him. Don't you understand what a miracle it is, that it erupted?"

Chrism cocked her jaw and said in a very precise tone, "I don't care about the stinking geyser! Just admit it, you like Will!"

"Please, let it go—I just—let it go."

"Why can't you give me an answer? I mean it's an easy one, really, or maybe you're too young to realize..."

Skylee had heard enough. She couldn't stand there another second listening to her cruel words. She glared at her and screamed, "Chrism, CHILL OUT!"

As Skylee turned to walk away she was shocked by the sudden silence. She peeked over her shoulder, wondering if her stepsister was sneaking up behind her. What she saw horrified her.

Her stepsister stood before her frozen in a thick layer of ice.

TWENTY

The Frozen Bear

"Chrism!" Skylee rushed back to her. "Oh, no, no, what did I do?"

Skylee let out a short high-pitched scream as she gazed inside and saw Chrism's motionless face. Placing her hands on the solid ice, she looked closer and realized that she was covered in something that looked like fur.

Will came running into the clearing. "Sky, what's wrong?" he called out as he quickly approached her.

"Help," she pleaded.

"What happened? We saw the geyser go off but..." his voice faltered as he did a double take at the chunk of ice. "Is that Chrism?"

"Yes! I was tired of hearing her gone on and on about—" she stopped and pointed to the frozen block that held her stepsister as a prisoner. "Oh, what have I done?"

Will started pounding on the ice. Skylee joined in and hoped that between the two of them, they could break Chrism out.

"Do you think she can breathe?" he asked, looking more closely at Chrism's frozen face.

"What? Hurry, Will, hurry," Skylee said desperately. "Chrism, hang on, please, hang on."

Skylee saw movement from the corner of her eye. Ann stepped into the clearing and looked around, Skylee waved at her, hoping she would see them. When their eyes met, Ann ran toward her.

"Will, your mom's here."

"That's good, cause I haven't made a dent in this ice," he said, still pounding away on the frozen block.

"We've got to do something!" Skylee said frantically.

"What's this?" Ann said as she jolted to a stop.

Glancing at Skylee, she pursed her lips in disapproval and placed her hands on the ice encasing Chrism. Then she spoke under her breath.

A warm breeze began to swirl around them, and as the ice melted Chrism fell to the ground. Skylee and Will exchanged shocked glances and then stared down at Chrism, who had shifted into a brown bear with the exception of her head.

"Ann," said Skylee her voice trembling with fear. "Is she all right, I mean..." her words faded as she watched in silence.

Ann didn't respond but continued to speak to Chrism softly. As the air grew warmer, Chrism's body began to return to normal.

Standing up, Ann surveyed the area, and said, "Will, get Chrism and head to that little clearing over there." Then she looked at Skylee. "I hope for your sake, that no one saw what just happened."

"I'm sorry, I-I didn't mean to do this."

"I know you didn't *mean* to," Ann said as she turned to face her. "But something like this isn't going to help your cause. They're watching you. How do you think it looks for you to use your power against your own sister, not to mention she's your Corporus?" Ann's expression changed from concern to frustration as her gaze locked on something behind Skylee.

Looking over her shoulder, Skylee locked eyes with Airon, who was standing there with his face set in stone. Then his eyes moved to Will as he led Chrism away.

"How long have you been standing there?" Ann asked. Airon just looked at her, saying nothing. After a brief pause, he turned and headed toward Will and Chrism. Ann reached out to stop him but he dodged her grasp. She exhaled loudly and called, "Airon."

"Do you think he saw?" asked Skylee.

"Of course, he saw," she said in an agitated tone. "Let's go, Chrism is going to be fine but now—she needs to be told."

Skylee followed Ann. Airon had already gathered Chrism in his arms to help warm her, along with wrapping her in his jacket. His face was still set in stone but his eyes were full of worry. Will stood over them, watching anxiously.

Ann knelt beside them. The air was still except for a small circle around Chrism. The warm breeze still swept over her body and carried a few leaves round and round. Finally her eyes fluttered opened.

"Is she all right?" asked Skylee worriedly.

"You're okay, just breathe." Ann said gently, griping Chrism's hand.

Chrism pointed to Skylee and whispered, "You...what..." her voice was ragged and barely audible.

Ann spoke in very calming tones. "Hey, look at me. That's right look at me. You're going to be fine. Just keep breathing, deep breaths," she said, demonstrating how to breathe in and out.

Chrism took deep breaths and closed her eyes. "What...happened?" she whispered.

"Just breathe," Ann spoke quietly, then turned and looked up at Skylee. "What did happen?"

"I didn't mean too. I never wanted to hurt her. It's just she was—" she stopped short as she glanced at Airon. His glare broke her resistance and tears flowed down her cheeks.

"Right, calm down, and tell me," Ann said as she rubbed one of Chrism's arms to help warm her.

"She was...she just kept asking about Will...and I didn't know what to say...I just wanted her to shut up and...I'm sorry, Chrism, I'm so sorry." Skylee wept.

"About Will, what would she want to know—never mind—not important right now," Ann quickly said as she looked up at Skylee and Will.

"She didn't mean to hurt her," he said, reaching out and pulling Skylee toward him. He patted her back gently as she sobbed uncontrollably into his chest.

Ann stood up. "I know she didn't mean to but she did. What if I hadn't been here? Chrism could have suffocated." Ann said matter-of-factly, then she leaned down and softly said, "Keep taking deep breaths, Chrism, you're going to be fine. Airon just keep that jacket wrapped around her."

Ann placed one hand on her hip and spoke directly to Skylee. "You have got to get a grip on your abilities. I have to say, quite impressive, the geyser, and now this. However, you have to remember that your emotions affect what happens around you. You can't just—"

Chrism interrupted as she grabbed Ann's pant leg and tugged. "Her abilities?" she whispered. "What are you talking about?" She looked up at Airon. "Do you know what she's talking about?"

Airon's expression was somber. He gave her a hug and spoke barely above a whisper, "I think she's going to try and explain."

"Right," Ann softly said, "I'm not sure where to start...but what you just experienced was Skylee's emotions run amuck."

"I don't understand, her emotions? How did her emotions turn me into an ice cube? You think you can really explain that?" Chrism stared at Ann incredulously.

Ann looked around. "Yes, I can. What you saw—uh, I just have to say that what I am about to tell you is secret and should not be repeated or discussed with anyone outside of this group. Can you keep it secret? I know that's a lot to ask but you'll understand once I tell you. So?"

"Sure," Chrism said as she glanced at Airon.

Airon's gaze went from Chrism to Will to Skylee and then slowly ended with Ann. He nodded in agreement.

Ann quickly explained about the Primortus world, only hitting the highlights. During her explanation Skylee slowly regained her composure. She watched as Chrism listened with her mouth half open and Airon looked as immobile as a marble bust.

"It's a lot to absorb, I know," Ann said. "Unfortunately there's more."

"More," Chrism said in a flabbergasted tone. "More about what?"

"Well, about you, Chrism."

"Wait, I'm not one am I?" she asked, looking somewhat like a child on Christmas morning. "I-I-I...what? I am?"

"No, you're not, but you do have a different power," said Skylee encouragingly, hoping to make Chrism less angry with her.

"That's right, you're not Primortus, you're," Ann said hesitantly. "You're a Corporus."

"That sounds disgusting," spat Chrism as she tried to sit up. "What kind of power do I have?"

"It's not disgusting," said Skylee. "I mean, as a Corporus your power can change you into anything."

"What?" exclaimed Chrism, looking around at all of them suspiciously. "What...does...that ...mean?"

Ann shared all the details about the Corporus and the abilities that she would possess. She told her that one of the reasons she survived the ice cocoon was that she had partially shifted into a bear.

"A bear...a freaking bear?" Chrism said through gritted teeth. "They get powers over the elements and I get to turn into animals!"

"Not just animals but any living thing," said Ann. "You're important to the Primortus world. You're a helpmate."

"No," Chrism shouted and struggled to stand up. Airon stood and lifted her to her feet. "No way! A helpmate to her? No, no, you said something about a Corporus has to be awakened. How?"

"You had to touch an Elementum that was in the possession of a Primortus," Ann said.

Chrism swayed. Airon seemed to be holding her up completely. Her eyes darted from Will to Skylee and then her brows went up. She pointed a finger at Skylee and said, "You, you did this to me—at the wedding—I touched your precious necklace and you freaked out."

"I didn't know," said Skylee earnestly. "I-I didn't know anything then, nothing, really. Even after I saw your birthmark glow, I wasn't sure what was happening."

Chrism's mouth flew open, her face was pale and she was visibly shaken. She placed a hand under the collar of her shirt, sliding it under the fabric to the birthmark on her shoulder.

"Take it back," she ordered. "Take it back. I can't believe you did this to me. You made this stupid diamond mark turn so dark. It was barely there before that day. Well, I don't want to be a Corporus, helpmate to anyone." She leaned into Airon. "Please make them take it back."

Airon looked blankly at Ann and finally spoke, "Well?"

She inhaled sharply. "No, there's no way to reverse it," she said wearily.

Chrism started sobbing and placed her hand on her chest. She glanced down, frowning, and said, "Where is my bracelet?"

"It must have fallen off," Skylee said, looking around.

"I'll go check where you..." Will paused. "Over there..." He headed to where Chrism had been frozen.

"I'm sorry all this has happened, please forgive me," Skylee pleaded, stepping closer to her.

"I need time...I can hardly believe all of this and I can't talk to anyone about it, except you all," Chrism whispered and stared at the ground. "So, I guess I'll have to forgive you—eventually."

Skylee felt such a relief wash over her that she leaped toward her sister and hugged her even though Airon never let go. "Thanks, I'm so glad you know. I'm just sorry it had to be this way."

"Uh well, I didn't find anything over there," said Will, coming back from the clearing. "Sorry."

"Great, just great," muttered Chrism.

"There is a little side effect that occurs, well—at first," stated Ann patting Chrism on the shoulder. "Until you learn to shift properly."

"Oh yeah, what is that?" she asked sarcastically.

"Sometimes when a young Corporus shifts back, they lose things," said Ann cautiously.

Chrism stood there for a while before she spoke, "Airon, take me back to the glider."

"Chrism," said Ann in a serious tone. "Remember..."

"I know, don't tell anyone," she snapped bitterly. "Besides, who would believe me? Come on Airon, before they tell us you're a Primortus or Corporus."

Ann's silence caused everyone to look at her.

"Well, I'm not, right, Ann?" said Airon quickly.

"Right," she confirmed in a calm, sure voice.

"Okay," said Airon before turning to leave. He held on to Chrism as they headed back toward the trail.

"One more thing, Chrism" Ann called out. "When you pass a snack stand, you're going to want to eat something with protein."

"Protein?" she asked as she briefly stopped walking.

"Yes, the shifting burns up your body's resources and you'll need to replenish them. You'll probably want to carry some of those Banquet Bars with you from now on."

"Ick!" sputtered Chrism. "Those things are gross. I hate them, why protein, why couldn't it be chocolate or something?" She leaned on Airon as they continued on toward the trail.

"Well, I thought that went amazingly well," said Ann with a smirk.

"Mum," Will said, looking up the trail and watching them go. "Airon didn't say much, he seemed upset. I'm a bit worried."

"I know you are but Airon has his own way of dealing with things," Ann said.

"I think Chrism hates me now," Skylee said, exhaling loudly.

Will took her hand and smiled. "Come on Sky, let's go. She'll come around. I mean look at me. I'm doing better with all of this, well, a little better."

Ann hooked her arm in Will's and the three of them followed behind Chrism and Airon.

The rest of day was quiet. Chrism hardly spoke and didn't even answer her V-phone. Skylee and Will tried to engage Airon in conversation but he mostly would just nod. He never left Chrism's side.

After a late lunch at the Geyser café, they hiked the rest of the trails, stopping to take in the sights. Skylee enjoyed crossing the wooden plank boardwalks. The sights fascinated her, for instance the Champagne Pool reminded her of a watermelon reversed with the green on the inside and the red rim on the outside. Near the end of the trail, they stopped on a particularly foul-smelling platform to view the Bird's Nest Crater. Skylee stepped up and read the sign...*Starlings, swallows, and Mynahs build nests here so that the heat can incubate the eggs.* As she looked at the many small holes in the crater's wall, she wondered if there were tiny fledglings inside.

Skylee noticed that her sister had only smiled once during the rest of their time at the park, it was when she heard they were all leaving Cook's Farm the next morning. They would be staying at the Bayview Château in Tongariro National Park. Her mom said they had burdened Zane long enough, but Skylee knew that wasn't the real reason. She was sure it had something to do with the G-files.

When they returned to the farm, a huge meal was waiting for them. Skylee was glad that Chrism seemed to be her old self as she spouted facts about Lord of the Rings all through dinner. Apparently, many of the cast and crew stayed at the Château.

Later that night, Skylee stood and looked out of her bedroom window. She wanted one last look at the moon over Rotorua Lake. The midnight blue sky was blanketed with thousands of stars and the silver crescent moon was gleaming. It was a beautiful sight. Skylee would never forget her time at Cook's farm, the place where she learned who her father truly was. Now, she had something in common with him, the world of the Primortus.

She glanced around the room at her sister, who was flopped out across her bed in peaceful slumber. Apparently being a helpmate wasn't going to cause her to lose any sleep. Skylee stepped over Chrism's suitcases and crawled into bed with one big regret. There hadn't been time to go back and investigate Zane's secret room with Will. She tossed and turned, unable to stop thinking about all the things she'd seen in that room.

Then she bolted upright and let out a loud sigh. It was now or never. Within seconds she was dressed in jeans and a sweatshirt. After putting on her jacket, she crept into Will's room and gently woke him up.

"What?" he said, sitting straight up. "What's wrong?"

"Nothing," whispered Skylee. "I just thought...now...might be a good time to..."

"To what?" Will asked, looking at her oddly.

"Oh, I—I mean, there's something I need to tell you," she nervously said as she sat down on the end of the bed with her arms crossed. "And you probably won't like it."

"Have at it."

"Well, a couple of days ago while I was getting a fax from Zane's office..." Skylee continued revealing that she had found a secret room. It took nearly ten minutes to explain everything as Will interrupted her on several occasions. When she had finished he sat quietly biting his lip.

"Listen, you know we're leaving in the morning," she said in frustration at his silence. "And I want you to go back with me."

"Zane's home," he said with furrowed brows. "We aren't exactly private detectives and this isn't a bloody Sherlock Holmes movie. We might get caught."

"Scared, are we? What happened to the adventurous side of you, Chief?" she goaded him, knowing full well he could never resist a challenge.

There was silence for a moment then Will shook his head and said, "You're unbelievable—oh all right, let's go Sherlock."

"Ok, Watson," Skylee said, unable to hide a rather smug smile.

Will started to get up, but abruptly stopped and motioned for her to look away. He grinned roguishly as she turned her back, which caused her to blush. A few minutes later, Will was fully dressed and holding a flashlight in each hand.

"Here, thought ya might need a torch," he said, handing one to her.

"Torch? Don't you mean flashlight? Honestly, you and your Aussie words. You know, you are an American."

"Only half—I know I haven't lived in Oz for a while but I haven't forgotten my mother tongue—so let's go mate."

They both laughed, then Will suggested they use the backdoor of the main house since it was closest to Zane's office. When they reached the office door it stood ajar, they tiptoed through, shutting it without a sound.

"Whoa, this place is a mess," Will whispered, sweeping his flashlight over the stacks of papers, books, and boxes. "Guess he's a bit of a packrat."

"Yeah—and just wait 'til you see this," she whispered back.

Skylee led Will to the back wall and shined her light on the glass case of knives. As he curiously glanced over the collection of daggers and blades, she noticed that the flashlight she had dropped on her earlier visit was back in its original spot.

She motioned to him, opened the secret door, and they both stepped inside. Will searched around and managed to find a string hanging from the ceiling. He tugged on it and a light came on.

"Let there be light," he quietly said, causing Skylee to giggle.

"Look at all these maps," she whispered. "And that one over there." She pointed to one labeled The Day.

Will pulled the door closed and moved closer to study the map. "Sky, this just shows the crack in the earth. There are lots of maps like this. I even saw one at the Memorial, you know, on your mum's wedding day."

"I know, but why would he have one here? And look," she said as she pointed to a smaller map, "at this one, I think this might be that island that vanished and these are of New Zealand." She heard the words as she said them and realized there really wasn't anything sinister about the maps.

"Yes, but Zane is helping your mum and Alex with their case. He could have these maps because..." Will paused. "Sky." He handed her some papers. "They're airplane diagrams. This one looks like the plane that crashed."

"Why would he—what do you think he's doing with these?"

"Not sure. Didn't you say something about some photographs? Where are they?"

"Oh that's right, I didn't have time to look at them before. They're over here." She walked to the opposite wall. "Right there." She tapped one of the pictures.

"It's you, it's us at the Sky Tower," whispered Will. "This is strange. Why would he have these?"

"Your mom maybe..."

"No, she didn't take these pictures. She's in some of them," he said as he walked slowly down the wall, examining each picture. Skylee followed him. Will stopped suddenly causing her to bump into him.

"Cripes."

"What?" she asked.

"Are you seeing this?" Will pointed to a flow chart that listed all of the events that had happened since the wedding. "It seems to be connecting everything to you."

She examined it carefully. A knot formed in her throat as she realized that Zane thought the events were centered on her.

"Will," she whispered. "You don't think that he knows about the Primortus, do you?"

"I don't know what to think," he said with a puzzled look. "I wonder—"

The sound of a phone ringing somewhere nearby interrupted him. He grabbed Skylee, reached, and turned off the overhead light. The room went black. They moved toward the door but stopped when they heard Zane come into the outer office as he answered his V-phone.

"Hello," he said in a gruff voice. "Yeah, still working on it..."

Skylee silently pulled Will backwards. She tugged him along, feeling her way down the wall by the door, until they reached the corner where they stood in the darkness. Suddenly, the door opened and a pale column of light invaded the small room. Skylee held onto Will's arm like a vise. They remained frozen in place, with their backs pressed against the wall as Zane looked in.

"I know, I said it was going to be taken care of...its taking longer than I thought," he said as he stepped back out and closed the door.

Skylee felt as if her heart had stopped.

TWENTY-ONE

The Stolen Box

The air in the tiny room was thick and humid. Skylee felt a bead of sweat slide down her backbone. She blinked and tried to adjust her eyes in the darkness. Narrow cracks of light appeared, outlining the doorframe. Shadows flickered on the walls as Zane, who was still talking on his phone, paced back and forth in the outer office. All Skylee could do was stand still and hold on to Will's arm while her pulse pounded loudly in her ears.

As she struggled to remain calm, her thoughts flashed back to the day she opened the gift from her father. A vivid memory of the mysterious stranger emerged in her mind. The haunting image of his tall, slender frame and angular features made her skin crawl. She had been terrified of him as she huddled in the darkened corner that day. *How did I manage to end up hiding in the shadows again?*

Skylee peered over in Will's direction. She could barely make out the silhouette of his face. It seemed as if he was scarcely breathing. A twinge of guilt rushed over her for talking him into coming along with her to explore the secret room. He wouldn't be there if it weren't for her, he would be safely sleeping in his bed. She wondered if he might be thinking the same thing.

Her thoughts were interrupted by Zane's muffled voice echoing through the door. She closed her eyes and strained to make out his words.

"No, no I haven't...I need more time," he said in an unusually high tone. "But I'm close, very close. Now, let me talk to—what? Why not? Hello...hello?"

Skylee and Will stood motionless and listened as Zane hung up the phone and let out an angry groan. After a silent pause that seemed like eternity they heard him click off the light and close the office door. Then his heavy footsteps faded away down the hallway. She released her grip on Will's arm and leaned against the wall with a sigh of relief.

"That was close," said Will with an odd little chuckle. "Let's go."

"Shhh, hold on. He might come back," whispered Skylee, gently switching on her flashlight.

"What was he talking about?" he whispered back.

"I couldn't make any sense of it, only that he's working on it—whatever *it* is. Oh, and that he needs more time," she spoke softly as she pointed her light on the desk. "But, I think it's pretty obvious he's up to something."

"Much as I hate to admit it, I reckon you're right. It is suspicious," Will quietly said as he turned on his flashlight and shined it around the room. "All of this seems..."

"Wait—wait a minute," she abruptly said. "What's that?"

"Sky, no, we should get out of here. He could come back at any minute."

"I know but I saw something. Shine your light over there."

On the desk she found a small wooden box covered with intricate carvings.

"Look at this," she said as she handed it to Will who examined it, squinting in the dimness. Skylee leaned in and watched as he turned the box over in his hands looking at each side. The soft glow from their flashlights formed little shadows around his eyes. He looked so serious and so unbearably handsome. As she gazed at him, she suddenly realized how close they were standing and her face warmed to a rosy glow. She quickly looked away and hoped he hadn't noticed.

"Did you see this?" asked Will, pointing at the carvings on the lid.

"What?" she said as she cleared her throat and stepped back slightly.

"This—this carving—doesn't it look like the lettering on your Elementum?" he said with a perplexed look as he shined a beam of light on the box.

Skylee's mouth fell open. She pulled out her necklace and compared the carvings.

"Oh my gosh, you're right," she gasped.

Will's eyes narrowed as he said, "Why would Zane have this?"

"Yeah, listen, this is too much of a coincidence. He must know about us. He might even be involved in the attacks. Why else would he keep all of this hidden in a secret room?"

"I don't know," Will said, chewing his lip. "Maybe we're jumping to the wrong conclusions and it's not as bad as it looks. What if he's only researching all the strange occurrences?"

Skylee didn't say a word. She merely shook her head, but her mind was made up. Zane was up to no good.

"Right then," murmured Will returning his attention to the box. "Let's see what's inside."

He tried several times to open it without success. Finally he raised his shoulders in a shrug and handed it back to Skylee who placed the box on the desk and shined her flashlight on it. She gently pulled on the lid and it popped open.

"Huh? How'd you do that?"

"Guess I have the magic touch," she said with a little giggle before looking down at the box again. "Whoa, look at this."

Inside was a spinning silver arrow. It was set upon a golden dial with markings around the edges. The arrow halted for a moment then began rapidly spinning again. Skylee picked it up, held it between them and they both silently stared down at it.

"Looks like a compass, doesn't it?" she asked.

"Yeah," he replied in a hushed tone. "But I've never seem a compass spin like that before."

"Well, whatever it is I think it must be connected to the Primortus—to us—in some way. Just look at the carvings," said Skylee, holding the box slightly closer to Will's face. "Do you think Zane would miss it, if we took—I mean borrowed it?"

"Yes, put it back," he said at once, pointing at the desk. "And we'd better get out of here, before we get caught."

She disappointedly closed the box and set it down. "Fine," she said.

"Good," he whispered with a satisfied smile. "Let's go."

They both turned to leave but as Will opened the door Skylee impulsively reached around, grabbed the box and stuffed it into her coat pocket. Then, as she followed Will out of the office, a knot formed in her stomach. While they tiptoed down the hallway, her hands began to shake and her mouth suddenly felt bone-dry. She couldn't believe she had actually stolen Zane's box. *Or is it?* she wondered. *Is it really his?* Something inside told her it wasn't.

Once outside the cool night air slightly eased her anxiety, although her mouth was still so dry she could barely swallow. She clasped Will's sleeve and they swiftly crossed the lawn between the main house and the cottage. With every few steps she glanced back over her shoulder. One of Zane's large dogs followed along behind them happily sniffing their path. When they were nearly to the cottage, Will surprised her by bursting into nervous laughter.

"What's so funny?" she asked breathlessly.

"If we—we'd been caught, what—what were you gonna do, eh?" Will said, bending forward and holding his stomach as he chuckled. "I mean he—he was so bloody close, I could've reached out and touched him."

"I don't know," Skylee admitted, giving him a playful punch on the arm. "I'm just glad we made it out of there, without being seen. Now, c'mon Watson—or maybe you prefer Chief, let's get inside."

"Oh no, you're not gonna start calling me either one of those—now—are you Skippy?"

Skylee snickered at him. It felt good to find a little humor in the situation. She slid her hand in her pocket and touched the box with her fingertips. If Will knew that she'd taken it he wouldn't be laughing, in fact he'd be really mad. So why bring it up, she was only going to examine it more closely, check the Humusara, and return it before they left the farm in the morning. No one would be the wiser.

When Skylee and Will reached the cottage they crept inside and quietly closed the door behind them. Neither one of them had noticed the large silhouette of a man watching them from a second story window of the main house.

* * * * * * *

A moment later, Will leaned against the doorframe and watched as Sky treaded softly down the hallway to her room. The cottage had been utterly silent when they entered, so they dared not speak to one another. Sky had simply reached out and given him a tender hug. As they embraced a wave of attraction had rushed over him, but he squelched it. If she only wanted him to be the "Watson" to her "Sherlock" then so be it. He couldn't care less.

Will frowned. *Cripes, what a lie.* In truth, he didn't want to be Sky's mystery solving sidekick, he wanted much more. Although, all the cloak and dagger stuff had been a lot more fun than he'd expected. There was something exhilarating about it. Why had he gotten such a high from their risky mission? *Its elementary my dear Watson,* Will thought to himself. *I was hiding in the dark, in the middle of night, in danger of being caught, with Sky clinging onto me.* Of course it was exciting.

But there was another reason Will's adrenaline was still pumping, a more sinister reason. From the instant he'd seen Zane's airplane diagrams, a nagging suspicion had taken hold of his mind. It felt like a seed of doubt had sprouted in his soul. Not only had a small plane like the one in the drawings almost killed Sky, a similar plane crash had taken his father's life. *Could Zane somehow be involved in dad's death?*

"That's crazy," he whispered with a deep sigh.

Will shook his head and looked around the cottage. A small fire smoldered in the fireplace, giving off a pale glow. He pulled the torch out of his pocket and clicked it on, shining the light down the dark hallway.

Seconds later, he stood at his mum's bedroom door contemplating whether he should knock or wait until daybreak. He needed advice about what he'd seen in Zane's office and his mother seemed like the most logical person to ask. Sky wouldn't like it, but he knew bloody well that they were in over their heads. Will took a deep breath and softly tapped on the door. In seconds he heard muffled sounds coming from inside.

"Will, is that you?" Ann asked, peeking out from the door as she put on her robe. "Are you alright?"

"Yeah, yeah sorry to wake you mum," he whispered, shifting his feet nervously. "I'm okay, but—something—we need to talk."

"Come in, come in," she said, motioning him into the room. "Has something happened?"

"Um, not exactly. You're probably gonna think this is weird, but how much do you know about Zane Cook?"

Ann's eyebrows shot up as she said, "Zane? Why? What's going on?"

The look on his mum's face stopped Will cold. *She knows something,* he thought. She stared at him with her large brown eyes and he suddenly remembered how many times she had kept secrets from him. Will tried to speak but he couldn't seem to get any words to come out. His mother had been keeping things from him, for years, maybe it was time for a few secrets of his own.

The room grew deathly still and they stared at one another. The only sound was a faint scraping noise coming from the window, where a branch moved up and down in the breeze.

"What's wrong?" his mum finally said in a concerned tone.

Will took a deep breath and let it out very slowly before he said, "No worries, I'm just struggling to understand a few things. And I'm hoping you can answer some questions that are nagging at me."

"Okay?" his mum said apprehensively.

"You and Sky's dad were friends, twenty years ago, right?"

"That's right."

"And her dad was also a close friend of Zane's back then, wasn't he?" asked Will, looking her straight in the eye.

"Yes," his mum said, moving her gaze to the floor.

"So, did you ever meet Zane back then?" Will prodded on while searching his mum's face for any reaction. "And what about dad, did he know Lee and Zane?"

"Wait a minute," she said looking up at him through narrowed eyes. "Why are you asking all these questions now, at such an ungodly hour? And why the sudden interest in Zane?"

At that very moment, Will decided not to tell his mother about what he'd seen in Zane's office. What good would it do? She was clearly still keeping secrets. Even if he did reveal that Zane had suspicious maps, diagrams and photos, she would probably just make up some lame excuse for it. It was obvious, he would have to figure out what Zane was up to on his own, starting with learning as much as possible about him.

"Come on mum," said Will, crossing his arms over his chest. "Are you going to answer all my questions with questions?"

"Will, I don't think you understand..."

"Too right," he broke in. "I don't and that's why I'm here. I'm asking for answers. Don't you think it's time? I can take it. I'm not a kid anymore."

"In that case, I think there are more important things for you to worry about than Zane Cook. For example, like understanding how to control your power," his mum said as she removed her Elementum and held it out to him. "Maybe it's time for you to have this. And maybe it's time for you to prove you're not a kid anymore."

Will swallowed hard and stared at the shiny amulet dangling before him. He was speechless.

* * * * * * *

At that same moment, Skylee sat cross-legged on her bed with the wooden box in one hand and her Humusara in the other. She laid them on the down comforter and removed her necklace, putting it into the book's cover. Feeling a mixture of guilt and excitement her fingers brushed across the brown leather.

"Now, for some answers," she said to herself, opening the book.

WHAM.

Chrism burst out of their bathroom door nearly knocking it off its hinges.

"GUESS WHAT? GUESS WHAT?" she shouted in a voice that sounded like a kid with a new toy.

"What?" gasped Skylee, slamming the book shut as she sprung up off of the bed. "Shh, do you know what time it is? Are you trying to wake the dead?"

"Funny, I heard you come back in and I won't even ask what you were up to at this hour. But I just had to tell somebody. I've been checking the weather on my V-phone and it's snowing in the mountains near the Château. Snow, do you know what that means?"

"Uh...let's see, frostbite?"

"No silly! Skiing, we can go skiing when we get to the Château. It'll be awesome. I love to ski. How about you, can you ski?"

"I wouldn't exactly say it's my best sport," Skylee said with a sudden flashback of herself sliding downhill face first.

"What? You've got to be kidding, it's so much fun and you know the best part is the fashionable outfits."

"Okay, well I guess I hadn't thought of that."

Chrism nodded happily. Then she looked down at the Elementum and box on the bed. One of her eyebrows went up as she asked, "What are you up to?"

Skylee followed her sister's gaze to the items on the bed. She really didn't want to tell her about the secret room, since she couldn't understand why Zane had a hidden office herself. She certainly wasn't going to reveal all the things she and Will had seen inside, but why shouldn't she tell her about the box. After all she was a Corporus, a helpmate, so maybe she could help.

"I found this over at the main house," said Skylee picking up the box and handing it to her.

"And you took it—without getting caught?" asked Chrism wide-eyed. "I'm impressed. Didn't think you had it in you."

"Well, yes but I am going to return it and I wouldn't have taken it, except, oh, just look at these carvings," said Skylee, pointing back and forth between the Elementum and the box.

"Wow," breathed Chrism eyeing the box with a mystified expression. "Zane had it, that's odd. Anything inside?"

Skylee nodded and handed the box to Chrism, who tried to open it.

"Darn, it's stuck," she said while vigorously pulling on the lid.

"Hey, careful! Let me try," Skylee insisted, wondering if it would open for her just like it had earlier.

Chrism tossed the box back to her with a look of frustration. Once again the box opened with ease when she lifted the lid. She noticed her sister's mouth fell open when she saw the shiny arrow spinning upon the golden dial.

"Let me see that," she said, snatching it out of Skylee's hand. "Hey, this is real gold."

"It is? How can you tell?" asked Skylee skeptically.

"Well, I happen to know a thing or two about precious metals. And this," Chrism thrust the box toward her face, "is definitely the real thing."

"Okay, okay I believe you, but I still don't know exactly *what* it is, she said as she placed her finger inside the box which was still in Chrism's hand. The moment she touched the golden dial it popped open, revealing the velvet lined compartment beneath. Skylee noticed there was an indention in the center, which was the same size as her Elementum. Both girl's eyes widened and they peered inside to find it was empty.

"I wonder what's supposed to be in there?" said Chrism.

"I think I know," she replied, reaching down to remove her necklace from the Humusara's cover."

Skylee held out her palm to Chrism, who handed her the box. They both stood staring down at it for a moment. Wondering if she should put the necklace inside, Skylee paused and dangled it by the chain above the box. She had seen what the Elementum and the Humusara could do. What if the necklace and the box created some kind of power?

Out of the blue there was a loud thumping sound at the window. Skylee held her finger up to her lips signaling Chrism to stay quiet. Then she quickly placed the box and necklace on the bed and rushed across the room to look outside. A large sheepdog ran back and forth, whipping its tail against the windowsill with each step.

"Whew, it's just a silly sheep—" Skylee stopped mid-word when she turned to see Chrism trying to pry open the box with a metal fingernail file.

Skylee's hands flew up to her mouth. Obviously Chrism had put her Elementum inside the box. She watched in disbelief as its chain swung from side to side while her sister forcefully poked the sharp point of the nail file into the edge of the box. There were deep gouges forming in the wood.

"STOP IT!" cried Skylee, dashing toward her and grasping the box. "What are you doing? Have you lost your mind? I won't be able to take this back. Zane will know that someone took it! What were you—"

"Skylee?" gasped Chrism looking down at the box.

"Are you listening to me?" she huffed furiously. "Don't you understand, you've messed up my chances of—"

"Skylee?" repeated Chrism with an expression of shocked disbelief.

"WHAT?" she asked, finally looking down at the box.

As she held it up she realized there wasn't a scratch on it. The unharmed wooden box was open. Her necklace rested safely inside.

"Did you see that?" Chrism asked as she stepped back and slumped down onto the bed. "As soon as you touched it, it opened up and um— like fixed itself. You did something to it, right? You used your power?"

"Well, I kind of—yeah—okay, it must have something to do with my powers," she said, feeling a little confused.

"Wait a minute, can you do it again?"

"Uh...I'm not sure."

"Here, let me see it," demanded Chrism as she stood and reached out for the box.

"Why?" said Skylee pulling it away.

"Come on, just take out your necklace and hand over the box. I want to see something."

Skylee reluctantly removed her Elementum and gave the box to her sister. Without the slightest warning Chrism placed it on the floor and grabbed one of her shoes from a nearby suitcase, slamming the spiked heel down on it. *KLUNK*! The box was amazingly strong. In fact it only received an indentation on the lid.

"No, no, no," groaned Skylee, shutting her eyes tightly.

"Now, let's see if you can fix it," she said, bending down to pick it up. "Here, take it."

Skylee opened her eyes and cringed as she looked at the dented wood. She carefully took the box from her sister and held it up between them. They watched in amazement as the damaged wood repaired itself.

"Cool," whispered Chrism. "Wish I had a power like that."

"Be careful what you wish for," she said still looking at the box. "I think it's time to see if the Humusara can explain what this thing really is."

"And you want me to leave, right?" asked Chrism with a frown.

"No, why don't you stay? Maybe you can help me figure it out—two heads are better than one."

Skylee smiled as her sister kneeled beside her at the foot of the bed. She noticed that Chrism's eyes lit up when she placed the Elementum in the Humusara's cover. It was good to finally be able to share what was happening with someone even though she worried a little about Chrism keeping her secrets. As soon as Skylee opened the Humusara words shimmered onto the page.

The arrow shall point to the true gift if you follow it with care.
For Brinfrost will be revealed by the one and only heir.

Skylee and Chrism looked wide-eyed at one another then back at the Humusara. They watched as the shimmering words slowly disappeared.

"Does it always do that?" asked Chrism curiously.

"Not always, but it's been happening more and more," she answered with a look of exasperation. "And the most frustrating part is trying to understand what it's telling me. The messages are sort of like riddles, they're written in code. I mean, what true gift? And who is the one and only heir? I sure hope it isn't me."

"Hate to tell you," said Chrism with a twisted grin. "But I think you could be on to something."

"That's encouraging," replied Skylee, smirking back at her sister. "Well, at least I know one thing—and I wouldn't have if I hadn't taken the box—Zane definitely is involved."

"That scraggily sheep farmer? You're kidding," scoffed Chrism.

For the next hour, Skylee and Chrism tried to make sense of why Zane had the box and what the message meant. They discussed all kinds of crazy theories, none of which seemed completely plausible. Then they talked about the things Hera had told Skylee. Chrism seemed shocked when she learned the Maori woman had been an Animus. She was even more surprised to discover there were two prophecies and that some of the Primortus considered Skylee to be an abomination.

"Why would they call you that?" asked Chrism in a soft voice.

"I think it's because my birth broke the rules," answered Skylee sadly. "You know, my dad already had a son and the Primortus aren't supposed to be able to have a second child...something about passing the power, I guess. I don't know."

They continued talking until they finally admitted they were too tired to figure it all out. It was almost sunrise when they went to bed.

What seemed like seconds later Skylee woke to the sound of tapping at her door. She pushed back the covers and jumped out of bed. As soon as her feet hit the floor she felt dizzy, her head pounded. Checking the clock on her bedside table, she realized she had only slept for two hours. Skylee glanced around the room and noticed that Chrism and most of her stuff was gone. She shuffled toward the door in a sluggish haze.

"Who is it?" she asked in a raspy tone.

"It's me," Will said from behind the door. "Are you ready? We're already packing up the glider."

Skylee looked down, she was wearing jeans and a crumpled tee shirt. She'd been so tired that she had fallen into bed without bothering to put on pajamas. She ran her hands through her long wavy hair and tried to straighten up her shirt before cracking open the door.

"Were you still asleep?" asked Will with a grin, his chocolate brown eyes peeking in at her. "Rough night, eh?"

"Yeah, I feel like I've been run over by a solarbus," she said with heavy eyes.

"Ha, I'm not exactly feeling top notch myself," he said, winking at her. "I didn't get any sleep at all. There was a little—uh—development after you left last night."

Will pointed to something on his chest and Skylee blinked and rubbed her eyes. As her blurry eyesight adjusted she could see two chains around his neck, each holding an amulet. She quickly identified one of them as his Maori necklace. Then ever so slowly her gazed focused in on the other necklace and she realized he was wearing an Elementum. Her hand immediately went to her chest where her Elementum rested beneath the thick fabric of her shirt.

"No, not yours," he said, shaking his head at her.

"So that's...?"

"Yup, mum gave it to me," he said slipping both necklaces back under the collar of his shirt. "And she took me out for some training this morning just before daylight. Bit of a surprise, huh?"

Skylee felt her heart speeding up. Confusion seemed to overtake her exhausted brain. It was so sudden. She stood in the doorway fighting back tears, unsure if they were from relief or joy. But why had Will decided to wear his Elementum now? He'd been fighting her for days, saying he wanted no part of being Primortus. She wondered what had changed his mind.

"Sky?" called Will anxiously. "Say something."

"I'm—I'm trying to," she responded weakly.

"Hey, I thought you'd be happy. Isn't this what you've been wanting me to do ever since you found out who or what we are?"

"Yes," Skylee said somewhat unconvincingly. "Yes, just give me a minute."

"You don't have a minute," he blurted out as he pointed a finger at his vintage watch. "If you don't hurry up you're gonna have the whole gang in here packing your bags for you."

Skylee exhaled loudly and shoved Will out of the door, which she swiftly shut. Spinning around, she zigzagged across the room gathering her things and stuffing them in her suitcase. Then she brushed her teeth and combed her hair at the same time, which was no small task, considering her long tangled mane.

After throwing on a fresh outfit and putting on her sneakers she scanned the room, making sure all of her belongings were at the door. She gathered up the rest of Chrism's things too, placing them alongside her own. At the very last minute she checked her backpack to make sure the Humusara was tucked into its hiding place, where she had put it before she fell asleep. As she peered inside Skylee spotted the wooden box resting atop the Humusara.

"Crap!"

In all the rush she had completely forgotten about the box. She grabbed it and shoved it into her coat pocket. Hopefully she would have a chance to return it once she got her stuff loaded into the glider. She scooped up her bags and took one last look around her room. She had left nothing behind. Despite all that had happened, she felt a tinge of sadness as she switched off the light and hurried out the door.

As soon as Skylee exited the cottage she was greeted by the realization that she wouldn't be putting the box back in Zane's office. Will, Airon and Chrism all stood at the edge of the porch clearly waiting on her. And to make matters worse her parents, Ann and Zane were standing near the back of the auto glider deep in conversation.

"I'll take that," said Will as he grabbed her suitcase and headed toward the van.

"Thanks" Skylee softly said, looking over at Zane. *Is it my imagination or is he staring at me?* she thought.

She looked down and placed her hand in her pocket. How could she sneak the box back now? Maybe if she claimed she needed to check one last time for school assignments. That might work.

Before Skylee could say a word her mother and Alex stepped up and informed her that they had been called away on assignment.

"Drake and Desoto have heard reports of another missing island and they've arranged to meet us on site," her mother said. "I could tell you where, but then..."

"I know, I know, you'd have to kill me," said Skylee in a deadpan voice.

"Ah, careful, we might have to make a secret agent out of you," her stepdad teased.

Usually Skylee would've responded with a witty comeback about the secret world of the G-files. However, since she was secretly hiding a box in her pocket that she had secretly taken from a secret office, the best she could do was shrug and change the subject.

"Are you sure that you're well enough to go mom?" she asked with genuine concern.

"I'm fine," her mother said reaching out and putting her arm around her. "Now that Ashley Hayes is in custody there's nothing to worry about. And I think it's time that you and Chrism see more of New Zealand and have some fun."

"For sure," interrupted Chrism as she stepped up to them. "It's time we get off the farm!"

Skylee noticed her stepdad chuckle at his daughter. Chrism did have a knack of stating the obvious. For once Skylee agreed with her, it was time they saw more of the North Island, but she had thought her mother would be with them. Going their separate ways seemed risky. How could she protect her if they weren't together? Everyone else might think the danger had passed because Ashley Hayes was in jail but Skylee knew there was another man lurking about. And she was beginning to wonder if it had been Brinfrost who had shown up at the wedding and attacked her at the tower. What she couldn't figure out was how Zane fit in.

"So, we all agree," her mother said cheerfully. "You'll go do some sightseeing and meet back up with us in Wellington. It'll only be for a few days."

"But mom, you haven't completely recovered from the—the—" Skylee didn't want to finish her sentence.

"You can trust me to take care of her," her stepdad said assuredly. "I promise to do a better job this time. I'll watch over her like a hawk."

Skylee watched as her stepdad and mom clasped hands. There were still bruises on her mother's arms and a long deep scratch on her neck. Skylee didn't like thinking about how close she came to losing her.

"Really honey," her mother insisted. "You're beginning to sound like a worrywart. Go have fun. We'll see you in a couple of days."

Skylee knew there was no use in arguing once her mother had made up her mind. She nodded in agreement. There were several minutes of small talk about where to meet in Wellington, after which they all began saying goodbye to one another. As she hugged her parents, Skylee was struck with the realization that she would not be returning the box. Then to her dismay, Zane approached her and held out his arms for a goodbye hug. She timidly moved toward him.

He loomed over her, so large that his shadow blocked the sunlight from her face. She felt like she was shrinking down into nothingness. Her heart was thumping wildly in her chest. His rigid arms swept around her and she looked up into his face. She thought she saw a wicked smile beneath his grizzly beard. He leaned his head down next to hers.

"I know what you saw...and what you took," Zane spoke in a deep hushed tone in her ear.

Skylee stood perfectly still as if she had been turned into stone. She didn't respond. What could she possibly say? He knew she had taken the box. As she looked in Will's direction she saw a worried expression on his face.

At that point, Zane released her from his embrace and in his usual booming voice said, "I'm sure I'll be seeing you again, soon."

TWENTY-TWO

The Château

After getting in the auto glider Skylee began trembling. She couldn't believe she had messed up so badly. Zane's words were still ringing in her ears. She desperately tried to conceal her emotions from Will, who seemed to be watching closely from his seat behind her.

It took them about an hour and a half to reach The Bayview Château Tongariro. And although Skylee was exhausted she couldn't sleep. She spent the entire trip trying to figure out how she was going to tell Will that she had taken the box. He would be furious, and he'd probably lecture like she was a child. She found herself imagining all the things he might say. *Didn't I tell you to put it back? Does anyone else know you took it? I can't believe you did that behind my back, blah, blah, blah.* By the time their glider soared over the flaxen colored field leading up to the hotel's front entrance, she was considering taking her little secret to the grave. Unfortunately, there was only one problem with that idea, a problem named Chrism.

As Skylee exited the vehicle she looked up at Mount Ruapehu. The snow covered volcano provided a magnificent backdrop for the Château. Her gazed rested on the elegant four-story structure. The 1920's era hotel was nestled in the shadow of three active volcanoes none of which had erupted since The Day.

Skylee followed Ann, Will, Airon and Chrism into the hotel lobby. Shiny crystal chandeliers hung in clusters high above her head. A large drape of red velvet gracefully swooped in the center of the ceiling. Plush furniture filled the entire reception area.

Standing at the front desk was a woman wearing a black and white polka dot dress with pointy-toed pumps. Her brown hair was flipped up on the ends and she wore a single strand of pearls around her neck.

"Omigosh, it's the Brady Bunch mom," Chrism whispered to Skylee.

"Who?" asked Skylee with a puzzled expression.

"The Brady Brunch mom, you know from that old TV show."

"Oh yeah, I think I saw it once or twice for my television history course," said Skylee quietly as they approached the registration desk.

"Welcome, Welcome to the Château Tongariro. I'm Ruth Tasman," the lady said in a singsong voice. "May I help you?"

"Yes," said Ann as she opened her V-phone, which displayed a hologram showing their reservation. "Hello Ms. Tasman. I'm Ann Butler."

"Oh, please call me Miss Ruth, everyone does," she said graciously. "I'm happy to have you staying with us."

"Thank you, um Miss Ruth," said Ann with a polite nod.

The Brady Brunch mom pointed to a large plate of cookies on the counter and smiling up at them said, "Please have some biscuits while I check you in."

Will and Airon dug in to the chocolate chip cookies while Miss Ruth worked on her halo-screen

"Theez-ur-goo-duh," Will said with his mouth full as he offered the plate to Skylee and Chrism.

"Thanks," both girls said together, snickering at him as they took a cookie.

Skylee took a big gooey bite and chewed slowly. She sighed as the warm chocolate chips melted in her mouth. Chrism, who had broken her cookie in two, was daintily nibbling on one half.

"Delicious," she said in between bites.

"Mmm, it sure is," said Skylee wiping a crumb from her lip. "But I was wondering, do you have any Luck-E-Chocs around here?"

"Oh, sorry, lovey," answered Ms. Ruth. "We don't."

Skylee's disappointment was interrupted as Chrism leaned toward her and very quietly said, "Hey, I've been thinking, you know, about that box."

Skylee almost choked on her cookie as she gasped. "Not now—not a good time."

"Not a good time for what?" muttered Will, gulping down another cookie.

"F-or-f-or—" stuttered Skylee trying to come up with something.

"For girl talk," spouted Chrism. "You know *girl* as in, not you."

"Course not," replied Will, shaking his head. "But, me and Airon were just curious. Weren't we, mate?"

"Nah," said Airon quickly. "Leave me out of it."

Chrism glanced over at him and momentarily flashed a triumphant smile, and then her gaze returned to Will. "I was simply pointing out that you can't seem to give us a moment of privacy, for goodness sakes. I mean, really do you mind?"

"Right-o," smirked Will, looking both annoyed and amused.

"Don't you take that tone with me," shot back Chrism, looking at him with fire in her eyes.

"Okay-okay Duchess, no worries," Airon said smoothly as he pulled Will away from her a few steps.

"Yeah Chrism, and remember," added Skylee. "We'll have plenty of time to talk since we're sharing a room."

At the mention of their rooms her sister's attention quickly shifted and as Skylee grabbed another cookie Chrism stepped up to the desk and said, "I was just wondering, Miss Ruth. Do you know which rooms the Lord of the Rings cast, uh, particularly Orlando Bloom, stayed in when they were here?"

"My goodness, that was years ago," Miss Ruth said whimsically. "You're the first young person to ask me about that in ages. Oh, I'm not sure which cast members stayed here, let me see, I might have some information on that. Lord of-the-rings, Orlando Bloom…"

"Ah, come on Duchess," Airon mischievously said, tapping Chrism on the shoulder. "Are you still hung up on that old bloke?"

Skylee and Will looked at each other and then at Chrism whose face was bright pink. Before her sister could respond Miss Ruth handed her a brochure, which was filled with information about the hotel including a section on the LOTR's cast members.

"Ooooh," said Chrism opening the brochure and eyeing a photo inside. "Here he is. Wasn't he gorgeous."

Airon gave a half laugh, half grunt and to Skylee's surprise she thought she saw a hint of jealously in his eyes.

Br-brr-bar-ruf. A high-pitched bark suddenly rang out from behind the counter. Skylee felt something brush past her leg. A furry black poodle bounded up and happily jumped up and down in front of Chrism.

"Oh, how cute!" she squealed as the little dog jumped up onto her arms nearly crushing the brochure.

"I can't believe it," Miss Ruth gasped. "This is Prissy. And well, she usually is very shy around strangers. And she almost never barks."

"Really?" asked Chrism, cuddling the dog and smiling.

Skylee watched as Miss Ruth gracefully dashed over to her sister. The poodle continued making high-pitched sounds.

"I don't know what's gotten into her. Well, normally she only allows me to hold her. This is such a surprise. Come here Prissy, come to mummy," she said reaching out take the dog from Chrism.

"Aww," said Airon. "Ya seem teh have a way with animals."

Chrism tousled his hair, gave him a pat and said, "You should know."

As Skylee watched Chrism and Airon smiling at one another she wasn't sure if they were talking about Chrism's new power or something else.

Ten minutes later, Skylee and Chrism tagged along behind the bellman down a long corridor toward their room. He was a stocky man, who looked comical in his tight fitting uniform. Yet he appeared to be struggling with the luggage trolley, which carried Chrism's pile of baggage and Skylee's lone suitcase. When they reached their room Skylee opened the door and Chrism breezed inside.

"Very nice," she said, inspecting the room. "Which bed do you want?"

"Doesn't matter, I'm so tired I think I could sleep standing up," said Skylee with a yawn.

Chrism threw herself down on the nearest bed. "Me too, I guess neither of us got much sleep after you showed me that—"

"Um, yeah," Skylee cut her off, looking over at the bellman, who was straining to lift one of Chrism's largest bags. "Maybe we should try going to bed early tonight."

"That's a good idea, we'll need our energy for skiing tomorrow."

"Er...right," said Skylee with a feeling of dread.

Before the bellman could finish unloading the heaping mound of bags, Chrism began excitedly reading facts from her brochure. *Not again*, thought Skylee. As her sister loudly recited LOTR's trivia, the man stacked her luggage at the foot of their beds.

"Oooh, and did you know they filmed the Mordor scenes here, on the volcano? It says because the black lava and eerie mist look otherworldly. But I don't see anything about which cast members were here—oh wait, it says they used the hotel's conference room as their headquarters. And did you know the opening battle on Mount Doom was filmed near the ski area?"

"Uh, no, I didn't," said Skylee smiling apologetically at the bellman as she handed him twenty U.S. dollars.

"Cheers," the man said, noticeably out of breath, as he quickly exited the room.

"Hey, Chrism," she said before her sister could pick up reading where she left off. "I was just wondering what I should wear tomorrow, you know for skiing? Are jeans and a sweater okay?"

"JEANS AND—no—don't you have a ski suit?" asked Chrism looking up and down at her clothes like they had just fallen out of a dump truck.

Skylee frowned and shook her head no. Chrism exhaled loudly, grabbed one of her largest suitcases and heaved it onto the bed. In seconds she had half a dozen ski suits with matching boots laid out across their beds.

"Let's see which one would look best with your blonde hair," said Chrism peering down at each suit before finally picking an expensive looking one up. "This one."

A few hours later, when the "Ski Suit Fashion Show" was over, Skylee gazed over at her sister and smiled. Chrism had fallen asleep wearing a pajama top and ski pants with a silly grin on her face, clutched in her hand was the LOTR's brochure. *She's one of a kind,* thought Skylee.

She looked around the room, which was scattered with clothing pretty much everywhere. It took her over thirty minutes to straighten it all up. Although she was exhausted she couldn't sleep, there were too many things racing around in her head. With a heavy sigh she decided to go down to the lobby and get a snack. She wished she had some Luck-E-Chocs but maybe she could get some hot chocolate. It might help her take a nap.

Skylee quietly slipped out of the room and headed down the corridor. She rounded the corner and almost collided with Shelley, who was standing on the landing looking pale and anxious.

"Oh!" she exclaimed breathlessly. "I was just—um, I suppose your wondering what I'm doing here."

"Well, yes," said Skylee. "Has something happened? Are you alright?"

She nodded. "I'm sorry to surprise you like this, but I'm here by order—we have to talk."

"By order, whose order?" Skylee asked, looking curiously at her. "Is this about what happened that day at the cable car?"

"Yes, in a way."

"How'd you do it? How'd you know about the note from my father?"

"It's complicated," replied Shelley with a somber look. "All of the powers that surround the Primortus are."

"You—you're a Primortus?"

"No, no I'm not. I'm well, something else. Are you aware of the others, the helpmates?"

"Yes," said Skylee, raising her eyebrows. "But I don't know that much, only that they're helpers with special abilities. Are you one of them?"

"I'm a Spiritus," said Shelley. "Nowadays we're called reapers."

Skylee gave her a startled look. "Like *dead* reaper?"

"I know it sounds a bit scary, but it's not…we got the nickname because we talk to the dead. Well, only certain ones, called the Mortalus, we bring messages to the Primortus from them."

"Who are the Mortalus?"

"They're the Primortus who have passed on," said Shelley patiently. "And we—"

"Wait—the dead Primortus?" Skylee quickly asked.

Shelley bobbed her head. "Mm-hm."

"So that's what happened at the cable car, that's what you did. Oh my gosh, was that a message from my father?"

"I'm sorry, I don't know. We Spiritus aren't always aware of who the message is from, especially when they speak directly through us, like that day."

"But it could have been him, right?"

"I suppose," Shelley said reluctantly. "Listen, there's something else. I have another message for you. It's from the Mortalus. And I think you should take it very seriously, okay?"

"Of course I will, but first let me ask you something. If the past Primortus speak to you, then can you take a message back to one of them? Like to my dad?"

"It just doesn't work that way," Shelley said, shaking her head. "We're messengers for the living."

"I don't understand. Are you saying the Spiritus can only deliver messages, and that's all?"

"No, we have other abilities. We also protect the secret of the Primortus. For example we can erase someone's memory or plant a thought in their mind."

There was silence.

"So you did that to me?" murmured Skylee.

"Of course not," she immediately assured her. "We can only erase memories or place thoughts in humans, never on a Primortus. And then, it's only if the person is in danger or if they might harm the Primortus in some way. I promise to explain it all to you later, but right now I should give you the message."

Chill bumps formed on Skylee's arms. "All right, are you going to um, well, do like before?"

"No, that only happens when one Mortalus takes control and speaks though me. This message is from the collective, all the Mortalus. Well, at least the ones who believe the ancient prophesy."

"Which one?"

"You already know about both of them?" Shelley asked sounding surprised. "So do you know about the powerful being who wields the power of the Elementum?"

"Brinfrost," she whispered, her tone hushed, almost reverent.

"So you do know of him?"

"An Animus told me he wants my Elementum."

"Yes, it's true and he seeks to control all of them. That's why the Mortalus want you to be prepared to face him. This is your destiny as the second born."

"I don't think I'm ready for that," said Skylee, feeling blood rush to her head.

At that moment the elevator down the hall opened. A short woman who was dressed in a white uniform stepped out pushing a serving cart. She passed by them, headed down the hall, knocked on a door, and called out, "Room service."

Shelley looked around nervously and said, "Come on, let's go outside so we can be sure no one is listening."

Skylee followed her to the elevator and they rode down in silence. Shelley's words were repeating over and over in her mind, *Brinfrost, second born*. The same words she'd heard before and seen in the Humusara.

DING! The elevator stopped, the shiny doors parted, and there stood Ann with Will standing by her side.

"Shelley, what are you doing here?" she asked in low voice.

"Hi Ann," Skylee brightly said as they exited the elevator. "I ran into Shelley upstairs and..."

Ann didn't let her finish. She motioned for them to follow her. They swiftly moved toward the front doors. Skylee saw Will trailing behind them with a confused expression on his face.

"What's going on?" he asked, once he caught up with her.

"I'm not really sure, but your mom isn't happy," she said, shrugging as she twisted her mouth into a half-frown. "And believe it or not, Shelley just told me she's a helpmate, a Spiritus."

Will put his hand on his forehead, and then slid it down his face slowly. "Who's helpmate is she?" he asked.

"She hasn't said yet."

As the four of them stepped outside, Skylee felt the sting of the cool night air on her cheeks. The farther they walked, the smaller the hotel looked beneath the snow-covered volcano. Shivering, Skylee crossed her arms over her chest. Once they were a good distance away from hotel, Ann stopped and glared at Shelley.

"What are you doing here?" she huffed.

"You know exactly why I'm here," retorted Shelley. "I'm doing what's been asked of me."

"Didn't I tell you to stay away from her," Ann said sharply. "I can handle this, or are you going behind my back like you did before the wedding?"

"What I did was for the best," insisted Shelley defensively. "Can't you see that? What if Skylee hadn't had her Elementum when her mum was taken? What do you think would have happened?"

"Well, maybe if you hadn't stuck your nose into things, *none* of this would have happened."

"That's ridiculous, if you'd done what we asked of you fourteen years ago she would be more prepared. Just accept it. She needs to know, Ann."

Skylee's head was spinning as she tried to follow what they were saying. She threw her hands up and cried, "Stop! Fourteen years ago! You knew each other fourteen years ago?"

"Mum?" asked Will as through it was the only word he could get out.

"Are you happy?" Ann said to Shelley through gritted teeth, ignoring Will's question. "What else are you going to tell them?"

"What I've been told to," she coolly replied. "It's my duty. And in case you've forgotten, you have a duty too."

"That's enough," Ann bitterly said, then she turned toward Skylee and her voice completely changed. "Listen Sweetie, it seems as if Shelley has forgotten that you aren't quite old enough to deal with some of this yet. Why don't you and Will go back inside so we can work this out. You have enough to worry about."

"She's right Sky. Come on," said Will, tugging at her sleeve.

Skylee took a step in his direction then something inside her snapped. Maybe it was lack of sleep, or the stress of Zane finding out she'd taken the box, or the threat of Brinfrost, but it finally overpowered her. All the feelings she'd been holding in for weeks seemed to explode from deep inside her.

"NO, WAIT A MINUTE," she shouted. "I'M SICK AND TIRED OF BEING TREATED LIKE A CHILD. IF I'M OLD ENOUGH TO FIGHT OFF WHOEVER IT WAS AT THE TOWER—TO STOP ASHLEY HAYES FROM KIDNAPPING MY MOM—TO HAVE TO FACE BRINFROST—I'M OLD ENOUGH TO KNOW WHAT'S GOING ON HERE!"

Will was standing beside her with his mouth half open and Shelley and Ann were staring blankly at her. Despite their shocked expressions, she was relieved by how good it felt to let out all those pent-up emotions.

Skylee took in a deep breath of cold air and said, "I just want to hear what she has to say."

"No, don't say a word," Ann blurted out, pointing her finger at Shelley before turning and looking at Skylee and Will. "Okay, I get it, I get it. But Sky, this isn't only about your age. There are things going on here that you and Will don't understand yet. I'm asking you to let me handle this—just for now—trust me."

Skylee felt like all the air had left her body. There was a long pause. For a split second she considered telling Ann no, that she wasn't going to wait, but all the fight had gone out of her and the exhaustion took over. As she nodded in agreement, a defeated expression covered Shelley's face.

"Okay, let's go Will," said Skylee in a weary tone. "It's cold out here."

"Y'all right?" he asked softly as they turned to go.

"Yeah, I'm just tired."

A light snow was beginning to fall as they walked back to the hotel in silence. Skylee held out her hand and watched as a few snowflakes drifted onto her palm, melting away as soon as they touched her skin. Will gave her a wink and stuck out his tongue to catch an icy crystal. She halfheartedly smiled at him then looked back over her shoulder at Ann and Shelley. The two women were still standing in the same place. She could tell from their tense postures that their dispute wasn't over.

Skylee was so exhausted and mixed up that she couldn't think straight. Her feet felt like blocks of ice shuffling on the ground beneath her.

When she and Will reached the lobby they quickly told one another goodbye without discussing what they'd heard. Unspoken questions hung in the air between them. On the way to her room, she began to wonder what Will might be thinking. He had seemed confused, especially when she agreed to leave his mom and Shelley alone. Perhaps she shouldn't have given up so quickly, perhaps she should have stayed and insisted on hearing the truth. She sighed and slumped her shoulders. She just hadn't been able be muster the energy to go up against Ann and find out what it all meant. *But I will...*Skylee told herself. *I need answers.*

TWENTY-THREE

The Avalanche

Early the next afternoon, Chrism ducked into a banquet room on her way to the hotel lobby. She needed a quiet place to use her V-phone. A quick check around told her that she was alone and that the expansive space seemed to be prepared for an elegant party. She walked between the rows of tables covered in white linen, crystal dishes and silver candles, which looked like they were just waiting to be lit. An enormous mirror filled the entire back wall.

Chrism glanced up and smiled when her eyes caught her reflection. *Fabulous,* she thought. *Yeah, this solar skiwear is worth every penny.* As she turned from side to side, admiring it she thought back to her very first ski suit. It had made her look like the Michelin man's daughter. Chrism giggled softly. Most people her age wouldn't even know who the Michelin man was, but she had seen his funny image in the pages of her vintage fashion magazines.

She wouldn't be caught dead in a ski suit like that now. But that had been only a few years after The Day, when she was about five or six, and everyone had to wear heavy clothing to go out during the winter. Even a thick down-filled coat wasn't warm enough back then. Thank goodness for the scientists who worked relentlessly and finally developed solar fabric. It was less bulky, much warmer and definitely more stylish.

She closed her eyes and leaned back against the wall, contemplating how much her life had changed in the last few weeks. *What are the odds, my new sister is a Primortus and I happen to be a Corporus?*

It seemed too coincidental. And she wondered about her brother, Michael. *Is he one too?* Perhaps she should call and find out, except if he wasn't he would think she'd lost her mind. She decided to put it off, at least for the time being, she already had enough to deal with thanks to Skylee.

Chrism was still finding it hard to accept that supernatural powers actually existed, let alone a power to shift into all sorts of creatures. In fact, that very morning she had awakened from a nightmare in which she had tried to change into a beautiful horse but ended up as an ugly potbellied pig. Everyone around her was pointing and laughing at her, including Skylee. *Where did she get off laughing at me!* she thought for a moment before rolling her eyes at herself in the mirror. *Geez, I'm losing my mind. It was just a dream.*

Finding out that her sister was considered to be an abomination by some of her own people bothered Chrism. She worried that she might be included on the Primortus "hit list" because she was Skylee's Corporus. She was determined to master her shifting to help protect herself and of course her sister. So she had devised a plan to achieve this goal and the first part was contacting her godfather. After all, Doc Muller was an animal specialist. With his expert advice she could pick out the ultimate animal to use as her primary form when shifting.

She gave herself two thumbs up in the mirror and mouthed *you go girl.* Glancing out of the doorway, she caught a glimpse of Skylee standing in the lobby. Her sister had worn the green solar ski suit that she had suggested. She had to admit it looked pretty good. Skylee had even worn her hair in a long braid pulled to the side, just the way she had shown her. Chrism watched as Will walked up and whispered something in her ear.

"He's probably telling her how great she is," Chrism sneered.

Will might've believed that Skylee was a sweet, honest girl, who could do no wrong. But Little Miss Prefect had a secret, and Chrism knew what it was...Miss Perfect had taken the box from Zane. She quietly chuckled, touching the screen of her V-phone.

"Hallo," rang out a deep voice as Doc Muller's hologram sprung up before her. He was wearing a simple white robe and stylish looking sunglasses.

"Doc," she cheerfully said. "Hey, it's me Chrism."

"How is it?" he said with a big grin. "Oh, I see...ya must be going skiing. Yer look'n very stylish in that fancy ski suit."

"Why thank you," Chrism said happily.

"What can I do for ya, sweet girl?"

"Well..." she hesitated briefly before chattering on, "I have a school project to pick an animal I would most like to be. Can you give me some advice? I mean tell me which animal you think would be a good choice. I need to know all about it and I thought you would be my best source."

"Ya be right about that. I love animals...they are my favorite things. So, ya need an animal," he said seriously.

"Yes," she said quickly nodding at him.

"Well, ya were never much for animals as I recall, except for those little ankle biters," said Dr. Muller with a smile. "Ya silly girls want to carry them around in a purse on your shoulder. Dog's have four paws, let them walk."

"I know—I know Doc but please, I really need to find an animal. I'm afraid I put this...um...assignment off and I'm running out of time."

"Okay, I'll help ya now-now, I can see the stress in yer eyes," he said. "How about a bunny? Those are cute, yes?"

"No," she said in frustration. "I want something strong and fast. Something that can defend itself, also, it has to look good."

"Hmmm," was all he said as he rubbed the whiskers of his closely shaved goatee. "I would say, from what ya have described, maybe one of the big cats would work for you. I know how you like fur," he chuckled.

Chrism laughed quietly. Time was of the essence. If she didn't arrive in the lobby soon, a search party would be gathered.

"Okay, big cats, like what?"

"Let's see, there's the lion."

"Too bland, you know, with all that beige fur."

"How about a Cheetah? They have spotted fur and are very fast."

"Nope, their bodies look funny. And aren't they only fast for a short period of time?"

"Yes, that's right. Well, there's always the man eater, a tiger?"

"Maybe...they are beautiful..." Chrism said, closing her eyes. Then a bright orange and black image of "Tony the Tiger" from an old commercial popped into her head.

"No, no, not a tiger but something like that except, I don't know— how about white fur? Is there something like that?"

"I think I might have one," he spoke with assurance. "A snow leopard, some have white fur with grey spots—they're strong, fierce, and very rare. They are also beautiful."

"Ohhh—snow leopards, I think I remember something about them. Can you email me information on them?"

"Sure, ya know I'd do anything for my favorite goddaughter."

"Doc Muller, you know I'm your only goddaughter."

"Yes, and my favorite," he said.

Chrism laughed aloud. She loved this man. "And you're my favorite godfather."

"Bless ya child, I'll send that snow leopard information right away, anything else?"

Chrism wished she could tell him about her situation, he would keep it secret and he would love to help her.

"Well, no nothing else," she said. "Thanks for the help, love you, oh and don't tell my dad about me calling."

"Why?" he asked, pulling his sunglasses down on his nose.

"He's got so much to think about and I don't want him to worry about—my school stuff."

"Hmmm, as you wish goddaughter. Goodbye."

"Bye"

Doc Muller's image disappeared and within seconds the file he promised began to download. She turned around and was surprised to see Airon leaning against the doorway. He looked like a professional ski instructor dressed in a blue and white ski suit, which made his eyes look even bluer. A pair of dark sunglasses was perched atop his head and his hair was tossed about, as if he had already gone down the slopes. She felt her face flush as their eyes met.

"Like what ya see?" Airon teased.

"What?" asked Chrism trying to act as if she didn't know what he meant.

Airon's mouth turned up on one corner as he moved slowly toward her. "Was that bloke on the phone the best man from the weddin'?"

"Oh, yes it was."

"What was he supposed teh keep quiet about?"

Chrism hesitated. Had he been standing there the whole time? She put her hands on her hips and exclaimed, "You know, it's rude to eavesdrop on someone's private conversation!"

"Again, what was he supposed teh keep secret, eh?" he pressed as he continued to move closer to her.

Chrism needed to say something but all she could think about was the determined look on Airon's face as he paced closer and closer. She backed up until she was nearly pressed against the wall.

"Ya do remember what Ann said, about keeping the Primortus world a secret," he stated as he tucked his sunglasses in the front of his suit and ran his fingers through his ruffled hair.

"If you must know, I called my godfather and whatever I tell him, he'll keep secret."

Airon stopped his approach abruptly a few feet from her, his face was set in stone except for a frown, which was slowly forming as he spoke, "Chrism, did ya tell him?"

She swallowed hard and felt her face grow warm. *Why is he talking to me like I'm an imbecile?*

"I asked ya a bloody question? Did ya tell him?" he said heatedly. He took one long step and was eye to eye with her, grasping both of her arms in a firm hold.

"No," breathed Chrism, trying to free herself from his grip. The struggle seemed to only make him clutch her tighter.

"We must keep this quiet, only discuss it among ourselves."

"I didn't tell him," she cried. "Now let go of me."

His expression relaxed as he released his grip. They stood there staring at each other until he spoke.

"Duchess," he said in a low soothing tone.

"What?" she replied more abruptly than she intended.

"I heard ya talkin' and—"

"And what?" Chrism interrupted. "You just assumed that I was sharing what I am now! I can't believe that you're acting like everyone else—like I'm..." Her eyes blurred. *Darn it, don't lose it now, not in front of him,* she thought. Chrism took a deep breath, squared her shoulders, and made a move to walk past him.

"Wait, Duchess," he said as he took her hand and held tight. "I'm not like everyone else...I shouldn't have jumped teh conclusions. It's just—"

"It's just—what?" She wanted him to hurry up and speak so she could get away from him before she lost it.

"I'm worried about ya and I'm not use teh feelin' that way," said Airon with furrowed brows.

"Sorry about your luck," she said facetiously.

"Hey, I'm tryin' teh be serious here," Airon spoke softly as he tucked a stray strand of her hair behind her ear.

Her anger at him was fading. She didn't understand why because he hadn't apologized for anything. He'd only sent her mixed signals. One minute he was all mad and the next he was looking at her tenderly with his steely blue eyes. *What's happening to me*, she asked herself. She needed to get away from him.

Chrism squeezed his hand, attempted to give him a smile and calmly said, "I'm fine, you don't have to worry about me."

"Yeah, yer fine," Airon said, looking unconvinced as he took a step back releasing her hand. "Well, I guess Will and Skippy are waitin' for us."

Chrism suddenly grabbed his hand and tightened her grip. "Airon...I..." she stuttered, slowly raising her eyes. "I'm not...really okay. I'm having a hard time, dealing with this Corporus thing."

Airon opened his mouth to respond but Chrism continued on, "I'm not sure who I am anymore. Before all this, I was pretty sure of where my life was headed. Now, everything is all messed up and tangled in the lives of other people and yet I feel alone. I-I feel like I'm a freak!"

Airon leaned down, placed his forehead against hers and said, "First, ya aren't a freak, well sometimes ya do act a little freakish—but definitely not a freak and second..." He straightened up and looked down at her. "Yer not alone. I'm not a Corporus so I reckon I don't understand all the things yer feelin' but I'm here. I'll help ya anyway I can if ya will only let me."

Chrism put her hands on each side of his face raising her eyes until they locked on to his. For the first time in days, she felt some of the pressure lift off her chest. She smiled and surprised herself as she reached up and gave Airon a gentle kiss on his cheek.

"I was so wrong about you," she whispered as she remembered the day she met him.

She had literally fallen into his arms. He had seemed so full of himself that she didn't want to be anywhere around him. But lately, especially since her change, he had treated her with more kindness than she thought possible.

"I feel the same way, Duchess," Airon admitted. "So, did your godfather give ya any good advice, ya know, about animals?"

"Yes, he did and I'm not telling you about it," she said teasingly. "You'll just have to wait and see what I've chosen."

"Is that right?" he smirked as he turned and tugged her behind him toward the lobby. Chrism felt like she was being pulled along on air. She finally had an ally. At least for now Airon was on her side.

* * * * * * *

Meanwhile, Skylee sat on a plush red sofa watching Miss Ruth scurry around the lobby, straightening up brochure racks, and throwing away litter. Will, who was dressed in black solar skiwear, was sitting next to her reading a sports magazine. His hair was neatly tucked beneath a wool ski cap with only a few wisps escaping at the corners of his ears. As she gazed over at him, Skylee felt a familiar flutter in her stomach. Quickly looking away she scanned the room.

The lobby was empty, except for the three of them. Several T-screens, which were mounted on the walls around the seating area, were broadcasting news of an unexplained explosion on Mount Ruapehu. Skylee silently read the print scrolling along the bottom of the screen.

MYSTERIOUS BLAST TRIGGERS AVALANCHE NEAR WHAKAPAPA SKI AREA... ACCORDING TO THE DEPARTMENT OF CONSERVATION NO VOLCANIC ERUPTION OCCURRED... OFFICIALS CONFIRM EXPLOSION WAS NOT PART OF AVALANCHE PREVENTION SYSTEM... LIFTS ARE CLOSED AND STAFF TEMPORARILY EVACUATED THE SKI AREA TO THE BAY VIEW CHÂTEAU TONGARIRO AT THE BASE OF THE MOUNTAIN...

Skylee looked around the lobby again. Only a few minutes earlier the entire lounge had been filled with people dressed in skiwear, carrying snowboards and skis. Miss Ruth had served hot chocolate while assuring everyone that the danger had passed. The room had quickly cleared when a shuttle bus arrived to take the evacuated skiers back to Whakapapa village.

Skylee glanced at her watch. Chrism and Airon were late. Apparently something had changed between those two. It seemed to have happened right after the "frozen bear fiasco" at The Thermal Park. Chrism was no longer insisting that Airon wasn't her type, and she was now acting quite smitten with him. Not that Skylee minded her switching her fixation from Will to Airon. She just hoped that Chrism wasn't going to hurt him. Likewise, Airon had better not hurt her sister. Either way would be a serious problem.

A series of shrill beeps came from the T-screens as another update on the avalanche was broadcast. Skylee had heard the first report while Chrism showered but she didn't mention it, knowing it would put her sister in a foul mood.

"Sky?" Will said, tapping her on the shoulder.

"Hum?"

"What are you thinking about?"

"The avalanche—OW!" she yelped. She felt searing pain as her Elementum heated against her skin. She pulled it out and held it by the chain. Her other hand rubbed the burnt area attempting to ease the pain.

"What's up?"

"This thing is on fire," Skylee said.

"Not good, is it?" Will asked as he glanced around.

"No I don't think so..." her voice faded as she glanced toward the front doors of the lobby. "Your mom doesn't even know what it means but I have a theory?"

"Eh?"

"I mean at first I thought it only got hot when trouble was near,"

"Yeah, that seems right."

"But it didn't heat up when my mom was in trouble," she said, turning her gaze from the door to the Elementum. "It went cold. She was in danger, but it was cold."

"Hmmm," Will murmured.

"And you were in danger too, when you were chasing that weird bloke, Ashley."

"Exactly—and it didn't heat up."

"And your theory?"

"Has a lot of holes in it," sighed Skylee.

"True," he chuckled. "But I reckon what ever temperature it is, hot or cold, we need to pay attention and be on the lookout for trouble."

"Maybe skiing isn't the safest thing for us to do," said Skylee, hoping that the ski lifts were still closed. "I mean it's so out in the open and anyone could get to us."

Will gave her a sideways glance, "That isn't going to stop Chrism from—"

"Hey you two," interrupted Miss Ruth. "I baked these cupcakes this morning. Would you like one?"

"Oh, thanks but I just had a late lunch," Skylee graciously declined as she tucked the Elementum between her ski suit and her jacket, making sure not to let it rest against her bare skin. Will took a cupcake and thanked Miss Ruth. Yesterday it was cookies and today a lovely silver platter was adorned with an arrangement of beautifully decorated cupcakes. *Miss Ruth really is like the Brady Bunch mother.* Skylee looked more closely at her. *Or maybe she's an android.* She just seemed a little too perfect. It kind of bugged Skylee that it was so hard to tell the difference between androids and humans.

"Well, okay loveys, I'll just leave the cupcakes here on the counter in case you change your mind," Miss Ruth said.

"Okay, thank you," Skylee said to her before turning to Will and resuming their conversion. "So, speaking of Chrism. I think we should talk to her and Airon about what happened with your mom and Shelley last night."

"Right, probably right," he said, devouring most of the cupcake in one bite.

"I mean, it would be good to get their input..." Skylee's voice faded.

"Mm–hm." Will nodded with his mouth full. He finished his cupcake in two more bites and then said, "No doubt you want their input on Zane as well."

"That's a good idea," Skylee chuckled. "I'm glad you came up with that."

"Yeah, me too," he said as he reached for another cupcake and began to eat it."

Skylee watched as he wolfed it down. "Good?" she asked playfully.

"Delicious," exclaimed Will. "I'll have to have another one, soon."

She knew he would too. He was like a bottomless pit when it came to food. Skylee heard someone excitedly talking and turned to see Airon and Chrism entering the lobby. Her sister looked like her old self, happy and carefree. Skylee had been worried about her. Over the last few days, Chrism's mood swings had reached an all time high. Skylee assumed it had something to do with her being a Corporus.

Everyone, well at least everyone who knew, seemed concerned about her and worried that she might shift in front of someone. Skylee's train of thought was interrupted as Miss Ruth's dog came barreling around the corner and pranced all around Chrism.

Chrism let out a sigh and squatted down to pet the frisky poodle.

"Hey, puppy," she said with a smile.

Prissy whined and yelped as Chrism continued to pet her. The little dog's mouth flew open and she began to howl. Skylee intently watched the interaction between Chrism and Prissy. Suddenly, the color drained from her sister's face.

"Duchess?" Airon said in a concern tone.

"Enough," Chrism mumbled, ignoring him as she pushed the dog away. She tried to stand up but Prissy bounced into her causing her to tumble back. "Ow!"

"Prissy, where are your manners?" cried Miss Ruth. "So sorry, Miss, I don't know what it is about you that my Prissy is so attracted too. Come on girl, let's go outside." But the dog continued to yowl and whimper. "Prissy, let's go," Miss Ruth said sternly as she reached down, plucked up the dog and carted her out the door.

"Geez," Chrism said as she glanced around. "Hey, stop staring at me. Okay, the dog likes me for some odd reason."

"Are you okay?" asked Skylee. "Did something just happen with that dog?"

"I don't want to talk about it," her sister said. "But well, I guess Ann didn't tell me about all of my abilities."

Will stepped up and said, "Yeah, mum has a habit of that."

"Wait a minute," said Skylee, gazing down at Chrism, who was still sitting on the floor, looking pale. "Are you talking about what I think you are? You can talk to animals?" She almost laughed as she heard the words pass from her lips.

"I *said* I don't' want to talk about it," snapped Chrism, getting up as Airon extended her a hand. "Thanks," she said as she accepted it and he pulled her up.

"My pleasure," he said.

Will chuckled. "Don't I remember *someone* calling you Dr. Doolittle once?" he teasingly said to Skylee, who gave him a subtle nod.

"Ha ha," Chrism sneered. "Are we ready to leave? I've been looking forward to this all day. Nothing better mess it up."

"The driver is…um…probably waiting for us outside," Skylee said as she stole a quick glanced at one of the T-screens, which was still scrolling breaking news about the avalanche.

"Something's wrong," grumbled Chrism. "What?"

"I don't want to say," Skylee answered, cringing slightly.

"As long as you're not going to tell me that we can't go skiing there shouldn't be a problem," she said seriously.

"Well—I guess I'd better not say it then," mumbled Skylee, pointing at the nearest T-screen.

"Crap!" shouted Chrism. "What happened? Great, an avalanche! Why does everything have to happen to me?" She stomped her foot and began bitterly complaining for what seemed like an hour but was probably only a few minutes. Then she suddenly stopped as if a light bulb had gone off in her head.

She turned, smiled cleverly at Skylee and said, "You, you can fix this, just blow the excess snow off the slopes."

"How am I supposed to do that?" she asked in a hushed tone.

Her sister just kept glaring at her. Skylee's jaw dropped as she realized what Chrism really meant. She actually wanted her to use her power to clear the slopes.

"No, no way—" Skylee sputtered as she looked around the empty lobby. "Listen, if I use my power like that something terrible could happen."

"Nothing's going to happen and besides your power is about savings lives," encouraged Chrism. "And this would save mine."

"Ya can't be serious, Duchess," Airon said, sounding astonished.

"Well I am, I need some fun time," she flippantly replied. Then she turned to Skylee and pleaded, "Do this for me, please."

"How can you ask me to do something like that?"

"Oh, I see, I'm supposed to help you but you can't do this one little thing for me?"

"Come on," interjected Will. "She can't, Mum said—"

"Darn it, Will, must you always be the good boy and do what *mummy* says?" snapped Chrism.

Everyone looked stunned.

"Humph," Will said as his jaw tightened. "I'm really not surprised that you would ask Sky to abuse her power."

"What's that supposed to mean?" Chrism asked as her face reddened.

Skylee bit her tongue. *He means you're acting like a spoiled brat,* she thought to herself.

"Duchess," Airon said as he put his arm around her sister's shoulder. "We shouldn't be discussing this here, that little dog and her owner might come back at any moment. Let's go check out the slopes and see what we find. Maybe they're not all closed."

Chrism glared at Will as Airon took her hand and proceeded to slowly draw her out the front doors of the hotel.

"She's a keeper," said Will with a sarcastic laugh.

Skylee giggled in agreement. She loved her new sister, but sometimes she could be a real pain. At that moment another kind of pain grabbed Skylee's attention, pulsating just above her heart. She tugged at the chain of her Elementum, repositioning the it.

"Will, it's happening again, my necklace—it's heating up."

"More than before?" he asked.

"Yes, maybe we should just go with them and take our chances."

Will smiled slightly and motioned for Skylee to go first. They stepped outside and climbed into the auto glider. Chrism and Airon were already seated in back, impatiently waiting for them. As they left the parking lot, Skylee felt a prickling sensation on the back of her neck as if someone was watching her. She recalled having that same feeling at the wedding. She glanced out of the back window just in time to see the silhouette of a tall man standing in the shadow of the hotel.

She blinked and looked again but he was out of sight. *It can't be him,* she thought...*unless he's following me.* Leaning back into her seat, she fastened her seatbelt as her pulse raced. Her Elementum was hotter than ever. She could barely think straight.

As their vehicle soared on, climbing up the mountain, she tried to convince herself that her imagination was running wild. After a while, her glances to the rear became less frequent. Slowly, her necklace cooled and her heart rate returned to normal. She looked across at Will, who was nervously biting his lip, obviously deep in thought. *Should I tell him?* she wondered. *Not unless I want him to call out the National Guard. Huh, does New Zealand even have a National Guard? Oh well, anyway, what are the chances of Brinfrost being here?*

* * * * * * *

A thin man, who was dressed in black skiwear, stepped out of the shadows and watched attentively as the teens boarded the auto glider. The corners of his mouth rose in a cruel grin. As the vehicle soared out of sight he looked down at Blaze, who was also wearing a dark colored ski suit.

"So, there's trouble with the four musketeers," Brinfrost said sneeringly. "Division among the ranks will only help to escalate my plan."

"Of c-course Master, t-trouble," stuttered Blaze as Brinfrost viciously glared at him.

"You useless moron, undoubtedly I performed one too many experiments on you," he coldly said, running his hands through his thick blonde hair. "Is that fear I see in your eyes?"

"N-no Master."

"You lie," he snarled. "I can see your fear and I know why."

"B-but, when I—"

"Shut up," he spat out. "It was simple. I gave you every step to take, every detail to set off that avalanche and you still managed to ruin my plans. You brainless imbecile!"

"M-Master, I d-did everything you s-said," Blaze stammered with fear dripping off each word. "It was s-set, b-but the weather—it s-snowed and—"

"Silence!" Brinfrost hissed. "Say another word and it will be your last. How did the bomb go off this morning? Did you change the timer?"

Blaze shook his head and cowered away as his Master grabbed his arm, dragging him to a private corner away from prying ears.

"I'm surrounded by idiots," he complained, rubbing his temples. "I suggest you work on getting Ashley out. I'm going to need someone with some brains."

"It won't b-be easy," said Blaze still cowering in fear. "He's b-being held in high s-security."

Brinfrost's nostrils flared. "I know, but with or without him I have plans for the Second Born. And you can mark my words...the Eleventh Elementum will be mine. If you screw up again," he warned, pointing his long bony finger down at his servant. "I'll bury you alive, literary."

"Yes M-Master," Blaze said in a low quivering voice.

TWENTY-FOUR

The Snow Leopard

Skylee, Will and Airon followed Chrism to the entrance of the ski lifts, but a large banner blocked their way. Chrism huffed dramatically and sullenly read the boldly printed words.

Whakapapa Ski Area Closed

Relief washed over Skylee for she had been granted her wish. She wouldn't have to spend the rest of the day spread-eagle on the snow while the others effortlessly skied down the mountain.

The four of them turned back and returned to the auto glider. Airon and Will chatted with the driver and after several minutes, it was decided that they would hike to Tawhai Falls. The driver took them back down the mountain and dropped them off at the trail. He left them with a flatmap, a solar-powered map that sent a continuous signal to the Rangers desk, which helped them keep track of their hikers.

Freshly fallen snow crunched beneath their feet as they started down the trail. The sun peeked out from behind a cloud and rays of light streamed through the trees, shimmering on their icy branches. Skylee breathed in the crisp, cold air.

"Wow, this is beautiful, isn't it?" she asked, looking back at Chrism, who was wearing a surly expression.

"It is," Will said just as a deer leapt across the trail ahead of them. They all stopped and watched it continue on its way through the trees.

"That was cool," said Skylee cheerfully. "Don't you think so, Chrism?"

Her sister replied by shrugging her shoulders. Skylee noticed Airon as he lifted Chrism's hand to his lips. As he gently kissed it, her sister smiled slightly at him.

"Ya know what I think," Airon said, looking attentively at her. "I reckon this might be a good time teh practice, Duchess. What'd ya say?"

She stopped and frowned at him. There was a long pause before she let out a deep sigh and said, "Fine, I'll try it."

She removed her ski jacket and handed it to Airon. Sitting down she took off her boots and instructed, "I really like these, please don't lose them...or my jacket."

Skylee, Will and Airon stepped back as Chrism began to shake. A low murmur came from her lips, which gave Skylee a chill. After a brief moment of silence, Chrism kneeled down and her body transformed like a rippling wave. It happened very quickly but Skylee thought she saw pain on her face right before the shift was complete.

"A snow leopard," Skylee exclaimed, blinking in surprise.

"Duchess, what a beaut," Airon said as if he were talking to a house cat. He handed Chrism's jacket and boots to Skylee as he squatted. "Come teh me, come on."

The imposing, large cat approached Airon guardedly, as her eyes scanned the surrounding area. Skylee wondered why she had picked a snow leopard. She certainly was beautiful but a rare sight in the wild.

"Yeah, yer a sweet kitty," whispered Airon while he rubbed behind her ears.

"Is she purring?" Will asked as he took a small stepped toward her.

"Actually, a snow leopard doesn't purr it's called chuffing," Skylee said. "It kinda sounds like a purr though."

The leopard rubbed her head against Airon and continued to chuff. Her long tail swished around before she flopped down and rolled over. Airon continued to speak to her as if she were a pet. She appeared to be completely comfortable with him.

Skylee smiled and reached toward the cat to touch her thick white fur. A low growl came from Chrism as she rolled onto her stomach. Skylee ignored the warning and placed her hand on her soft fur. *HISSS!* Skylee jerked her hand back as the cat rose swiftly, hunched down and twitched her tail.

"Hey," Skylee said startlingly. "Why'd she do that?"

"Don't know but it might be best if ya stay back," Airon said calmly as he patted the snow covered ground beside him. "Here, lay back down, Duchess, I thought we were having a moment." She leaned into Airon and rolled her head up and down on his shoulder.

Skylee tried again to pet her, but she stood up and shook her head while she pawed the ground, leaving a large rut in the snow. Then she took a step toward Skylee.

"Come on, now..." Skylee gasped and held her hands out in front of her. "Please..."

"Back off, Chrism," Will insisted as he moved forward.

She snarled at Skylee and Will, revealing massively sharp teeth. Skylee swallowed hard and wondered if her sister would actually attack them.

"Sky," said Will as the big cat drew closer. "Use the Elementum and make her change back. I'm not sure if she knows what she's doing."

"I don't know—Can I do that? Maybe if we use both our Elementums," Skylee said.

"I'm not wearing mine," he said, sounding alarmed. "Go ahead, try it at least, I mean you're the one who sort of created this beast. You ought to be able to control her."

Skylee grabbed her Elementum, held it out in front of her and spoke in a trembling voice, "Okay, that's enough, change back."

"Come on kitty," Airon softy said as he scooted closer and tried to gently grab hold of her fur. Chrism looked back at Airon and flung her tail around knocking him backwards.

"Airon, please talk her down," said Skylee, backing up. "She's freaking me out!"

Will stepped in front of Skylee, "Chrism, come on, stop this."

She wailed loudly and leapt over the two of them knocking them to the ground. She bounded through the snow and disappeared leaving only large paw prints behind her.

Skylee watched as Airon jumped up and ran after Chrism leaving her and Will sprawled out on the ground in stunned silence.

* * * * * * *

The leopard dashed through the woods, leaping over snow-filled ditches and downed trees. Chrism let out a loud wail that filled the forest. She had nearly shifted back when Skylee held the Elementum in front of her. It had taken almost all her strength to resist. She growled angrily as her destiny played out in her mind. *Will I always be under her control?*

Racing onward, she tried to get lost in the rush. All of a sudden, a sharp pain jabbed at her, causing her to stumble. Her huge paws gripped the icy ground, and she continued to run. *Stay focused,* she told herself. But there was no way to stop it. She didn't want to go back to human form, not after knowing what it was like to run free across the snow. However, the pain was too great, which caused her to unwillingly drop down and crawl on her belly.

Her body shook violently. She curled up, wrapping her tail around her face, waiting for it to finish. Now, half human and half leopard, her ears twitched as footsteps approached. A hand reached out to her. She was weak and frightened and lashed out with her sharp claws to warn the intruder.

"Easy, Duchess," said a startled voice.

Realizing it was Airon, she raised her head and glanced in his direction. Blood trickled down his arm, staining the white snow.

"No," she softly whimpered as she finally returned to human form. "Did I...?" She struggled to sit up, tried to reach out to him, but stopped when she saw him hold up a hand to halt her.

"No," he said sharply.

"I didn't mean to hurt you," she cried. "I didn't realize it was you. Are you badly hurt?"

"No—I'm not—but ya seem teh have lost the top of yer ski suit and if ya sit up any more..." his voice faded off and he turned his back to her.

She looked down to find that her ski top was indeed missing. *Of all things, it had to be my top,* she thought. *Well, guess it could be worse...I could've lost my bra.* She wrapped her arms around her legs as she pulled them to her chest. She felt her face flush as embarrassment flowed through her body.

"I slashed your arm," she said as her voice cracked. "I'm so sorry."

"It's all right, nothing but a scratch," Airon said glancing over his shoulder. Before Chrism could argue, he removed his ski jacket and then his solar shirt, leaving him in an undershirt. He handed his shirt to her. "Put this on, Duchess. You're shiverin'."

She took his shirt in one hand and fumbled around trying to put it on without revealing too much of her bare flesh. Airon took the shirt from her and slipped it over her head pulling it down completely covering both her arms.

"Just slip yer arms through the holes," he instructed. She did as he said, and then he laid his jacket over her shoulders.

"Wait," she weakly cried. "You need your jacket—you'll freeze."

"I won't, yer the one shakin'. Keep it wrapped around ya for now."

Chrism looked up and saw that they were only a few hundred feet away from the waterfall. White water crashed over black lava rocks into a deep pool below. Even in her weakened state the beauty of their surroundings astounded her.

Airon reached in the pocket of his jacket, still draped around her, and pulled out a Banquet Bar. She eyed it and although she still found them disgusting she could barely resist the temptation to grab it and poke the whole thing in her mouth. It was a surprising urge, which she chalked up to her feeling so weak.

"Is that for me?"

"This?" he teased. "Nah, it's for me, besides, I thought ya hated these bars. And I'm starvin' after chasing ya across the width of New Zealand."

Chrism knew he was joking but tears formed in the corners of her eyes.

"Duchess," he spoke tenderly. "Don't cry—of course this is for ya." He handed her the bar after pulling the wrapper down.

She timidly smiled, took it, and began to eat.

"Are ya startin' to warm up?" he asked, rubbing her arms with his hands.

"A bit—I mean, yes, here put your jacket on," Chrism insisted as she took another bite of the bar. "I've got your shirt. I'll be fine."

"No worries, keep it for a little while longer. I'm not cold at all."

Chrism saw him flinch as he tugged the coat up around her neck.

"You're still bleeding," she said with her mouth full.

"It's nothin'," he said as he reached down, taking a handful of snow to wash the scratch.

Chrism's gaze went higher and she spotted the ink on his arm. Her brows went up in surprise as she remembered the horrible things she had said about tattoos. She reached out and traced the shape with her finger. It was an artistic cross with an Old English letter on each side. An 'A' and a 'C'—she pulled her hand back, wondering what they stood for.

"That's our initials," she whispered quietly.

"What?"

Chrism gasped. *Did I say that out loud?* she thought as her face turned red. "I...umm...I just meant...well, A and C, those are the initials of our first names."

Airon glanced down at his arm and the corner of his mouth lifted. "I guess yer right about that, Duchess. So ya like it, and ya think these are *our* initials?"

"I didn't mean that—you had them put on—for—to—" she stuttered. Chrism was so embarrassed. She knew he'd gotten the tattoo right after they met surely it couldn't represent the two of them.

Airon let out a huge laugh. Even though she felt humiliated, she loved the sound of his laughter. She couldn't remember hearing him let go like that before.

"I didn't realize that ya could turn that many shades of red."

"Yes you did," she said quietly. "You make be blush all the time." Chrism shut her mouth tight. She had already inserted both feet and she didn't need to give him any more ammunition.

"Actually, they're the initials of my parents, Allison and Conner," he said as he regained his composure.

Chrism could hear pain in his voice as he said their names even though he tried to conceal it.

Airon stared out into the forest and in a low somber voice said, "We argued—my father and me—before he left on the trip with Uncle Gab. I wanted to go along but he insisted I stay with Will. I was so mad at him and even mad at my mum because she agreed with him."

Chrism watched as his gaze fixed on the snowy ground. "After they died, I felt guilty—still feel guilty about that. When I heard they had been killed, I..."

"Airon," Chrism spoke softly as she placed her hand on his shoulder. "Parents and kids argue. It's what they do. I'm sure they knew that you loved them."

Airon took a deep breath and turned toward her. His face grew dark and tense and he spoke bitterly, "That's what people say because they're uncomfortable with the topic."

"No," Chrism choked back a sob. "I'm not like...*those people.* I believe your parents loved you and that they knew you loved them. Please don't start treating me like I'm..."

"Duchess, I've heard that from so many people," he said dismissively.

Chrism held back a strong urge to blast him for being rude to her. She decided to take the high road, after all, he had opened up to her about his parents, and she could see it was still a tender subject for him.

"So, you really do have a tattoo," she said, trying to lighten his mood.

"I wanted—needed somethin' of them teh carry with me..." He looked at his arm and almost instantly his intense expression was gone. He paused for a moment then continued, "Anyway, my granddad suggested the tattoo, so I got it. Of course, Ann doesn't know and I would appreciate it if ya didn't tell her."

"I won't tell her," she said as she touched the tattoo lightly with her fingers. "Did it hurt?"

Airon shook his head.

"I like the cross. It's really intricate."

"Celtic," he said quickly and then remained quiet.

She felt a little disappointment that he had stopped talking. She thought about the initials and realized that if they became a real item that those initials could represent them, too. She sighed heavily. *Good grief, I'm losing it,* she thought, burying her face in her hands.

"It'll be all right, Duchess," said Airon. He placed a hand under her chin, raising her head up. She lifted her eyelids and looked up at him. "It's just a scratch, eh. I've been hurt a lot worse just clowning around. Like I said, no worries, just finish eatin' that or I'm gonna eat it."

Chrism bit off a chuck of the disgustingly chewy stuff then offered the last bite to him but he motioned for her to finish it. She had barely swallowed when he leaned in and brushed her lips with his.

"Mmm," Airon said against her lips. "...tastes like chicken."

Chrism giggled and wrapped her arms around his neck.

* * * * * * *

"How far did she run?" Skylee asked, breathing heavily as she trudged across the snow.

Up ahead, the mist of the waterfall came into view.

"The paw prints are getting closer together, that means she slowed down and there...those are Airon's foot prints, I believe," said Will.

"Wait." Skylee stopped abruptly. "Did you hear that?"

"Yeah, I think I heard something—maybe it's just the sound of the falls."

"No, no that sounded like a giggle. It sounded like Chrism, giggling."

"Well, that's promising," Will said looking intrigued.

"I think it came from over there," she said pointing to an area near the waterfall.

Will stepped out of the forest onto the trail and stopped causing Skylee to plow straight into him.

"Ow! Hey, why'd you sto—" Skylee gasped as she spotted Airon and Chrism.

The two of them were so tightly embraced in a kiss that Skylee couldn't tell where one ended and the other began. She felt as if her eyes were glued to the scene. Skylee didn't know how long she stood there staring at them, or what made her finally look away.

The next thing she knew she was standing face to face with Will. The only things keeping them from touching were Chrism's boots and ski jacket, which were still clutched tightly to her chest. It was like the air around her was gone and she found it hard to breathe.

She looked at Will and her heart faltered. Somewhere deep inside her mind was an image of him kissing her just like Airon was kissing Chrism. Her eyes locked on his lips and she impulsively leaned in toward him.

"Sky," Will whispered uncertainly as he took her face in his hands.

Skylee's breathe caught in her throat. She closed her eyes and waited.

"WHAT? Are you kidding me?" bellowed Chrism, shattering the moment.

Skylee felt like a bucket of cold water had been dumped on her head. Her knees were weak and she felt light-headed. *What am I doing? I can't believe it, I actually urged him on.* A flood of confusing emotions swept over her.

"Sky, I...I..." Will's voice faded, he cleared his throat and stepped away, looking totally disorientated.

Skylee smiled at him timidly as he released her. She was surprised and thankful that her legs held her up. She glanced at Chrism and caught her sister's expression of annoyance.

"Ahem, we were worried when you didn't come back," said Skylee averting her eyes away from her sister. "So we came looking for you."

"I can see that," groaned Chrism.

"Sorry to interrupt," Will said nervously shuffling his feet on the snow.

"Yeah, great timing, mate," grumbled Airon as he stood up. "Skippy, can ya toss those boots over here, huh?"

"Oh, sure," she said as she walked in their direction, stumbling a few times on her way. "Here's your jacket too. Airon, where's your solar shirt? You must be freezing."

"Not likely," joked Will who seemed to have regained his composure and was now grinning like a crazed mental patient.

Skylee turned and frowned at him and his smile faded.

"Not that it's any of your business but I lost my shirt," barked Chrism, glaring at them. "And Airon kindly gave me his and his ski jacket."

"And I would do it again," he quietly said, winking at her.

"Put your jacket on, Airon," insisted Chrism as she handed it to him and slipped her boots on.

"Whoa, mate, you cut yourself," said Will, pointing at Airon's arm.

"What?" Skylee said in alarm. "Where?"

"It's nothing," assured Airon as he struggled to put on his jacket.

"Wait!" demanded Skylee, grasping his sleeve so he couldn't pull it up. "How did you get that?"

"I did it," admitted Chrism in a guilt-ridden tone as Airon helped her up and hugged her.

"It's only a scratch," he insisted finally putting on his jacket.

"Chrism," Skylee blurted out. "You need to be—"

"Don't," Chrism interrupted her. "Don't start. I feel bad enough without having you scold me as if you're my *mother*."

"I...okay then," she said, knowing it was better to say nothing.

Will stepped forward and looked at his watch. "It's getting late. We'd better get back to the hotel. Mum wants us to have an early dinner with her." He looked at Chrism and Airon. "Oh and—Sky and I have a few things to discuss with you two."

Chrism took Airon's hand. "As long as it isn't about me,"

"I like discussing ya," Airon teased.

"Come on then, let's go," she said as she smiled and rolled her eyes at him flirtingly.

The four of them quietly walked back up the trail. Skylee felt as if her thoughts were scattered in all directions like the tiny snowflakes in the air around her. She thought about how close she had come to kissing Will, and about the man she had seen before they left the Château. Then she thought about how her Humusara had been repeating the same message over and over, about how the arrow would lead her to the gift, and Brinfrost would be revealed. And that thought led her to remember what Zane had said to her before she left the farm...*I'm sure I'll be seeing you again, soon*...and that made her wonder how Will would react to the fact that she had secretly taken the box from Zane's office, which made her think...*I almost kissed Will.*

* * * * * * *

The clock on Skylee's V-Phone said five-thirty when Chrism came out of the bathroom. She was decked out in a dark purple dress, which draped over her body like a glove. After everything that happened in the woods, she comes out looking like she's ready to hit the runway at a fashion show. *Geez, how does she do that?* wondered Skylee. She looked down at her own pale blue skirt and simple cream blouse feeling a bit under dressed.

"Is that what you're wearing?" Chrism asked, sashaying to the large mirror.

"Yes," she answered quickly. "We need to go, Ann said to be there at five-thirty sharp. We're late."

Chrism rolled her eyes and said, "Only by a few minutes."

"She said it was important. I think it's more stuff about the Primortus. She even set it up in a private dining room."

"Keep it together little sis. I'm ready, let's go."

Chrism opened the door and both girls headed down the hall. They took the elevator to the first floor. As they made their way to dining room, Skylee's thoughts turned to how close she had come to kissing Will. If her sister hadn't interrupted them, it would have been her first kiss. Her cheeks grew hot as she imagined a different outcome.

"Here we are," Chrism said, glancing at her. "Are you all right? You look a little flushed."

"I'm fine. Let's go in."

The door opened suddenly, and Will stood before them with a look of surprise on his face. Skylee looked down, hoping he couldn't tell what she had just been thinking.

"There you two are," he said with a slight frown. "Mum was sending me up to get you."

"No need," Chrism said as she walked past him and made a beeline for Airon. "We're here now, so the party can begin!"

"Yer lookin' good," Airon said to her.

"You don't look so bad yourself," her sister replied, smiling brightly at him.

Skylee gazed up shyly at Will. "Sorry," she said, jerking her head toward Chrism. "Beauty takes time."

Will laughed and shut the door as Skylee came further into the room.

"Okay, everyone," Ann said. "Please have a seat." She passed her hand through the air, motioning toward the chairs. Skylee and Will sat on one side of the table with Chrism and Airon directly across from them. Ann remained standing at the head of the table, her hands gripping the chair in front of her.

"Are you going to tell us about that conversation with Shelley?" Skylee asked.

"No, I'm not," Ann said sharply.

"But I'm really want to know," insisted Skylee. "And so does Will."

"I'm afraid you didn't hear me the first time," Ann said sternly as her eyes bore into Skylee. "I'm not going to discuss that. End of subject."

Skylee frowned and folded her arms across her chest. *What is up with her? Why is she talking to me like that*, she wondered. *And why didn't anyone else join in.* She looked around the table and everyone was either fiddling with their silverware or refolding their napkins.

"There are extra place settings here," Chrism said. "Is someone else coming?"

"That's right, two more will be joining us."

"Who?" Will asked curiously.

At that same moment, the door opened and in stepped Levy and Hawk. Skylee took note that Will's curiosity had immediately changed to a definite look of disapproval.

"Hey," Hawk said, walking up to the table in jeans and a fitted dark green shirt. "Cool, just in time for dinner!" He pulled the chair out next to Skylee and sat down.

"Hey, hi," she replied, fumbling her words. *What is wrong with me?*

"I've asked Levy and Hawk to join us today because they are—" The hotel servers interrupted Ann as they came through the door bearing food. They placed it quickly on a side table by the wall. The aroma filled the room making Skylee's tummy rumble.

"Someone's hungry," teased Hawk as he gently elbowed her.

Again she felt her face flush.

"That's good," Ann said, dismissing the servers. "We'll take it from here. Thank you."

"Yes ma'am," one of them said as they all left the room, shutting the door behind them.

"I say let's get our food and we'll discuss the reason for this gathering while we eat," Ann suggested.

Skylee wondered what she was going to tell them since it certainly wasn't going to be about Shelley. She had thought she was going to learn more about the Primortus, but it didn't seem likely with Levy and Hawk joining them.

Hawk was last to return to the table, and his plate was piled high with food. He smiled at Skylee as he sat down and said, "I'm a growing boy."

"Well, the boy part is right," grumbled Will under his breath.

Skylee glanced nervously at Hawk, but he hadn't seemed to hear.

"Okay, sit down Hawk," Ann said. "We only have this room for a few hours."

"Mum, what's going on?"

"I need to tell you all something about Levy."

"He's your boyfriend," Chrism said excitedly. "I knew it!"

"What?" Will asked, stopping in mid chew.

"No, he's not my boyfriend," Ann said. "He's my Corporus."

The room became deafeningly quiet. Airon shook his head while Will's mouth hung open. Chrism frowned no doubt thinking Ann was not telling the truth and Hawk continued eating.

"He's you're Corporus," Skylee asked, her voice oddly high. "For how long?"

"Since I was a young Primortus," Ann said. "Not much older than all of you."

Will let out a gasp and his fist landed on the table, hard.

"I know this is a lot to take in," Levy said looking at him. "But with everything that's going on, your mom and I decided all of you needed to know."

"Why didn't you tell me before?" Will asked, looking angrily at his mom. "When you first told us about the Primortus."

"William," she said. "I have my reasons and—well I'm not going to discuss them. But I am telling you now."

"And Hawk?" Skylee asked as she glanced at him.

"I'm not activated yet," Hawk said. "But I hope to be soon. I really wanted to be your Corporus, Sky, but it seems your sister beat me to it."

"Careful what you wish for," Chrism responded sarcastically.

"Really?" Skylee said. "You wanted to be mine—my Corporus?"

"Remember at the wedding, I touched your necklace," he said with raised eyebrows.

"Yes," she replied with a nod. She could feel Will's eyes on her.

"That's what I was doing." Hawk gave her a huge grin and then returned to his food.

Wow, he could have been my Corporus, she thought as she looked over at Will. Her smile faded quickly. He was glaring at Hawk with fire in his eyes. It was a long time before he looked away.

As everyone continued to eat, the discussion stayed centered on the events since their arrival in New Zealand. Much of it was old news to

Skylee but she tried to listen hoping to hear something new. She did learn that Hawk and his dad were traveling in a home-glider, that way they could be where ever Ann was but not in full view.

After they finished dessert, Ann stood up, "Levy, thanks for coming. Hawk you too. If you want to stay at the hotel I think they might have some vacancies, since the avalanche scared people off."

"No thanks," Levy said, leaning in and kissing her on the cheek. "We have our home on wheels outside."

"Yeah," Hawk said. "It's like we never leave home."

"Must get boring," Chrism said. "Riding in that thing all day."

"I guess it depends on what you're doing while riding in it," Hawk said in return.

"Well, that makes sense. Come on, I'll walk you out," Ann said as she led Levy from the room.

Hawk followed them, but not before turning and giving Skylee a huge grin.

"Did he just wink at you?" Chrism asked with a smirk.

"No, he just smiled," she said, chancing a peek at Will, who was now looking down sullenly at his plate. "Hey, I think we should meet in our room in say ten minutes. We have a lot to talk about."

Will and Airon exchanged a look, and nodded in agreement.

Later in their room, Skylee, Chrism and Airon chatted while waiting on Will. Her sister stood at the mirror, fussing with her hair and Airon was leaned back casually on the dresser beside her.

"Wow, can you believe it?" Skylee said, sitting down on the edge of her bed. "Hawk wanted to be my Corporus."

"No...I can't," Chrism said in a heavy voice as she turned toward her. "You wish it were him instead of me, don't you?"

"What? No," Skylee said. "I'm glad it's you." But in truth she wondered if it would have been easier to have Hawk as her Corporus. *What am I thinking?* she inwardly scolded herself. *I'm sure Will wouldn't like it.*

"I don't believe you!" her sister exclaimed.

"Hey," Airon spoke up. "Duchess, of course she's glad ya beat him to it. I know I am."

"If you say so," said Chrism, flopping down on the bed across from Skylee. "Never mind, I'm just too tired to care. But I bet Hawk wouldn't have kept quiet about you lifting that box from Zane's office."

"What box?" Will said, coming into the room.

"I can't believe you just said that," Skylee snapped at Chrism. "You *promised*."

"Sorry," her sister said quietly.

"I'm with Will," said Airon. "What box?"

Everyone looked at Skylee waiting for her reply. *Good grief, there's nothing I can say that's going to make them understand*, she thought. *Now, I kinda understand what Ann has been feeling.* She stood up and walked over to her backpack. Then she reached in and pulled out the item in question.

"This box," she said holding it out in the palm of her hand.

"Sky…" Will said in a shocked tone. "You took it? What's he gonna think when he finds it missing?"

"Well," she said hesitantly. "He knows."

Will and Airon moved toward her and both gazed curiously at the box. She handed it over to Will, who looked at it for a moment, and then gave it to Airon. As they passed it back and forth between them, examining it closely, she finally came clean about what Zane had said to her before they left the farm. It took a few minutes, because Airon and Chrism kept stopping her to ask questions. When she shared her theory about her mom's G-file case possibly being connected to Zane they looked surprised. Skylee noticed Will was completely silent the whole time. His jaw was clamped taut and a vein near his left temple had begun to pulse.

"And ya knew about this?" Airon asked, turning to Chrism. "Why didn't ya say anything?"

"Hey, don't get mad at me," her sister said. "She asked me not to say anything so I didn't—well until tonight—I didn't mean to blurt it out…"

"I'm glad you all know," Skylee said hoping she would eventually feel that way. "Now we can move past this and talk about Brinfrost and Shelley."

"What does Shelley have to do with this?" asked her sister.

"She's a Spiritus," Will said, still looking at Skylee.

"I should've known. Man, everyone we know is something," Chrism said, looking disillusioned.

Skylee felt a sense of relief as she told them about Shelley completing the words in her father's note. She had hoped Will would chime in as she described the argument between his mom and Shelley, but he remained silent. So she tried to explain that she had only taken the box because it had the same lettering as the carving on her Elementum.

"My Humusara practically told me I'm supposed to have it," she insisted.

No one responded. Taking that as a sign of agreement she continued on, telling them that she had needed to find out more given that Ashley was not the man at the tower.

"It seems pretty obvious," declared Skylee. "Whoever he was, he wanted my necklace. And since Zane had the box he might be involved in the attacks."

"I don't think so," Airon said, shaking his head slowly. "Of course, findin' out more is somethin' we all want. But ya should have told us, Skippy. We need to work together. Maybe we could've all gone and talked to Zane about it."

"Well, I agree with Sky about him," Chrism said. "I mean he is creepy and it wouldn't surprise me if he came and killed all of us in our sleep."

"Aw, Chrism," Airon said, sounding exasperated.

There was a long pause as Will paced around the room, then he stopped suddenly and said, "I think Zane may be up to something. I just can't pinpoint it. And now that he knows you took that box, we all need to be on the look out."

"Cripes, who we need to be lookin' out for is the bloke with the knife," Airon said loudly. "He's the one after Skippy's Elementum." He threw up his hands and walked out of the room. Chrism gave Skylee a look of dismay as she followed after him.

"Will," Skylee said cautiously, gazing down at the box, which was still in his hand. "I really believe I was supposed to take that."

"It's not so much that you took it," he said, handing the box back to her. "It's that you didn't tell me about it." He raised his hand to stop her from speaking. "And I don't think you would have, not if Chrism hadn't spilled the beans. Mum said that you need to be careful, to not give the Primortus any more reasons to doubt you. I don't want to hear you're sorry or any other reasons why you did what you did or why you didn't tell me. I'm going to my room, goodnight."

"Will," she said barely audible. She had seen the pain in his eyes as he left. *I've really screwed things up now*, she thought to herself as she slumped back on her bed. Her head throbbed so she closed her eyes and somehow drifted off to sleep.

It was nearly midnight when Skylee awoke to the sound of Chrism snoring. She hadn't even heard her come back into their room. Skylee got up and tiptoed past her sister's bed, sitting down quietly on the window seat. Pulling a wooly throw over her lap, she took in the beauty of the view. The moonlight cast a soft blue sheen across the fresh snow. She touched the frosty edge of the window and watched her fingertips melt little circles in the ice. Shivering, she drew in a deep breath.

"What are you doing?" a sleepy voice asked from across the room.

"Oh, sorry Chrism, I couldn't sleep," said Skylee softly. "I didn't mean to wake you up."

"Whatever," her sister mumbled as she rolled over.

Skylee shook her head, and then looked down, realizing she was still wearing her skirt and blouse. As quietly as possible, she dug her pajamas from her bag, slipped into the bathroom, and got ready for bed. A few moments later, she crawled under the covers and stared up at the ceiling.

TWENTY-FIVE

The Museum

The next three days crawled by at a snail's pace. Skylee knew that it wasn't because of the gloomy skies, or the hours of cold rain that had melted away the beautiful snow, resulting in another shut down of the ski area, which nearly emptied the Château of its guests, or because she had played phone tag with her mom at least a dozen times, ending in a weird texting relay wherein she learned nothing new at all, and it wasn't even because of the silent treatment she had been receiving from everyone except Chrism. No, time had seemed to slow down thanks to Ann.

Her dear aunt, who had become suspiciously fixated on giving her schoolwork, in fact, each and every time Skylee had tried to ask her about Shelley, she received another assignment. She was currently up to four essays, five math quizzes, two book reports and a biology exam. She was so bogged down with her studies that she hadn't spent any time at all with her Humusara, and slipping out to practice with her Elementum was out of the question.

Skylee assumed Will had also been imprisoned in his own virtual schoolroom. Of course she had no way of knowing this, since she was pretty much cross-eyed and brain-dead. Nevertheless, even in her condition she noticed that Will had been extremely busy with important things like staring at the walls, scowling at the floor, and walking in the opposite direction.

Then there was the fact that Shelley's whereabouts were a complete mystery. Skylee had tried contacting her and leaving several messages on her voicemail, with no response. After texting her at least half a dozen times she finally received a reply, which read: Sorry I had to leave. Ann knows why. She sent back a long text, full of questions, to which Shelley replied: Ask Ann. She will explain. Skylee then typed in two words on her V-phone: Fat Chance. But she never sent it.

Meanwhile, Chrism and Airon were extremely chummy which made her kind of nervous. Not that she wished them any ill will, but because the two of them had what Skylee liked to call a love/hate relationship. So this newly developed, all love all the time phase seemed unnatural. Frankly, it was downright unsettling since she knew there was the possibility of them reaching an all hate-all the time phase. If that happened Skylee might have to use her freezing power again, on both of them.

At half past five the next morning Skylee awoke and found she was too excited to go back to sleep. The previous evening she had finally received word from her mom and Alex. She was to meet them in Wellington at the Te Papa Museum, accompanied as always by Ann, Will, Chrism and Airon.

By a quarter to seven, Skylee had showered, woken up Chrism (which was not a pleasant task), gotten dressed, packed her bags, and eaten breakfast. She took a second and mentally ticked off a list of what she would need for her day: *jacket—check, V-phone—check, walking shoes—check, Elementum—check.* Then she stopped and thought about the box. Rummaging through her backpack, she retrieved it, unceremoniously stuffing it into the pocket of her jacket.

At seven o'clock on the dot Skylee went downstairs. She could see the newly risen sun shining in through the lobby windows. The rain had finally ended and it looked like a perfect day for their journey into the city. She stood by the hotel entrance waiting for the others to show up, checking the time on her V-phone every few minutes. Exactly thirty-seven minutes later they set out for Wellington.

"I don't know why we had to get up so early," whined Chrism, twisting around to look groggily at Skylee, who was sitting in the back of the auto glider with a large space between herself and Will. "We aren't meeting Dad and Janis until dinner. Couldn't we have waited and seen the museum tomorrow?"

"It's because they're on a tight schedule. We're going with them to Picton tomorrow. You know, they *are* here on a G-file case," said Skylee.

"Geeee...faaaaa....les...yeah," Chrism said through a huge yawn.

Skylee watched as her sister turned back around in her seat and laid her head on Airon's shoulder. *Yep, guess they're still in the all love phase,* she thought. Then she looked down at the wide gap on the seat beside her and then back up at Will. *No love there,* said a little voice in her head.

A sense of excitement rose as they reached the outskirts of Wellington. The airspace around them grew busier. They merged their way into a constant flow of vehicles, which carried them to a main street in the middle of town, where they hovered along near the pavement below. The sidewalks were heavily populated, teeming with men, women, and children, all dressed in an extraordinary array of clothing. Skylee had never seen this many people in one place.

She had once read that Wellington was the tenth most populated city in the world. After The Day people from all over the globe migrated to the area because it was one of the least damaged places on earth. The city never even lost electrical power.

The colorful crowd fascinated Skylee, who was peering out of the window. Men in business suits were briskly walking while talking on their V-phones, ladies dressed in brightly colored coats, also on their phones, were holding expensive looking leather briefcases. There were shopkeepers carrying trays or pushing carts filled with merchandise, children in school uniforms, priest and monks, old couples walking hand in hand, and even a few beggars in tattered clothing. At one point she thought she saw a man who resembled Zane and her heart leapt into her throat. *Is that him?* she wondered. Then she shook herself mentally and thought, *not every farmer with a scruffy beard is Zane Cook.*

A moment later Skylee caught sight of a nicely dressed woman holding a cute little dog. The pair reminded her of Miss Ruth and Prissy. As their auto glider made a second sweep around the block, in search of parking, Skylee replayed their departure from the Château in her mind. At the very last minute Prissy leapt into the vehicle chasing after Chrism. Everyone tried to catch the flying ball of fur as she dodged and sprinted her way from the front to the rear of the vehicle. In the end, Chrism managed to nab the dog, whispering something in her ear before she handed her back to Miss Ruth. They drove off leaving a teary-eyed, whimpering Prissy in her relieved owner's arms.

"Sky-lee," a voiced sang out.

"What?" she faintly asked, being brought back to the present.

"You gonna stay in there?" her sister asked in a hopeful tone. "I mean we could call Dad and tell him we would rather do something else. I just think this whole museum thing is going to be boring. Really, what kind of excitement is there in a museum—a bunch of pictures, wall plaques, stuffed dead things..."

Skylee glanced around and realized she was the only passenger remaining in the vehicle. She quickly jumped out and enthusiastically said, "Oh, I want to see the museum."

"Great," mumbled Chrism, sounding both annoyed and disappointed.

Skylee stretched her arms above her head and sighed deeply. The ride there had been a very long two and half hours. The thick tension exuding from Will reminded her of the years right after The Day. Even though she had been a small child, she remembered the dense, smoke-filled air had made it hard to breathe. That was exactly how she had felt while sitting there with him. Taking a few deep breaths to clear her head, she tried to convince herself that everything would be all right between them.

Relax, she thought. She was finally at the Te Papa Museum, which she had looked forward to visiting from the moment she found out they were coming to New Zealand. *I'm going to enjoy this day, no matter what,* Skylee promised herself.

She joined the others, with Ann in the lead, and they walked along a crowded sidewalk for twenty minutes, until at last they reached the museum. The sun peeked out from behind a cloud and cast a warm glow on the structure. The building's assorted geometric shapes blended into one magnificent design with a tall rounded facade on the left and a huge charcoal gray wall to the right. Above the entrance was a big w-shaped turquoise canopy.

Skylee looked across the expansive stone courtyard and saw three large boulders in front of the gray wall. On the opposite side, standing out spectacularly against the beige colored wall was a gigantic tree, which was sculpted from dark bronze. Though Skylee couldn't see what was written below, she could tell it was a memorial for The Day. They set off towards it, weaving their way through the crowd. Skylee picked up fragments of conversation, in a variety of foreign languages, as they went.

Will was the first to reach the sculpture followed closely by Skylee, Ann, Airon, and Chrism. At the base of the towering tree were dozens of carved roots on which names had been engraved. An inscription was on the thick trunk of the tree.

Day of Disaster Memorial
Here are recorded the New Zealanders lost on The Day
Te Papa Museum - Our place - a testament of survival
Standing near the Wellington fault line

Skylee already knew the building was sitting almost directly on a fault line. It had been built on huge rubber springs, which were like shock absorbers, making it earthquake resistant. Although if the same kind of shift in the earth's crust had happened here, as it did in many places on The Day, everything inside would surely have been lost.

How long Skylee stood there, gazing at the memorial and reading name after name, she didn't know. She found herself wondering if her birth, the birth of The Second Born Primortus had caused the death of each and every name before her. But when she finally looked up into the soft white clouds another name seemed to swim before her eyes— *Lee Porter.*

"Can we go see something else? This is boring," Chrism complained.

Ann frowned. "Well, all right then. Let's go," she said, waving for them to follow her. Skylee tore her eyes away from the memorial and slowly trailed after them.

"This is just as beautiful as I remember," said Ann as she pulled a camera out of her purse and began taking pictures. "Don't you think?"

"Sure," muttered Chrism as her eyes scanned the massive building, "and really large."

"It has six floors of exhibits," Skylee said with excitement.

"Do we have to go through the whole thing?" asked Chrism as she pursed her lips.

"Come on, Duchess," Airon said as he took her hand and guided her toward the door. "I'll help ya get through it."

"Bite me," said Chrism out of the corner of her mouth.

"They're quite a pair...and very entertaining," said Ann, snapping their photo as she followed after them.

Skylee smiled slightly at the exchange. She looked at Will and found him staring at her. Their eyes locked on each other for only a second.

"Will," Skylee said hesitantly. "You're not still mad at me about the box, are you?"

"I don't think we should talk about it here," he said coolly.

"But if you'll just listen, I can—" she began, pausing as he held up his hand between them.

"No," he said stubbornly. "You kept it secret all that time. It can wait."

Skylee was dumbfounded. It was enough to make her want to freeze him out of her life, like he had done to her. All at once, she felt a cold breeze flow down her right arm and into her hand. Looking down, she saw a tiny swirl of ice on her palm. In surprise she glanced up at Will, who raised his eyebrows.

"Are you planning on using that on me?" he boldly asked.

"No! Sorry," she whispered, fiercely rubbing the side of her jeans to warm up her hand.

They both looked around but no one seemed to notice anything. Skylee stared down at her feet. She felt like a complete failure. Now Will was upset with her for keeping secrets *and* being a total mess up with her power.

"We should go in," he said heavily.

"But, I—why are you acting like this? I still want to explain."

"Not now," he said, giving her a glum look as he walked past her and followed the others through the entrance doors.

Skylee took a deep breath. Her chest ached in reaction to his coldness toward her. She stood outside the massive doors of the museum and tried to compose herself. Gradually, she felt her chest getting warmer, much warmer, and then too warm.

She placed her hand over her Elementum, slowly turning in a circle to scan the area. Nothing seemed out of place. Yet, she felt a sense of foreboding. After all she had been through, it was best to stay alert.

As she entered the museum she spotted Chrism in an intense discussion on her V-phone. Her sister was pacing back and forth, vehemently shaking her head. Every few seconds she heard her say, *no, no, no.* Skylee wondered who was on the phone and what was being said to make her so unhappy. She would know soon enough.

Skylee glanced around the entry foyer and observed Will and his mom, who were deep in conversation as they stood beside a massive stone ball, which was spinning inside a fountain. As much as she hated to admit it she felt a twinge of resentment. He could share the Primortus world with her. Skylee really wished she could to talk to her mom about it. Especially now that she believed the G-file investigation was connected to all the things that had been happening to them.

It seemed strange to Skylee that her mom didn't know about the Primortus world already. After all, she had been married to one.

Shelley had said something about erasing memories, she thought, *what if—no she wouldn't have.* Skylee tried to push that thought out of her mind.

It certainly didn't seem fair that her mom was in the dark about it. She and Alex needed all the facts right now, but in the back of Skylee's mind she worried that knowing would put them in more danger. She sighed as she rubbed her temples trying to ease the pain that was growing in her head.

Her lips formed a grimace as her short talk with Shelley reentered her mind. Brinfrost was coming for her Elementum. What was she supposed to do to stop it? If only her dad had lived, things would be different for her now. He would have prepared her, trained her, and guided her.

Chrism plodded toward Skylee and snapped shut her V-phone.

"What's going on?" asked Skylee. "I mean—you look upset."

"Upset! That's an understatement," barked Chrism. "My dad, in his infinite wisdom, has asked ME to watch those two brats so their parents can attend some meeting. Can you believe that? What lucky star am I standing under?"

"The twins...they're here...in New Zealand?" asked Skylee in surprise. She caught movement to her right as Ann and Will walked up to them.

"Yes, of all the places," complained Chrism. "I can't do this. They'll probably destroy the museum!"

"Did I hear you correctly," asked Will. "Your cousins, Gaby and Izzy are coming here?"

"You heard right," cried Chrism miserably.

"It'll be fine, with all of us here to help," assured Ann, who had a faint grin on her face.

"Sure," Skylee agreed, trying her best to sound and look cheerful. Although deep in her mind she secretly worried that the twins might live up to their nickname. If truth be told, Chrism was right. The "twins of mass destruction" were precisely that—a cute little duo of demolition.

"Are they here now?" Will asked, looking around.

"No, but their parents are going to drop them off soon—So, Airon?" Chrism asked in a high-pitched voice, "Will you go with me to get them? They're supposed to drop them off out front somewhere."

"Duchess, I don't do rug rats," he announced, folding his arms across his chest.

"Please," she said sweetly, batting her eyelids at him. "I would have to stand out there all by myself...in a strange place."

"Ya won't be by yourself," teased Airon. "There are blokes all over the place."

"Airon," she pleaded, pursing her lips into a small pout.

Skylee watched as Airon lowered his head and took a deep breath.

"Well Duchess, I reckon we're takin' some rug rats for a little walkabout then," he said as he hooked his arm through Chrism's and ushered her toward the entrance of the museum.

Skylee watched them go and chuckled at Airon's admission of defeat.

"Pathetic," said Will, staring openmouthed at the glass doors as they exited. "Who is that guy and where'd he put my best mate?"

"Well," said Ann in a completely deadpan voice. "I'm thinking invasion of the body snatchers...or he's in love."

Both Skylee and Will laughed. It was the first lighthearted moment they had shared for days. An awkward pause hung in the air.

"Listen you two," Ann abruptly said. "I don't know what you're fighting about, but we're not going to have much fun today if this feud continues. I suggest you call a truce." She didn't wait for them to respond. She walked across the entry area into the gift shop.

"She's right," said Skylee, turning slowly toward Will. "So, how about it—truce?"

He tilted his head and looked at her with one eyebrow arched upward.

"Or, I could try to baby talk you," she said in a sweet high voice. "And as a last resort I might even try battling my eyelashes and doing that pouty thing. But I warn you I'm not as good as Chrism so I'll probably just end up looking like I have a bug in my eye and a bee sting on my lip."

Will stared at her for a second, then a small snort escaped his mouth and he broke into laughter.

"It's not that funny," blurted Skylee in relief as she smacked him on the arm. She felt like a heavy weight had been lifted from her shoulders. It was almost as if the last week had never happened. But deep down she knew that it had.

Minutes later, they found Ann and shared the news of their truce. Then the three of them set out to explore the museum.

TWENTY-SIX

A Helpmate Resists

"So, what should we see first?" asked Ann as they climbed a long staircase, which led to the information desk.

"I don't know let's see if we can find a map," said Skylee. "A person could get seriously lost in a place like this."

After studying the map Will insisted on heading straight to the Colossal Squid display, which was located in the Mountain and Sea Exhibit. They spent nearly an hour learning about New Zealand's plants and animals. Then, as Will and his mom turned back to gawk a little longer at the giant squid, Skylee decided to go in search of The Day of Disaster Exhibit.

She rounded a corner and paused in front of a large wooden statue, which reminded her of the warriors she had seen at the Maori Village. She gazed up at his intricately carved features. The powerful looking face had bulging eyes and his long tongue protruded from his mouth. She leaned in and examined the circular tattoos, which covered his entire face from forehead to chin.

Stepping back to take in the full view, she came to a stop right in the path of a tall blonde woman who was hurrying by with a huge stack of documents haphazardly balanced in her arms. On impact the papers flew up in the air and scattered across the floor. It looked a little like a ticker tape parade, without the floats and clowns.

"Ah! Pardon me," the woman cried, trying to hold on to the remaining papers in her hands.

"Oh, no," said Skylee as she attempted to catch some of the papers flying around the room. "I am so sorry—I was looking at—here let me help."

Skylee and the woman started gathering papers. As they picked them up, she noticed that most of them were covered in strange lettering.

Is this hieroglyphics? she wondered. *It kind of reminds me of...*

As she continued picking up papers, Skylee decided the woman might be just the right person to ask about the markings on the box.

"Here," said Skylee graciously as she offered her the papers. "Again, I'm very sorry. I hope I didn't ruin anything."

The woman stood, politely smiled and straightened her designer suit with one hand. Her hair was swept back in an elaborate twist and she wore stylish eyeglasses. As Skylee smiled back at her she noticed the woman's friendly brown eyes.

"No problem, I mean, I wasn't watching where I was going either," the woman said, accepting the papers. "I get so caught up in my research that everything else around me just disappears."

"I guess I did the same thing with this statue," Skylee said, and then she looked down and pointed to the stack of papers. "I couldn't help but notice the strange writing on that paperwork. Is it a certain language?"

"No, not just one but a variety of languages. I study them, hobby of mine," replied the woman, nodding courteously at her. "Hi, my name's Rachel Cara."

"Skylee Porter," she said, extending her hand.

Rachel carefully cradled her papers in one arm and reached out with the other. As their hands intertwined, Skylee felt a familiar tingling sensation.

No... no... no...This can't be happening...She's a Primortus.

"What did you say?" asked Skylee, tightening her grip.

She knows...I have to get out of here. Rachel had a panicked look on her face as she jerked her hand out of Skylee's grip.

"Sorry, but I didn't say anything," she quickly said in a quivering voice.

Skylee blinked and shook her head. She had heard it, not audibly but in her mind, exactly the same way she had heard Hera's voice. Before she could say a word, Rachel nervously turned her head and Skylee saw a mark behind her ear. It was an arrow.

"Are you an Animus?" Skylee asked just above a whisper.

"Why...why don't...you people...just...just leave me alone," Rachel stammered in fear.

"Um, are you afraid, of *me*? You know what I am, right?"

"Yes," she said as her breath caught in her throat. "I know and I-I don't want anything to do with you. You're—you're evil."

"What?" said Skylee in shock. "I'm not evil. We're here, you and me, to help the ear—"

"No, don't say that...please," she pleaded. "I can't go through this again."

"I don't know what you're talking about," said Skylee in disbelief. "I'm not trying to hurt you or anything."

"Okay, then," Rachel said, sounding both unconvinced and nervous. "You'll have to excuse me, I must get back to work."

"But I...have something that I would like you to look at...to see if you could decipher a symbol on it." Skylee said, reaching into the pocket of her jacket for the box.

"No, I can't," insisted Rachel, shaking her head as she backed up slowly, then she quickly turned and raced away.

"Wait!" Skylee yelled as she watched the woman disappear into the crowd.

She paused for a moment, debating whether she should follow. It was a short debate. What were the chances of her meeting someone else who could tell her about the box? Edging her way through a group of Japanese tourists who were crowded around an exhibit, she made it to the doorway only to be greeted by Will.

"Hey, where ya going? I saw you talking to a woman. Who was she?" Will asked. "You all right?"

"Yeah, I wasn't paying attention and bumped into her," replied Skylee, darting her eyes around the exhibit hall.

"Oh okay, isn't this place epic?" he asked excitedly. "Did you see that giant squid? Wouldn't want to be out surfing and run in to that bad boy."

Skylee nodded absentmindedly at him and without a word started off in the direction where she had last seen Rachel.

"Hey, where are you going?" Will said as he reached out for her arm but missed.

"I'll be back in a minute." She looked past Will's shoulder and noticed the Lavatory sign. "Bathroom, I really have to go."

"Er—thanks for sharing that," he said as she took off. "Sky—hang on..."

Skylee heard Will calling her but she rushed through the crowd searching all around, until she came to the far end of the museum. Rachel was gone. She sighed in disappointment. As she slowly turned in circles, trying desperately to find her, she stuck in hand in her pocket and fumbled with the box.

"Where is she?" she whispered to herself.

Checking the time on her V-phone, she considered going back to find Will. But at the moment she didn't need him to tell her all the reasons she shouldn't show Rachel the box. And standing around doing nothing wasn't going to get her any answers. She headed back through the exhibit hall seeking out a museum worker.

"Excuse me," she said to a man, who was wearing a nametag that read Te Papa Volunteer.

He was extremely short, probably no more than five feet one or two, and his absurdly thick glasses were perched high on the bridge of his pointy nose. What was left of his thin gray hair had been combed over to cover a shiny bald spot.

"Yes miss," he warmly responded as his huge magnified eyes widened. "Great heavens! You're the girl that fell off the Sky Tower! Aren't you?"

"Um, yes," she said, shuffling her feet uncomfortably. It had been quite some time since anyone had recognized her.

"My goodness, Sky tower girl! Of course I saw all the news reports about it," he said loudly. "Terrible thing, just terrible. I knew right away it was you, I never forget a face, especially one as pretty as yours. Did they ever find out what happened? I mean how'd you fall? Was there really a boy who broke your heart?"

"Ah well, it's a really long story. I wouldn't want to bore you with the details."

"Oh, I wouldn't be bored. But then, I understand if you'd rather not talk about it. I'm sure it was ghastly falling off like that. You poor thing," he said, looking up at her, eyes bulging like a goldfish staring out of its fishbowl.

"Um, thanks," said Skylee, unsure of what else to say. "So, I was just wondering do you know a woman named Rachel Cara? Does she work here?"

"No, Professor Cara doesn't really work here. She's one of our volunteer researchers, so I do know her, well, know of her."

"Oh, would you happen to know where she is?"

He looked at his watch. "Hmm, I'm not sure, but I often see her in the archive reading room about this time of day, except for when she's working out here with her students."

"Thanks. What direction is that?" asked Skylee.

She did her best to follow his directions, climbing the stairs one level, and then roaming through a maze of exhibit rooms. After wandering around for at least twenty minutes she turned back and began retracing her steps. As she passed by an open doorway she heard crying and followed the sound down a hallway. At the end of the wall, Rachel stood with her forehead pressed against a window. Her eyes were swollen and her expression was not just sadness but fear. *Maybe I shouldn't bother her,* thought Skylee, *but if not now...when?*

"Ahem, Professor? Um, Rachel," Skylee called softly. "I know you're upset but please I...I don't mean to bother you I just want your help."

"Please leave me alone," she said wiping her eyes and sniffing. "I don't want anything to do with it."

"But, if you would just take a look at this box," Skylee said as she took it out of her pocket. "I promise I'll leave you alone. I think that since you're an Animus and you've studied ancient languages you might have an idea as to what these symbols are—they're right here."

Rachel sniffed again, and then gave the box a sideways glance before closing her eyes and taking a deep breath. She looked toward the open door as if she was considering bolting through it.

"Please," Skylee begged.

"I...I..." stuttered Rachel. "If I look at it, you promise to leave me alone?"

"Yes," assured Skylee. "I won't bother you again."

"Okay, let me see it," said Rachel, dabbing her tear-streaked face before she stood up straight and held out her hand.

"Have you seen a box like this before?" Skylee asked as she laid it in her palm.

"No," Rachel whispered but her red eyes stared intently at the wooden box as she turned it over carefully.

"This," said Skylee, pointing to the lettering, "is some sort of ancient writing. But the symbols here are unusual. I'm not sure what they mean."

Rachel held it closer and squinted. "Does this open?"

"Yes," said Skylee as she lifted the lid. "So far I've been the only one to get it open."

They both stared down at it. As always, the shiny arrow spun around the golden dial.

"Hmm, this looks like some kind of directional device, maybe a compass of some sort."

"But it just keeps spinning."

"Well, maybe it's broken..." Rachel replied softly. She examined it closer as she gently ran her fingertips over the symbols.

"Captivating, isn't it," said Skylee.

All of a sudden Rachel shut the box hard and spoke unemotionally, "You want to know what these markings are, I believe this symbol could be the number seven."

"Really, how do you know that?" Skylee said excitedly as she looked at the box. "Can you explain the markings to me?"

"Yes," said Rachel, exhaling loudly. She glanced at Skylee then her large moist eyes locked onto the box. "It looks a little like Glagolitic or possibly Proto-Sinaitic..." she continued on, describing in detail what she believed the symbols were.

It all sounded like Greek to Skylee. "Wait, you can read it?"

"Not exactly, but based on the morphology, I can somewhat decipher it."

"O...kay, so, you're sure it's a seven?" Skylee said pointing at the carving.

"This is just an educated guess," Rachel said, handing it back to her.

Skylee's eyes met Rachel's as she asked, "It makes sense though and you're sure you've not seen a box like this before?"

"That's right I haven't," said Rachel hesitantly. "But...I have seen symbols like that number before...long ago..."

"Really? Where?"

"It was on an amulet," she said barely above a whisper.

Amulet, she thought as she shifted the box to her left hand and reached for the chain around her neck. If she showed her the Elementum, Rachel might be able to tell her more about its carvings. Her fingers hooked around the chain but she paused as Ann's warning rang through her mind. She could see Will giving her that "don't do it" look which annoyed her. But Brinfrost was coming soon, it was worth the risk.

She took a deep breath, pulled out her Elementum and asked, "Like this one? Look, it has markings on it sort of like the one on the box."

Rachel's brows furrowed as she leaned in to study the necklace. Her mouth opened, and then closed.

"So, the symbols here," Skylee said. "Are they a number?"

"Yes, the number eleven."

"Eleven," said Skylee curiously. "Well, I know the lettering here means 'protect life.' Did the amulet—the one you saw before—have something like this written on it too?"

Skylee looked up and saw Rachel's expression darken, her breathing appeared labored.

"Hey," Skylee said as she gently clutched her arm.

I don't understand this, she isn't like him... Skylee realized she was hearing Rachel thoughts again. *This girl is different... he didn't protect life...he destroyed it...*

Suddenly an image raced across Skylee's mind of a man, not more than twenty years old, being ripped to pieces by some sort of machine. His scream was broken as each swipe was made. Blood gushed from his wounds as he tried to speak. Skylee felt herself being hurled forward, as if she were kneeling by his side. It felt like her hands were trying to stop the bleeding. Then just as abruptly as the vision began it was over.

"Oh, Rachel," she whispered as a tear slide down her cheek.

Who is this girl? Did he send her? Skylee heard in her mind. Closing her eyes, she tried to concentrate on what Rachel was thinking. Then another image flashed through her mind. A chain with a dark amulet hung around the neck of man. It looked burnt and twisted. And there were symbols on its face, although she couldn't see them clearly. She desperately wanted to see who was wearing the necklace, but she could only see the man's chin.

"Who is he?" whispered Skylee with a shudder.

"What are you doing?" Rachel shrieked as she jerked her arm back. "You have no right to be in my head."

"I'm—I'm sorry," Skylee stammered as she reached for her again.

"Don't touch me!" she snapped, flinching away from her.

Skylee kept her hands close to her sides and said, "It's not something I can control. If I caused you pain I didn't mean to. I really am sorry."

"Sorry, you're sorry," cried Rachel disbelievingly as she pointed to Skylee's Elementum. "You have no clue what evil surrounds that thing. No clue as to what lies ahead for you and for those you care about."

"I don't understand, this isn't evil, I use this for good," Skylee pleaded.

"You're wrong," she huffed as she began to back away. "I've experience the *good* that it can do. It kills."

"Why would you..." Skylee began, pausing as her thoughts went to Brinfrost. "Wait—the amulet that I saw—"

"You saw that?"

"Do you remember who had it?" Skylee said, ignoring her question. "What's his name?"

Rachel slowly raised her eyes from gazing at the necklace until they were level with Skylee's. There was such a look of fear and anger on her face that Skylee clutched her Elementum.

"Please, can you tell me who has that dark amulet? It's important."

"No," said Rachel. "I can't help—I'm leaving. I gave you the information you asked for. You promised to leave me alone. Don't follow me, don't talk to me again."

Skylee stood helplessly as she watched her walk away. She glanced at the box quickly before slipping it back into her pocket. The horror of the images from Rachel's thoughts repeated in her mind. *Who could do something like that? No wonder she was terrified,* she thought. Skylee had felt Rachel's pain. The wounded man must have been someone she cared for deeply. Thoughts exploded in her mind like fireworks going in all directions. *Is that what Brinfrost is going to do to me? Hurt the people I love? I can't let that happen. I'm not sure I can do this. What if she's right? No, she's not. The Primortus are—*

"Ahhhh." Skylee jumped as she felt a hand on her shoulder.

"Sorry," Will chuckled. "What's going on? I've been looking everywhere for you."

"Nothing," she said as she turned to stare in the direction of Rachel's retreat. "Nothing..."

"Cripes, I can't believe it!" he scoffed. "You're keeping more secrets." Will turned to leave.

"Hey, I'm not keeping secrets," she quickly said. But she knew that was a lie, sort of.

He took a couple of steps then spun around and said, "You're not? I know you didn't go to the bathroom, Sky. And I can tell by the look on your face, something happened here. There are real dangers out there, maybe even here. I'm beginning to believe that you want to do this all alone without any help, especially mine."

"Don't be ridiculous," she snapped, moving closer to him and lowering her voice. "When Brinfrost shows up it'll take all of us to stop it."

"Is that right? So, what happened in here?"

"Nothing happened, really and I'm okay." She wanted to tell him but not right then and there. Skylee knew he was still mad about the box and he wouldn't understand her reasons for following Rachel alone.

Will shook his head and chewed his lower lip.

"Okay, I'm not exactly fine, I mean, yes something happened but I can't tell you here. It needs to be in private." She hoped that would appease him.

"Keep it secret, right?" he said as he reached out and lightly yanked on her Elementum. Skylee drew in a sharp breath as she realized it was in plain sight. He looked at her sharply then let the necklace drop back against her shirt.

"Right," said Skylee as she tucked it in her top.

Will shook his head, exhaled slowly and said, "Listen, I came looking for you to tell you Chrism's having a hard time with the twins. I think she's about to lose it."

"When it comes to the twins, it is only a matter of time," she lightheartedly said, trying to ease the tension between them.

Together they set out in search of them. Descending the stairs, they proceeded along a hallway checking for them in each room. As they entered the third exhibit room, loud yelling and squealing bounced off the walls.

"Looks like we found them," said Will in a droll tone.

"Oh joy," smirked Skylee as she watched the twins running wildly through the exhibits with Chrism right behind them.

"If you two don't stop!" her sister exclaimed.

"What? You can't do nothing to us," said Gaby boldly.

"Yeah," agreed Izzy.

Chrism's reached out and grabbed both girls by the collar of their jackets. As she dragged them away from the exhibits, they twisted their bodies until they had squirmed free and took off again.

"This is going to be bad," Skylee said under her breath.

"You know, I think I'll let you handle this one," said Will, pausing briefly as if he were waiting for an argument. "Good then, I'll be right over here, um, let's see, reading that fascinating looking wall plaque."

"Coward."

A grin flashed across his face. Skylee sighed loudly at him then without a word she headed toward Chrism. She couldn't blame him for retreating to safer ground. Although she was equally amused and surprised to see him back away from a challenge, considering how fearless he usually was in the face of danger.

Out of the corner of her eye Skylee caught sight of her red-faced sister. She wished that Chrism's big brother, Michael, would magically appear and stop the craziness. But that kind of stuff only happened in the movies, so she braced herself and walked straight into the battle zone to try and help defuse the situation before it erupted into World War III. After all she was the second born, whatever that meant.

"Hey, come on you two," Skylee said loudly. The twins and Chrism both stopped in their tracks and looked at her.

Skylee smiled at the effect she had on them and said, "This is a very special place and the things here are—"

"Old" Gaby said.

"Yeah, they're old," laughed Izzy.

"Well, yes they're old but much more than that," Skylee spoke sweetly through gritted teeth. "They're also rare and shouldn't be—"

Her sentence was interrupted as the two red headed torpedo's laughed and took off.

"ARRGH," growled Chrism.

Skylee turned sharply and gaped at her.

"Why are you looking at me like that?"

"I heard you growl and—"

"You thought I was going to, uh...do that *thing* I can do?"

"Well, yeah."

Chrism rolled her eyes then planted a wicked grin on her face and said, "Hey, that might not be a bad idea! I could change into something that would scare them so bad."

"No," said Skylee horrified that her sister might actually do it. "Don't, please..."

"Oh for crying out loud," smirked Chrism. "Calm down, I'm not going to, *you know*. Besides, I like my outfit much more than any of these exhibits."

"And because there are a lot of people around," insisted Skylee.

"Yeah," she shrugged her shoulders. "That too."

Skylee looked around and noticed several people scowling disapprovingly at the twins, who had their faces pressed against a glass display case, which was boldly marked DO NOT TOUCH.

"Where's Airon?" Skylee asked as she tapped the girls on the shoulder, in an unsuccessful attempt to stop them from smearing theirs hands up and down the glass.

"I sent him to get Ann, maybe she can control—" she stopped mid-sentence as the twins took off across the exhibit hall at full speed. "Oh no, HEY! Stop, you can't go down there!"

A loud noise erupted from the other side of the room. As Skylee turned, she saw the twins running through the middle of an exhibit. Gaby bumped into one of the tall wooden sculptures, which caused it to tilt. As Izzy passed by, she too pushed on the tilting sculpture. The massive artifact began its decent right toward a petite young woman who stood beneath it.

Skylee watched in horror as the small woman's eyes widened with fear. Then surprisingly and almost immediately the sculpture stopped falling. A wave of relief washed over Skylee.

A pair of hands had come around the artifact and placed it back in the upright position. Skylee smiled brightly when she saw that Will had come to the rescue. But her face changed from joy to confusion as the woman wrapped both arms around him. And he, in turn, put his arms around her.

Skylee watched them and noticed that the girl was wearing a very extravagant outfit that even Chrism wouldn't dare wear. Her snug fitting skirt was much too short in Skylee's opinion and her shiny blouse didn't leave much to the imagination. From the way Will was leaning over her, she appeared to be only about five feet tall. In fact, everything about her was short, including her trendy pixie hair cut.

After the hug fest finally ended, the girl took Will's hand and talked to him for quite some time. It wouldn't have bothered her except he had the same stupid grin on his face he did when he first met Shelley.

Skylee decided it didn't matter. If he wanted to make an idiot of himself, that was his business. She turned her attention to the other side of the room and tried to see where the twins had gone. She was determined to ignore the embarrassing display between Will and that woman. Laughter rang out and she whipped her head around and saw the two of them, laughing like they were old friends.

Skylee couldn't take her eyes off of them. Her stomach flipped as she tried to focus on what was causing her to feel this way. She shook her head in denial as the girl pulled Will's head down, kissed him on both of his blushing cheeks and ended with a full on kiss to his lips.

Exasperated, Skylee let out a loud sigh. What happened next was so fast that no one, including Skylee knew how she did it. A waterfall exhibit, which was just to her right, burst into the air like a geyser. It formed a wave, flew out of the basin and drenched the young woman who shrieked in surprised. People nearby gasped loudly and a few ran for the exits. The twins finally stopped their mischief.

"COOL!" they both squealed.

"Oh no," Skylee whispered to herself. "Don't..."

The remaining water immediately flew back onto the exhibit. Will, who had been spared from the deluge, cocked his head and glared back at her

"Well, well," taunted Chrism. "Look at you, using your power or should I say abusing your power."

"I didn't mean too," Skylee said.

"Oh, I think you did," sneered Chrism. "And I'm not the only one."

"Skylee," Ann said sternly as she rushed up to her. "Was that you? What are you thinking? There are people all around."

"I...I'm not..." stuttered Skylee.

The realization hit her. She had let her emotions control her power. In shame, Skylee looked down at the floor, avoiding Ann's glare.

"I'm disappointed in you," Ann said. "Our powers are not to be used like that—ever!"

"I know but," said Skylee quietly. "It wasn't on purpose."

"We'll discuss this later," Ann said as the twins rushed by her. She reached out and managed to grab both of them by their hands and led them out of the exhibit area only glancing back at Skylee once.

"I can't say I wouldn't have done the same thing," said Chrism with a pretentious look. "Jealousy can get the best of you."

"I'm not jealous."

"Sure you're not. You just keep telling yourself that and maybe—no that won't change it either," laughed Chrism. "Well, I'm going to go and see if Ann can control those two monsters. By the way, Will's headed this way and he looks really mad."

"He does," Skylee murmured as she lowered her eyes, just taking a peek to see his approach. "Don't go."

Chrism smiled coyly at her sister as she turned and walked away leaving her to face him alone.

"What are you doing?" Will asked in a stern voice.

"I...I..." Skylee stuttered, frantically trying to come up with an explanation for her blunder. "It just happened and why are you just assuming I did it?"

"Who else would have done that?" he snapped back. "Besides, you did something just like that at the wedding with that punch bowl."

Skylee opened her mouth to answer then shut it just as fast. She closed her eyes and inhaled slowly. She had abused her powers, so what was there to say.

"Are you going to tell me why you did that?"

"I...well, I don't..." Skylee's words faded. She wasn't going to tell him Chrism's theory even though it might be correct.

"What has gotten into you lately?"

"Look, I just think that she—that girl was a bit too grateful and trying to take advantage of you."

"Oh her. Too grateful, how so?" asked Will, who was still frowning although his voice sounded strangely amused.

"Well, she hugged you—way too long. I mean really."

Will's frown twitched slightly. "All that over a hug? You would risk our secret being revealed over a HUG?"

"Yes—No," she muttered.

"Well, which is it?"

"You kissed her," she blurted out.

"I...kissed...her," he said slowly with a slight grin. "If I remember correctly, because I happened to be there, she kissed me."

"Same thing."

"Really?" he asked in a sly tone.

"And then you had that stupid grin on your face and I swear it looked like you were drooling."

"Yes go on," he said as he smiled at her. "I was drooling...and?"

"Well, you were embarrassing yourself."

"So you drenched that pretty young lady to stop me from embarrassing myself?'

"Sure,' she said realizing it was as good an excuse as any she could come up with. At least it was better than the real reason.

"Huh, I find that hard to believe," he said shrewdly.

"And who said she was pretty? You think she's pretty?" Skylee's voice cracked.

Will suddenly smiled very mischievously and said, "You know, I think you're jealous."

"I am not," she said, trying to convince herself. "Why would I be?"

She watched as Will leaned in and smiled even more widely.

"Sky's jealous...I like the sound of that," he taunted.

She stared at him trying to appear calm even though her insides were wreaking havoc on her.

"Cat got your tongue? Hmmm, since your silent, I can only assume that I'm right...you're jealous."

"Uggh," Skylee grunted and turned to leave but she bumped right into Airon.

"Skippy, watch yer step," Airon said as he caught her by the arm. "Ya all right? Ya look flustered."

"Just let me go," snapped Skylee, trying to wiggle out of his grip.

"She jealous," Will simply stated with a silly grin on his face.

"Jealous," Airon said as his brows arched. "Ya don't say!"

"I am not!" she shouted. She shoved Airon's hand away and stomped into the hall but not before she heard both of them sniggering.

TWENTY-SEVEN

The Confessions

After Sky's quick departure, Will followed Airon from one exhibit to another, passing by life-sized holograms of all sorts of animals. But his mind was still on Sky's reaction to the girl who had kissed him. He grinned. *So maybe I didn't imagine it that day in the forest,* he thought. *Maybe Sky really did want me to kiss her.* His grin faded as he let out a soft huff. *Girls are so confusing.*

Will eventually found himself surrounded by sea creatures, some of which looked amazingly real and others that were actual bones or fossils. His cousin stopped under the skeleton of a blue pygmy whale, which seemed to hover in midair. As Will gazed up at the suspended monstrosity, he wondered how something big enough to fill the entire ceiling could be called a pygmy. Lots of words weren't exactly what they seemed. The word friend fell into that category.

"Now, mate," Airon said as he placed a hand on Will's shoulder. "I need to discuss something serious with ya."

"What's that?" Will asked sincerely, giving Airon his full attention. *Did he and Chrism have a fall out?* he wondered. *Or had Zane contacted him about Sky taking that stupid box?*

"I'm in major need of some tucker. How about ya?"

"Cripes," Will responded with a great sigh of relief. "I thought it was something—never mind—food, yeah, you know me, hollow leg."

"Too true," his cousin said in agreement. "So, where to?"

"I noticed a café on the first floor and I think there's a coffee shop somewhere on the fourth."

"Do ya even need to ask?" Airon declared with raised eyebrows. "I want real tucker not tea and crumpets."

"To the first floor it is then," Will cheerfully said, motioning toward the stairs.

As they made their way to the stairway, they passed by a couple of men dressed in custodial uniforms, who were examining the waterfall exhibit. Will laughed inwardly, wondering how they would explain the incident. The young lady who had received the drenching stood near what appeared to be an office door, surrounded by a couple of women. As his eyes meet hers, she winked at Will with a bright smile.

"Who's that?" Airon whispered, looking at her with a wicked glimmer in his eyes.

"That's the girl Sky nearly drowned," answered Will, who was amused to discover his cousin wasn't completely wrapped around Chrism's finger. "Her name's Mimi, she's French."

"That shelia's a beaut," Airon said. "I just don't understand how a bloke like ya can manage to draw the attention of someone who looks like that, especially when I'm not around to catch her eye first," Airon teased.

"That's easy," boasted Will mockingly. "My charming yet manly personality."

"Always the joker," said Airon giving him a slight push. They bantered back and forth a few more rounds as they descended the stairs to the first floor.

"Excuse me," said a short, muscular, redheaded man, who was standing a couple of steps from the bottom of the staircase. "Did you f-find it?"

Will stopped and glanced in confusion at Airon. Then he looked at the stocky fellow. "Sorry, I'm not sure I understand. Did you lose something?"

"Shh...not lost. Did you f-find the pen?" he said, looking around anxiously. "You have to f-follow the pen. Then you c-can s-stop him."

"Stop who," asked Airon, taking a step closer to him.

"H-hurry or it will b-be too late," the short man said, turning and scurrying away.

"Wait," called Will, but the man was already headed into the exhibit hall. "Should we go after him?" he asked Airon.

"I don't know. Who is he? Have ya ever seen him before?"

"No, I'm sure I haven't, a guy like that is hard to forget."

"Yeah, the bloke kinda stands out in a crowd. What was that he said about a pen?"

"Nah, it couldn't be," said Will.

"What's goin' on in that pea-brain of yers?"

Will scowled at him and said, "Remember that pen that Alex found in the plane wreckage? Oh yeah...that was before you got here. Well anyway, there was a pen. It was burned badly, nah, I doubt it has anything to do with it. That bloke was a little off."

"Mate, I'm not sure he was all there. Too many steroids, if ya ask me. Come on I'm stravin'."

Will nodded and they moved along, but he still had a nagging feeling in the back of his mind about the little muscle man.

A moment later, they walked through the open doorway of the café and followed the curved counter around to place their orders. Will looked up at the menu above the checkout scanner as they waited for the customers in front of them to move along. After a brief discussion on what they wanted to eat, Airon stepped up to the counter. A plump-cheeked woman dressed in a white uniform greeted them.

"G'day, she said. "May I take your order?"

"I'll have the beef sanger and chips with a large soda," Airon rattled off then pointed toward Will.

"Same—wait, except give me the turkey sandwich," added Will.

After Airon waved his V-phone over the scanner to pay for their meals, the lady handed them each a tray and they stepped down to await their food.

Will precariously balanced his meal as the two of them found a table. While they ate Will explained the circumstances that had led to the newest development with Sky. Somehow during their conversation, Airon changed the subject and began to convey what he had gone through while babysitting the twins with Chrism.

As his cousin spoke the minutes crept by. Will stared at the floor and counted the tiles, unable to calm his racing thoughts. He tried to focus on what Airon was saying but his mind kept returning to Sky, to the secrets she had kept from him, the mixed signals she had sent his way, and above all to his feelings for her. She had clearly been jealous, and he should be glad. A part of him was. But another part, a far more sensible part, couldn't forget that she had rejected him. Nothing could erase the hollow feeling in the pit of his stomach every time he thought of it.

"Mate!" Airon said kicking Will's foot under the table.

"What—sorry, what did you say?"

"I said that the twins could be cloned and used as a means of birth control," Airon said pausing to take a sip of his soda. "Ya agree?"

"Maybe..." Will mumbled.

"Really?" Airon questioned with a confused look on his face. "What's with all the bloody daydreaming? Seems like ya never hear a word I say anymore. Where's yer mind at?"

"Where else," Will answered cramming a few fries in his mouth. "I mean, she said she just wants to be friends, and then she—"

"I know what yer saying, mate," Airon interrupted him before he could finish. "But what nearly happened between you two on the hike. Well, that's a step away from *friends.*"

Will mulled Airon's words over for a few seconds. "I wish that were true but I can't figure out what she wants! She keeps me on edge and with all the secrets going on I'm not sure I can trust her anymore."

"Sure ya can trust her, its Skippy," insisted Airon, looking somewhat surprised.

Will didn't argue with him, but his head filled with thoughts. *I tried to tell her how I feel and she pushed me away. Maybe I should just let it be, move on to someone else. Someone like Mimi, she's pretty—not as pretty as Sky, but she seemed to like me well enough. That's what I'll do. We'll see how Sky likes that.*

Will took a sip of his soda determined to move on, but he knew that would never happen, not as long as there was still hope for him and Sky.

"Hey, here comes yer mum," said Airon, waving her over to their table.

"Hey boys," said Ann, smiling at Will as she sat across from him and next to Airon. "Let me just say, Will, that I'm proud of you. I know you stopped that water fiasco before Sky could do anymore damage. Thank goodness you're wearing the Elem—well—I'll just call it a necklace. But seriously, you handled it well. You're progressing faster than I thought you would."

"He's a bright boy," Airon teased.

"Not in the mood, mate," Will gruffly said to Airon, and then he gave his mother a quick grin. "Thanks, mum, but I didn't do it to be heroic, I just didn't want to get wet and mess up my hair."

Ann raised her eyebrows and said, "Self preservation is a good trait to have and you prevented it from being much worse."

"Possibly," Will mumbled.

And then, out of nowhere his Elementum grew cold against his chest. Could it be because his mum was talking to him about it or something else? He started to ask her but she spoke first.

"William, you did save the day and that's a good thing," Ann stated in an insistent tone. She reached across the table, picked up Will's drink, and took a long sip before continuing, "On another note, I just don't understand what's going on with Sky. Do you think it's because things are so tense between the two of you?"

"Part of her problem is me," said Will hesitantly, keeping his eyes focused on his sandwich. "I...well I—"

"You what?" his mum asked.

"I told her I have feelings for her," he blurted out, peeking up to see her reaction.

"Of course you do," Ann said. "You two practically grew up together."

"I don't think he means *brotherly* feelin's," informed Airon.

"I see," Ann said coolly. "And her response to that was?"

"She didn't want to go there," Will answered, his mouth suddenly going dry.

"Good," his mum said, letting out a long breath.

"But today, she seemed like she wanted—wait," he said. "What do you mean 'good'?"

"Son, I never dreamed in a million years that you and Sky would have *feelings* for each other," she said. "I mean you too have known each other since you were both babies. When did this all start?"

"I think I've known for some time now," he answered. "I'm just not sure what she's really feeling."

"I'm sorry," Ann said, shaking her head slowly. "But you need to put a stop to those *feelings*."

"Why?" asked Will as he looked from his mother to Airon, who was staring down at the table solemnly.

Ann rubbed her temples for a moment, and then said, "It's forbidden for two Primortus to be together, because a child from two of our kind would have too much power. It's one of our sacred rules."

"That's crazy," he said. "They have too many rules! My feelings for Sky aren't any of their business. I can't just snap my fingers and change how I feel about her. Even Airon thinks it's a good idea."

"You encouraged this?" Ann sharply asked, looking at his cousin.

Airon shrugged and kept eating.

"Will, you've got to let this go. You don't want the Provectus to have more reason to doubt her. She's going to need their help to defeat Brinfrost."

Anger rose inside him. If his mum hadn't kept secrets, he wouldn't be in the middle of this mess. And it didn't change anything. *I still want to be with Sky,* he told himself defiantly, b*ut what if the Provectus abandon her because of me. I can't risk it.*

"Well, if you really want to know what I think is bothering her," said Will in frustration. He could still feel the cool sensation of his Elementum. "It's the fact that you've been avoiding her. She has a lot of questions."

"I know she does."

"And as a matter of fact so do I," he continued as his voice grew louder. "If you had told us about it none of this might have happened." *Maybe...*

"Not so loud," Airon mumbled with his mouth full of food.

"Yes, let's try to keep it down," Ann spoke softly. "But you're right, son. It's my fault."

Will sat there dumbfounded. Had he heard her correctly? Suddenly his necklace being cold didn't seem as important. He looked over at Airon, who raised his eyebrows and made a befuddled face. His mum went on without missing a beat.

"I have been avoiding her...and you. I just wasn't ready to answer all your questions. That's why I doled out so much schoolwork. I was hoping it would keep you all too busy."

"Why would you do that? Why not just tell us what we need to know?" Will asked, in frustration.

"I'm sorry, I should have done a lot of things differently like preparing you and Sky when you were younger. But when your father was killed, everything changed for me. I-I was upset because I wasn't warned of that storm in enough time to stop it."

Ann paused taking another sip of Will's drink and then she continued, "Your father died because of me. With all the power that I possess, I couldn't save him. So, I became defiant even though I was supposed to help Sky get ready for her calling. I just couldn't do it, to either one of you. It was foolish of me, but I didn't want you to be a part of the Primortus anymore."

"How could you feel that way? Unfortunately, I am part of it and so is Sky," Will said, looking back and forth between his mum and Airon with bewilderment. *And now I love her and you're telling me we can't be together.*

"Yes, you are a part of it and I knew deep in my heart that I couldn't stop it from happening so I did my best to delay it. That was a mistake. The danger came anyway and now things are in motion that can't be stopped. I'm sorry Will, for everything, for all of it."

"You should have told us about all this," said Will in a harsher tone than he had intended.

"Easy, mate," said Airon with a frown.

"No, it's all right Airon," said Ann. "I understand. There are so many things I should have done. I may not be able to change the past, but I can help with the present. Will, you had some questions that night at the farm and I turned you away. So ask me now, but just remember that some questions might be better discussed in private and with Sky present."

Will once again became aware of the cold amulet against his skin. He watched his mum struggle to keep her emotions intact as she folded and unfolded her napkin repeatedly. He knew she was upset. Over the years, he had learned to read the signs. He had to, since his mum had always kept things to herself.

"So Will," Airon said. "Ya have any questions?"

"Yeah, I do," he sighed deeply and said, "I want to know more about these rules you seem to keep telling me about after the fact—but I don't want to talk about me and Sky right now. What I'd like to know—because it's been bothering me ever since that night that you turned me away—did dad know Zane?"

His mum sighed and said, "In a way, their paths crossed on a few occasions. But they were more like acquaintances not what I would call friends."

"Do you think Zane could've had something to do with dad's death?"

"Mate, what are ya saying?" asked Airon, sounding disappointed.

"No, I don't think he had anything to do with it," Ann stopped and her brows furrowed. She looked down, folded her napkin some more and exhaled loudly. "He's more involved than you know. But I trust him. It's his story and not my place to share it. I think when it comes to *our world*, the more you know the more danger you're in." Ann looked sadly at Will. "I've learned the hard way. I brought your dad into this and I have a sickening feeling that's what caused the plane crash."

"Aunt Ann," Airon said, shaking his head slowly. "I don't think that's what happened."

"Mum, it's not your fault."

Ann laughed quietly as she closed her eyes. "I have told myself that over and over. But I felt lost and I needed to blame someone."

"So, what you're saying is you blame yourself," Will said in a concerned tone.

"I guess I have," Ann replied. "What happened today with Sky's power mishap is really my fault. Keeping secrets from you all hasn't kept you safe. I'm not going to do that anymore. Brinfrost is out there and he seems bent on coming after Sky. Tomorrow, the real training will start."

"So, you're sure Zane had nothing to do with their death?" Will asked again.

"Mate, come on," said Airon crossly. "She said no. Yer dad and my parents are dead, just let it go."

Will saw an expression cross his cousin's face that he hadn't seen in a long time, it was one of anger and hurt. He watched as Airon fought to reel in his emotions. Will thought back to the weeks following the funeral. Even now Will believed that he had never really gotten over the death of his parents."

His mum reached over and patted Airon's hand. Will realized that she could sense his cousin's pain as well. She had been the one to break through the wall Airon had built around himself.

Ann turned her attention to Will, who was finding it harder and harder to ignore the icy cold of the Elementum. She gave him a concerned look and said, "What's this fixation on Zane?"

"There are just things…things about him that…that bother me," Will stammered as he realized he couldn't wait another second to ask her about the freezing amulet. "Wait, mum is there any reason that—" he stopped and lowered his voice. "Why would the Elementum be cold right now?"

"What?" breathed Ann. "It's cold? We need to find Sky. She could be in danger."

"Why?" asked Will as his heart rate quickened.

"I thought you knew, it turns cold as a warning or because there's an urgent message."

Will frowned. "Cold? I thought it turns hot when it's a warning?"

"No, only Sky's Elementum does that. Listen, our Humusara will be able to tell us more. I'm going to go get it out of the glider."

"You'll need your Elementum," Will said as he reached around his neck to remove it.

"No," his mum stopped him. "You might need it, if she's in trouble. I'll call you when I get back inside and meet up with you. Hopefully, you'll find her before we have to look in the book."

"Where's Chrism?" Airon quickly asked as he stood up.

"When the twin's parents arrived, she took off," said Ann, also jumping to her feet. "I assumed she would seek you out."

"I'm calling Sky, maybe she's with her," Will said as he pulled his V-phone out of his pocket. He dialed her number. "She's not answering."

"Cripes, Chrism isn't either," Airon said, redialing.

"We need to find them, now," Ann insisted. "Go on and find her, I'm going to the parking garage. Hey you two be…"

Will didn't hear the rest of what his mum said as he took off in search of Sky and Chrism with Airon right on his heels.

TWENTY-EIGHT

The Silver Arrow

"Jealous," Skylee mumbled to herself. "That's just great."

She was in a fairly large exhibit room seated on a bench by the wall. Tucking her unruly blonde hair behind her ears, she closed her eyes and let out a long slow breath.

"Who are you talking to?" said a familiar voice.

Skylee opened her eyes to see her sister sitting down on the bench beside her.

"You having a bad day?" asked Chrism.

"Yeah," she said, wondering what her sister was up to.

"Me too," she sighed. "Those twins are freaks of nature. I mean really—look at me, I'm normal—well better than normal—but they are supposedly of the same gene pool. I just don't get it. How can they be so horrible? It's just frustrating."

Skylee dropped her head down to her knees and muttered, "I can see how hard that must be for you."

"It's good that you understand, Airon thinks I'm overreacting. Sometimes I just don't get him. But do you think I am?"

"No, course not," she mumbled through her fingers in an unconvincing tone.

Chrism rolled her eyes at her and looked away.

"You know, I thought the snake exhibit was scary, but that right there is the scariest bird I have ever seen," said Chrism as she pointed up at a life-sized replica hanging overhead. "Why do you think they arranged it to look like that?"

"Haast," Skylee said, sitting up and looking at it.

"What?" asked Chrism as she gave her a strange look.

"It's a haast eagle, a bird of prey," Skylee said. "A bird species that once lived in New Zealand."

"And…"

"It was the largest eagle with a wing span of nine to ten feet. That's a pretty small span for a bird that weighed around twenty-five pounds. Its main source of food, the moa bird was killed out, and so now, the haast is extinct too. It's sad, don't you think?"

"You know, my question was rhetorical. I really didn't expect a lecture on wildlife."

Skylee sighed as she leaned forward again and let her head rest on the palms of her hands.

"Gosh, you're like Wikipedia with arms and legs," teased Chrism.

"I was just trying to...oh never mind. Yeah it's scary looking."

"It really is, but I've seen scarier. Like have you ever seen that old, old movie called *Snakes on a Plane*? Now that made my skin crawl. And then there's *Anaconda*, which was a bit fake but can you imagine being attacked by a huge vicious snake like that."

"Did you come in here just to make my day go from bad to worse?" Skylee mumbled.

"Ah come on, sis. Where's your sense of humor?"

As Skylee tilted her head to stare at Chrism she wondered the same thing. Where was her sense of humor? Sitting up slowly, she ran her fingertip along the scar on her arm and realized that part of it was still splattered at the Sky Tower. Some of it was spread out on Zane's field where the plane had crashed, and the rest was lying in the forest where her mother nearly died.

"So, go ahead. Spill it," insisted Chrism. "I can tell something's on your mind. And I am your big sister now."

"Okay, you're right," Skylee admitted. "It bother's me. All the stuff that's happened and I still can't control my power. I mean I don't know why I made a fool of myself over Will kissing that girl."

"Are you sure about that?" her sister asked in a soft voice. "I think you *do* know."

Skylee stared at her defiantly for a moment. "Oh all right! I like him! Does that make you happy? I like Will or maybe even more than that...I love him." *There, you said it,* she thought as relief and shock washed over her.

"Finally!" her sister said in a high, excited voice. "Of course I knew it all along. But now we can really talk. You know...about me and Airon...and you and Will. Has he kissed you yet?"

"I, well I guess I almost kissed him," Skylee said self-consciously. "Sort of."

"Huh?" said Chrism with a funny look on her face.

"Remember that day when you turned into a leopard?"

"How could I forget it...oh is that when it happened?"

"Yes, but you interrupted us and..." Skylee paused and looked at her sister, not sure of what to say.

Chrism's hand went to her mouth, and then she lowered it and said, "I didn't know. Sorry. Well, what about now, have you told him how you feel?"

"No," she said. "I can't. I don't think it's a good idea."

"Why not?"

"You wouldn't understand."

"Try me."

"I can't let myself get that close to him. If I do, I'm sure I'll lose him."

"You mean, uh, you're afraid things won't last between you?"

"In a way, I almost feel like I have a curse when it comes to getting attached to someone. I guess it stems from my childhood. For a while, it seemed like everyone I got close to died...Gracie, Will's dad, Airon's parents."

"It's not your fault," said Chrism so sincerely that Skylee almost believed it was true. "If that's all that's bothering you, you've got to put it out of your mind. You aren't cursed. You know that, right?"

"I guess, but lately after finding out I'm the Second Born and apparently considered to be an abomination, it makes me wonder. Just today I met a Helpmate who was afraid of me. She seemed to be threatened by me."

"You? Why? So, who was she?" asked Chrism.

Before Skylee knew it she had filled her in on both conversations with Rachel. She sat quietly and waited for her sister to respond. And surprisingly, she already felt a little better.

"Wow, so this Rachel's an Animus," Chrism remarked. "Like that lady at the village?"

"That's right," said Skylee. "And I have a strong feeling that this one knows a lot more than she was willing to say. I saw a man wearing an amulet in her thoughts but she blocked me before I could see his face."

Chrism raised her eyebrows and said, "You could see her thoughts?"

"Yeah, almost like I was her."

Chrism's expression was a mixture of curiosity and worry. "You haven't been seeing my thoughts, have you?"

Skylee didn't say a word. *Unbelievable,* she thought, *once again the world revolves around Chrism.*

"You have?" she asked, looking mortified.

"No," Skylee quickly exclaimed. "It's never happened before. That's the first time."

"Good, my thoughts are private."

"Trust me, I don't want to see your thoughts," said Skylee. "And you're missing the point. I don't know why I saw hers."

"I'm sure you asked her what it meant, but I take it she didn't explain it."

Skylee shook her head as her Elementum warmed on her skin. Then she reached into her pocket, pulled out the box and opened it. She held it in front of Chrism and said, "She did tell me what this symbol is. She said it was a number...number seven."

"That's an *odd* number," chuckled Chrism staring at the box.

Skylee didn't laugh, since her sister had already pointed out her loss of humor. They both sat in silence and watched the silver arrow spin one way then another.

"Has it done that before? Changing directions like that?" asked Chrism.

"Hmmm, no, it hasn't. It's always just spun around in a circle."

Suddenly the arrow stopped. Skylee and Chrism shared a quick glance and then both looked in the direction it pointed.

"I know it hasn't done *that* before," said Skylee as she stood and slowly turned around, watching as the arrow continued to point in the same direction. Then she looked at her sister with her jaw agape.

"What do you think that means?" asked Chrism, peering curiously at the box.

"Well, maybe we should follow it," whispered Skylee. "The Humusara did say it would lead to a gift."

"Yes, but it also said something about revealing Brinfrost."

Skylee hesitated, thinking...*if we follow the arrow it might lead us to him. Bad idea...and if I'm right about my necklace, he could be nearby. But why would my Humusara tell me to follow it? My book wouldn't lead me into danger.* She placed her hand on her chest and felt the heat of her Elementum. Her eyes returned to the box. The arrow was still pointing in the same direction. Then her curiosity got the better of her.

"I say we follow it. Things like this happen for a reason, right, so, I think we're supposed to follow. It could lead us to whatever the gift is. And it could be something to help us defeat Brinfrost or at least give us some information on whom or what he is."

"I don't know," said Chrism with narrowed eyes.

"Okay, here's what we'll do. The moment we see anyone suspicious we'll turn back. That way we can make sure nothing bad happens."

"All right but shouldn't we get the guys?" asked Chrism, looking anxious.

"Not yet, let's just go with it." Skylee said as she headed out of the exhibit room and started down the hallway.

"Hey, I think we should get someone," said Chrism, quickly catching up with her. "What if it does take us to Brinfrost? We should have Airon or Will with us. Both of them would be great."

"Yeah, you're probably right. I just don't want to lose our place here. The arrow could start spinning again any moment now. Can you call them and maybe have them meet us?"

"Sure, okay." Chrism pulled out her V-phone and moved her fingers smoothly across its face. She frowned and repeated the process. "That's strange."

"What?" asked Skylee, not stopping.

"The call isn't going through. It's like we have no service but all the bars are showing, weird."

"Well, here try mine." Skylee dug her V-phone out of her pocket and handed it to Chrism without ever taking her eyes off the arrow.

Chrism pressed a few keystrokes and sighed. "Yours isn't working either, here." She handed it back.

"Keep trying on yours, but I think we should carry on," Skylee said as she continued following the arrow, which was rotating slightly with each turn she made.

It guided them across the landing to the staircase where, after trying several floors they decided it was leading them up. On the fifth floor, they zigzagged through a maze of galleries lined with paintings, turning in so many different directions that Skylee hoped they could find their way back. Then she realized they might be on the wrong floor, so they followed the signs back to the stairs and took them down. On the second floor, they eventually found themselves in a long corridor.

"All these halls look the same," Chrism said, looking past Skylee nervously.

"Yeah, it's confusing."

When they reached the end of the hall, they stood before a large double door, which was labeled restricted area.

Skylee glanced at her sister and shrugged. "Should I open it?" she asked.

"Well, I guess so, we've come this far," said Chrism.

"Here goes," she said, tugging on the handle. The door did not budge. So she pushed on it several times and then tugged at the handle even harder with no luck.

"It must be locked," whispered Chrism.

"Yeah, but this is where the arrow is pointing. Right at this door," Skylee said as she glanced over her shoulder down the deserted hallway.

"Here let me try," said Chrism. She barely touched the door and it flew open. "Whoa, that's weird."

Skylee gave Chrism an uneasy look before stepping cautiously through the open door. She felt her sister's hand grip her shoulder.

"It's so dark, I can't see a thing," said Chrism from behind her.

Skylee glanced at her and said, "Hey use your phone light."

"Use yours, I'm gonna try to call Airon again," said Chrism in frustration as she frantically punched in numbers on her phone. "It's still not working. What's the arrow doing? Can you see it in here?"

"Not really, there isn't enough light, even with my V-phone. I'm gonna step back into the hall." Skylee took one step toward the door and it slammed shut causing her to jump.

She caught hold of Chrism's hand as the overhead lights began to flicker at the other end of the room. Brief flashes of light sporadically lit up the cavernous room like lightning illuminating a dark sky. Skylee squeezed her sister's hand as she saw quick glimpses of their surroundings. Wooden crates with shipping labels were stacked high along one wall and shelves filled with smaller boxes lined the other. A large crate, which was sitting on a forklift in the center of the room, had been cracked open and Styrofoam peanuts littered the floor around it. An extraordinary array of artifacts, including carved statues, ancient looking pottery and what appeared to be large fossils were scattered about the area.

All of a sudden, the lights went off completely.

In the darkness, Skylee flinched as pain struck her from two sources. First, Chrism crushed her hand so hard that she thought her fingers might break. And second, her Elementum instantly felt as hot as fire against her skin.

"Ouch," she cried, pulling it outside of her shirt by its chain.

At that moment, a section of lights at the opposite end of the room flickered once, and then stayed on.

"Oh no! Is that thing heating up?" Chrism asked, blinking to adjust her eyes as she looked at it like it might ignite into flames at any second.

"Um, yeah," Skylee said anxiously. "And—and Chrism could you let go of my hand I can't feel my fingers anymore."

"Oh...sorry," she whispered, quickly letting go.

The fearful look on her face made Skylee feel terrible. A knot grew in her stomach as she realized that the two of them following the arrow alone definitely hadn't been a bright idea.

"Your necklace—that's not a good sign, is it?" asked Chrism in a small frightened voice.

"No, it's not. Plus, I think we need to get out of here. I mean, who turned the lights on?"

"Hmmm, I don't know. What's the arrow doing?"

Skylee had almost forgot she was still holding it. She stared down at it and saw that it was pointing to the far corner of the room. All she could see there was a stack of wooden crates.

"I wonder, maybe Rachel was right. You know, this thing might be broken or something," said Skylee.

"Well, I wish it hadn't brought us here cause this whole place is creepy with all of this stuff lying around. You don't think there's a mummy in here, do you?"

"I hope there is *only* a mummy in here, they're dead and can't hurt us."

"What!" shrieked Chrism, abruptly turning toward Skylee, who was nearly knocked off her feet. "Have you not seen the movies where the mummy rises and kills everyone?"

"Seriously," moaned Skylee, wondering what planet her sister was from. Surely Chrism knew movies weren't real. She shook her head and decided not to argue the point. She knew from previous experience that she could never win against her sister's thought process. Besides, her mind was still fixed on why the arrow would lead them on a wild goose chase. Why had they ended up in an unattended storage area and why was her necklace hot again? One thing was sure, they didn't need to hang around in there any longer. She shoved the box into her pocket and looked around.

"Hey, over there. Another door. Let's see if we can get out that way," said Skylee, motioning toward the lighted area of the room.

They were half way across the room when Skylee caught movement out of the corner of her eye.

"Chrism," she whispered very softly.

"Hey, a janitor," said her sister as she headed toward a man who stood near the corner, facing away from them. He was wearing coveralls and sweeping the floor.

"Wait," Skylee said as she made a failed attempt to grab her arm.

"Excuse me sir," Chrism said. "Can you tell us how to get back to the main part of the museum? We were talking and must have taken a wrong turn. We didn't realize…"

Her words faltered to a halt as a shrill sound echoed around the room. Someone was whistling.

"Is that—" gasped Chrism as she slowly stepped back toward Skylee.

"Yes, it's the tune we heard after the wedding," she replied quietly. "Let's get out of here."

"You don't have to tell me twice," whispered Chrism.

"You two shouldn't be in this part of the museum," scolded the man as he slightly turned toward them but continued to sweep with his head down. "You could get hurt."

And then, Skylee winced in agonizing pain, as her Elementum grew even hotter. She gasped, and the man looked up. As she stared into the black eyes that had been haunting her for weeks, she knew who he was…Brinfrost.

TWENTY-NINE

Brinfrost

The air in the room suddenly seemed heavy. Skylee could barely breathe. Her mind raced with thoughts...*How can I face him now? I still haven't learned to control my powers. I was a fool to follow that arrow. And now Chrism's in danger too.*

Skylee clutched Chrism's hand and held tightly as they stepped cautiously toward the door. Brinfrost watched their movement but didn't come after them. Within ten feet of their escape, a loud, rumbling noise met their ears.

"What's that?" shrieked her sister.

Skylee glanced over her shoulder and saw an unmanned forklift racing toward them. She lunged sideways and desperately tried to shove Chrism out of the way.

The forklift barreled a path straight at them. The impact pitched Skylee forward in what felt like dreadful slow motion that couldn't be stopped.

Fa-thud. The sickening sound of her left knee cracking on the floor vibrated in her ears. She rolled onto her side and hugged her knee to her chest. Tears filled her eyes as pain wound its way up her body and exploded in her head. Panic swelled inside her as she remembered Brinfrost was still in the room.

"Chrism," she groaned through the nausea caused by the pain. "Where are you?" Skylee sat up and looked around wildly for her sister but all she saw was her V-phone lying on the floor.

The stench of exhaust fumes from the forklift swirled around Skylee's head. She grabbed hold of a nearby crate and managed to pull herself up. Balancing on one leg, she held on till some of the queasiness lifted.

"Lose something?" asked Brinfrost tauntingly.

The hair on the back of her neck stood up at the sound of his voice. Skylee turned and couldn't believe her eyes. Her unconscious sister dangled from the crook of his elbow.

"Let her go!" she shouted and wrenched in pain as she stepped forward.

"That's really up to you, Skylee," he said smoothly as he pulled his arm tighter around her sister's neck.

His black eyes bore into hers. He looked much like she remembered, tall and thin with eerily smooth skin. She couldn't move a muscle. Her pulse pounded loudly in her head. And all the while the heat from her Elementum burned fiercely through her shirt.

"What do you want?" she asked as her voice cracked.

"Lots of things," he mocked. His face twisted in a hideous grin as he snarled, "Let us start with your Elementum...bring it to me."

"You know I can't."

"Then your little helper, here, will die," he said in a cold sounding voice.

Gurgling noises escaped Chrism's mouth as he tightened his grip.

"Wait!" pleaded Skylee desperately.

They stared at each other in silence as she recalled the words in her Humusara...*Brinfrost will be revealed by the one and only heir...*then she remembered Hera's words...*protect it at all costs.*

Skylee inhaled a deep shuddering breath and made her choice. Centering all her attention on Brinfrost, she thrust her hands towards him. Instantly a powerful gust of wind hit him square in the face, knocking him and Chrism backward a few steps. While he tried to regain his stance, Skylee managed to hobble along the side of the crate, moving closer to them.

"So, that's how you want to play," he said, darting his eyes behind her.

Skylee turned just in time to see a nail gun fly past her and into his hand like metal to a magnet.

Ping...ping...

"Ow!" Skylee flinched as a nail pierced her ear. More nails sailed by her head hitting the wall behind her as she ducked. Touching her ear, she felt her punctured skin as a trickle of blood ran down her neck.

"Now," he said, pointing the gun at Chrism's head. "Let's see if your pet bleeds like you do."

"Wait!" Skylee gasped. "Just wait, she's not part of this. Just let her go, this is between us."

"That's right and you know what you have to do," he said. "Give me the Elementum and I'll let go of her."

Skylee carefully cupped her hand over her searing hot Elementum and said, "If I give this to you, you'll let her go, unharmed?"

She actually had no intention of giving it to him. Protecting the necklace now felt like a part of her soul. And she needed it to help Chrism.

Brinfrost's lips curled menacingly as he lowered the gun and in what seemed both a question and a statement, said, "Yes."

Skylee exhaled loudly and limped toward him keeping her eyes on her sister. She didn't take time to think. She acted, forming a tight fist, which she quickly released in the direction of his feet. At once, a whirling wind came up from the floor. The scattered packing peanuts took flight and circled rapidly around him, like a snowy tornado. He swung his arms violently, dropping the gun. Without pausing, Skylee lunged forward and grabbed Chrism's arm pulling her out of his grip. But her limp, unconscious sister went straight to the floor.

"I see that you have chosen," he said as he once again took hold of her sister. "Say good-bye."

"No...don't," pleaded Skylee as the packing material floated downward, settling at his feet.

Brinfrost seized Chrism around the neck with both hands. In the process, Skylee saw something hanging from his neck. It looked very much like her necklace but dark and twisted just like the amulet in Rachel's thoughts. She wondered if it was his power source like the Elementum was hers.

"Why do you need my necklace when you already have one of your own?" she asked.

"You and I both know that without an Elementum you're powerless."

"But, I don't understand. Have I done something to...to...why are you..." Skylee's voice trailed off as she struggled to find the right words to keep him talking.

"Don't be foolish," he said. "Give me the necklace or I'm going to snap her neck in two!"

This was exactly what Rachel had warned her about, Brinfrost hurting the ones she loved. Her only hope of saving Chrism was to make him turn all his attention on her. She fought to keep the tears back as she reached behind her neck and took the clasp in her hands. Skylee saw his black eyes flash with excitement.

The next few minutes came in a blur. Chrism's eyes flew open as he tightened his grip around her neck. To Skylee's surprise, her sister gave her a wink. *She's going to shift,* she thought. Although, she had never felt so afraid in her life, she gathered all her courage and dropped her hands.

"I WON'T!" she said boldly. "It's mine."

Skylee glared at him as he shook her sister violently.

At that moment, Chrism shifted into an enormous snake. Her large round head rose up and struck.

"Ahh...ahhh!" he cried out as her long reptilian body twisted around and bit down on his wrist.

The bite was so fierce that Skylee heard his flesh tear as blood gushed from the wound. His shrill scream ripped through the air, sending a jolt of fear over her entire body. Then Brinfrost doubled over in pain and Chrism released her bite, sliding down to the floor.

"Get out!" Skylee yelled to her.

She slithered toward the door, and instead of fleeing to safety, she coiled into strike mode. Even in shifted form, Chrism was still Chrism. As Skylee turned to face him, she heard a hissing noise above her head.

"Just stay out of—" she stopped and quickly glanced over her shoulder. To her amazement, her sister was still coiled by the door. Then movement overhead caught her eye and she looked up just in time to see a live electrical wire ripping away from the ceiling. It whipped around and brushed her arm causing her body to involuntarily tremble as it knocked her off her feet.

"Noooo," she moaned as she landed on her injured knee. Struggling to stand, she saw the wire winding its way behind Brinfrost. It hovered there.

Skylee knew what she had to do. Summoning every ounce of strength, she dug deep within until she felt the ground shuddering beneath her feet. A long, low rumble that sounded like distant thunder rose up from the floor and the entire room began to ripple. For a moment she lost her balance, then she instantly felt something stabilizing her like invisible hands were holding her up. Maybe her Elementum was protecting her. She looked up just in time to see the concrete at the far end of the room snap upward with such force that a long crack spread across the floor, moving toward Brinfrost.

As the rumbling grew louder, the wire circled back aiming directly at Chrism.

"Aaugh..." screamed Skylee as the wire struck her sister, who was no longer coiled but slithering wildly along the wall.

Taking a deep breath, Skylee willed the fracture in the floor to widen. To her great surprise a look of fear flashed across Brinfrost's face.

"Ehh!" he shrieked, slipping downward into the gapping crevice with only his head and shoulders visible.

Wasting no time, she lifted her hands and drew them together, making the crevice tighten around him. Then she swung around to check the wire, which was now motionless on the floor. She glanced back down and saw him struggling to free himself.

In a flash, small objects came hurdling toward her from every direction. She ducked and swayed as various pieces of pottery and metal tools flew past. Then she realized the items seemed to be unable to touch her, as if an unseen safety net was around her. Once again something was protecting her.

Drawing strength from its power, Skylee moved closer to Brinfrost. "I will never give you my father's Elementum," she vowed.

Brinfrost stopped struggling and peered at her with his black eyes. "It's already mine."

As a shudder ran through her, from the corner of her eye she saw Chrism, who, still in snake form, was weakly swaying to avoid being pelted. Hobbling as fast as she could toward the door, she swooped up Chrism's slithery body, threw it over her shoulder and barreled out.

"This isn't over..." Brinfrost screamed in fury as the door shut behind them.

Skylee didn't glance back, she just kept limping down the hallway. "I can't believe it, we're still alive," she said breathlessly.

As they entered an exhibit room, she heard people screaming. Glancing around, she watched them race out of both exits. She wasn't sure if it was because they thought there had been an earthquake or because she had a huge snake wrapped around her neck. Her sister was now dangling there lifeless, which made Skylee's shoulders slump forward, but she could still feel Chrism breathing. Slowing her pace, the reality of what they had just experienced began to sink in.

"Sky! Skylee!" she heard in the distance.

Oh no...did Brinfrost followed us?

The room seemed to spin around her. She staggered forward, her knees buckled and she collapsed to the floor. Exhausted she let go of Chrism, who slid down beside her.

As she lay there, a shrill siren pierced the air, and then a garbled voice sounded over the loudspeakers. Her pulse thundered so loudly that she could barely make out the words. *This is an emergency...please evacuate the building...*

Skylee flinched as she felt a hand cradle her head. Her eyes flew open and she saw Will's blurry outline. He spoke but his words didn't reach her ears. She closed her eyes hoping to stop the hammering in her head. He pulled her closer with her head resting in the crook of his arm. Her eyes fluttered opened and Will's face came into focus.

"Chrism," she whispered.

"Airon's with her," he said. "She's fine."

Skylee turned and saw Airon embracing her sister, who was curled up in his lap, still in the form of a snake.

In spite of Skylee's pain a giggle escaped her mouth. "That's not something you see everyday."

"Yeah, he's got it bad," chuckled Will. Then his face grew serious as he pushed her hair away from her punctured ear. "Sky, what happened?"

"Brinfrost—tried to kill us," she said in a barely audible voice. "I didn't think we were going to make it. He wanted me to give him my Elementum."

"I see you didn't," he said, eyeing it.

"Of course not. I used it against him," she said, smiling weakly.

"Did you..." he paused, leaned closer and whispered, "...kill him?"

"I don't think so."

"Doesn't matter, as long you're all right." Will glanced down at her amulet and said, "I realize now that I shouldn't have fought it, shouldn't have discouraged you. I should have been there with you."

"Do you mean it?" she said looking up at him in surprise.

"Yes," he said, lifting his Elementum by its chain to let it rest on the fabric of his shirt. "Don't you think it's time I accept what I am?"

Skylee brushed her fingers over his amulet. *Finally,* she thought, locking eyes with him. She reached up and touched his cheek. They were finally both on the same page about the Primortus. Maybe they could be on the same page about other things.

"Will," she said as her heart sped up. *Just tell him.*
"What is it?"
"I shouldn't have fought it either," she whispered.
He smiled and lowered his face toward hers.

Meet the Authors

J.L. Bond (left) and Val Richards (right) met in college in Clarksville TN., where Val excelled in Math and J.L excelled in creative ways to talk Val out of going to class. A few years later...okay, more than a few, they found themselves living about an hour away from one another in Florida and joined forces to write the Primortus Chronicles, A fantasy-adventure series. Nowadays, J.L. likes to remind Val that math isn't necessary for writing.